PROXY WAR

DAVID BRUNS

J.R. OLSON

Severn River Publishing
www.SevernRiverBooks.com

ISBN: 978-1-64875-615-3 (Paperback)

ALSO BY BRUNS AND OLSON

The Command and Control Series

Command and Control

Counter Strike

Order of Battle

Threat Axis

Covert Action

Proxy War

Line of Succession

Also by the Authors

Weapons of Mass Deception

Jihadi Apprentice

Rules of Engagement

The Pandora Deception

For Jen

1

10 kilometers northwest of Chaknak, Uzbekistan

Harrison Kohl's legs had gone numb an hour ago. He flexed his toes and shifted his position on the icy rock ledge. A fresh gust of biting wind made his eyes tear up. His thick socks, long underwear, and other cold weather gear had long since lost the battle against the bitter cold of the Central Asian winter night.

Overhead, diamond stars studded the night sky, and the Milky Way billowed across the blackness like silvery dust. The crescent of a waning moon shone scant light on the narrow valley three hundred meters below.

Harrison and his two companions had been in this rocky niche for over three hours, watching the work of the men in the valley. He raised the night vision binoculars, studying their target for the hundredth time. The railroad bridge spanned a half-kilometer-wide gorge some hundred meters deep. The floor of the valley was thick with scrub brush and boulders—perfect cover for the approach of the resistance fighters.

This section of the Chinese-built railroad, part of Beijing's Belt and Road Initiative, ran across the narrow plains west of Dushanbe, Tajikistan, before it punched across the border into Uzbekistan. From there, the railroad snaked north on its way to Karshi, Uzbekistan, around snow-covered peaks, through tunnels, and across bridges like this one.

But this bridge was special. According to the Joint Warfare Analysis Center this was the most vulnerable point in the entire section of rail line between Dushanbe and Karshi. Harrison had read the entire report and the JWAC analysis was mind-numbingly thorough. The document included the type of trestle bridge, the distance from the nearest repair depot, availability of the steel required for the new supports, even a soil analysis that indicated the Chinese engineers would be forced to repour at least half of the footings if the demolition plan was executed correctly. It concluded if this bridge were destroyed, it would take the Chinese over three months to rebuild it, possibly much longer.

They were buying time, Harrison knew. Time, he hoped, for a new administration in Washington to take over and start to actually support the resistance fighters in Central Asia. As CIA liaison officer, Harrison saw how much these fighters needed, and deserved, US support.

The Chinese referred to the resistance as the Seljuk Islamic Front, a terrorist group, but that label was just another aspect of the massive Chinese disinformation campaign across the region. On this winter night, however, Beijing's propaganda was the last thing on Harrison's mind. With shaking hands, he raised the glasses again and studied the pair of tents erected next to the tracks.

The Chinese were not fools. They knew how critical this rail line was to their supply lines in the region.

Smoking metal chimneys poked out of the canvas roofs, one of which served as a bunk house and the other a combination mess tent and command post. He'd watched this PLA encampment so much in the last two weeks that he knew every aspect of the soldiers' routines.

Six PLA soldiers did a three-day rotation at the site before they were taken back to the forward operating base in Dushanbe and a relief security team was flown in.

Harrison shook his head. This was the worst kind of duty. Stuck in the middle of nowhere, freezing your balls off, staring at a big steel bridge for two-hour rotations. The soldiers patrolled in pairs. They hunched in their jackets, stamped their booted feet against the cold, and did their time until they could get back into the warm tent.

Today was the third day of their rotation. Dawn was only a few hours away and the thoughts of the PLA soldiers on guard duty would be on the hot food and hotter showers that awaited them back at their home base.

By now, Harrison could recognize individual soldiers. He'd even assigned them names. The two on duty now were Acne Boy and Birth Control Glasses, so named for the black, heavy-framed glasses the young man wore.

They were just kids, he realized. Recruits. Maybe eighteen or nineteen years old.

Acne Boy told a joke and BC Glasses roared with laughter, his long frame doubling over. Their squad leader was in the warm command post and both of them had leaned their QBZ-95 assault rifles against the bridge railing. They had their gloved hands buried in their jacket pockets. Their breaths smoked white in the cold air.

"Harrison." Akhmet Orazov's voice rumbled under the whistle of the wind. "What's the status of the charges?"

Harrison moved the field of view below the laughing PLA soldiers into the darkness of the valley. The illuminated image picked out the twelve trestles beneath the ruler-straight dark line of the railroad surface. He counted the winking dots that speckled the steel structures. As he watched, another light came on and he saw one of Orazov's men start to climb down the steel beams. Using a blinking infrared light to signal that the charge was set had been Harrison's idea.

"Eighteen charges set," he reported. His whole arm shook with cold as he handed Orazov the night vision binoculars.

Orazov accepted the glasses and raised them to his eyes with steady hands.

"If we'd had these in Afghanistan, I think we could have beaten the Muj," the older man said quietly as he scanned the rail bridge.

Harrison studied Akhmet in the dim light. The older man had ice on his beard, but the cold did not seem to bother him.

"Sanjar," Orazov said, without lowering the glasses.

"Yes, sir." Sanjar's normally perky voice sounded thin and shaky.

On the other side of Akhmet, Sanjar Umarov had contorted his thin frame into a ball to conserve his body heat. Wavy black hair flowed out from under the knit cap on his head, and his brown skin was pasty with cold. His breath came out in puffs of frozen vapor.

Managing Sanjar was usually a challenge. The kid had boundless energy—Harrison was sure he had ADHD—and he loved to talk. When they'd hiked into their overwatch position, Sanjar had carried the heavy SV-98 Russian-made sniper rifle, and Harrison had humped in a single Stinger shoulder-fired surface-to-air missile. Akhmet carried his own AK-74M, the field radio, and the remote detonator.

Once they were in position, Akhmet forbade Sanjar from speaking. Since Harrison was not about to give up the night vision glasses, Sanjar had unpacked the sniper rifle and used the high-powered optical scope to watch the valley below. Then the bone-chilling cold took its toll on the young man. The big rifle lay on the open case.

"Get a status on the train," Akhmet ordered.

Sanjar unwound his arms and used his teeth to pull off one glove so he could work the radio controls.

"Almost done setting the charges." Akhmet's gray eyes gleamed in the dimness. "The idea to use IR lights on the charges was a good one, Harrison. I like it."

Harrison experienced a tingle of warmth. Akhmet Orazov was not a man who gave praise often. For the leader of the resistance movement, *I like it* was the equivalent of an enthusiastic high five.

In the six weeks he'd been embedded as the CIA liaison officer to the resistance in Central Asia, Harrison spent almost all of his waking moments with Akhmet and his lieutenants. Without realizing it, he was receiving a master class in guerilla warfare. But the leader's influence on Harrison went beyond battlefield tactics and fighting skills. Orazov knew how to inspire the men and women who rallied to his cause, how to spur them to give more than they even realized they possessed.

They called him Ussat. Harrison, who was fluent in Russian, assumed the word was slang for *boss*. Only later did he learn that *ussat* meant *master* in the Turkmen language. For Harrison, the term held a double meaning. Orazov was more than just a leader of men. He was their master. Moreover, the word was drawn from Orazov's native tongue, one of dozens of languages spoken inside the multiethnic resistance force—another sign of respect.

Orazov was Russian-trained and had fought with the Spetsnaz in Afghanistan. Although he was in his late sixties, Harrison had seen no sign of challenge in any of the resistance fighters he'd met. It wasn't fear, he realized, it was respect. Every fighter under Orazov's leadership knew that Ussat would never order them to do something he would not do himself.

Harrison heard the soft tempo of Sanjar's voice increase. He and Orazov turned to the younger man.

"Report," Orazov said.

"The train." Sanjar seemed to have forgotten how cold he was. "Ten minutes, no more."

Harrison checked his watch. 2337. Right on time.

Orazov spoke softly into his handheld radio, warning the six-man demolition team of the time they had left. Harrison peered through the glasses, watching the last man reach the concrete base of the trestle and jump down. He raised his field of view up to the embankment. The PLA patrol was oblivious to the impending attack. Harrison swept the glasses back down to the structure, counting the winking lights.

Twenty-four. All the charges were in place and armed.

In the distance, Harrison heard the thin bellow of a train whistle.

His heart beat faster, the aching cold forgotten. This bold plan to take the fight to the enemy was going to work.

He panned the glasses back across the bridge, picking out the PLA soldiers. Acne Boy had crossed the embankment to the edge of the structure. He spread his legs and fumbled with his zipper, preparing to relieve himself over the side of the bridge. As he dug into his trousers, something below him seemed to catch his eye. He stopped rooting in his pants and instead thrust his bare hand into a pocket and pulled out a pair of mini binoculars. He raised them to his eyes.

Harrison cursed. "Ussat," he said in an urgent whisper.

No answer. He looked over and saw that Akhmet had settled the long barrel of the sniper rifle into the cup of his left hand. The green light of the night scope ghosted his right eye.

"I see him," Orazov replied. His voice was even, breathing regular.

Harrison brought up the glasses again. Acne Boy bent over the railing, staring down into the valley, binoculars pressed to his face. The young man straightened and turned to look for BC Glasses.

Harrison was concentrating so hard he barely registered the sound of the suppressed shot.

Orazov's bullet took the target on his left shoulder blade, traversed diagonally across the chest cavity, and exited at his right shoulder. Harrison saw the spray of blood and flesh. The body twisted, like a pirouette, and toppled over the edge of the railing.

BC Glasses was ten meters distant, on the other side of the embankment and facing the other way. He turned around—perhaps he'd heard the shot or Acne Boy cried out. He trudged up the shallow slope and across the tracks to where his companion had been just a moment ago.

He looked at the abandoned rifle, then bent down and picked up the binoculars off the frozen ground. His face crumpled into a scowl and he called out for Acne Boy.

Harrison heard Orazov curse and take aim again.

BC started to peer over the railing, then his head turned sharply to the right.

The blast of the train whistle echoed through the valley and the roar of diesel engines reached Harrison's ears. The light from the locomotive rounded the bend and bore down on the bridge.

Harrison sat up. Next to him, Orazov flipped the cover off the remote detonator and snapped the switch forward. Two green lights energized. The charges were armed.

The train slowed as it approached the bridge. The engineer gave a short horn blast and BC Glasses waved, his missing companion temporarily forgotten. The locomotive rolled onto the bridge span.

Orazov's finger hovered over the red button on the side of the detonator. His eyes were locked on the progress of the train. Harrison saw him draw a breath and hold it.

Seconds passed as the train crawled across the span. When the locomotive was two car lengths from the end of the bridge, Orazov depressed the red button.

A red light on the face of the detonator blinked three times, then stayed on.

For a full second, nothing happened.

The explosions came like fiery punches in the night. Staccato booms, followed by bursts of flame in the blackness under the train. The shock wave ricocheted around the narrow valley.

The track dissolved underneath the still-moving train.

The charges were designed to take out the middle of the span, then the sides. The center of the train was sucked down into the valley, dragging down the front and tail ends of the long line of cars. Harrison watched the engineers in the locomotive try to scramble out of the cab. One moved across the side of the engine like a spider and made a leap for the embankment.

After the gut punch of the explosions, the rest of the destruction unfolded in slow motion. The locomotive wailed as it tried to power forward, but it was pulled slowly backward. It teetered on the downward slope of the rail line, then fell.

The sound was terrible. The screech of brakes, the roar of the locomotive engines, the tearing sound of rending metal.

And then the secondary explosions began. The train carried munitions to the PLA forces in the western part of Central Asia, another key element of the JWAC analysis report. The rail cars crashed to earth and ripples of fiery detonations illuminated the valley.

Sanjar was on his feet, cheering, fists pumping the air. His young face was alight with joy and the reflected glow of the burning train. More cars fell and the mayhem expanded.

In the spaces of time between the detonations, Harrison heard a new sound. The rhythmic beat of rotor blades. Two Harbin Z-19 attack helos burst through the smoke of the burning train and dove into the narrow valley. Instinctively, Harrison hit the dirt next to Akhmet. He heard the angry *bzzzt* of the 23mm cannons as the helos attacked the demolition team.

How did they get here so fast? Harrison wondered. The JWAC report gave them a twenty-minute window before the PLA air assets would be able to respond, but no more than five minutes had passed since the explosion.

He peeked over the ledge as one of the helos rose up to reposition for another strafing run.

The SV-98 rifle boomed to Harrison's right. He and Orazov looked over at the same time. Sanjar fired the heavy sniper rifle from a standing position, the force of the recoil from the heavy-caliber weapon nearly knocking his thin frame to the ground. He recovered his stance, took aim and fired again at the PLA helo. Flame spouted from the muzzle like a flare.

The Z-19 interrupted its ascent, banked toward them.

"Get down!" Orazov threw himself at Sanjar, driving them both behind a boulder.

The rock face above them exploded as the Z-19 unleashed the cannons on the side of the mountain. Chunks of rock and debris rained down.

Harrison rolled. His hands found the case containing the Stinger missile. His fingers scrabbled at the latches.

The helo pilot had seen something, but he was firing blind. Any second now, the pilot would see their ledge and launch a missile. End of story. No amount of shelter would protect them from that. If the explosion didn't kill them, the rockslide would. Harrison would die on the side of an icy mountain in the middle of nowhere.

Frantically, he dragged the Stinger missile launcher from the case. Like all of Orazov's men, he had trained on the weaponry over and over again until it was second nature. He slammed home the battery pack and snapped up the aiming mechanism. His right hand disengaged the safety and snaked around the trigger. His left index finger found the uncage switch to open the cover on the front of the breech.

Harrison rolled up to kneeling position and aimed. He pressed his face against the side of the launcher, listening for the lock-on tone.

One Mississippi.

Nothing.

Two Mississippi.

No tone. His heart sounded like a freight train in his ears.

The sensor next to his cheekbone buzzed with the lock-on tone.

Harrison pulled the trigger and closed his eyes.

A great gout of flame and smoke blasted out behind him. If the pilot didn't know where they were, Harrison had just lit a bonfire. The missile shot out of the canister, blazing in the night like a Roman candle.

A split second later, the helo exploded. The force of the blast knocked Harrison on his ass. He lay stunned, staring into the night sky. Stars swam in his wavering vision.

He felt hands lift him to his feet, half carry, half drag him off the ledge and up the slope. He stumbled, then found his footing. He laced his fingers into the webbing on Akhmet's pack and let the older man lead him to safety. He felt like he was on fire and chilled to the bone at the same time.

Harrison didn't know how long they walked, but he sensed that the wind had died down, and there was a musty smell.

They were back in the cave, he realized.

Akhmet helped him sit, then he turned on his headlamp. Harrison winced in the bright light. The older man pressed a canteen into his hand and Harrison drank.

"Hold still." His fingers gently probed Harrison's face. "You have burns on your face from the explosion."

He led Harrison to a rolled-out blanket on the rocky floor. "Sleep. We're staying here for the day. The PLA will be looking for us."

Harrison stretched out. His head felt like it was about to split in two. Akhmet crouched next to him, grinning.

"What's so funny?"

"Merry Christmas, Harrison."

Harrison squinted at the face of his watch.

December 25. Christmas Day.

The older man punched him on the shoulder. "Was Santa good to you this year?"

2

Ayni Air Base, 50 kilometers west of Dushanbe, Tajikistan

Senior Colonel Kang Hao stood at attention, eyes forward. His gaze looked past the rank of men in front of him, over the rounded shoulders of his new commanding officer, Major General Wong, to the picture window behind the man pacing at the front of the room.

The view was magnificent, like something from a historical drama. A snow-swept plain rolled away from the fenced edge of the PLA base toward a snowy mountain range. Morning sun fired the peaks with golden light.

Since he'd only arrived here this morning, he wasn't even sure what mountain range he was looking at, but it was beautiful. Ayni Air Base was a hive of military activity, with thousands of PLA troops in transit, a massive supply depot, and a fortified Huawei regional communications center.

The General pacing at the front of the room had arrived on the same morning flight as Kang. But while Kang occupied a jumpseat in the crowded rear of the aircraft, Lieutenant General Cheng, Commander of the Western Theater, lounged in a VIP pod in the front of the cargo bay.

Cheng reached the office wall and turned on his heel. The General's uniform was tailored and spotless. Ranks of ribbons sparked color across his breast. He'd shaved since they landed and his gelled hair gleamed like polished obsidian. The man was on the shorter side, with a powerful compact build, and Kang guessed he was no more than fifty.

Young for a three-star general, which meant that he came from a politically connected family. He was what Kang's father would have called a toy soldier. The elder Kang had spent a career in the PLA as an infantryman. His oft-stated paternal hope was that his only son would follow in his chosen career.

Kang did not disappoint. Not only did he join the People's Liberation Army, but he was accepted to the National Defence University in Beijing, the Chinese equivalent of West Point, and graduated with top marks. From there, he entered the elite special operations forces where he'd spent his entire career.

Until forty-eight hours ago, he'd been in command of the irregular warfare operations section for Special Forces Unit Falcon, based in Chengdu. He'd received urgent orders to report to Major General Wong in Dushanbe.

Like everyone, he'd closely followed the PLA's progress in fortifying the Central Asian countries to protect the vital Belt and Road infrastructure projects from the terrorist organization known as the Seljuk Islamic Front. He'd read the intel reports from the field boasting how the Chinese forces had cowed the SIF into submission.

But what Kang found when he landed was chaos.

The base was in lockdown, which delayed their landing and enraged General Cheng. Once on the ground, Kang discovered that the SIF had struck only the night before, bombing a key railroad bridge and severing the only rail connection between Tajikistan and Uzbekistan. Kang had not even had time to find the quartermaster before he was summoned to the office of his new commanding officer.

Still clad in the same wrinkled field uniform that he'd slept in, Kang was ordered to fall in next to his fellow senior officers. General Wong called the group to attention and General Cheng stalked in.

Then the shouting began.

"The sloppiness of your operation, General," Cheng began, "has damaged our reputation with the Party and is endangering the security of our holdings in Central Asia."

When Kang attended the National Defence University, leadership courses were mandatory. One of the tenets of leadership was to praise in public and reprimand in private. Lieutenant General Cheng must have been out sick that day.

The thirty-minute diatribe delivered to the commanding officer and his senior staff was petty and unprofessional. Cheng sneered when he spoke, all the while pacing as if he was lecturing a child. He also made sure he spoke in a loud enough voice that everyone outside the office would be able to hear him. Kang knew that even a base as large as Ayni was still a small community with a well-oiled rumor mill. By the time the office door opened again, the entire base would have heard that the CO and his senior staff had been chewed out by a direct representative from Beijing.

Behind his impassive exterior, Kang's stomach roiled with disgust. Cheng's petty display was nothing more than an elaborate show to divert blame for the terrorist attack onto General Wong. It was designed to humiliate, to be talked about among the troops and drag down morale. It was how weak leaders covered their asses. If the problem was solved, Cheng could claim that his criticism had had the desired effect. If more attacks happened, Cheng would be able to point the Party minders to Wong's history of incompetence as the root cause of the failure. Then he'd replace Wong and start the process over.

Men like Cheng were political animals, pathologically ambitious and allergic to blame of any kind. In Cheng's mind, the failure was always someone else's fault.

Kang tuned out the diatribe and instead watched the play of light on the distant mountains.

General Cheng paced across his view, waving his arms. His voice reached the next level of intensity and Kang realized he was working up to a big finish.

Disgusting. Ineffective. Unprofessional.

"If you can't do this job, Wong," he concluded, "I will find someone who can. Do I make myself clear?"

"Yes, General," Wong replied in a quiet voice.

"Very well, then." Cheng wheeled and marched to the door already being opened by his aide. Kang heard someone call the outer office to attention and then the door closed behind him.

The dozen men remaining in the room, all of them colonels and above, were still at attention. The humiliation of their commanding officer hung in the air like an offending odor. Everyone sensed it, but no one acknowledged it.

"Dismissed," said General Wong in a subdued voice. He gave the order without turning around. The officers broke ranks, hurrying toward the exit. No one wanted to stay here. No one wanted to carry the stink of failure beyond the door.

Wong walked toward his desk and the panorama window. "Senior Colonel Kang," he called over his shoulder. "Please stay behind."

Kang checked his stride, letting the others pass. The door closed again and Kang turned toward the desk. He glanced down at his wrinkled uniform and ran his hand over his stubbled jaw. Not a great first impression for his new commanding officer, but he supposed the man had other things on his mind at the moment.

Wong had taken a seat and spun the chair to face the window. Kang centered himself in front of the desk, came to attention and saluted. "Senior Colonel Kang Hao, reporting for duty, sir."

Outside, a breeze chased a screen of white across the mountains. The blowing snow crystals sparkled in the sun.

Without turning the chair, Wong replied, "At ease, Senior Colonel." Then he sighed as if it pained him to tear his gaze away from the view and spun to face Kang.

Major General Wong was in his mid-sixties. He had a thick shock of iron-gray hair and sagging facial features. His generous mouth was turned down at the corners and his shoulders slumped. When he looked up, Kang was surprised to see that his eyes were bright and alert.

"I'm sorry you had to see that, Senior Colonel," he said.

"Yes, sir." Kang kept his voice noncommittal.

"You probably haven't even been briefed yet about what happened."

"No, sir."

Wong got to his feet and walked to an interactive tabletop display against a wall. He touched a button on the console, and a 3D representation sprang to life. Wong expertly manipulated the controls to zoom in on a section of mountains bisected by a rail line. The legend in the lower right-hand corner told Kang he was looking at a five-square-kilometer section. The railroad passed over a narrow gorge about half a kilometer wide.

"Last night," Wong said, "the terrorists attacked this span." He touched the console again and still photos overlaid the 3D map.

The rail bridge was destroyed. What trestles remained were twisted and scorched. The blackened skeleton of a freight train littered the bottom of the ravine. There was ample evidence of secondary explosions. A munitions train, Kang realized.

"They timed their attack to coincide with the arrival of a freight train carrying ammunition to the western operating bases. The placement of the charges was precise, and the resulting damage extensive. Our engineering corps says that it will take at least a month for us to rebuild that span, maybe more, depending on the weather. There's also an issue with availability of the replacement trestles."

"I didn't know the terrorist forces were that sophisticated, sir." Kang recognized a well-executed attack when he saw one.

"Neither did I," Wong replied in a dull voice.

"Did they have outside assistance, sir?" Kang asked cautiously.

Wong grimaced at the display. "The MSS says no. They just got lucky."

Kang said nothing, but Wong's face betrayed his real thoughts. There was always a brotherly tension between the Ministry of State Security and military intelligence. Yes, they were all members of the same Party, but they were not always on the same team. Kang wondered how cooperative the MSS was being in this case.

"Are you going to ask me if I believe them, Senior Colonel?"

Kang chose not to take the bait. Instead, he asked, "Why am I here, sir?"

The General studied him, a faint smile tracing his thick lips. "They said you were a no-nonsense officer who could handle a tough assignment with little direction."

"May I ask who *they* are, sir?" Kang replied.

Wong ignored the question. "I need time, Senior Colonel."

"Time, sir?"

Again, Wong did not answer. Instead, he turned back to the window. "Do you know who had this office before me?"

"I've never been here before, sir."

"General Gao," Wong replied with a tone of reverence. "The Hero of Tashkent."

This time Kang was silent out of respect. Lieutenant General Gao had died a hero's death, defending the General Secretary himself against an assassin's bullet. Kang had been at the man's funeral in Beijing, remembered seeing the casket being carried by an honor guard through the Great Hall of the People.

"I had no idea, sir."

"The Hero of Tashkent will not die in vain, Senior Colonel, but I need you to buy me time."

"Sir, you've lost me. Time for what?"

Wong looked at him with fresh eyes. "They didn't brief you at all, did they?"

Again, Kang wondered about the mysterious *they*. "No, sir."

Wong turned back to the interactive map. He zoomed out so that the field of view showed the entire region from western China to the Caspian Sea. The Belt and Road project showed as a thick blue line worming its way through the mountains and across the plains of Central Asia. Depots and hubs in cities showed up as dots. He touched the console again and a wavy blue shadow expanded on either side of the line. It bulged out in some areas and thinned down to almost nothing in others.

"The real power of the Belt and Road is not concrete and steel," Wong began. "It's data. It's the surveillance network. Cameras, drones, mobile phone towers, satellites, every possible monitoring device we can install, all working together to form a perfect shield."

Kang had seen this kind of network before, in Xinjiang when the Party had to deal with the Uighurs. But that was a controlled area where the Party could place surveillance nodes anywhere they wished and the population was forced to carry state-issued devices. This was a hundred times larger and spanned multiple borders and languages. There was no Great Firewall to keep the outside world at bay.

"I know what you're thinking, Senior Colonel. It's impossible...but it's not. Not for *Yuanjian*."

The General said the word *foresight*, as if it should mean something, but Kang was at a loss. Meanwhile, General Wong was just warming to his subject.

"The Huawei network is designed to be the infrastructure backbone. It's everywhere. Every day we're adding new sensors, new nodes, more capability."

"But, sir," Kang interrupted. "More data does not solve the problem. All that data has to be processed and analyzed and—"

"Turned into actionable intel, I know, Senior Colonel. That's what Foresight does."

"So, Foresight is an analysis tool."

Wong chuckled. "Foresight is so much more, Senior Colonel," he replied in an urgent voice. "Foresight is an artificial intelligence. If we feed it enough data, it will predict the moves of our enemies."

Kang tried to contain his disappointment. He'd heard these promises before. An AI would take the place of flesh-and-blood leaders, dispensing perfect orders to the battlefield like dog treats.

"You don't believe me?" Wong challenged.

Kang kept his voice neutral. "I do not, sir. It's a science fiction fantasy."

The corners of Wong's lips turned up. "What if I told you it almost prevented the attack last night?"

Kang was tired now. He made no attempt to hide his skepticism.

Wong turned back to the console. He was animated now. It showed in the way his fingers moved across the keyboard.

A technocrat, Kang thought with disgust. In the last fifteen years, the PLA had expanded at a rapid clip, bringing on technology and capability that had taken the West over fifty years to develop. Nuclear submarines, hypersonic missiles, unmanned vessels, next-gen fighters, all powered by gushers of money from Beijing.

In the midst of all this growth, a breed of officer developed who believed that every battlefield problem could be solved with a new gadget. In this futuristic vision of the People's Liberation Army, people were not the solution, people were the problem.

Kang stifled a sigh. A better rifle, a faster helo, more secure comms were welcome additions to his life, but AI was a bridge too far.

If Wong noticed Kang's reservations, he didn't show it.

"At 2335, Foresight predicted an attack on the rail line in the section between Atkamar and Chala Mazar, both of which are in Uzbekistan. We did not have an exact location, but I put attack helos in the air. They were intercepting the train when the attack happened. The flight time from Ayni to the scene of the attack is more than twenty minutes. They were on scene in less than five. They engaged the enemy."

"And did they kill them?" Kang asked.

Wong shook his head. "One helo was destroyed by a shoulder-fired missile and the terrorists got away. But you're missing the point, Senior Colonel."

"I don't think I am, sir. The bridge was attacked, the munitions train destroyed, we lost a valuable air asset—and the enemy got away."

"Foresight *worked*!" Wong's face was red. "It predicted the attack. It wasn't perfect, but it worked."

Kang let his silence be his answer.

"I will make you a believer," Wong said. "Until then, I need you to buy me time. Every day, we bring more sensors online and Foresight learns more about the enemy. She's hungry for information. I just need time to feed her, train her. Do you understand what I'm asking for?"

Kang wanted to roll his eyes or sigh or somehow display his disgust in a vaguely respectful manner, but he did none of those things. He looked from the console to his new boss. This was the hand he was dealt and he would play the game to the best of his ability.

You are a professional soldier, he thought. If there's one thing you know how to do it's hunt down enemies of the State. Let this computer jockey play with his AI while Kang got down to the business of killing.

He smiled grimly. "I understand, sir."

3

Chevy Chase, Maryland

Don mounted the wide brick steps of the substantial Georgian-style home. He made sure his face was visible to the camera mounted at eye level as he touched the doorbell. Deep inside the house, he heard the melody of "Silver Bells."

Custom doorbell, he thought. I guess that's how the other half lives.

He turned toward the yard, nearly a half-acre of closely cropped Kentucky bluegrass, ending abruptly at an eight-foot brick wall that matched the house material. His chauffeured Suburban idled on the cross-hatched pavers that made up the driveway and circular courtyard.

Don stamped his feet against the chill. It was a gray day and raw with dampness. Christmas Day, and if the weather report was to be believed, they might just have a white Christmas after all.

He heard the front door open and Don turned.

The girl who stood in the open door might have been six or seven—Don had little experience judging the ages of children. Her hair was in braided pigtails, and blue eyes blazed at him from behind round glasses. She wore a bright red sweater whose front was almost entirely consumed by the face of a neon-green Grinch with glued-on googly eyes.

"May I help you?" She smiled brightly and Don could see she was missing two front teeth. "I bet you're here to see Gran."

"Sophie," said a quiet male voice behind her. "Please let Mr. Riley inside."

When Sophie opened the door wide enough for Don to enter, he saw the Secret Service agent standing behind her. Don nodded a greeting and the man gave him a bemused smile.

"Did you bring a sweater?" Sophie asked as she shut the door. "You have to wear an ugly sweater on Christmas. It's a rule."

Before Don could answer, the agent intervened again. "Sophie, please escort Mr. Riley to the kitchen."

"Yes, Randy." The girl led Don deeper into the house. They passed under a curving staircase, entering a living room with vaulted ceilings and an enormous lighted Christmas tree. Four children playing a board game did not look up. Sophie next led him to a family room with two televisions. A romantic comedy held the rapt attention of three teenage girls and an older woman. Two men and two adolescent boys played a video game on the other TV.

Sophie pushed through a swinging door into a country-style kitchen. "Gran," she called out, "Mr. Riley is here to see you."

President-elect Eleanor Cashman turned away from the six-burner stainless steel stove. Don was used to seeing the Senator in a professional setting. Ash-blond hair carefully styled, perfect makeup, and dressed in a conservative business suit. If Don had not seen this version of Eleanor Cashman himself, he would not have believed it.

The Senator wore no makeup and her hair was held back by a set of foam reindeer antlers with a banner that read *Merry Xmas* swinging between them. She wore a baggy sweater with the sleeves pushed up to her elbows. The handmade garment had faded from red to a splotchy pink, but the front had been enhanced with ample glitter and LED lights that spelled out L-O-V-E in rapid, blinking succession.

"Hello, Donald," Cashman said. "Merry Christmas."

"Merry Christmas, ma'am."

"I helped Gran fix her sweater," Sophie announced. "Do you like it?"

"I love it," Don replied. "It's very unique."

Cashman nodded at the agent. "Thank you, Sophie. I need to speak with Mr. Riley for a few moments. I'll bring the soft pretzels out when they're ready."

"I'll secure the room, ma'am." The agent held the door for the girl.

Cashman plucked a pair of red reading glasses off the counter and used them to peer into a pot boiling on the stove. She fished out what looked like lumps of dough and placed them on a baking sheet. After scattering a handful of salt over the wet dough and sliding the sheet in the oven, she turned back to Don.

"You have my undivided attention for"—she consulted the timer on the oven—"twelve minutes. Then chaos will ensue. My soft pretzels are world famous." She offered a warm but wistful smile. "One last hurrah before I start the new job, I guess. I don't see myself baking too much in the White House."

"I'll be brief, ma'am," Don said.

"So what brings you to my humble home on Christmas Day, Donald?"

"There's been a development in Central Asia, ma'am."

"Remind me. Is the word *development* code for good news or bad?"

"The resistance movement led by Akhmet Orazov conducted a successful attack on a Chinese railroad bridge last night. The bridge span and a freight train carrying munitions were destroyed."

Cashman pursed her lips. "This is the operation where you have an embedded case officer? Was he there?"

"Harrison Kohl, ma'am. He was present at the attack. There were no casualties on the resistance side. In addition to the bridge and the train, the PLA lost a Harbin Z-19 attack helicopter that was shot down by a Stinger shoulder-fired missile."

Cashman frowned. "Can anything be traced back to us?"

Don shook his head. "All indications are that it was a clean operation."

"That all sounds positive, Donald, yet I detect a note of dissatisfaction in your tone."

Don cleared his throat. "I just think we need to calibrate our expectations relative to our current level of support. This attack, while successful, will only inconvenience the PLA. If we want to effect real change in the region, we need to put in place a secure logistics pipeline that can allow the resistance forces to take the fight to the PLA."

"And we're not doing that now?"

"No, ma'am." Don did not elaborate. He let the silence hang in the air.

"Let me guess: President Serrano does not want to get involved." Cashman cast a glance at the oven timer. "He promised me support on this. Are you suggesting that the current administration is not honoring that promise?"

"I'm saying it's complicated, Madam President-elect. But I do have a suggestion that would help the situation. One I think President Serrano might support."

"Do tell, Donald."

He took a breath, resolving to lay out the case calmly and concisely. "The issue we have is one of scale, ma'am. For us to get enough arms into the region to make a difference, we need multiple secure routes."

"Why do I feel like you're about to drop a shoe, Donald?"

"We need to use the Russians, ma'am. It's the cleanest, safest way for us to move supplies into Central Asia."

Cashman straightened. Her lips hardened into a thin line. "Absolutely not."

"Please hear me out, ma'am—"

"You know my feelings here, Mr. Riley. Russia cannot be trusted. All along I have suspected that President Sokolov's buddy act with Serrano did not represent a real change of heart. You know what he did in the run-up to the last election in Russia. The apple does not fall far from the tree, and in my view, there is no difference between Vitaly Luchnik and his nephew, Nikolay Sokolov."

"That may be true, Madam President-elect." Don tried to banish the pleading note in his voice. "But in this case our interests are aligned. Russia wants the PLA out of Central Asia just as much as we do—maybe more. Competition for influence in the region is at stake, and President Sokolov knows it."

"Donald, I want nothing to do with Nikolay Sokolov and Russia. Can you imagine how it would look for me if that news became public? Pushing back against Russia was a cornerstone of my campaign. Now, you're asking me to abandon that before I'm even in the Oval Office?"

Don thought about all the hard choices he'd seen President Serrano make early in his first term. Campaign promises were aspirations, made with the best of intentions and limited insight. Governing was about practical realities and compromise.

"I think you should consider it, ma'am," Don said. "I can work up some options. We can keep this compartmentalized—"

"The answer is no, Donald. Find another way to get the job done."

Don held in a sigh.

"What about the Chinese General?" Cashman asked. "What's the status with exploiting that avenue?"

Don had rescued—*kidnapped* was probably a better word—an unconscious General Gao from the chaos of the PLA false flag attack in Samarkand. After treatment at Walter Reed for his gunshot wound, Gao had been relocated to a secure CIA facility in northeastern Pennsylvania to recuperate. The General claimed to have privileged access to the Chinese secure network in Central Asia, something which Don could use to aid Orazov's resistance effort.

But there was a price: Gao wanted his family extracted from China before he would cooperate.

"That plan is on hold right now, ma'am," Don reported.

The timer on the oven beeped, interrupting their conversation. Cashman busied herself with removing the soft pretzels from the oven and sliding them onto a cooling rack. The kitchen filled with the smell of baking bread. Don's stomach rumbled, reminding him that he hadn't eaten anything all day.

Cashman placed the empty baking sheet into the sink. "The President doesn't want to do it. Is that what you're saying, Donald?"

"The President has not given the authorization to move forward, ma'am." Don kept his tone neutral. If there was a difference of opinion between Serrano and his incoming replacement, Don wanted no part of it.

A flash of irritation crossed Cashman's face, then disappeared.

"Pretzels are out of the oven!" she sang out.

The door burst open and the kitchen filled with laughing, pushing children ranging from Sophie to a man nearly Don's age.

"Thank you for coming all this way, Donald," Cashman said. The wistful smile was back as she watched the horde attack her baked goods.

"Of course, Madam President-elect."

"Things are going to change, Donald. I hope you're ready for that." She handed him a soft pretzel on a paper napkin. "Randy will show you out."

Don followed the Secret Service agent to the front door. "Merry Christmas, Mr. Riley."

"Merry Christmas."

Don stopped on the front step. A fat snowflake drifted down as he bit into the soft pretzel. It was warm and chewy, with a sprinkling of coarse salt on the crisp exterior.

The sifting snow made him think of Harrison Kohl on assignment in the wintry mountains of Central Asia. He'd promised Harrison that the resistance would get the weapons they needed to fight the Chinese, and he was going to keep that promise. The Russian option made the most sense, but at least for now, that was off the table. He'd just have to find another way.

Don popped the last of the pretzel into his mouth and descended the steps.

4

Grand Kremlin Palace, Moscow, Russia

"We're ready whenever you are, Mr. President." The disembodied voice of the director came from the darkness beyond the bright lights.

Nikolay Sokolov locked his attention on the glass eye of the camera lens located just below the red dot that indicated they were recording.

Spine straight, shoulders square, eyes level, lips slightly upturned at the corners. Not a smile exactly, just a subtle indication of his innate kindness and concern for his fellow Russian citizens.

"My fellow countrymen," he began. His voice was calm and confident, exactly what people expected in their leader. "Let me be the first to wish you a happy New Year."

Federov claimed his speechwriter could make Stalin sound like Mother Teresa, and Nikolay had to admit the woman had skills.

In his private moments, he acknowledged to himself that the last year had been an abomination of his values. Fair elections had gone out the window with Konstantin Zaitsev's girlfriend. Independence of the press expired when he turned Federov's security services loose on the media. But the clincher, the pinnacle example of how much he'd changed, was when he personally put a bullet in Uncle Vitaly's brain.

These were the thoughts that raced through his mind as Nikolay Sokolov, newly elected to a full six-year term as President of the Russian Federation, delivered the annual New Year's address to the nation.

I did what was necessary, he told himself. I did it for my country. I did it to *save* my country.

He stared straight into the camera lens and he said the words of the speechwriter with sincerity and conviction. He ended the broadcast with a quiet smile and sincere wishes for a wonderful Novy God and a prosperous year to come.

The red light above the glass eye winked out. The director said, "Cut!" and it was over.

The harsh lights were extinguished, leaving spots of color in Nikolay's vision. He stood and turned back to view the Hall of the Order of St. Andrew. The room extended for thirty meters, a perfect backdrop of vaulted ceilings and square columns crusted with golden figurines. Up until the end of the nineteenth century, this had been a throne room. Nikolay imagined the very spot where he'd been sitting only moments before had once held a pedestal and a carved throne decorated with precious stones. He wondered how the tsars felt about their grip on power, if they ever entertained second thoughts about the things they had done in service of their country.

"A masterful job, Mr. President." The director emerged from behind the camera. "I do have a few notes, sir, if you would like another take."

Nikolay felt his lip curling at the man's sycophantic tone, but the buzz of his mobile phone distracted him. He turned away abruptly and raised the phone to his ear.

"Da."

"Mr. President." Vladimir Federov's voice was a light tenor, bordering on feminine, at odds with the immense power wielded by the head of the Russian Federal Security Services.

"Vladimir, happy New Year."

"I wonder if I might impose on you to visit me at my office, sir."

His *office* was Federov-speak for the Lubyanka Building.

"I have a car waiting, Mr. President," he continued. "The matter is time sensitive."

Federov's circumspect tone made Nikolay resist the obvious question of why he was being invited to visit a prison on New Year's Day. The fact that the FSB head was taking precautions despite the security measures on Nikolay's private mobile phone spoke volumes.

He cast a look back at the director, who still waited, clipboard in hand. Nikolay slipped his phone into his breast pocket. "We're finished here."

"Mr. President, I have a few recommendations—"

"I'm needed elsewhere," Nikolay interrupted.

"But another take would ensure—"

"I have read the speech three times. You called my last performance—what was the word you used?"

The director colored. "*Masterful*, Mr. President."

"Exactly. Masterful. Do you really require a fourth recording?"

"It's not a matter of *needing* another, sir. I like to have an extra take just in case."

Nikolay stared at the man, letting the phrase *just in case* hang in the air. The director found sudden interest in his shoes.

"I can work with the recordings I already have, sir," he said finally.

"I expect perfection," Nikolay replied softly. "I'll be watching tonight."

The threat was unnecessary, but it gave Nikolay a thrill. The director paled, and the electric sensation of pleasure in Nikolay's chest increased.

For all the fear that the name *Lubyanka* instilled in the Russian populace, at first glance the structure itself looked like just another government office building. The Neo-Baroque edifice wore a façade of yellow brick and overlooked a square of the same name in the Meshchansky District of Moscow.

But the fear of this address was well-founded. Although Lubyanka had started life as the headquarters of an insurance company, the location had been home to the secret police of Catherine the Great, the offices of the KGB, and finally the headquarters of the FSB.

It also housed Lubyanka Prison, which was Nikolay's destination.

The interrogation room was a square box with soundproofed walls and harsh fluorescent lights. What had once been white surfaces—walls, ceiling, linoleum floor—were now a shade of dingy gray from years of use and cigarette smoke. The only furniture in the room was a sturdy steel table, bolted to the floor, and two chairs on either side of it. The air reeked of disinfectant. And fear.

Nikolay studied the man shackled to the table through the mirrored glass. He looked vaguely familiar, but Nikolay could not place him, and he knew this was probably a test by Federov.

The prisoner was in his late thirties, with broad shoulders, a square face, and dark eyes, which were fixed on the mirror. He was well dressed in a dark blue business suit, white shirt, and flawlessly knotted red silk tie. Draped across the chair to his right lay a camel hair overcoat and a cashmere scarf. He appeared alert, but not nervous—an unusual response to an unexpected trip to Lubyanka.

Nikolay cast a sidelong glance at Federov. In contrast to the vigorous good health of the man inside the interrogation room, the FSB chief looked pallid and worn. Federov had always been a big man, but in the last few months, he seemed to have deflated. His neck did not fill out the collar of his shirt and his pale skin looked waxy. Nikolay started to ask him if he felt all right, but then reconsidered.

Instead, he said, "I give up, Vladimir, who is our guest?"

Federov answered without looking away from the mirror. "Sergei Musayev, heir to the—"

"Transneft oil conglomerate," Nikolay finished. He remembered the younger man now. A Russian mother from a connected Moscow family married into the Kazakh oil dynasty at the ripe age of seventeen to a man thirty years her elder. The woman—Nikolay could not remember her name —bore her new husband one son, then moved back to Moscow.

Sergei, the progeny of the arranged marriage, divided his time between Moscow and Astana, the capital of Kazakhstan. He'd grown up in two worlds, equally comfortable in both. Nikolay recalled that young Sergei had a reputation as a playboy in his twenties but had since turned his attention to Kazakh politics.

"What is he doing here?" Nikolay asked.

Federov allowed a ghost of a smile. "Young Sergei has shown very poor judgment, Mr. President. He was swept up in a sting operation last night."

It was just like Federov to dribble out the information. "Can you be more specific, Vladimir?"

"We had intel that the Free Nations were planning a New Year's Day demonstration. Naturally, we decided to preempt the unpleasantness with a demonstration of our own."

The Free Nations of Post-Russian Forum was a collection of small regional ethnic groups who had been advocating for independence from Moscow since the fall of the Soviet Union. Because none of the smaller groups held enough political clout on their own, they formed a coalition. The group was rarely violent, but in Federov's heightened state of political alert, every group was under new scrutiny.

"And?" Nikolay was getting tired of this game.

"I have evidence that Sergei is funding the Free Nations movement."

Nikolay let the comment hang in the air as he studied their unconcerned prisoner. "Sergei has been a very bad boy."

"Quite so, Mr. President."

Now Nikolay understood the urgency of Federov's call. Sergei Musayev was the perfect candidate. It took resources to track down and prosecute every fringe group who might want to disrupt the work of the State. Instead of going after all of them, a much more efficient method was to find someone who could serve as an example, a test case. To be effective, the candidate needed to be a public figure, but not so well-known that his prosecution would create counterdemonstrations. It was better if he was rich—classism always played well with the public—and had some political connections but was not too well-connected.

Nikolay smiled as he studied the handsome face in the next room. Musayev was practically Kazakh royalty, but not as well known in Russia. His arrest and prosecution would also give Nikolay a way to show he was being tough with the southern border states. Another way to push back against the undercurrent of discontent about the rising Chinese influence in Central Asia.

"Have you announced his arrest yet?" Nikolay asked. It was hard to keep the excitement out of his tone.

"No, Mr. President." The words were said in such a way that it made Nikolay look at the FSB chief.

Federov smiled. Not a pretty sight on his sagging features, but his eyes held a spark.

"What is it, Vladimir?"

"I would like you to consider another option for our comrade in the next room."

Comrade? Nikolay thought. What the hell is he getting at?

"Sergei is very close to the President of Kazakhstan, sir. *Very* close. I have it on good authority that he might even be in the running to be the *next* President of Kazakhstan. With the proper support, of course, and appropriate mentoring."

Nikolay turned back to the mirror. Sergei Musayev yawned. It was an affect, but it showed he was a man who could keep his composure under pressure. The type of man who could be relied upon. The type of man who could be a spy. Nikolay's spy inside the Kazakh President's office.

It was a brilliant idea, but if this idea was going to work, Nikolay needed leverage.

Next to him, Federov's smile widened as he watched Nikolay put the pieces of the plan together in his head.

"How is Sergei's relationship with his mother?" Nikolay asked.

Federov's grin turned ghoulish. "Very close, Mr. President. I am told he would do anything for his *mamochka*."

"Have Sergei's mother picked up, Vladimir. And then let's make Sergei an offer he cannot refuse."

5

Samarkand, Uzbekistan

As acting President of the nascent Central Asian Union, Timur Ganiev was sure of only one thing: if you put a Tajik, a Kyrgyz, an Uzbek, and a Turkman in a room for five minutes, they would not be able to agree on the color of the sky.

If you multiplied their number by a factor of twenty and added in a few dozen government staffers and consultants for good measure, you would get the same result—only louder. They all spoke Russian, the common tongue from their legacy of occupation by the former Soviet Union, but in the background Timur could distinguish any of the dozens of ethnic languages that populated the region.

A young Tajik firebrand occupied the podium overlooking the Congressional Committee General Assembly. He had wavy dark hair, piercing eyes, and a strident voice that seemed to have only one volume.

"The first order of business for this august body must be to sponsor a referendum on the occupation of our homeland..."

His voice was lost in a chorus of angry shouts. From his position on the dais at the head of the room, Timur surveyed the delegates. Including staffers and security, there were some four hundred men and women seated in the General Assembly. He wondered idly how many of the shouters were in the pay of the Chinese.

The scene before him was exactly what the Chinese wanted. Chaos. Gridlock. Faction against faction. Anything went, as long as whatever was said had no tangible effects on the People's Liberation Army investment of the Central Asian republics.

The Committee for the Constitution of the Central Asian Union had taken over the resort known as the Silk Road Samarkand. Located on the outskirts of the city, the resort boasted some of the best hotels and restaurants in the region, not to mention a brand-new Congress Center with 28,000 square meters of meeting space.

The entire resort had been repurposed as the new home of the Central Asian Union, but the Congress Center was the crown jewel of the new government. Each Central Asian republic had their own set of spacious offices and meeting rooms, and delegates were housed in the luxury Regency Amir Temur hotel—where Timur had the penthouse suite. This afternoon was the conclusion of the final General Assembly session of the second Constitutional Committee Conference. By tonight, the delegates would all scatter. Most would travel back to their separate republics to report back on their progress in negotiating a constitution for the Central Asian Union. They would write reports and give speeches, but in truth, there had been no progress.

Timur allowed his gaze to wander over the well-appointed conference hall. He took in all the details: the thick carpets, the linen-covered tables, the coffee-and-tea bar along the wall and the laden tables in the back of the hall, constantly replenished with sweets and pastries between meals.

Strange, he mused. No one ever asked who paid for all this luxury. The hotels, the food, the limousines, the meeting rooms. He supposed they all assumed that the host country of Uzbekistan was footing the bill. It was what the Chinese wanted everyone to think and Timur was content to let the delegates believe the white lie.

It was all in service of the greater good, he told himself.

The fiery Tajik at the podium managed to outshout his detractors. "The presence of Chinese military troops in our homeland is a violation of our sovereignty. They must be removed immediately!" He leveled an accusing finger at Timur. "The actions of one man cannot be allowed to stand in for the voices of our people."

Timur allowed a tight smile at the reprimand. The young man's voice disappeared into roaring chaos again.

The speaker was right, of course, Timur reflected. He alone had invited China to provide security for the republics in the form of the People's Liberation Army. In the aftermath of a terrorist attack in Samarkand in November, Timur assumed political authority for an entire region. The people—many of whom were in this room—had just let him do it.

The light in front of the speaker's podium changed from green to red, indicating the speaker's time was expired. The young Tajik protested that he should be allowed more time, but the chairman of the proceedings was unmoved by his entreaties.

Chairman Firuz Sharipov rapped his gavel and called for order. He stared sternly at the assembly until he achieved some level of control.

"The honorable representative from Uzbekistan is allotted three minutes," Sharipov announced, punctuating his remark with another rap of the gavel. He cast a sidelong glance at Timur, and out of sight of the assembly, tapped his wristwatch.

Timur nodded once, barely perceptible to the audience. After this delegate, Sharipov would adjourn the meeting for a two-week break.

Of all the people in the room, Firuz Sharipov was possibly the only person Timur believed was acting in the true interest of the Central Asian Union. The younger man was in his early thirties, with a close-cropped beard and thin face. He had skin the color of milk and startling green eyes that drank in details like a sponge. He was fluent in Russian, English, and his native Kyrgyz, as well as conversational in most of the dialects spoken in the polyglot chamber.

But Sharipov's greatest trait was his loyalty to Timur Ganiev's vision of a Central Asian Union.

More discord on the floor of the assembly broke into Timur's thoughts. This speaker was proposing calling elections for the Central Asian Union before they proceeded with the congressional congress. The topic was another crowd favorite and destined to end in failure.

The ugly truth was that there were enough people in this room who did not want progress at all. Not the dictators who held power in the individual republics, not the Russians, not the Chinese. The constitutional committee proceeding was a living example of the contrasts at work. They debated their own future in the Russian language, inside a building paid for by the Chinese.

The tragedy was that no one apart from Timur seemed to recognize the irony of the situation.

That wasn't entirely true, he knew. Firuz Sharipov was an honest man and a steady presence. Timur noted how his Vice President gathered around him like-minded politicians from across the region. Slowly, carefully, he was building a coalition that one day might realize the dream of a true Central Asian Union.

Timur shifted in his chair, suddenly uncomfortable. In Sharipov's vision, the leader of that future Union was Timur himself.

When he looked at his reflection in the mirror every morning, he told himself that the ends justified the means. The CAU was a vision worth fighting for. Worth lying for.

The cold truth was that Timur Ganiev was a traitor, a Chinese agent. His plea for the PLA to quell the terrorist violence in Central Asia had not been a cry for help from an embattled leader as he'd told the world. He was carrying out an order from the Chinese Minister of State Security. In the chaos following a staged terrorist attack on the Jade Spike ceremony, Timur called for an invasion of his own country. His words also gave license to the lie. Because of him, the Chinese were the saviors of Central Asia in the eyes of the world, not invaders.

He looked out over the shouting delegates. These men and women had about as much chance of forming a true Central Asian Union as a classroom of preschoolers had in building a rocket ship to Mars.

Chaos. Bought and paid for. Just what his Chinese handler wanted.

A woman, blond hair pulled into a ponytail, edged into his field of view. A camera crew trailed her as she maneuvered near the speaker's podium.

She pointed to the lectern, angling her hand to indicate the shot she wanted. The Chinese cameraman knelt on the ground to get the angle.

Nicole Nipper. He'd even dragged a foreign reporter into his lie. What was he thinking when he'd asked her to stay? It hadn't been that hard, not really. Nicole was here for Nicole. She was a journalist following a story, and he was the story.

He watched her graceful movements as she wove her way through the delegates. She was a beautiful woman and he was a lonely man, but try as he might, Nicole had never let him get too close. She shadowed him wherever he went, recording device on and camera crew never far behind, but she always maintained distance from her subject.

Friends, yes. Lovers, no—at least, not yet.

The delegate's time was drawing to a close. The light would turn red any second now. Sharipov turned to Timur.

"Mr. President, do I have your permission to adjourn these proceedings?"

"Mr. Chairman," Timur said in a voice loud enough that it would be recorded in the official proceedings. "You may adjourn this session of the Committee for the Constitution of the Central Asian Union."

A moment later, the Chairman gaveled the committee into adjournment. Timur rose, smiling, clapping his hands in seeming appreciation for the hard work of the delegates. He saw Nicole's camera man aiming at the dais and he squared his shoulders.

He released a long-held sigh of relief. A two-week respite from the all-day General Assembly meetings. Working groups would continue during the break, but Timur would be mostly out of the public eye.

The hardest part about living a lie was the juggling. He could hold most people at a distance, but the people he had to face on a daily basis—like Nicole and Sharipov—were the most difficult for him.

And then there was Jimmy Li.

His MSS handler was an arrogant ass who demanded much and gave little in return. His contempt told Timur all he needed to know about their relationship. They owned him. It was not a case of if Timur would follow orders, it was only how quickly he would execute Beijing's bidding.

If Timur's treachery was exposed, he was a dead man. He knew it and Jimmy reminded him every time they met.

One day, he told himself during his morning communes with his reflection, his sacrifice will have been worth it. The Central Asian Union will be a reality. The ends will justify his means.

But even that rationalization rang hollow now. With every day that passed, the PLA's grip on Central Asia grew tighter. They were never going to leave. It was only a matter of time before his homeland was just another province of the Middle Kingdom.

As he made his way off the dais, Sharipov ran interference for Timur with the delegates. Everyone wanted something from him.

Only a moment of your time, Mr. President.

Have you considered my proposal, Mr. President?

Most days, he would entertain a few requests from carefully screened individuals. He would listen and offer suggestions, perhaps agree to release a public statement. Timur wondered how many of them were being paid off by Jimmy Li and the MSS, how many were tests of his loyalty planted by the MSS.

If he stopped to think about the lies built on lies, it made his head hurt.

This afternoon, he merely waved at the delegates behind the cordon and strode into the winter sunshine. His two-man security detail fell into step behind him at a respectful distance. Foot traffic was light outside and a walk across the wide plaza in front of the Congress Center allowed him to stretch his legs. The wind blew from the west, bringing the chill of the steppes into the luxury resort. The fresh breeze felt good after the stuffiness of the assembly room. Timur breathed deeply and lengthened his stride.

"Mr. President!" called a woman's voice from behind him.

He knew the voice and welcomed the sound. He turned, gave a nod to his security team to let Nicole Nipper approach. Her camera crew was nowhere in sight. Good, he thought. A private chat with a beautiful woman was a nice way to end his day.

She trotted up to him, her face flushed from exertion. She wore cargo pants and a work shirt, rolled up at the sleeves and open at the neck. When she smiled, the expression lit up her face, making her seem even more attractive.

"Nicole, what a pleasant surprise." He turned on his heel. "Walk with me."

She fell into step beside him but said nothing. He found that odd for a reporter. Rather than ask question after question, she often stayed silent and let him speak.

"What can I do for you, Nicole?"

Another beat of silence. "How does it feel?"

"How does what feel?"

"This is the second session of the Constitutional Committee and there's been no progress. How does that make you feel?"

Timur laughed. "I think we're making great progress behind the scenes. The draft language looks excellent. The next committee meeting will be very eventful, I think."

"You said that before this meeting," Nicole replied. "I have it on tape."

They reached the edge of the plaza, and Timur's limo crawled to a stop next to the curb. Before the driver could get out, Timur opened his own door. "May I give you a ride, Nicole?"

She looked at him with a searching expression, then got in and slid across the back seat. Timur followed and closed the door behind him. The vehicle pulled away smoothly, entering the queue departing the center.

Nicole took a digital recorder from her pocket and placed it on the seat between them. "You haven't answered my question, Mr. President."

Timur stared at the recorder, then looked out the window. Delegates hurried along the sidewalk, some headed for the airport, some for the train station. All headed home for the break.

He suddenly felt lonely. He turned to Nicole. "Have dinner with me tonight."

The invitation surprised her, and he saw her guard go up. But then she did something unexpected. Nicole turned off the recorder and took his hand.

"I'm worried about you," she said.

Her hand was warm, but even he could sense it was the touch of a friend, not the caress of a lover.

"What does that mean?" Timur said. He started to pull his hand away, but her touch felt wonderful. He realized how much he craved human contact.

"How long can you keep this up?" she said. "You are not single-handedly responsible for the birth of a nation. I can help. You can trust me."

Trust. There was that word again. He suddenly wanted to tell her everything. His treachery, his lies—but, no, that could never happen.

"Have dinner with me tonight," he said again. "As friends," he added.

Nicole hesitated, then nodded. "As friends."

6

Ayni Air Base, Dushanbe, Tajikistan

Senior Colonel Kang studied the aerial view of the tiny Uzbek hamlet of Suvlisay. On the screen, the town appeared as a pocket of green tucked between folds of steep brown mountains. Twenty or so houses, two-story structures of stone and concrete, were scattered amidst shade trees. A shallow river snaked a path through the town and it seemed every square meter outside the town limits was occupied by some type of agriculture. His eyes ran over the straight rows of an orchard, shorn fields of harvested wheat, and pastures dotted with wandering cows, sheep, and goats.

Kang raised his gaze from the computer screen to where a PLA second lieutenant fidgeted. "Tell me again," he said.

The sweaty young man's voice had a breathy quality that betrayed his nervousness. "SIGINT intercepted a call from a mobile phone originating from this dwelling." On the screen, he'd dropped a red pin over a house in the center of the village. "The number is linked to a possible insurgent."

"Did signals intel recover any of the voice transmission?" Kang asked.

"No, sir. Only metadata."

Kang let the silence unwind as he zoomed out on the map. There was one main road that followed the river into the town. A few dusty tracks climbed into the hills. The village looked like a peaceful place, but looks could be deceiving.

"What is your proposed plan of action, Lieutenant?"

"The system recommends a search-and-seizure operation for insurgent weapons."

Kang felt a twinge of irritation and he let it show. "I didn't ask you what the system recommended. I asked for *your* plan."

The young officer flushed. "I concur with the Foresight recommendation, sir. Request permission to execute a search for illegal weapons."

Kang hesitated. This officer, this kid, was as green as they came. Fresh out of infantry school and eager to make his bones in the field. Excess ambition and lack of experience was a dangerous combination.

Still, it was low risk. Prior to this single intercept from a low-flying drone, there had never been any indication of insurgent activity in this town. Nor was the location a good place to cache weapons for the insurgents. If the town of Suvlisay was a staging area, it was a poor one. It was not near anything and the village had only one road in and out.

No, Kang decided, the predictive AI was wrong. This operation was a waste of time. It might, however, be a useful training opportunity for the young lieutenant and his men. As an added bonus, General Wong would get the satisfaction of seeing Kang following the operational recommendations of his pet AI. It never hurt to keep the boss happy.

"Tell me how you would perform the search, Lieutenant," Kang said.

The young man cleared his throat. "Well, sir, I would position a platoon on the south side of the town." He used a stylus to draw a yellow line on the road that ran by the river.

Kang listened to the brief, offering suggestions along the way. It was a simple plan, something not even a brand-new infantry officer could screw up. Place a platoon on either end of the village along the road while the third platoon, led by Second Lieutenant Li, entered the town to conduct a search.

"When you're inside the town, set up a security perimeter and ask permission to search the property, Lieutenant," Kang said. "If the owner refuses, you insist. Politely. If he still refuses, you take him into temporary custody and perform the search anyway. Do you understand?"

Li nodded vigorously. "Yes, Senior Colonel." His face was flushed and he was clearly excited.

"Above all, you must be calm and professional. Your men will follow your lead."

"I will not let you down, sir."

Kang nodded. "I want regular updates, Lieutenant. If you find anything —anything at all—that is linked to the SIF, you contact me immediately. I am thirty minutes away by helicopter."

"Yes, sir." Second Lieutenant Li saluted.

General Wong's face filled the screen of the tablet in Kang's hands. His cheeks were flushed red with anger.

"How could you let this happen?" he shouted. Kang turned down the volume in his headset.

"No excuse, sir." Kang clamped his jaw shut.

"Well, you'd better find an excuse, Senior Colonel. This sloppiness will not go over well in Beijing."

"Yes, sir. I'll be on site in the next ten minutes. I'll report back as soon as I have the facts."

With a final grimace at the camera, General Wong severed the connection.

Kang seethed. He directed his gaze out the window of the Z-20 helicopter to the brown mountains rolling out beneath them like the folds of a wooly blanket. Sunlight kissed the peaks while shadows pooled in the deep valleys.

The pilot swung in his seat and pointed down as the helo banked and descended.

The village of Suvlisay still looked like a peaceful place. From the air, there was no sign of what had transpired less than an hour ago.

The helicopter leveled out as it moved up the valley. Kang could see fields of winter grains on either side of the dirt track that led into the town. They passed over a platoon of Chinese soldiers, and Kang spied an army-green Mengshi command vehicle parked next to an orchard. A uniformed soldier waved his arms at the incoming aircraft.

The helo slowed, descended. Kang pulled open the door and jumped to the ground. Behind him, the aircraft powered down.

Second Lieutenant Li came to attention and saluted. Kang returned the salute without breaking stride, heading for the waiting vehicle. Li ran to catch up, entering the car from the opposite side.

"Drive," Kang barked at the driver. Then he turned his attention to the sweating lieutenant. "Do you have it?"

"Yes, sir." Li handed him a memory chip the size of his thumbnail. "The video feeds from all the body cams are there."

Normally, all the video footage from individual soldiers could be viewed live, but Li's company had not been outfitted with the latest model of body cameras. The older versions needed their recordings downloaded to view them.

Kang snapped the memory chip into the slot on his tablet and ran the program to integrate all of the individual feeds into one cohesive video. A dialogue box on the tablet asked him if he wanted to upload the compiled video to the network. Kang hesitated, then touched the box to decline. He might as well see what he was dealing with before he shared it with his chain of command.

"Sir?" Li said.

"What?" Kang replied.

"It was self-defense, sir. We were fired on by the enemy."

Kang ignored him and started the video.

A jerky shot of a view through a windshield. Kang looked up and saw it was the same road they were on now, except on the video they were moving much faster. The picture swayed as the Mengshi took a corner and swerved. Someone in the video shouted and voices responded in a chorus. Soldiers getting pumped up, Kang realized.

The video lurched as the car skidded to a stop next to a two-story stone-and-cinder-block house. When the doors opened, dust enveloped the emerging soldiers. They were all shouting now and Kang saw Li directing his men to set up a security perimeter. He was keyed up, but he looked to be in control and the execution of the perimeter was textbook perfect. Kang relaxed.

Maybe he exaggerated, Kang thought. Maybe it's not as bad as I thought.

Then the screen changed and Kang realized he was seeing Li's video feed.

"Tell him I want to search his house," Li said to his interpreter, a young Tajik who looked every bit as inexperienced as the PLA officer giving him orders.

The interpreter spoke with an older man who became more agitated as the conversation developed, shaking his head, his voice rising. More locals crowded around the older man. They were dressed in a hodgepodge of native and Western clothing. A polyester warm-up jacket over homespun pants and Nike sneakers. All of them wore hats of some kind. Knit caps, baseball caps, a girl in a floppy sunhat adorned with an enormous yellow flower. All of them yelled at the interpreter, who wilted under their disapproval.

Lieutenant Li on the video was out of his depth and getting frustrated. He spoke sharply to the interpreter and the man amped up his response to the crowd of townspeople.

There was a shout behind him and Li's point of view spun wildly before settling on a scene that made Kang cringe.

A young native man, a teenager, was flat on his back in the dust, a bloody gash across his forehead. He did not move. A PLA infantryman wrestled with another local, this one much larger than the thin young man in the dirt. As Kang watched, the Uzbek threw an elbow and caught the PLA soldier in the jaw. The soldier let go of his rifle. The Uzbek assailant stepped back as if surprised that he'd won the fight so easily. He bent down to pick up the fallen weapon.

In that moment, everything went sideways. Kang could not look away. A second PLA soldier realized what had happened and shouted. Kang saw his rifle come up. The Uzbek man saw it, too. In one smooth motion, he spun and pulled the trigger on the weapon he had just picked up.

The *pop-pop-pop* sounded like a tinny drum in the speakers of the tablet. Screams, more gunfire from multiple sources. Lieutenant Li's body cam dropped to the ground as he took cover. The young officer screamed at his men to stop firing.

The car drew to a halt and Kang paused the video. Through the windshield, he recognized the stone house from the recording. The road opened into a small town square fronted by a series of houses. A group of four PLA soldiers had a crowd of villagers on their knees against a stone wall. All of them young men, several with bruised faces.

A tall tree, bare of leaves, hung over the edge of the stone house. In the dirt under the tree, Kang made out six bodies. He swore under his breath as he turned to Li. "What did you find on your search?"

"Nothing, sir." Li swallowed. "I searched the house thoroughly and all of the adjoining houses. We found four hunting rifles. Soviet-made, bolt action."

"That's all?"

Li had trouble meeting Kang's gaze. "That's all, sir."

"Come with me." Kang got out of the car and slammed the door behind him. He did not wait as he stalked over to the bodies lined up under the tree.

Four men, late teens or early twenties, a middle-aged woman, and the girl from the video with the yellow flower on her floppy sunhat. She had a look of surprise on her face and a dark red stain on her blouse.

"Get a tarp and cover these bodies, Lieutenant," he ordered.

As Li hurried away, Kang fought down the anger surging in his gut. He had no one to blame but himself for this mess. He'd allowed that stupid AI program to dictate field actions. Li and his men were poorly trained and he'd sent them in anyway.

A stupid mistake. *His* stupid mistake.

He watched two soldiers unfurl a green tarp over the bodies of the villagers. Li returned to his side, breathing heavily.

"How many injured?" Kang asked.

"Three of my men were injured, sir. One seriously."

Kang looked at the men still on their knees next to the wall. "How many locals?"

Li hesitated. "Eight, sir. Mostly minor. They're being treated by the medical unit now."

Six dead, eight injured out of a town of what—he looked around—a hundred people? This was the kind of disaster that made recruiting for the terrorists an easy job. Time for some damage control.

"I want to speak to the man in the video," Kang said. "The one whose house you searched."

The old man was being held with the men at the stone wall. Kang watched as the interpreter spoke to the man and helped him to his feet. Kang walked until they were out of earshot of the rest of the prisoners—and out of sight of the dead bodies.

It was tough to say exactly how old the man was. With his sunburned skin and weathered features, Kang could have made a case for late forties or early seventies. His eyes were sharp, flitting from Kang to Li as he accepted a cigarette from the interpreter. He sucked in the smoke, held it, then blew it out in a long stream.

The sun was going down, shadows filling the valley. He said something to the interpreter, jerking his head back toward the way they had come.

"He says to let his people go free," the interpreter said.

"Are any of his people part of the SIF?" Kang asked.

The old man shook his head before the interpreter even asked the question.

"Why did we pick up a mobile phone transmission that linked someone in this town to the SIF? Tell him I'll know if he's lying."

"I'm not lying," the old man said through the interpreter. He looked at Kang. "No SIF here," he said in English.

Lieutenant Li started to speak, but Kang stopped him.

"I'm sorry for your loss," Kang said to the old man in English.

The man finished his cigarette and flicked it away. Then he leaned over and spat in the dirt at Kang's feet.

"Go back to China," he said, and turned his back on Kang.

7

Suvlisay, Uzbekistan

Harrison ducked involuntarily as the Harbin Z-20 helo flew over his observation post in the mountains overlooking the tiny Uzbek town. He raised the field glasses and followed the aircraft.

"We've got reinforcements coming in," he said to Sanjar.

There was no answer.

The helo made a wide circle around the narrow valley, then hovered next to an orchard and landed. The door opened and a uniformed man got out, striding across the close-cropped field. Harrison focused the glasses and hit the record button.

The PLA officer who'd overseen the raid on the town rushed up and popped a crisp salute. The senior officer walked past him and got into the waiting Mengshi. If you took away the red Chinese flag, the vehicle looked like a carbon copy of an American Humvee.

"Looks like a senior officer," Harrison continued. "I snapped his picture."

Still no answer. Harrison turned. Sanjar sat with his back to the wall, staring at a mobile phone cradled in his hands.

"You okay, buddy?" Harrison tried to make his tone sound reassuring.

Sanjar looked up, his normally cheerful face tight with worry. "It's my fault."

"Look, you were following orders and the whole thing got out of hand." Harrison tried to keep his tone light. "It's...complicated."

Except it wasn't complicated. What had started as a simple test to measure the PLA signals-collection capability had turned into a bloodbath. Down in the town square, innocent people lost their lives because of a simple phone call.

In the aftermath of the railroad bridge bombing, Akhmet had become convinced that the faster than expected PLA response was not a coincidence. He believed that they possessed a much more sophisticated signals-collection capability than the CIA analysis team had led him to believe.

So the former Soviet fighter devised a test to prove his theory.

Earlier that day, Sanjar had walked into the small town. He had a coffee at a makeshift bar and made a fifteen-second phone call on a burner phone to a number that they knew the PLA had already captured. When he climbed back into the observation post an hour later, he was full of energy and told Harrison all about the little town.

Suvlisay had been chosen specifically because it wasn't a central location. If the PLA was able to capture and process a mobile phone signal out here, then their collection capabilities were advanced well beyond the current CIA assessments.

Harrison and Sanjar were ordered to remain in the area overnight and observe any enemy response—although Harrison suspected he was there more as a babysitter for Sanjar than as an observer. A single mobile phone hit in an out of the way location like this one should not have warranted much of a response from the PLA. At most, Akhmet expected a visiting patrol and possibly a search.

At two in the afternoon, three PLA platoons arrived in the valley. Two of the platoons took up positions on the roads leading in and out of Suvlisay. Harrison watched the officer in charge fumble his way through the evolution. The troops were regular infantry, probably conscripts. There was a lot of saluting and shouting, but no one seemed to be in charge. It took the young second lieutenant over an hour to get his people organized and lead a convoy into the town itself.

Harrison got a little chill when the PLA officer disembarked from the Mengshi outside the stone house where Sanjar had made the phone call. He stood in the center of the dirt square shouting orders to his men, who scrambled around finding firing positions.

A haze of dust hung in the air when the officer approached an older man sitting under the tree outside the stone house. Harrison could not see faces at this distance, but the body language of the PLA soldiers told him all he needed to know. They were stiff and held their weapons at the ready. When they spoke to each other, they shouted. A sense of nervous tension increased as the townspeople gathered in the square, crowding around the soldiers.

At first, the old man didn't even get to his feet when the officer approached. But as the conversation went on, the old man grew more agitated, especially when the officer pointed at his house. He wished he could hear what they were saying.

Harrison looked back at Sanjar. The kid was playing a video game on his phone, his jaw slack, brow furrowed in concentration.

Back in the square, the situation was not improving. The PLA officer was leaning in and shouting at the interpreter, who was in turn passing on the urgency of the message to the old man.

It went off the rails fast. Harrison saw a burst of dust and trained his glasses away from the conversation. A shot rang out, at this distance it sounded like a pop. A split second later, a cascade of gunfire, like a string of firecrackers, rang out. Dust devils rose across the square as people ran. He heard screams, then distant shouts as the PLA officer tried to reestablish control.

Sanjar was at Harrison's elbow. He could hear the kid's breath, loud and raspy. "What's happening, Harrison?"

"It's...hard to see," Harrison replied. "There's a lot of..."

The dust cleared and Harrison got a sick feeling in his stomach. He saw people sprawled in the dirt. One wore a bright red knit cap, and a girl had a floppy straw sunhat. Neither moved. A PLA soldier squirmed under a tree, holding his belly and screaming.

"Oh, God," Harrison muttered. This was not supposed to happen.

"Harrison, what is—"

Harrison passed the binoculars to Sanjar. He watched the kid's Adam's apple bob as he focused on the scene below. His breath turned ragged. He sat back on his heels, his eyes wide.

"I did this," he said.

"No." Harrison gripped his shoulders. "The Chinese did this. Not you." He helped the kid to the back of the concealed cliff serving as an observation post and put a canteen in his hand. Then he went back to the glasses.

He watched the PLA soldiers rampage through the houses around the town square. They probably called it a search, but it was really payback. They threw furniture in the street, broke windows, and piled household goods in the doorway. A dog barked and a PLA soldier shot him. Harrison saw some of them eating loaves of bread they'd stolen from the houses.

They piled the corpses under the big tree and herded all of the men who had been in the square against a stone wall. They forced them to kneel and put their hands on top of their heads. Harrison held his breath, wondering if he was about to see a mass execution.

It was less than an hour later that the helo arrived. The tone of the raid changed as soon as the senior officer was on scene. He watched the interview with the old man. He saw the old man flick away his cigarette and spit at the officer's feet.

Harrison held his breath, waiting for a reaction. An insult like that one could get the Uzbek man jailed, or worse.

But nothing happened. The PLA officer walked away.

Smart move, Harrison thought as he refocused the glasses and took another still shot of the PLA senior colonel. Whoever this guy was, he was a professional.

When it was dark, he rousted Sanjar and they made their way around the mountain, away from Suvlisay. It was a two-hour journey back to Akhmet's base camp.

Akhmet was a busy man these days. Most of his time was spent receiving visitors. Harrison was in very few of these meetings, but he understood that the former Spetsnaz officer was setting up resistance cells across the region. He'd once had a front row seat as the Soviets fell to a smaller, less capable insurgent force in Afghanistan. All the lessons he'd learned in defeat were now part of his toolkit as he created an insurgency against the Chinese military.

Akhmet's trusted cadre of handpicked leaders were scattered across the four nations of the Central Asian Union, operating from safe houses and camps in the mountains. These leaders formed cells of no more than four men, mostly recruited from the local population and military deserters. Compartmentalization of information was key to his strategy. As recruits entered into the ranks of the resistance, the cells divided, ensuring that no single man knew more than one or two other cells.

Coordination was done face-to-face or by messenger, hence the steady stream of visitors for Akhmet. It was slow and time consuming, but it kept them off the PLA surveillance network. Cell phones and secure apps were available, but they relied on the Chinese Huawei network for connection and were only used in case of emergencies.

When Harrison and Sanjar arrived after midnight, Akhmet asked to see him immediately.

The older man listened to the entire recounting without interruption, his hooded eyes studying the CIA officer. Harrison was used to the scrutiny now. When Akhmet did something, he did it with his full attention.

When Harrison was finished, Akhmet looked into the embers of the fire. "What are your conclusions?"

"Our assessment of the PLA collections and analysis capability are inaccurate," Harrison said.

Akhmet grunted.

"You think there's more?" Harrison asked.

"Maybe." Akhmet shrugged. "You said they wanted to search the house. That's when the argument started?"

"That's what it looked like."

"Why would the PLA send three platoons of soldiers into the middle of nowhere on the basis of a single mobile phone call?"

"What do you think it means, Ussat?"

Akhmet grinned at him, a sudden slash of white teeth in his weathered face. "You're the intelligence analyst. You tell me."

Harrison considered the question. They'd chosen Suvlisay because of its remote location. There was no resistance activity in the area. The mobile phone call was the only possible trigger for the PLA raid.

"Those people suffered because of our actions, Ussat."

The lines on Akhmet's face deepened in the dim light. "They bring their own undoing."

"What does that mean?" The words came out more forcefully than he'd planned.

Akhmet seemed unperturbed by Harrison's harsh tone. "For every senseless killing, the PLA creates ten new resistance fighters. They are our best recruiting tool."

Harrison felt his anger rising. Akhmet's eyes narrowed.

"This is war, Harrison. We use all the tools at our disposal."

Harrison stood up. "I have to go."

Akhmet checked him at the door. "The PLA response was not logical, Harrison. You saw it yourself. I need you to find out why. That is what the CIA can do for us."

8

Washington, DC

The West Wing of the White House buzzed with activity. Staffers, smartphones and laptops clutched in their hands, rushed past him. Hand trucks piled high with boxes clogged the narrow hallways. Every television in every office was tuned to the White House Press Room, where President Serrano's press secretary was delivering her final briefing of the term.

It was the end of an era, Don realized with no small amount of nostalgia. He'd spent eight years with the current President, but tomorrow, at 1201, all that would change when Eleanor Cashman took the oath of office.

Don knew how rare a truly peaceful transfer of power was in the world and he was proud to be part of the process.

Listen to yourself, he thought. You sound like you're narrating a documentary. Get your head in the game.

Don had business in the West Wing this morning. Serrano was still President for another day and he'd summoned Don to the White House for reasons unknown. In Don's experience with Serrano, that was not usually a good sign.

The President's executive assistant smiled at him when he arrived outside the Oval Office. Her desk was bare except for a small stack of file folders and her computer.

"How good to see you, Don," she said. "You can go right in. He's expecting you."

Don tugged on the handle of the soundproofed door, and the heavy panel swung open easily. He let the door close behind him.

Outgoing President Ricardo Serrano was seated at the Resolute desk, pen in hand. The windows behind him were flooded with light, casting a warm glow into the room. The desk blotter was empty save for a single sheet of paper and an envelope. As Don entered, Serrano signed the bottom of the page. He looked up and grinned.

"I'll be right with you, Don. Have a seat and pour a coffee for both of us, please."

He sounded relaxed, his voice warm. Don poured two coffees and added a splash of cream to his cup. He perched on the sofa and watched as the President carefully folded the sheet of paper and put it into an envelope. Serrano opened the top drawer of the desk and placed the envelope inside.

He sprang out of his chair in a burst of youthful energy and strode to the sitting area, waving for Don to stay seated. He cocked his head toward the desk.

"I remember the letter my predecessor left for me," he said. "I thought I knew what I was doing. Turns out, I didn't know anything." He shook his head ruefully. "There's no handbook for this job. Every day something happens that no one has ever seen before. A brand-new opportunity to make a difference."

The soon-to-be former President was in a good mood. Considering some of the meetings he'd had in this office, Don thought that was a very generous way to look at the job of Leader of the Free World.

Serrano sipped his coffee. "You probably want to know why I asked you to come in."

"Yes, sir," Don replied.

Serrano drew a folded sheet of paper from his inner pocket and passed it to Don.

Don unfolded the page and scanned the contents. It was a handwritten letter from Russian President Nikolay Sokolov that began with *Dear Ric.*

Don looked up. "This looks personal, sir."

Serrano crossed his legs, leaned back in his chair. "It is. Nikolay sent it in the diplomatic pouch in a sealed envelope with instructions for the Russian ambassador to deliver it to me personally. It arrived this morning."

"May I?" Don asked.

Serrano nodded.

Dear Ric—

We've come a long way since our first meeting at the peace accord in Helsinki. That seems like such a long time ago.

I regret that we were not able to work together more closely in the past year. I always thought we made a good team, but even the best partners are subject to circumstances beyond our control. I trust that history will judge us for the good we have done.

I thank you for your assistance these past years in helping me to offer a new future to my people. I am in your debt.

My sincere wishes for a peaceful retirement. I hope we can meet again someday, when we are old men, and look with pride on the world we have helped to make.

You have been a good leader to your people and a good friend to me.

Sincerely—

Nikolay

Don read the letter twice before he looked up.

"Well?" Serrano asked.

"It seems like a heartfelt letter to a friend, Mr. President."

"What does the analyst in you have to say about this note, Don?"

Don perused the page again before he answered. "He opens with your time together in Helsinki. Arguably, that moment was the closest that Russia and the United States have been since the end of the Cold War. You used that bond to protect our Navy from the Chinese when we were searching for the lost nukes. President Sokolov called on you to return the favor and help him in Central Asia last year."

Serrano's face soured at Don's last observation. "I fear our help to a friend in need was too little, too late."

"I think he acknowledges that fact, Mr. President. He says: *even the best partners are subject to circumstances beyond our control.* He knows you did what you could."

"Did we, Don?" Serrano's expression turned grave. In that moment, Don could see how the office had aged the man. His styled hair was more gray than black now and permanent worry lines etched the skin around his eyes and the corners of his mouth.

"Sir, I—"

Serrano waved his hand. "You don't have to answer that." He leaned forward and raised the silver coffeepot to ask if Don wanted a refill. Don held out his cup and saucer, grateful for the distraction.

"There's a line about history judging us," Serrano said.

Don consulted the page again. "I trust that history will judge us for the good we have done," he read aloud.

"That's the one," Serrano agreed. "What do you make of it?"

Don hesitated and the President noticed. "Give it to me straight, Riley. I only have a few hours left in office. You have nothing to fear from telling me the unvarnished truth."

"The reports we're getting out of Russia are not good, sir," Don began. "If even half of them are true, then Nikolay Sokolov has...changed."

"Did he really assassinate his uncle?"

Don nodded. "We believe that's the case, Mr. President. The election he won was not free or fair, either. That's been confirmed."

Serrano sighed. "Why? Your best guess, please."

"I believe that President Sokolov did what he thought he had to do to stay in power. When I read that line, sir." Don picked up the letter. "*I trust that history will judge us for the good we have done*. I hear him saying that the ends justify the means. That he felt he truly had no choice except to take the actions he did to ensure Russia's future."

Serrano was silent for a long moment. The bright winter sunshine dimmed as a cloud passed in front of the sun.

"Will he stop?" Serrano asked. "Does he have an off-ramp?"

Don evaded the question. "His biggest issue right now is Central Asia, Mr. President. The Chinese are in a strong position and rising. If Russia loses any more influence there, it endangers their economy in the long-term."

"Cashman's not going to lift a finger to help Nikolay, is she?"

"I think President-elect Cashman has made her feelings about the Russian Federation very clear, sir. In my dealings with her, she has not been open to reconsidering her position."

Serrano's lips twisted. "I guess a change in leadership falls under circumstances beyond our control." His tone was bitter, resigned.

There was a knock at the door and the executive assistant poked her head in. "Your next appointment is here, Mr. President."

Serrano held up two fingers to indicate another two minutes. She shut the door behind her.

"One last thing, Don. When I was brand-new in this job, I wanted to fix Venezuela. It was a campaign promise and I thought we could make a difference. What did you tell me?"

"Based on our intelligence assessment, I told you it was a bad idea, sir."

"That's right, you did." Serrano's eyes locked on his. "Apply that same filter to Central Asia, Don. What does your analytical mind tell you?"

Don cleared his throat. "My analytical mind tells me that any decisions about our involvement in Central Asia are above my pay grade, sir."

"Fair enough," Serrano said, "but answer me this: What does a win look like in Central Asia?"

It wasn't really a question, Don knew. Geopolitics was like wrestling a balloon animal. When you squeezed one part of the animal, another area expanded. It was a constant balance between diplomacy and strength.

Serrano stood suddenly and held out his hand.

"You're a good man, Don Riley. You've never been afraid to tell me the truth. I want you to give President Cashman the same respect."

For the last time, Don pressed his palm into the President's hand. His grip was as firm as ever. A lump formed in Don's throat.

"I promise, sir."

9

Samarkand, Uzbekistan

Timur groped at the bedside table for the ringing phone. He held the receiver to his ear.

"Good morning, Mr. President." The mocking voice spoke English with an American accent.

Timur focused on the red numbers of the clock on the bedside table. 0218.

"What do you want, Jimmy?" he growled.

"I want you in the lobby in one hour, Mr. President. There is work to be done that requires the deft hand of a seasoned politician."

The line went dead.

Timur dropped the receiver into the cradle and rolled onto his back. He felt his lips curl in disgust.

When he'd first met the Chinese Minister of State Security at a World Health Organization event, Yan Tao had been gracious, even deferential. Timur recalled feeling gratified by the attention from such an important figure in the Chinese government.

The casual contact turned into an invitation to dinner, then a consulting job for Timur in the Central Asian region bordering western

China. There were more trips, more money, and more dinners filled with heady discussions of Timur's plans to improve the healthcare system not only in his own country but across all of Central Asia.

Meanwhile, Chinese infrastructure projects flowered across the region. As the projects became deeply embedded in local communities, Timur heard stories of local politicians taking bribes. He recalled his disgust at those petty, grasping men.

Then came the first ask, a request for confidential details about the latest census. It was a small favor, and considering all that the Minister had done for Timur, he fulfilled the request almost without a second thought. Over the following weeks and months, there were more requests, some asking him to make calls to close friends on behalf of the Chinese, but they were always followed by additional donations to Timur's medical initiatives in Central Asia. Timur obliged, but he also asked to see his friend the Minister.

"I'm feeling uncomfortable about some of the things your people are asking of me," Timur said over a fine dinner at an exclusive Tashkent restaurant.

The Minister sipped his tea and nodded. "I see."

"I'm glad you understand, Tao," Timur said.

"I thought you wanted to help your people," the Minister continued as if Timur had not replied. "I thought you wanted to break down the artificial political boundaries that separate the indigenous peoples of this region."

"Of course I do!" Timur put down his wineglass. He'd spoken about the concept of a unified Central Asian region with the Minister dozens of times.

"Then why won't you cooperate? I am only trying to help you, my friend."

Timur started to reply, but paused as the Minister extracted a folded paper from his breast pocket and slid it across the table. It contained an accounting, down to the last cent, of everything the Minister had given Timur over the last twenty-four months. Every lucrative consulting contract, every trip on a private jet, every hotel stay and dinner, every donation to Timur's nonprofit. There was even a gift of an *ikat*, the ornate silken wall hanging that reminded him of his late wife. It hung on the wall of his sitting room.

The total was staggering. Timur looked across the table at the Minister. "What is this?"

"It's an investment, my friend. Now that we understand each other, the real work can begin."

Timur swallowed, the expensive wine soured in his stomach. He knew without even being told what the Minister meant. He was being given a choice. On one side of the scale was money, influence, and power in exchange for his cooperation. Weighing against that bargain was reputational ruin. If this ledger of his involvement with the Chinese government ever became public, Timur's position as leader in the region was in jeopardy. His carefully cultivated network of contacts around the world would see him as a fraud.

"You can do so much good for the world," the Minister said softly. "I just want to help."

That was the moment when Timur Ganiev became a Chinese asset.

He did not protest that he was being blackmailed or become indignant. Instead, he made an affirmative choice: he would take Chinese money, but he would be different than the greedy politicians he so disdained. For him, this was not about personal gain. He would use Chinese money and influence to change the world for the better.

Their arrangement was different after that dinner. The flow of money became a regular deposit in a numbered account in Dubai. The requests became regular as well, but they were manageable for a man in Timur's position. The Chinese also boosted his social presence, just enough to keep his cause of unity prominent in regional discussions.

And then there was Jimmy Li. Because the Minister was a busy man, he delegated day-to-day control of his newest asset. Jimmy's cover was as an oil and gas executive in Tashkent. For Timur, the fact that he and Jimmy did not reside in the same city was the only redeeming aspect of their relationship.

His new handler was an arrogant young prick who insisted on being called by his American nickname and loved to speak in American slang. He treated Timur with the contempt of a man who had betrayed his people and Timur hated him for it.

At least his personal interactions with Jimmy were minimal these days. In his role as acting President of the Central Asian Union, he and Jimmy were rarely seen together.

Which made Jimmy's phone call to Timur's hotel room at two o'clock in the morning all the more significant. With a sigh, Timur rolled out of bed and made his way in the dark to the bathroom.

The penthouse bathroom was a vast expanse of heated marble floor with a walk-in shower and steam room, a separate area for toilet and bidet, and an entire wall of mirrors above dual sinks and an expansive makeup counter. He splashed water on his face and studied his reflection in the mirror. His head ached from the two bottles of wine he'd drunk with Nicole the evening before and he chased two Tylenol with a large glass of water.

As always, Nicole had ignored his heavy hints that she could spend the night with him. This time, it was for the best. If she had stayed, he wondered how he would have explained Jimmy's early morning call.

Timur knew something was very wrong as soon as he arrived in the lobby at two minutes past three. Jimmy was already there, fifteen minutes early. Jimmy was never early.

Timur's second clue was that Nicole wasn't there. Nicole was supposed to be shadowing him on all official business of the CAU.

"Good, you're early," Jimmy said curtly. "Let's roll." As he turned toward a waiting trio of black Range Rovers, Timur noticed that Jimmy's normally styled hair was a mess and he looked like he'd slept in his clothes.

When Timur climbed into the back of the car next to Jimmy, he saw that the front seats were occupied by armed PLA soldiers.

"What's going on?" Timur asked.

The car sped away from the hotel entrance. "We have a two-hour drive, Mr. President. Take a nap. You're going to need it."

They drove due south on the M39, which only deepened the mystery for Timur. Two hours south would put them deep into the Qashqadaryo river basin. His sense of unease increased when they left the agricultural region and headed east, directly into the mountains. There were no major cities in those mountains. He tried to look up a map on his phone but kept losing the signal.

The sky grew pale as they entered a narrow green valley. Cultivated fields and orchards were wedged between the verge of the two-lane highway and steep mountain slopes. Nothing went to waste in this part of Uzbekistan. Every square meter of arable land was in use to support the inhabitants of this valley. The PLA convoy sped past a donkey cart laden with sheafs of golden winter wheat. The animal's steady tread did not falter. The farmer did not look up.

The mountains crowded closer together and the vehicles slowed as they entered what Timur judged to be the last town in this narrow valley. He caught a glimpse of a hand-painted road sign.

Suvlisay. Timur had never heard of the place.

The cars rolled into a crude town square and stopped. The driver and passenger got out of the vehicle, leaving Timur alone with Jimmy. In the wan morning light, Jimmy's face looked lined and haggard. His dark hair hung in his eyes.

"There was an incident here yesterday," Jimmy said.

Timur looked out the window. He saw pairs of PLA soldiers posted at both sides of the town square. "What kind of incident?"

"The kind where civilians get killed," Jimmy snapped.

Timur put the PLA presence together with the remote location. "Tell me what happened."

"There was a signals intercept of a mobile phone linked to a known terrorist," Jimmy said. "The regional commander authorized a search. It got out of hand."

"What are you talking about? What terrorist organization?"

"The SIF—"

"There is no SIF, Jimmy," Timur snapped, anger coloring his voice. "There never was. You people made it up, remember? That was how I convinced the world to let you invade my country. You were going to fight a terrorist organization that *you* invented."

Jimmy's sigh broke a long silence. "There's a resistance, Timur. A real one. We're calling them the SIF because—"

Timur laughed. To his own ears, his laugh sounded braying and harsh, but he didn't care. "That is rich, Jimmy. First, you invent a terrorist group as an excuse to invade my country, which in turn creates an actual terrorist group."

"Shut up," Jimmy hissed. "You're here to settle things down."

That made Timur stop laughing. "What exactly am I settling?"

Timur spied a PLA officer striding across the town square. He was on the shorter side, but well-built, and he walked with forceful purpose. Jimmy saw him as well and he smiled thinly at Timur. He opened the car door. "You're here to negotiate damages, Mr. President."

Jimmy was out of the car before Timur could say anything else, so he followed. The morning air was chill and a stiff wind blew down the valley. Jimmy shook hands with the PLA officer and turned to Timur.

"Mr. President," he said with a slight bow, "may I present Senior Colonel Kang. He is in command of our counterterrorism mission against the SIF in the Central Asian Union."

The officer's handshake was firm and professional. "Good morning, Mr. President. Thank you for coming on short notice. We are anxious to have this matter resolved quickly."

Timur cut a glare at Jimmy. "Of course, Senior Colonel."

"Our host is anxious to meet you, sir," the officer continued. "If you'll follow me."

Kang led Timur into the largest stone house on the square. They entered a small sitting room populated with a low table flanked by wooden benches, both of which were covered with bright embroidered cloth. The wall behind the table was decorated in a tile mosaic of red, blue, and yellow in an intricate star pattern. A gray-bearded man, his head covered with a plain white *doppa*, immediately stood and rushed to meet them.

"Timur," he said in a low voice full of reverence. He spoke in Uzbek, the language of these mountains. "You honor my home with your presence."

Timur extended his hand, and the old man grasped it with vigor. "Salaam," Timur said. "*Tanishganimdan hursandan*," he added, adopting a formal reply to the man's greeting. It was the proper way to show deference to the man opening his home to an important political figure.

The house was filled with the smells of *plov* cooking and the table was already laid with tea service, sweets, and dried fruits. Timur's stomach growled as the man ushered him to a chair.

As he scanned the room, Timur noticed a few details out of place. The bench the old man occupied had been hastily repaired with a mismatched leg. A cabinet with a glass front had two panes missing and there was a bullet hole in the tile mosaic on the wall.

The PLA officer and Jimmy took a seat on the bench next to Timur, but the old man's undivided attention remained on his countryman. He poured tea for Timur, but the amount of liquid barely covered the bottom of the glass.

Timur saw the two Chinese men exchange a puzzled look, but nodded his thanks. It was Uzbek tradition: the more honored the guest, the less the amount of tea in his glass. This was high praise from the village elder.

"May I have some more?" he asked, again following tradition. This time the old man filled the cup.

These things were not to be rushed. Thirty minutes passed before Timur steered the conversation to the PLA raid. He kept the conversation in Uzbek, both of them ignoring the Chinese men, as Timur extracted the story from the old man.

Six dead...houses searched. What were the Chinese thinking? The thought of foreign soldiers killing his countrymen made him sick at heart. And angry.

When he was satisfied he had the full story, he turned to the PLA senior colonel. "I've gained this man's trust," he said in English. "What do you want me to do?"

Jimmy answered, "Make it go away. Negotiate a number for his time and we'll pay him off."

The PLA officer ignored Jimmy. He studied Timur with cold eyes. "I need information."

The old man watched their exchange and there was hatred in the elder's eyes. Whatever the colonel wanted, Timur would have a difficult time getting it from the old man.

"What kind of information?" he asked.

"The SIF was here," the PLA officer said. "I want to know who they talked to and why."

Timur let out a short laugh. "You're serious?"

The officer frowned and started to say something, but Jimmy interrupted. "The senior colonel wants to know about the SIF, Mr. President. I assured him of your full cooperation." Jimmy's gaze signaled caution to Timur.

Then Timur understood. Even a high-ranking officer like this senior colonel thought the SIF was real. He'd assumed that Jimmy was referring to the SIF in case someone was listening, but that wasn't it at all. The Chinese secret service had taken the ruse so far that they'd even fooled their own military.

Timur filed that fact away in his brain and smiled at Kang. "My apologies, Senior Colonel Kang. I will be happy to help in any way I can."

Then he asked the old man for more tea.

10

The White House, Washington, DC

The first meeting of the National Security Council of the new administration took place at 0800 on January 21st, the day after the inauguration of President Eleanor Cashman.

The Situation Room was standing room only. The fact that almost everyone was new amplified the closeness of the room. Typical National Security Council meetings were structured, often routine affairs, but the atmosphere today was charged with anticipation and no small measure of chaotic energy. Don wasn't surprised. Everyone in the room had the same goal: to make a good first impression—or at least, not screw up in their first interaction with the new President. Some eyed each other warily, as competitors. Others looked ready to be collaborative. But the currency of the moment was their new leader's attention and favor.

President Cashman swept into the room at precisely 0800, her Chief of Staff and the Vice President in tow. She was dressed in a dark blue tailored pant suit with a light-pink pinstripe and matching blouse. At her neck, she wore a simple gold crucifix.

She stood silently at the head of the long table, fingertips pressed on the dark wood, running her eyes around the horseshoe of expectant faces.

It felt to Don like everyone in the room was holding their breath, himself included.

"Please, take your seats," she said finally.

She let the rolling of chairs and rustle of paper die away until everyone's attention came back to her. Again, she let the silence extend until the only sound in the room was the gentle *whoosh* of the air-conditioning system.

When President Cashman spoke, her voice was controlled and firm. "Action this day," she announced. She let her eyes pass over the faces of the principals seated at the main table. Don, from his vantage point behind acting CIA Director Carroll Brooks, followed her gaze.

The Vice President sat to Cashman's right. Next to him was the new National Security Advisor, Todd Spencer. Don knew Spencer by reputation only, but he hoped he might establish a better relationship with him than he'd had with Valentina Florez. Next to Spencer was acting Secretary of State Abel Cartwright. His spare features seemed tailor-made for the role, as did his experience. Cartwright had previously served as ambassador to both China and Russia.

On Don's side of the table, to the President's left, were the Chairman of the Joint Chiefs, the new acting Secretary of Defense, and Carroll Brooks.

"Action this day," Cashman said again, her voice carrying through the quiet room. "That will be the motto of this administration with respect to national security. I want to establish a bias for action. I do not want to sit on the sidelines and wait to see what happens tomorrow, I want the United States to meet our adversaries head on. Today. Now. On their home front, not ours. On my watch, the way we will succeed is by taking the fight to our enemies."

She paused, her eyes scanning the faces as if daring someone to disagree with her. "I've watched for years as America reacted, over and over again, to crises not of our making. I've watched every administration fail to think strategically about what the world should look like in our lifetime, and then craft a national security strategy that pursues that desired outcome."

In this moment, Don was glad he didn't have Carroll's job. The President spoke as if they lived in a world of clear choices, black and white. If Don knew anything after his over two decades of service to the nation, it was that the real world was a whole lot of gray. Sometimes the best choice was the least bad option.

Cashman was no fool, Don knew. He'd seen her operate as part of the Gang of Eight when he'd briefed the group on CIA covert actions. When the time came, she would dive into the gray with the rest of them.

"Let me be more specific." Cashman laced her elegant fingers together and laid them across a leather folio on the table in front of her. "What I have seen out of Russia in the last year disturbs me greatly. In my view, there is no difference between Vitaly Luchnik and his handpicked successor, Nikolay Sokolov."

Don winced. Considering that Nikolay had not only ousted his uncle from power but had later assassinated him, Cashman was playing fast and loose with the facts.

"As to the People's Republic of China, our intelligence reports paint a very clear picture of their activities in Central Asia. The Chinese have done an excellent job of erecting a political shield around their invasion, but I will not sit by and let the people of Central Asia fall under the yoke of Chinese communism."

When she finished, acting Secretary of State Abel Cartwright was the first to speak. "I wholeheartedly agree with your sentiments, Madam President. The threat from the Chinese Communist Party has never been greater. Our only option is to push back firmly and aggressively against both China and Sokolov's Russia."

If Don had hoped that a former ambassador to both Russia and China would help moderate President Cashman's binary positions on those countries, he now saw those hopes dwindling. Even in this relatively private setting, Cartwright clearly saw his job was not as a voice of counsel but as one of unwavering support for the President's position.

The President's gaze fell on the acting Secretary of Defense. Robert Gable was on the shorter side and a little heavy. He had florid features and a carefully trimmed fringe of white hair, but Don had heard this unassuming exterior masked a consummate Washington insider.

"Secretary of Defense?" Cashman asked. "Do you have anything to add?"

Gable shook his head firmly. "Peace through strength, ma'am," he said.

"I believe diplomacy is our first—and best—line of defense, but we will stand ready to back up your words with force, if necessary. As long as we commit to funding the finest military in the world, you'll have it if you need it."

The Chairman, seated next to the SECDEF, nodded as if for emphasis.

A careful answer, Don thought, surveying the room with fresh eyes. He realized that Gable and the Chairman of the Joint Chiefs were probably the least hawkish people of the new administration.

The President turned the meeting over to the National Security Advisor, who rotated a series of briefers to the podium for updates around the globe. When they arrived at Central Asia, the President stopped him.

"I'd like to hear what the CIA has to say about our ongoing operation in the region," she said. "I'd say there's a high likelihood that this will be the first test of my administration."

"Of course, ma'am," Spencer replied shortly, clearly annoyed that the spotlight had moved away from him.

"I've asked Don Riley to have an update available, ma'am," Carroll said.

The President smiled as Don stood and walked to the podium. "Good morning, Donald."

"Good morning, Madam President." Don called up his first slide, which was a map of Central Asia. Red dots showed PLA forward operating bases and blue lines the Belt and Road infrastructure network. "Since the Chinese began moving forces into the Central Asian region in November—"

"Let me stop you right there, Donald," President Cashman said. "I want to make one thing clear: I'm not a fan of euphemisms. What's going on in Central Asia is nothing less than an invasion of multiple sovereign nations by the People's Liberation Army. Let's call things what they really are, please."

Don felt the heat of embarrassment rising on his neck.

"Yes, ma'am," he said. "Since the PLA *invasion* of Central Asia in November, we've had a CIA field operative embedded with the resistance forces. We've been able to provide a limited supply of weapons into the region, as allowed under the previous administration. Per your direction, we've made preparations to dramatically ramp up covert weapons shipments to the resistance forces."

The map did most of the explanation for him. "As you can see, our supply routes are limited. To the west, we have a narrow window through Armenia and Azerbaijan across the Caspian Sea. Armenia has shifted away from Russia's orbit, which works in our favor. Azerbaijan remains firmly connected to Turkey, our NATO ally, which is also to our benefit."

He moved the red dot of his laser pointer counterclockwise around the map.

"To the south and east, we have Iran, Afghanistan, and China, none of which are viable options for volume supply of weapons. The northern half of the region is bordered by Kazakhstan and the Russian Federation. That, in my view, is our best option."

He touched a button on the remote slide advancer to update the slide with a series of red arrows cutting across the Russian border into Kazakhstan. "The most effective way to move supplies into Central Asia is by partnering with the Russians. This move would keep the Russians in our camp and let us play them off against the Chinese. Putting the Chinese on their back foot in Central Asia is in the national interest of the Russian Federation, as it is for the United States. With the right incentives, I believe we could bring them on board."

Don paused. The room was coldly silent.

"I don't think you've taken my message to heart, Mr. Riley," the President said, her voice clipped with annoyance. "I do not wish to have the Russians involved in anything we do in this administration. That includes covert operations."

"We could accomplish the same thing if we partner exclusively with Kazakhstan," the National Security Advisor said. "The land border between Kazakhstan and Central Asia is huge."

"There's two issues with that approach," Don replied. "The first is security. With the volume of shipments planned, it's very likely the Russians will find out. If we include them up front, they're part of the solution. If we box them out, and they find out, they could become part of the problem. They could endanger the security of the entire operation."

"In my opinion, Madam President," Spencer said, "I think that's a risk worth taking. We'd be better served by partnering solely with the Kazakhs and leaving the Russians out of it."

Spencer was rewarded with a nod from Cashman.

"All these choices are trade-offs between speed and effectiveness," Don pressed. "If we want to get the most weaponry into the hands of the rebels in the most effective time frame, we need to maximize our options. If we use Russia, we have land routes into the region. Otherwise, everything has to come in via air to a limited number of airports. A Kazakhstan-only approach puts the entire operation at higher risk."

Carroll Brooks cleared her throat. "We understand your concerns about partnering with the Russian Federation, Madam President. We will make our plans accordingly."

She threw a warning glance at Don. Her message was clear: *Drop the Russia talk. Now.*

NSA Spencer eagerly took back control of the meeting following Don's briefing and ran through another round of national security issues. When Don was called on to give updates, he kept his answers as short as possible. There were a lot of ears in the room, belonging to a lot of people he didn't know.

When the meeting ended, the President signaled Don and Carroll to stay behind with the National Security Advisor. They convened at the President's end of the table, with Don and Carroll facing Spencer across the table.

"I'm sorry to be short with you about my decision on Russia, Donald," the President began, "but I hope I've made myself clear. I want as much separation as possible from Nikolay Sokolov and his ilk. This operation in Central Asia has to work, but it has to work on my terms."

"Well said, Madam President," NSA Spencer said.

Don's face grew warm again. He had never seen eye to eye with Valentina Florez, Spencer's predecessor in the National Security Advisor position, and he didn't see things getting appreciably better with this change in management.

"That said, I want to open a new front against China," the President said. "In our last meeting, Donald, I asked you about the status of using the Chinese defector to open up a cyber front against the PLA. I believe President Serrano was reluctant to do what was necessary to exploit that resource."

Don let Carroll take the question. This one was above his pay grade.

"Yes, ma'am. General Gao wants his family with him in the United States before he will fully cooperate with us. President Serrano considered that operation to be outside his sphere of comfort."

Sphere of comfort? Don mused. Where did she pull that one from?

"And what do you think, Director?" the President asked.

Carroll hesitated. She'd only been in the Director's chair for a month, and she had a grueling Senate confirmation on her calendar. Pulling off a covert extraction operation on the Chinese mainland would be a major coup, but failure would be a career-ending event.

"It is possible, ma'am. But the risk is significant."

"And the reward?" the President asked. "Is the reward worth the risk?"

"At this point, we've had no success in penetrating the Huawei network in the Central Asian region, Madam President," Carroll replied carefully. "I'm confident we'll get there, but it will take time. If this Chinese General can deliver what he claims, it would get us there more quickly."

"So, what is your recommendation, *acting* Director?" the President asked.

"I say give the job to Riley, ma'am. If anyone can pull it off, it's him."

The President smiled at Don and he got the impression she was enjoying his obvious discomfort. "Congratulations, Donald."

11

Moscow, Russia

"I apologize for my appearance, Mr. President," said Vladimir Federov. "I came straight from the airport."

It was nearly midnight. They were seated in Nikolay's personal office in the President's private residence adjacent to the Kremlin. Everything in the room reminded Nikolay of his late Uncle Vitaly. The heavy wooden desk with the stained leather blotter, the armchairs where Federov now sat, the map of the Russian Federation hand-painted along one entire wall of the room. Nikolay had changed nothing since his uncle's demise.

He knew Federov's apology was probably meant for the way he was dressed. The FSB chief was back from a five-day visit to Turkmenistan to assess both the PLA forces in the region and the resistance to the invaders. He wore tan cargo pants, combat boots, and an army-green campaign sweater, all of which were worn, dirty and wrinkled. But Nikolay was more worried about Federov's physical appearance.

The man hunched forward as if his spine struggled under the weight of his barrel-shaped torso. His haggard face told of sleepless nights and his lips were the color of frozen liver.

Nikolay waved away the apology. Federov could show up in his birthday suit for all he cared—as long as he brought his President some good news for once.

"Did you find him?" Nikolay asked.

The *him* was Akhmet Orazov, leader of the resistance to the PLA invasion of Central Asia. Nikolay had met Orazov only once. Unfortunately, the details of the meeting were masked by an alcohol-induced fuzziness. He remembered the sharp sting of embarrassment he'd felt at the dressing down he'd received from the man, and the red-hot rush of anger at the public setting of their clash. The CSTO meeting in Dushanbe, Tajikistan, had been less than a year ago, but it seemed like much longer. So much had changed since that night when he'd let Orazov get the better of him.

He pictured the man in his mind's eye. Short, he recalled, and older—mid-sixties, he guessed—but fit and ready for action. Still a soldier after decades away from active service. A deadly fighter, according to Federov.

And the attitude. Nikolay remembered the attitude most of all. Forceful, but not condescending, Orazov put the Russian President in his place with plain facts and measured confidence. Most of all, he'd told the truth, which was more than the assembled politicians in the room that night had been willing to do.

At the time, Orazov's attitude had enraged Nikolay. Now he was glad the Turkmen fighter was on his side. That same obstinance would be a formidable weapon against the PLA.

The enemy of my enemy is my friend.

"I found him," the FSB chief said in a raspy voice. "He agreed to meet with me." He coughed into his closed fist, and Nikolay detected the gurgle of heavy liquid in the older man's chest.

"Are you well, Vladimir?" Nikolay asked. He stood and poured the FSB chief a glass of vodka.

"I'm fine, Mr. President." Federov took a sip from the proffered glass and made an attempt to sit up straighter. "I'm just tired. It was a difficult trip."

Nikolay put aside his concern. There was no time for that now. He leaned forward, placing his elbows on the desk. "Tell me."

"It is worse than I feared, Mr. President," Federov began. "The Chinese have a significant presence in the region, much more extensive than our sources have led us to believe, I'm afraid."

As he began to reel off numbers of troops and armaments at locations in the republics of Central Asia, Nikolay walked to the wall map. He knew few of these places, but he placed his index finger on each location as Federov named them as if his sense of touch somehow gave him better context.

Ayni Air Base, outside Dushanbe, was division strength, including attack and transport helicopters as well as four squadrons of fighters and ground attack aircraft. Between the capital of Uzbekistan in Tashkent and the proposed capital of the Central Asian Union in Samarkand, there were a total of three divisions, mostly conscripted forces with less experience. Bishkek, a critical logistics hub, was reinforced by two divisions of PLA ground troops, with accompanying attack and transport helicopters. The PLA had even managed to move battalion strength forces as far west as Turkmenistan.

Everything was connected by the damned Belt and Road infrastructure network.

Nikolay cursed his lack of intelligence assets in the region. The situation was so dire that he was forced to send the head of the FSB into the field to ensure he received accurate information. It was ludicrous...and it was his own fault. Yes, Uncle Vitaly had underinvested in the region, but had Nikolay done any better?

No, instead of doing the job himself, he'd asked the Americans for help. Stupid, he chastised himself. And for his shortsightedness, he was now paying the price.

Federov's voice cut into Nikolay's runaway thoughts. "There's more."

Nicolay turned from the map. That tone of voice told him he hadn't heard the worst part yet.

From an open manila folder, Federov handed over an 8x10 photograph. The picture had been taken using a night vision camera. Even in the low-quality image, Nikolay recognized the stocky figure of Akhmet Orazov. He was deep in conversation with another man. Thinner, about the same height, and similarly dressed in well-used paramilitary gear, but clearly not from the region.

"The man on the right is Harrison Kohl," Federov said.

A German, Nikolay thought. The Europeans were getting involved—

"He's CIA, Mr. President, and he's been embedded with the resistance forces since the start of the PLA operation."

Nikolay studied the photograph of two men in conversation. Orazov had his hand on his chin, listening. The CIA officer spoke with intensity, his hands caught in midair as he made a point.

"What do we know about him?" Nikolay asked.

Federov heaved his shoulders into a shrug. "Not enough, sir. He is a trusted confidante of Orazov. I am told the CIA agent was present at the bombing of the railroad bridge in late December. There is a story circulating that he was the one who shot down the PLA helicopter."

Nikolay looked at the photo with new eyes. The two men leaned together as they spoke, suggesting some level of intimacy, the way one might get close to a personal friend. Nikolay suspected a man like Orazov would not trust easily, so what was the connection between these two men? How was it possible that the American CIA not only had an asset embedded with the resistance fighters but had direct access to the leader of the resistance?

"Did Orazov acknowledge this relationship with the Americans?"

Federov shook his head.

Nikolay chewed his lip in thought. The CIA was already there. He needed to act swiftly. "What did Orazov say to our proposal?"

Federov shifted in his seat, his eyes veered away from Nikolay's face. "I have some distressing news on that front, Mr. President."

From the same folder, Federov extracted a thin sheaf of stapled pages and handed it to the Russian President. Nikolay scanned the first page executive summary, his eyes locking on keywords: *corruption...graft...depleted reserves*. Hot blood thundered in his temples.

He flipped the page. The next sheet was a series of bar graphs comparing reported military inventory to actual verified stockpiles. He scanned the headings. Russian ammunition stocks and small arms were at thirty-eight percent of what had been reported in the most recent Ministry of Defense inventory.

His eyes traveled down the page. Only twenty-nine percent of Russian fighter jets were fully operational. Long-range aviation transport assets were higher, close to sixty percent operational, but both of these branches of the Aerospace Forces were using cannibalized spare parts to keep their planes flying.

Tanks...forty-one percent operational, but they lacked ammunition, spare parts, and fuel. Artillery, both towed and self-propelled, showed the same level of operational readiness as tanks, but Federov's marginalia indicated his skepticism of these numbers.

Nikolay looked up. "How?" he whispered.

Federov's eyes stayed on the floor. "I am investigating, sir," he said quietly. "The operation required to hide corruption of this scale was extensive."

Uncle Vitaly's legacy, Nikolay mused. A paper army. If this report was to be believed, of all the money he'd poured into the Russian military machine since the conclusion of the Ukraine War, at least half of it was wasted. Stolen. The word *corruption* seemed inadequate. He should have seen this coming...

Nikolay's temper flared. *They* should have seen this coming. Was Fedorov slipping or was he part of the corruption?

He pushed the thought from his mind. Federov had been nothing but loyal to Nikolay, but how had he missed this? He assessed with fresh eyes Federov's haggard appearance, his travel-stained clothes. Had he asked too much of this man? If Federov was not part of the corruption, was he up to the task of rooting it out?

Nikolay wanted to throw the report against the wall and scream, but he controlled his anger. With measured paces, he crossed the room and took his seat behind the desk. He laced his fingers together, laid them upon the blotter, and studied the old man before him.

Federov's eyes remained on the floor.

"Look at me, Vladimir," Nikolay said.

The whites of his crystalline brown eyes were stained red. Nikolay saw the anguish there. "Mr. President, I—"

"We don't have time for apologies, Vladimir. I need to know what to do. I need your counsel, my friend."

A spasm of emotion crossed Federov's face. Fear, embarrassment, anger? Nikolay failed to identify the expression before it was gone.

"What would my uncle do in this situation?" Nikolay asked.

That, at least, was a starting point. Together, the two men looked at Russia's southern flank on the wall map and the answer was plain.

Kazakhstan. Everything depended on Kazakhstan.

It was really a question of scale. The land mass of Kazakhstan was so large that the Central Asian republics of Turkmenistan, Tajikistan, Uzbekistan, and Kyrgyzstan could all fit within its borders with room to spare. The border between the two countries was over 7600 kilometers long. There were critical business connections as well. The oil and gas pipelines, water reserves, and the Russian space program at the Baikonur Cosmodrome were irreplaceable elements of his country's economy. Without a secure Kazakhstan, the Russian Federation's near abroad was a disaster for Nikolay.

Yet the Chinese had chosen to stay out of Kazakhstan and focus on their interests in the remainder of Central Asia.

Nikolay was living on borrowed time, he realized. The Chinese were expanding their empire on a timetable. Once they had the Central Asian republics under control, they would turn their gaze northward to Kazakhstan. And then the southern flank of the Russian Federation would be at risk.

The map told the story—unless he changed the narrative. Nikolay pinched his lip as he studied the map, his brain racing.

Orazov's resistance forces were running a Fabian strategy against their Chinese invaders. There was no way they could take on the PLA in a fair fight, so they used guerilla warfare, wearing down their enemy through small, continuous attacks. Ultimately, the Chinese would crush the resistance. The question was not if the Chinese would dominate, but when. Critical support from Russia could add months to the PLA invasion timetable. Months for Nikolay to come up with a new plan to secure his southern flank.

He turned to Federov. "I want you to give Orazov whatever he needs. If you need to take it from active-duty forces, so be it. We need the resistance fighters to hold out as long as possible against the PLA."

Federov rose to his feet, swaying slightly. "I understand, Mr. President."

"We need to solidify our position in Kazakhstan, Vladimir. Quickly."

"I agree, sir."

"When is Sergei Musayev next in Moscow?" Nikolay asked.

Federov consulted his mobile phone. "Next month. He's here for a board meeting."

Nikolay walked back to the map. He traced the Kazakhstan border with his index finger. The red paint was rough to the touch.

They had kept their asset in the Kazakh government in reserve long enough. It was time to make a play.

"I think Sergei's mother is about to come down with a very serious illness. She needs her son by her side. Immediately."

Federov's voice had more vigor than before.

"It shall be done, Mr. President."

12

Caspian Sea, 25 kilometers southeast of Karagel, Turkmenistan

In the dark sky of a new moon, it was hard to tell where the beach ended and the water began. The Caspian Sea was a sheet of black glass stretching away from the shore, the gentle surf a barely audible shushing sound in the darkness.

Harrison, seated in the cab of one of the cargo trucks with the comms set on his lap, felt exposed. A dozen trucks parked on the beach with nothing around them but sand and water for miles and miles. All it would take was one Chinese drone to fly by and it was all over.

For the hundredth time, he checked the settings on the comms set. The lid was up on the black carbon fiber case, revealing a laptop with a handset. The dimmed screen listed off system parameters in ghostly letters. The ultra-secure laser communications device had a solid lock on a satellite.

Ready to receive, read the last line of the display, followed by a blinking cursor.

A breeze, heavy with moisture, blew through the open window, leaving a film of salt residue on Harrison's cheek. A sea on the edge of a desert felt out of place.

He heard footsteps in the sand outside the truck and Akhmet's bearded face loomed in the open window. His gray beard showed white in the faint light of the LED display.

"Nothing yet, Ussat," Harrison said in a whisper to the unasked question.

He listened to Akhmet's breathing. Three beats passed while the older man considered the situation. He knew better than anyone the risk of their operation being exposed. His life and the lives of his men depended on the promptness and security of the CIA.

"Five more minutes," Akhmet said.

"Yes, sir," Harrison replied. He made note of the time. 0218. The delivery was thirteen minutes late. For security reasons, the exact coordinates had been passed to the resistance forces only three hours prior. Here on the deserted shore of the Caspian Sea, they would receive their next arms shipment from the CIA.

The LED screen flickered and Harrison heard, "Rover, this is Rubber Ducky, over?" The voice had an American accent, slightly distorted by the warble of the secure digital comms.

In spite of the tension, Harrison chuckled. The line and drawling accent sounded like something from the 1970s citizen's band radio craze.

He snatched up the handset and pressed the transmit button. "This is Rover. I read you, Ducky."

"Roger that, Rover. I am ten miles out, approaching from the southwest. Approximately three mikes out from your position. Energize the beacon, over."

He leaned out the window. "Turn on the beacon. Orient to the southwest."

The IR beacon had been set up on a foldable tripod, the face of the device screened except for a thirty-degree arc.

"Beacon is on, Harrison," someone called out of the dark.

"Ducky, this is Rover. Beacon energized."

"I see it, Rover. I'm coming around for a final approach."

Harrison popped open the truck door and jumped to the sand. A seaborne delivery had made little sense to Harrison from the beginning, but Langley had insisted and Akhmet wanted the delivery enough to risk the operation.

He heard the drone of a prop-driven aircraft, the sound growing louder and deepening as the cargo plane descended. He heard the zip of pontoon floats hitting flat water and the roar of engines drawing closer. A small wave crashed ashore, the crest a creamy white in the dim light.

Harrison borrowed the night vision glasses from Sanjar, who was trembling with excitement, and focused on the seaplane.

"I'll be damned," he muttered to himself.

He'd heard that US Special Operations Command had built and tested an amphibious version of the C-130 Hercules, but he'd never seen one. The four-engine military cargo plane rode atop a pair of pontoons each the size and shape of a sleek power boat. As he watched, the aircraft coasted to a stop on the water about a hundred meters from shore, then used the variable pitch propellers to turn the plane 180 degrees. The rear cargo ramp lowered, red light spilling into the darkness.

Harrison waded into the water toward the aircraft. Behind him, he heard Akhmet organizing his men into a double file to receive the shipment. Truck engines roared to life as the drivers prepared to reposition their vehicles.

The water rose to the middle of Harrison's rib cage by the time he reached the edge of the lowered cargo ramp. A hand reached down and Harrison took it, feeling himself being pulled from the water. He crawled up the steel ramp and stood, water streaming from his wet clothes.

"You look like a drowned rat, Harrison." Tom Stellner's voice rose above the drone of the idling propellers. Harrison gave the man a bear hug. Stellner was dressed in paramilitary gear, body armor, and a SIG Sauer 9mm rode on his right hip. He had a bulky pair of headsets around his neck.

"Tom," Harrison replied, fighting down a wave of nostalgia for his former life. "Where's Meyers?" He looked deeper into the cargo hold. Stellner and Meyers, both former spec ops soldiers, always worked as a team. Inside the CIA, they were referred to as S&M.

Stellner barked out a laugh. "Stupid ass got himself a serious case of shingles. Serves him right for not getting the shots. Riley grounded him for this op. I'm flying solo—I kinda like it." He tried to smile and failed. Harrison could tell he was worried about his partner.

Akhmet's men reached the ramp, water up to their armpits. "We're ready to unload," Harrison said, eyeing the line of crates in the cargo hold. This was not going to be easy. The crates got larger as they moved toward the front of the plane. The last row of crates were as tall as he was.

Stellner seemed to read his mind. "Don't worry, man. Check this out." He signaled to the flight crew. Harrison watched them ease the first pallet down the ramp. When it got to the water, they motioned for Akhmet's men to move back, then they ripped a cord from the side of the pallet. With a sharp hiss of air, pontoons on either side of the pallet expanded.

They floated the crate into the water toward two of Akhmet's men, who guided the package toward the shore. By the time they were out of the way, the loadmaster had a second pallet at the bottom of the ramp. He triggered the inflation of the pontoons and the cargo disappeared toward shore.

Stellner tugged at his arm. "C'mon, I gotta show you something."

Harrison followed him to the front of the plane, where Stellner had dismantled one of the largest crates. In the dim red light, Harrison could make out what looked like an all-terrain vehicle, but instead of wheels it had a pair of pods at each corner of the vehicle.

"What is it?" he asked.

Stellner laid his hand on the handlebar. "This, my friend, is the most fun you can have with your clothes on. It's a jet bike, brought to you courtesy of Falchion Labs."

Harrison knew Falchion had bought the assets of the now-defunct Sentinel Holdings, and he supposed that meant the Sentinel R&D department as well.

Stellner was already unfastening the toggles holding the machine to the pallet. "Don told me I should give you a test drive if the security situation was good, so what do you say?" He handed Harrison a helmet.

The queue of pallets was making its way down the cargo bay toward the ramp. Stellner manhandled the jet bike off the pallet and rolled it down the side of the bay on a set of retractable wheels. He positioned it at the top of the ramp and motioned everyone to step back. Harrison put on the helmet and climbed on.

Stellner toggled the control panel. The machine vibrated. A moisture-laden windstorm filled the back of the plane and Harrison felt the vehicle levitate off the deck. It was a weird, trembling sensation. A little unstable, like riding a horse for the first time.

Stellner angled the nose of the jet bike down the ramp and they rode atop the water, sprays of moisture shrouding them like a cloud.

Stellner's voice sounded in his helmet. "What do you think?" His voice was clear, the whine of the small jet engines negated through noise-suppressing headphones embedded in his helmet.

"Good, I guess," Harrison replied, but he thought to himself: What the hell is Akhmet going to do with a glorified jet ski?

Stellner's mocking chuckle rang loud in Harrison's ears. "Hang on. I'm about to give you a religious experience."

When Stellner opened up the throttle, Harrison felt like he'd been punched in the stomach. He hung on for dear life as the jet bike rocketed across the water, ran up the beach, and entered the open desert. On the heads-up display in his helmet, Harrison watched their speed spool up to over one hundred miles per hour in just a few seconds.

They slowed down to about fifty, and Stellner entered a wide turn. Dark sand unspooled beneath them in a blur.

Stellner talked him through how to use eyescan to access the screens in the HUD, settling on a line drawing of the jet bike. Each corner of the bike had two independent thrusters, each about the size of a small trashcan. The readings showed power levels, fuel, altitude, and heading. There was a separate screen for autopilot and navigation.

"It's fly-by-wire," Stellner explained. "You can even program it with waypoints for self-driving."

"Terrain following?" Harrison asked.

"Please, Harrison," Stellner said. "Only the best for you."

Harrison saw a new screen activate on the HUD. Stellner highlighted the menu selection that read TERFOLL, and set it for two meters.

The unit descended to ground level, kicking up a dust cloud. The bike rose smoothly over a dune and raced down the following side at fifty miles per hour. Stellner sat up straight and folded his arms across his chest. "Look, Ma, no hands."

"Okay, okay," Harrison said. "I get it."

"You know, man. I don't think you believe me, but I've got one last trick to show you."

He gripped the handlebars and pulled back. The jet bike left the top of the next dune at a forty-five-degree angle and kept going. Stellner leveled them off at two thousand feet, aiming the vehicle out over the Caspian Sea.

Harrison checked the clock on the HUD. They'd been gone for fifteen minutes. "I believe you, Tom," he said. "Time to head back."

Stellner used the waypoint feature on the map screen to guide them back to the waiting trucks. As he settled the jet bike on the sand, Harrison asked, "How many of these can I get?"

"There's four in this shipment, plus another six in production at Falchion. Don said you'd figure out how to use them. Got any bright ideas yet?"

Harrison swung off the seat and pulled off the helmet. His legs trembled from the adrenaline of the ride. Akhmet approached, his sharp eyes glinting as he studied the new vehicle. He held out his hand to Stellner, who pushed it aside and hugged him instead.

Stellner broke the embrace with Akhmet and wrapped up Harrison. "Stay safe, brother," He waded into the surf, then turned and called out. "Can I tell Don you thought of something?"

Harrison rested a hand on the curved windscreen of the space-age vehicle. "Oh, yeah, you can tell Don I have big plans for these puppies."

13

Undisclosed location, Northeastern Pennsylvania, United States

Don could have flown from Washington, DC, to Scranton, Pennsylvania, and rented a car for the last leg of the trip. Instead, he chose to take a chauffeured car, figuring it would give him time to think.

He got more thinking time than he bargained for. A trip that should have taken four and a half hours ended up taking closer to six. Yet, even with all that extra thinking time, he'd spent most of the trip staring out the window at the wet snow blanketing the barren winter countryside.

The roads got worse as they reached the Pocono Mountains and deteriorated further when they left the main highway. The secondary roads had not been plowed yet and his driver navigated the country lanes with care. When they made the final turn onto the dirt road that led to the CIA safe house, Don felt the SUV fishtail. They descended into trees, the road following a winding brook to a small bungalow. The driver pulled into the unplowed parking lot and put the SUV into park. He let out a sigh. "We're here, sir."

Next to the bungalow-turned-guardhouse, a hand-painted sign read: Welcome to Frosty Valley.

Don had heard that Sam, the CIA caretaker, had found the sign in the barn on the property and restored it. Among the staff, the name had stuck. The Ranch was now officially on the CIA books as Frosty Valley.

Don stepped into six inches of heavy wet snow. In addition to forgetting to bring a hat or scarf, he was wearing dress shoes. Very wet dress shoes now. He hurried to the door of the small house and let himself in. The man seated behind a desk in what had once been a sitting room had an array of security monitors mounted on one wall and a flat-screen TV on the other. His desk held a laptop, secure landline, and a charging station for handheld radios. Behind him Don glimpsed a galley-style kitchen and a hall leading to a bunkroom.

As Don entered and stamped the clumped snow from his feet and trousers, the man behind the desk rose. He was dressed casually in jeans and a heavy sweater, and he was armed with a Glock 19.

"Good afternoon, Mr. Riley. Heck of a storm out there."

Don forced a smile. "Not fit for man or beast. I'm here to see the General."

The security man already had the radio raised to his lips. "Of course, sir. I'll get Sam to drive you down." He nodded at the kitchen. "Fresh coffee, if you're interested."

Don was interested. He poured himself a cup and held the mug between his chilled fingers—he'd forgotten gloves, too—as he waited, contemplating the accumulating snow outside. He still had not solved the problem that had been bugging him all day: Did he believe the captured PLA General could deliver what he promised?

Common sense said no. While the General had surely once had access to the Huawei network in Central Asia, the security service would have revoked his credentials by now. But General Gao Yichen was adamant that he had a way into the ultra-secure Huawei network. He would transfer access to the CIA if they agreed to his terms: they had to extract his family from China and bring them to America.

This is a fool's errand, Don thought. And yet he, the fool, was here because his President had ordered him to do the deal. The smart move would be to pawn off the task on someone below him and hope for the best, but Don couldn't do that. He was not about to delegate failure. If this operation was going to blow up on his watch, it would be from decisions of his own choosing.

Sam, the caretaker, came through the door in a whirl of snowflakes. He was covered from head to toe in caked wet snow, only his eyes showing from a gap between his muffler and his wool cap. He ripped off a glove. "Mr. Riley, it's good to see you again."

Don shook his offered hand. The man's grip was firm, his hand warm. He put down his coffee cup. "I'm ready whenever you are."

Sam's eyes raked over Don's appearance. Car-length coat, dress shoes, no hat, no gloves, no scarf. "Just a minute, sir." He went to a cardboard box next to the coatrack and rummaged, emerging with a plaid woolen hunter's cap complete with ear flaps, a lengthy crocheted neon-green and gold scarf, and red mittens. "It's not exactly the height of fashion, sir, but it'll keep you warm."

Don's only thought as he put on the scavenged gear was that he hoped the General would not see him in this getup.

Fully outfitted for the weather, they plunged into the snowstorm. The snow stung Don's eyes to the point that he imitated Sam, taking another turn of the scarf around his face so only his eyes showed. They climbed into a Polaris Xpedition utility vehicle and Sam drove into the seething wall of white.

It was disorienting for Don. He made out the dim shape of the farmhouse passing on their right. He glimpsed glowing yellow windows, then the building was lost behind a veil of snow. Sam took a right turn and pulled up next to a set of wooden stairs. He leaned toward Don. "I'll give you ten minutes to get yourself situated, then I'll bring the General around."

Don nodded his thanks and got out.

"Good luck, sir," Sam called as he drove off.

The building known as "The Studio" on the CIA compound had once been an artist's workshop. There was a woodstove at one end and high ceilings with skylights. Hidden cameras and listening devices were secreted among the rafters. The heavy planks of the wooden floor were worn smooth. The only furniture in the room was a pair of leather armchairs angled toward the large picture window that took up most of one wall.

Inside, Don stamped his feet on the doormat and hung his winter gear on a coatrack. The atmosphere was warm to the point of stuffiness—or maybe that was just his discomfort manifesting. He paced to the picture window. Outside, everything was buried under a layer of snow, all the rough edges and dirt and dead plants made shapeless and smooth under a blanket of white.

Don turned when he heard the door open.

In the three months since Don had last seen him, General Gao Yichen of the People's Liberation Army had put on some weight and grown his hair longer. He wore a red-and-black checked lumberjack shirt under a thick winter coat, and blue jeans with heavy work boots. He stopped when he saw Don, and a flicker of suspicion crossed his face.

"Mr. Riley." His English was more natural. He'd lost some of the flat tonals of his native Mandarin. "What an unexpected surprise." He took his time hanging up his hat and coat.

"You're looking well, General."

Don went through the niceties of offering tea and busied himself with boiling water and making small talk. Mugs in hand, they settled into opposing armchairs.

Gao took the lead on the conversation, touching on the weather and sports. It seemed the PLA General had become a fan of NHL hockey during his stay at Frosty Valley. Don watched him carefully, wondering how best to start this very delicate conversation he'd traveled all this way to have.

When all else fails, Don thought, tell the truth.

"I'm here to offer you a deal, General," Don said, interrupting the man's monologue about the Minnesota Wild hockey team.

Gao sat back in his chair. When he did not respond, Don plunged ahead.

"The problem is I don't know if I can trust you."

Gao's eyes narrowed. Still, he said nothing. The General was a political animal, and a careful one. He was looking for the trap.

"You claim you have a foolproof way to get into the Huawei network, but I don't believe you. You've been gone for months. Beijing has pronounced you dead. They even staged a funeral, despite not having your body. I cannot accept that any security service would not have revoked your access by now."

Then Gao did something Don did not expect. He smiled. Not a secret smile, but a broad toothy grin. "They cannot revoke something they do not know about, Mr. Riley."

Don felt the frustrations of the day catch up with him. "No more games, Gao," he snapped. "If you want to see your family again, you need to convince me that you can deliver what I need."

Gao pursed his lips. "Fair enough. Access to the Huawei network was carefully controlled. For my level of access, there was a password and a biometric scan. My actions on the network were monitored continuously. As you say, I am very confident that those access codes have been revoked."

Don sighed. Just as he feared, the General had been bluffing.

"But." Gao grinned again. "I had another way to access the system."

"Go on," Don said.

Gao steepled his fingers. Don could see him relaxing into his chair. The man was enjoying this little display of power.

"Captain Fang—you remember her?" he asked.

Don recalled the PLA captain, the one who had tried to finish the job of assassinating Gao. Tom Stellner had put her down with a clean shot to the head. She was the reason why Don had snatched Gao in the first place. He could not understand why the PLA wanted to assassinate one of their own. "I remember her," Don replied.

"You recall the informant that gave us the tip about the Jade Spike ceremony? The one who was killed on the dam?"

Don nodded, unsure where this was going.

"When Xiaomei—Captain Fang, I mean—accessed the Huawei network for that operation, she didn't want the MSS to know what we were doing. She used a back door to get into the system. It was a simple DOS prompt and a password. No biometrics, no monitoring."

Gao laced his fingers together and rested them on his belly. "I have the password. And no one else knows about it."

"How can you be so sure no one else knows about it?" Don pressed.

Gao shifted in his chair, his face reddened.

"Toward the end of our, um, relationship, Captain Fang confided this information to me in an intimate setting."

Don sat back in his chair. Pillow talk. Captain Fang was dead, but she was never supposed to die. Gao was supposed to die. The secret access to the network died with Fang.

It wasn't a foolproof plan. There was always the chance that the unauthorized access had been discovered and patched, but it was a damn sight better option than anything else he had right now.

"Let's say I believe you," Don said. "Let's say I have the authority to launch an operation to get your family out of China. How do you propose we do that?"

Gao leaned forward. "I have an idea."

14

Chaoyang Park, Beijing, China

Gao Mei Lin picked idly at the cuticles of her left hand. She drew blood, but it didn't matter. Her nails were a mess already. She hadn't had a manicure in months and had no plans to get one anytime soon.

"Mama, look!" Lixin called from the play set. The boy placed one mitten on a handhold of the kiddie climbing wall and raised one foot to the first plastic nub of fake rock. His dark eyes lit up with daring enthusiasm. He was almost three now and getting more adventurous every day.

Mei Lin shook her head and pointed her finger at the ground. The boy obeyed his mother, then set off to explore the maypole. The nylon of his winter coat made a whisking sound as he milled his arms forward.

Mei Lin snugged her own wool hat around her ears and checked on Bai. Only the baby's pinched face showed from beneath a mound of blankets and a hooded snowsuit.

They were good children and she was a lucky woman, she knew that. She had a beautiful apartment in a desirable neighborhood in Beijing, fully paid for by the Party, and she had Yichen's pension to live on. Both of the children were on the list for the most sought-after private schools in the country. All of her needs were satisfied—except for one.

She missed her husband.

When Mei Lin recalled how she had acted toward Yichen, she felt nothing but shame. She'd harped on him about accepting the job in Central Asia. She'd accused him of being unfaithful to her without any evidence and she'd kept the children away from their father out of spite.

Her eyes stung as she looked at the baby. Bai would never know her father, would not have a single memory of him to carry with her in this life. She hoped Lixin would remember him, but she suspected any real memories the child might retain would be wrapped up in the media attention.

The Hero of Taiwan, the Hero of Tashkent, the Hero of Samarkand. Lixin had been at her side for the state funeral of his father, his young eyes wide with wonder. He would remember General Gao Yichen as a great man, a hero of the Party, but would he remember the kind, gentle man that she had known and loved?

Mei Lin watched her boy race to the base of the kiddie slide and bang his mittens on the polished surface. He would remember none of those things, and it was all her fault.

She drew in a long, shaky breath, welcoming the winter air into her lungs, and held it. Then she let it out in a fierce blast.

Grow up, she told herself. You're a widow now, but you're a mother first. Yichen's memory must live through you.

Mei Lin got up from the park bench and paced briskly along the walk that bordered the children's play area. She swung her arms to get her circulation going.

She liked to come to the park early before the other children arrived, most of them accompanied by nannies. Mei Lin did not like the pitying stares she got from those women, most of them younger than her and less educated.

It wasn't just nannies, either. In the months since Yichen's death, her circle of friends contracted. It was partly her fault. When Yichen's name was in the news every day, calls flooded in. Everyone wanted to see her and be seen with her.

But those first weeks were hard for Mei Lin and she pushed them all away, preferring to grieve in private with her children. The attention peaked with the funeral. It was surreal to see herself on state television, her eyes red with tears, gripping Lixin's hand. She watched recordings of the programs obsessively, trying to recall how it felt in the moment. The actual event was only a series of vague impressions in her memory.

The smooth polished surface of her husband's coffin. The smell of flowers—so many flowers everywhere. The precision metronome of the honor guard's footsteps on the pavement. The boom of the gun salute. The doughy face of the General Secretary filling her vision, his peppermint breath, his fleshy hands enclosing hers.

Your husband was a great man...

Then it was all over. The funeral, the television cameras, the phone calls and emails, the posts on social media lauding her husband as a hero. All that disappeared as the world moved on.

Mei Lin was a widow with two small children. Alone.

"What is her name?" said a voice.

Mei Lin spun around to see a woman bending over Bai's stroller. She looked young and was dressed like a university student in jeans, ankle boots, and a shabby chic plaid jacket and matching cap. Mei Lin rushed forward and seized the handle of the stroller, jostling the baby awake.

"I'm sorry, I didn't mean to startle you," the young woman said as Bai started to cry. "She's beautiful."

"It's fine." Mei Lin met the other woman's eyes, sure that she would be recognized any second now. When that happened, the woman would either start to fawn or make an excuse to get as far away from her as possible.

Lixin rushed over and crashed into his mother's leg, wrapping his arms around her thigh. He peered shyly up at the stranger. To her surprise, the young woman crouched down to her son's height and spoke. "My name is Emi. What's yours?"

"Lixin," the boy said.

Emi extended her hand. Her bare fingers were long and elegant with nails painted a soft pink. "I am very pleased to meet you, Lixin."

The boy placed his mittened hand in hers and she solemnly shook his hand.

"What is your sister's name?" she asked.

"Baby Bai."

Emi feigned a look of surprise. "That is a beautiful name. Did you pick it out?"

Lixin nodded.

In spite of herself, Mei Lin laughed. "You did not. You were hardly speaking when she was born!"

Emi got to her feet in a single, fluid motion, like a dancer. She held out her hand. "Your children are adorable. You must be very proud of them."

Mei Lin was suddenly ashamed of her ragged cuticles and unpainted nails. She shook the proffered hand quickly, then busied herself with extracting the baby from the stroller. Cradling the child with one arm, Mei Lin dug into the diaper bag for a bottle.

"Can I hold her?" Emi asked.

Normally, Mei Lin would have made some excuse. But for some reason, she found herself trusting this stranger. Emi expertly cradled the baby's head as she held the child close. As Mei Lin devoted her attention to finding the missing bottle of formula, Emi sat down on the park bench and calmed the baby. When Mei Lin looked up again, Bai was quiet and Lixin was seated next to Emi on the bench. They all watched her.

Mei Lin held out the bottle. "Would you like to feed her?"

Emi stretched out an arm and craned her neck to see the face of her wristwatch. "I'd love to, but I'm afraid I need to run." She stood and handed the now-content Bai to Mei Lin. The baby latched onto the nipple of the bottle and sucked contentedly.

"It was lovely to meet you, Mei Lin," the young woman said. "Maybe we'll run into one another again."

"I'd like that," Mei Lin said—and she meant it.

She and Lixin watched Emi walk toward the busy street bordering the park. The woman pulled out a phone and held it to her ear.

"She was nice," Mei Lin said to her son. The boy nodded agreement.

The winter sun felt a little warmer after that. Bai finished her bottle and let out a healthy burp. Lixin leaned against his mother's arm. He did not argue when she said it was time to go. He held her hand as they walked through the park and crossed the street to their apartment building. Inside the lobby, she let Lixin push the button to call the elevator.

On the ride up to their apartment, Mei Lin thought about the woman in the park. She didn't recall telling the woman her name, but she'd known it. Maybe Emi had recognized Mei Lin after all and was just being nice to her. The encounter left her oddly hopeful that her luck was changing.

In the apartment, she turned on cartoons for Lixin while she went to change Bai. The child was asleep again, so Mei Lin carefully removed the blankets and lifted her from the stroller. In the baby's room, the blinds were drawn. She laid her on the changing table and unzipped the pink fleece onesie.

On the sleeping baby's chest lay a square of folded paper.

Mei Lin picked it up. The paper, still warm from being nestled against Bai's chest, was folded into quarters. It crinkled as she opened it and held it to the light coming in from the hallway.

Her breath caught. Her mouth went dry. The characters were carefully drawn ideograms in black ink on cheap white paper. She recognized the handwriting.

It was from her dead husband.

15

INDOPACOM Headquarters, Camp H. M. Smith, Oahu, Hawaii

Commander Janet Everett pulled her car into the visitors parking lot. Between the accident on Moanalua Road and the queue waiting to get into the base, she was late.

Although she'd not been told the reason for this sudden summons to the headquarters building for the Indo-Pacific Command, her years of Navy experience told her that this was not some routine briefing. Her submarine, the USS *Illinois*, was about to get a special assignment, probably a big one.

And she was late.

Janet seized her uniform cap off the passenger seat of her Volvo EX30 and stepped into a brilliant Hawaiian afternoon. A gentle breeze blew in off the Pacific, and sunlight danced on the water, but she had no time to admire the beautiful setting. She clamped the cap on her head and jogged toward the entrance of the headquarters building.

An ensign dressed in summer whites rushed to meet her. She was a tall thin black woman with round glasses that gave her an owlish look. She came to an abrupt stop and popped a smart salute.

"Ensign Jennifer Wallace, ma'am," she said in a rush. "I've been assigned to escort you to the meeting room." She handed Janet a visitor's badge.

A personal escort. This was a new one. Janet returned the salute and followed the young officer through the automatic double doors. The young woman quickstepped across the lobby with Janet in tow, headed for the elevators.

Inside the elevator, she scanned her badge over the sensor and stabbed at the button for one of the high-security lower floors. Ensign Wallace faced Janet. "Ma'am, I hope I'm not out of line, but I've admired your career for a long time. I'm headed to Nuclear Power school in June."

"You're stashed here before you start training?"

"Yes, ma'am." The elevator door opened and the young officer led Janet deeper into the building.

As only the second female submarine captain in the fleet, Janet was used to young women approaching her. Over the last decade, as women became more common in the once male-only submarine service, Janet had witnessed —and encouraged—the development of an informal support network for her fellow female submariners. In private moments, she joked that if there was an Old Boys' Club, it was only fair for women to form a Young Girls' Network.

She put aside her own anxiety about the mysterious meeting long enough to give the young woman a shot of encouragement. "Work hard, Ensign Wallace. We need you out there."

She stood a little straighter. "Yes, ma'am."

Wallace left Janet with the Marine guard outside a secure conference room. As the guard checked her ID and signed her in, Janet said, "Good luck, Wallace. Let me know how you do at Nuke School. I mean that."

"I will, ma'am."

"You're all set, Commander." The Marine held the door for her.

When Janet stepped into the conference room, two things struck her. First, there was a lot of brass in the room. Second, no one was smiling. She could feel the tension in the air.

A lot of unhappy high-ranking officers gathered together...what could go wrong?

She scanned the room, clocking the senior officers she recognized. Commander of Submarine Force, Pacific, Rear Admiral Lawrence Candy, known to submariners as "The Candyman," was a tall, spare man who always seemed to be sucking on a piece of hard candy. Submarine captains who'd been underway with him reported that he chewed the candy when things got tense.

The Candyman was deep in conversation with three other men. Janet recognized her boss, Captain Reed, Commander of Submarine Squadron One, and INDOPACOM J2 Intel Officer, Rear Admiral Jesse Cone. The J3 Ops Director was an Army officer, Major General Leif Knecht.

None of the men had staffers in the room, which only intensified Janet's curiosity. This was undoubtedly a highly classified mission, and as the only submarine captain in the room, her boat had been selected. Janet suppressed a smile as she nodded to her boss.

Another knot of three men clustered around the briefing podium. One was a Navy commander like her and the other was a lieutenant. They screened a third man standing behind the lectern. The commander stepped aside and Janet spotted Don Riley.

Don looked up just as she saw him. Janet crossed the room in three strides and wrapped him in a hug. "Don, what are you doing here?"

He smiled at her, but it was forced. "I was in the neighborhood."

Janet realized their reunion had stopped all conversation in the room. The Navy Commander, who was wearing the SEAL trident insignia on his summer white uniform, deadpanned, "Something you wanna share with us, Mr. Riley?"

Don turned pink with embarrassment. "Janet—Commander Everett, I mean—and I go way back. We worked together in DC."

The Navy SEAL raised an eyebrow at Janet. "Is that right? You were a spook, Commander?" He held out his hand to Janet. "Bill James."

Janet knew the name. Commander "Wild Bill" James was CO of SEAL Delivery Vehicle Team One and a legend in the tight-knit special ops community.

James clapped his hand on the shoulder of the Navy SEAL lieutenant. "This is Trevor Rantz, Commander Everett. Goes by T-Bone in the field.

One of my finest. I expect you to bring him back in the same condition I lent him to you."

"I'm afraid you have the advantage on me," Janet said. "I don't know what this is about yet."

"Neither do I," a deep voice said from behind her. Janet heard the crunching of hard candy. "I'd like to get on with the briefing, Mr. Riley. If the CIA wants to borrow one of my submarines, I'd like to know what we're getting ourselves into."

"Of course, Admiral," Don replied.

Janet took a seat between Lieutenant T-Bone Rantz and Commodore Reed, whose normally jovial face was tight and unsmiling. He leaned toward her and spoke in a low voice.

"The boss is not happy, Janet. We found out this morning that your boat is being assigned to an unknown operation in the South China Sea. Straight from the White House. If you've got a clue about what's happening, I'd like to know now."

"It's all news to me, sir." Janet held his gaze to make sure that he knew she was being straight with him. Because of her service with Don in the CIA, there were redactions in her service record that senior officers sometimes found annoying.

That said, she knew that Don had specially requested her boat for this operation and that thrilled her.

Don put up a slide on the screen that read OPERATION GHOST CRAB in bold black letters.

"The operation I'm going to take you through this afternoon is classified as top secret and falls under the US Navy's submarine reconnaissance program. To fully brief this special access program, I'm going to need each of you to sign the NDA in front of you."

In the quiet room, Janet heard another piece of hard candy getting ground to bits. There was a pause as everyone scanned the document and scribbled their signature at the bottom of the page. Don collected the sheets and filed them away in his secure briefcase.

Back at the podium, Don shifted the screen to an image of Hainan Island in the South China Sea. "The objective of Ghost Crab is a covert human extraction from this area." He zoomed in on the eastern shore of the island to a nature preserve marked in green. There was a hotel complex adjacent to the green zone.

"The subjects will be staying at this resort. The top-level plan is to deploy a five-man SEAL team in a delivery vehicle from the USS *Illinois* just outside of international waters. The SDV will make an approach to shore. At the two-kilometer mark, they will deploy a zodiac and continue onto the beach where they will meet and exfil the subjects."

The room remained silent as everyone absorbed the mission scope.

Wild Bill James spoke first. "How many passengers are we taking off the beach?"

"Three," Don replied.

James nodded. "I'd expect the Chinese security to be pretty tight in this area. Why use a zodiac at all? We can make a final approach in the water and piggyback the passengers out using a spare set of breathing apparatus."

Don shook his head. "That's not going to be possible. Two of the passengers are children."

The Candyman demolished a fresh piece of hard candy in a single bite. "Did you say children, Mr. Riley?"

"Yes, sir. The boy is about three years old. The girl is less than a year. The third passenger is their mother." Don hesitated.

"Do you have another shoe to drop, Mr. Riley?" Cellophane crinkled as the Candyman unwrapped fresh ammunition. "Do it now, please."

"The mother does not know she's being extracted, Admiral."

"Great." Wild Bill said in a dry tone. "So, now we're kidnappers."

Major General Knecht cleared his throat. "Look, I think we all know the score here. The White House and SECDEF have already signed off on this, so it's going to happen. Mr. Riley's a messenger and we can shoot him if we want, but I suggest we hear him out first."

"Thank you, General," Don said. "This operation is vital for national security. I do not for a second underestimate the risks here, but I believe it is possible."

The Candyman nodded. "Show us how, Mr. Riley."

Don had spent a good part of his career as a briefer. Despite his rocky start with an unfriendly audience, Janet was impressed with how he managed the room. He'd done his homework and she could feel the senior officers around her getting more comfortable with the scenario.

When he opened it up for questions, Janet leaned toward the commodore. "Sir, is it okay with you if I ask for some additional hardware?"

He cracked a smile, another sign that Don was winning the room over. "Ask for whatever you want, Janet. The CIA's giving us a blank check."

She raised her hand. "DARPA's been testing a new surveillance asset called a Waterbug. It's basically a tube-launched sail drone with a satellite link. If we could deploy two units, we could have a real-time tactical picture for the duration of the operation."

"How would you recover them, Captain?" the INDOPACOM J2 asked.

"We wouldn't," Janet replied. "When everyone is safely back on board, I'd give the order to sail to a predesignated point and scuttle."

"That's a pretty expensive disposable sensor," the J2 groused.

"It's a lot less expensive than buying a brand-new submarine, Jesse," the Candyman said. "Give the captain whatever she wants if she thinks it'll help. We'll have one shot at this objective."

"What else?" Don asked.

Wild Bill cast a sidelong glance at Lieutenant Rantz, his mission commander. "I think we need to assign a doctor to T-Bone's crew. We're gonna need to drug those kids to get them off the beach, maybe the mother, too. If someone starts screaming, I'm gonna have men on the beach with their asses hanging in the wind."

Don nodded. "We have some suggestions in that department, sir. I'll get you a full briefing."

"There's one thing you haven't mentioned yet, Mr. Riley," the J2 said. "Timing. When does this have to happen?"

"Gotta be a new moon," Wild Bill said. "If we're using a zodiac, that's just common sense."

Janet did the mental math. A fast transit from Hawaii across the Pacific to Guam was ten days, then they'd have to pick up the SEAL team and dock the SDV to the hull of her boat. Add another four days, then a slow transit down to Hainan Island. Add a week.

Don named the date. "That means the *Illinois* will have to depart no later than—"

"Day after tomorrow," Janet said.

Don smiled. "Correct."

The Candyman rapped his knuckles on the table as he stood. "Captain Everett, you have your orders." He pulverized another piece of candy and grinned at her. "Good hunting."

16

Astana, Kazakhstan

Until this moment, Nikolay Sokolov had never understood the term *new money*. But here, deep in the Ak Orda Presidential Palace in the heart of the Kazakh capital city, he understood.

In Moscow, Russian wealth and imperial history had coexisted for a thousand years. Wealth oozed from the paving stones of Red Square and history colored the minarets of the Kremlin. Everywhere one turned in his own capital city, the glory of Mother Russia was on display in parks, fountains, plazas, and buildings. It was part of the Russian identity.

But the capital of Kazakhstan was like a land of imagination, a country of pretenders. The Ak Orda building and grounds had as much in common with Moscow as Disney Land had with the Palace of Versailles. After all, the pretentious palace was barely a quarter century old.

But what really rankled Nikolay was that none of this would have been possible without Russian money. It was Russia that had developed the natural resources of this country. Russian money that transformed a country of Kazakh sheep herders into a modern republic and all the trappings of wealth that went along with that status.

In that sense, Nikolay reasoned, this city belonged to Russia, and by extension, to him. It also meant that the man who sat across from Nikolay at the dining table belonged to him as well.

But that was perhaps not the way to approach the young, reform-minded President of Kazakhstan.

Their last meeting had not gone well. No, that was being too generous. Their last face-to-face encounter had been an unmitigated disaster. After three days of careful—and fruitless—negotiation over an economic agreement, a drunken Nikolay had called out Karimov at the final dinner of the CSTO.

Nikolay had been right, he still believed that, but righteousness and diplomacy rarely coexisted. Federov had counseled restraint and Nikolay ignored his closest advisor. The fallout had taken the better part of a year to repair.

He studied the man across the table, wondering how much of their last interaction the Kazakh President recalled. Karimov was in his early forties, with coiffed hair and slim European-style eyeglasses that gave him the look of a modern technocrat leader of a rising republic.

We have so much in common, Nikolay reflected. They both represented a younger, fresher brand of leadership and a strong vision of a bright future. They should be friends. They should be allies. But if the day was an indicator, the Kazakh President did not want a warm relationship with his Russian neighbor.

Nikolay's one-day visit to the capital of Kazakhstan had been a full one. Meetings, photo ops, a carefully staged press conference, and a military parade had kept both men occupied. Even when they were together, Karimov seemed more interested in his phone than in the President of the Russian Federation.

All day, Federov kept up the pressure on their intelligence asset to secure a private meeting between the two Presidents. The best he was able to get was a few moments after the official dinner. The two men would be left alone at the dining table after the room cleared.

And here they were. The moment of truth. Nikolay experienced more than a twinge of embarrassment at being put in a subordinate position to the leader of a former Soviet satellite state.

Swallow your pride, he told himself. You need to repair this relationship for the good of your country.

"More wine, Mr. President?" Karimov interrupted Nikolay's careening thoughts. He held up a bottle of red wine. "The finest of my country. We've cultivated a new strain of Saperavi grapes to intensify the color and taste of the finished product."

Without waiting for a reply, he poured a healthy measure into Nikolay's empty glass. The wine was ink dark and the scent of ripe red fruit reached his nose.

Maybe this was an attempt at common ground, Nikolay realized. He held out his hand for the bottle. "May I?" he asked.

"Of course."

Nikolay noted an asterisk next to the Saperavi grape variety on the label. He turned the bottle, scanning the details for the meaning of the asterisk. At the bottom of the label, below the marketing description, health warning, and alcohol content, he found what he was looking for in Russian:

These Saperavi grapes have been genetically modified for flavor and color intensity by Sozhou Labs, Shanghai, People's Republic of China.

Nikolay cursed to himself. The Chinese had even infected the wine industry here.

Karimov held his wineglass up to the light of the chandelier and squinted. He swirled the contents and stuffed his nose deep into the bowl of the glass. He closed his eyes and drew in a deep breath. "I smell spices... cinnamon and cassis. Blackberry and plum...a hint of licorice."

He opened his eyes as if inviting Nikolay to join in. The Russian President looked at him with a pitying glance. What a raging ass, he thought.

Karimov's glance flattened. He put down his wineglass with studied care and lifted his phone. The light of the screen reflected in his glasses. He looked up abruptly.

"I apologize, Mr. President. I have another meeting starting in fifteen minutes. Sergei said you had a private matter to discuss with me. He said it was urgent."

Nikolay gritted his teeth, reminding himself again that he needed this man's help. If he was going to influence the resistance to the Chinese invasion of Central Asia, he needed the cooperation of Kazakhstan.

"I have a proposal," he began, "concerning the ongoing conflict in the Central Asian region." He paused, hoping for a reaction.

He did not get one. "Go on," Karimov said in a deadpan voice.

"I feel it's my duty, as the leading power in the region, to provide support to the resistance movement against the PLA," Nikolay continued.

He stopped again, hoping for some sign of agreement. A nod, a leaning forward to indicate interest. But Karimov just stared.

"My people have been in contact with the leader of the resistance. He welcomes my support—our support—of his cause. I am preparing substantial weapons shipments, but what I lack is sufficient supply routes."

Another pause. No response.

"I need your help, Miras," he concluded. "The most efficient access to the region is through Kazakhstan."

Karimov broke eye contact now, his eyes straying around the dining room. He seemed to focus on something behind Nikolay, and the Russian President resisted the urge to turn around. He kept his gaze steady on the other man.

Karimov shifted in his seat, cleared his throat. "I fear you place me in an awkward position, Mr. President."

"Please, call me Nikolay. We are old friends fighting the same enemy."

The offer of intimacy only seemed to make Karimov more uncomfortable. "Kazakhstan is in a difficult position, Nikolay. We are a country between two great powers. We share considerable borders with both China and Russia. I see my role as..." His voice trailed off as he seemed to search for words. "A balancing act between two great nations."

Karimov was sweating now.

"I'm sure you'll understand," he continued, his voice picking up speed as if trying to get the words out faster. "I must decline this request."

Nikolay felt as if he'd been slapped. "You're refusing me? This is in our shared interest. I'm only asking for transit through your country."

Karimov made a choking sound. "I cannot take sides, Mr. President. Surely, you understand."

Nikolay did not understand, but before he could speak, Karimov leaped to his feet.

"I must be going, Mr. President. Have a safe trip back to Moscow." He snatched his phone from the table and practically ran out of the room.

Nikolay was alone. His ears rang in the silence. He sat back in his chair, his body heavy, his mind still unable to process what had just happened.

He, the President of the Russian Federation, had been snubbed by a former vassal of the Soviet Union. It was so far beyond comprehension as to be laughable.

But it had happened.

His pulse roared in his ears like pounding surf. He stood suddenly, his hands clenched. Nikolay gripped the wine bottle by the neck and hurled it at the wall. The glass shattered, red wine sprayed across the yellow wallpaper, bloodred drips ran down the wall. He swiped his hand and his wineglass soared after the bottle.

He had played the part of the diplomat. He had sought to persuade and flatter to get what he wanted—and he had failed. Worse, he had embarrassed himself and his country.

No more, he vowed. One did not snub the Russian Federation and get away with it. There would be consequences.

Nikolay's hand shook with rage as he extracted his mobile phone from his breast pocket. He dialed Federov.

"Get the plane ready. I want to be in the air within the hour."

17

Karshi-Khanabad Air Base, 12 kilometers east of Karshi, Uzbekistan

They called the place K2—at least that was the nickname the Americans gave to Karshi-Khanabad Air Base. But Harrison knew it had been a long time since an American had set foot inside the perimeter of the military compound.

Back in the early 2000s, K2 had been an FOB for Operation Enduring Freedom, the US action against Afghanistan after 9/11. There had once been seven thousand US military personnel and support staff here.

But all that was ancient history. Today, K2 was officially the home of the Uzbek 60th Separate Mixed Aviation Brigade. Unofficially, it was a key PLA air base in the region and home to the largest Chinese helicopter maintenance depot in Central Asia.

From his overlook position, Harrison raised his night vision field glasses and studied the landscape below. According to the US DOD base survey map spread out on the ground before him, K2's single runway ran east-west and was 1.5 miles long. He followed the runway to the hangars, located to the north of the airstrip. Both of the sheet metal buildings had been expanded by the Chinese construction crews to allow space for the simultaneous teardown of up to six PLA helicopters. The door of one of the hangars was ajar, halogen overhead lights illuminating the deadly profile of a partially dismantled Z-19 attack helo.

The hangar was empty of maintenance personnel. It was after 0200, and the Chinese ran a two-shift maintenance schedule on the base. That was one of the observations they'd made from the twenty-four-hour surveillance Akhmet had placed on the base for the last three weeks.

Harrison counted the fleet of PLA military helos parked on the concrete apron outside the two hangars. Twenty-eight, mostly the newer Z-19s, but a few of the older Z-10 models were mixed in. Sixteen Z-20 utility helicopters and seven of the older Z-18s were also on the ramp. Akhmet's men estimated there were at least two dozen Chengdu GJ-1 unmanned aerial vehicles housed in the second hangar. These were aerial recon models, unarmed but still a vital part of the PLA surveillance network that blanketed the region.

He shifted his field of view to the right and focused on the massive cargo plane parked alone on the apron at the end of the runway. This was the other piece of intel gleaned from Akhmet's long-term surveillance effort.

Maintenance depots needed a constant resupply of spare parts and technical personnel. Every Thursday, like clockwork, a fully stocked Y-20 cargo plane arrived from Beijing. It landed at K2 at 1600 and departed the next morning at 0600. The unloading operation took a few hours and the aircrew reconfigured the cargo bay for passengers—the return flight was almost exclusively military personnel returning to China.

Harrison picked out the security team that patrolled the maintenance facility at night. There were always two teams of two military police officers on roaming patrol. Another pair of guards occupied an office in a squat building located adjacent to one of the hangars. The building was a new one-story structure with three roll-up overhead doors like a garage.

Harrison had assumed the building was used to house the security jeeps, but they were always parked outside, next to the office. Curious, he'd checked the records from the surveillance team and determined that no one had ever seen the garage doors open.

Harrison lowered his glasses and turned on a red night-light. He focused it on the survey map at his feet, his finger tracing a narrow line that ran parallel to the airstrip. When the PLA expanded the base, they'd put in new underground utilities on the north side of the airstrip to support the expanded facilities. Their engineers also installed a new drainage system, abandoning the concrete trench the Americans had dug on the southern side of the airstrip, the side closest to Harrison.

His finger followed the line on the map to where it made a forty-five-degree turn, angling toward the foothills. It terminated in a drainage pond barely twenty meters from the perimeter fence. At this moment, twelve of Akhmet's best men waited on the opposite side of the fence.

Harrison blew out a breath, glancing over at Akhmet. The older man squatted on the ground, hunched forward like a bird of prey, night vision glasses pressed to his eyes. He lowered the binoculars and his head swiveled toward Harrison.

"We are ready," he said.

"Yes, Ussat," Harrison replied. He tried his best to project confidence. Akhmet deserved his support, even if Harrison privately believed they were overreaching.

The plan to attack the PLA base was audacious—or stupid, depending on your point of view. Washington's view was the latter, but Akhmet brushed their concerns aside.

"We need a bold strike against the enemy," he insisted. "Something to inspire our recruits."

That was another thing that rankled the DC crowd. Akhmet was cagey about the scope of his operation. Only he knew how many cells existed in the resistance movement and he was content to keep it that way. Although he gladly accepted the American offers of intelligence and weapons, he did not reciprocate with information and he did not take orders from the United States.

This dynamic put Harrison uncomfortably in the middle. Even as he defended Akhmet to the Beltway crew in his communications with Don, he pleaded with the resistance leader to be more cooperative and not take so many risks.

Harrison saw Akhmet check his watch. He thought he could see the older man's posture tighten. His own muscles felt taut as bowstrings.

"Five minutes," Akhmet announced.

The resistance fighters were under strict rules of radio silence. The attack was on a timetable. The only way the plan could be altered was if Akhmet himself used the radio to give direct orders.

The first wave was a distraction, designed to draw the attention of the PLA security forces and allow Akhmet's fighters to penetrate the airfield fence and enter the abandoned drainage ditch. Using this cover, the fighters could advance to within easy range of the parked PLA aircraft for the second wave of the attack. Using Javelins and Mk 19 grenade launchers, the close-in attack would decimate the fleet of PLA helos and the maintenance facilities. From the overlook position in the foothills, Akhmet's third attack force would provide air defenses using Stinger shoulder-fired missiles and cover fire using small arms to allow the close-in fighting force to retreat.

It all looked great—on paper. But the reality of what they were about to do loomed large in Harrison's mind. Less than fifty men were about to attack a base with thousands of enemy soldiers and hundreds of tons of military ordnance. If they somehow lost the element of surprise, they would be crushed like a bug on the sidewalk.

He slipped an earpiece into his right ear and raised the glasses again. The sound of the PLA voice communications frequency murmured in his ear. At this early morning hour, the only people on the radio were security personnel. They broadcast in the clear in Mandarin. He didn't know the language, but boredom was universal. The reports were routine, sleepy.

He saw Akhmet look at his watch again and Harrison shivered. Not from cold but from excitement. He focused his glasses on the southwest quadrant. That was where they'd be coming from. As he fine-tuned the magnification on the glasses, time seemed to slow down.

He heard them before he saw them. A high-pitched whine on the edge of hearing, a communal drone like a swarm of bees.

"There!" Akhmet pointed into the sky and Harrison realized he'd assumed the jet bikes would arrive at ground level.

They entered the airspace over the base at about two hundred feet, Harrison guessed, and moving at least eighty miles an hour. Their passage in the night sky left ghostly white contrails. The four jet bikes dove at the tarmac together and the sound of gunfire reached his free ear. He saw sparks of light as the bikes fired on the parked aircraft. Harrison swung his glasses to the right. The infiltration had already begun. The second team was through the fence and at the drainage ditch.

An explosion erupted on the airfield just as the earpiece in his right ear came to life. The sleepiness in the voices evaporated, replaced by shouts of panic. The wail of an air raid siren floated over the valley.

A blast of digital noise sounded in his ear, so loud that Harrison ripped the earpiece out. "What was that?" he demanded of the radio operator.

"I don't know," the young man replied. "Some kind of computer-generated signal, I think."

The noise vaguely reminded Harrison of an old-fashioned modem, like in the days of dial-up internet, but that made no sense. He put the earpiece back in and focused his glasses on the airfield just in time to see the jet bikes blast back down the valley the way they had come. A pair of PLA Z-19 Harbins roared after them. That was expected. There was always a helo crew on ready-5 standby and they'd managed to get in the air very fast.

"Let them go," Akhmet called. Although the Z-19s were sitting ducks for Stinger missiles, they were no danger to the jet bikes. Akhmet wanted to keep their position hidden until the second wave started.

Below them, the airfield blazed with light, alive with activity. Men leaped off vehicles before they stopped, racing toward their aircraft. If they gave the PLA fifteen minutes, they'd have every functioning chopper in the air.

But that was not going to happen, Harrison thought. Any second now the real attack would start.

"What the hell is that?" the radio operator said in a loud voice. He pointed a finger at the airfield.

Harrison followed his gaze, swinging his glasses to the right.

The vehicle looked like a mini-tank. It left the concrete apron at speed, its tracked wheels throwing up a cloud of dust. There were at least a dozen of them and they advanced in a V-formation.

A bright explosion painted the night sky, then another, and another as

Akhmet's fighters opened fire on the air base from the cover of the drainage ditch.

Harrison's gaze ping-ponged back and forth between the airfield and the approaching miniature tanks. He didn't see any drivers on the vehicles, but they maintained a perfect formation.

At the first volley of Javelin missiles from the cover of the drainage ditch, the enemy formation changed course. The group of vehicles wheeled to the right, reforming on the lead tank and heading directly for Akhmet's fighters. Machine guns mounted on the vehicles opened fire, raking heavy-caliber rounds across the lip of the drainage ditch.

"Attack!" Akhmet's voice roared out loud and over the radio. "Bravo team, fall back now. That's an order!"

From a few meters away, Harrison heard the *punk-punk* of a Mk 19 grenade launcher being put into action. The whoosh and fiery backblast of shoulder-launched Javelins lit up the hillside. Their position was exposed now.

In the melee, Harrison looked down at his watch. Eight minutes had elapsed. How had the PLA responded that fast? It was not possible.

Another blast of the piercing computer noise echoed over the PLA comms network.

The fleet of mini-tanks advancing on the pinned-down fighters split. A formation of three continued their advance on the drainage ditch, but the rest peeled off to the left.

Toward Harrison's position.

They increased speed, kicking up dirt and dust. The mini-tanks reached the perimeter fence and rammed through it, still firing. Incoming automatic weapons fire zipped across the hillside, tearing up the earth. Harrison hit the deck. The gritty, rocky soil ground into the side of his face.

Whatever those things were, there was no way the vehicles would be able to climb the steep rocky hillside to their position. Even as he tried to convince himself, a finger of doubt wormed its way into his consciousness.

"Retreat," Akhmet called. "All hands, retreat."

Harrison gripped the survey map and crawled to the back of their hide out. The incoming gunfire made a *zip-crack* sound as bullets passed overhead. One .50-caliber round impacted above Harrison's head, blasting stone into shrapnel.

Harrison slid on his belly into the cleft of rock that was the exit. Outside, with a wall of rocky mountain at his back, he stood. The chill night wind was cool on his sweaty face.

He turned on his red-light headlamp and ran down the hill toward his vehicle.

18

Karshi-Khanabad Air Base, 12 kilometers east of Karshi, Uzbekistan

Senior Colonel Kang walked the concrete airstrip with measured steps. The dawn was hidden behind heavy overcast skies that seemed to press down over the airbase, adding to the feeling of oppression.

The gray morning light did nothing to soften the destruction around him. He walked past the charred skeleton of a Z-19 Harbin helicopter, tendrils of firefighting foam clinging to planar surfaces like dirty snow. The air reeked of charred metal and aviation fuel.

"Total losses?" he asked, his voice toneless.

"Six Z-19s were completely destroyed, sir. Four more are damaged but salvageable," replied the base commander, a junior colonel. The man's face alternated between anger and fear. He could see his career swirling in the toilet bowl and there was nothing he could do about it. Base security was his responsibility.

Maybe the man would be court-martialed, maybe not. What occupied Kang's attention at this moment was how fortunate the PLA had been.

Wordlessly, he held out his hand and felt a tablet being placed in his palm. He compared the marked up aerial image on the screen to his surroundings.

He faced the southwest, where the first wave of the attack had come. Some sort of aerial assault using high-speed weapons. They had come in under the radar, then popped up and attacked from above, like a cruise missile. Except it wasn't a missile. A helicopter? Kang dismissed the idea. There was no way the SIF had helos in their weapons inventory.

He'd worry about that later. Whatever the vehicle, the first wave had been a diversion.

He rotated his body to the left, where the rebel forces had penetrated the perimeter of the base. He walked forward, off the concrete apron and into the grass. As he walked toward the drainage ditch, the air grew sweeter. His breath steamed in the morning chill. He could hear the base commander stumbling along behind him, but he ignored the man. He'd failed in his duty, and his career would suffer the consequences.

Kang reached his destination. The edge of the concrete ditch was chipped from bullet strikes and the grass was shredded under the tracks of the autonomous fighting vehicles. Blood stained the dirty concrete. Kang counted twelve positions.

He turned around to face the airstrip. The hangars rose over the blackened wrecks of the burned-out helos. To his right, a few hundred yards away, the massive Y-20 cargo plane squatted on the concrete, untouched by enemy fire.

It was a clear field of fire from here to the airstrip where dozens of parked helos sat like roosting pigeons. This enemy was clearly well organized and well armed—Kang had seen the US-manufactured Javelin missiles recovered from the fight—but they had only managed to destroy or damage ten PLA helicopters. Meanwhile, the Y-20 cargo plane, an enormous target, escaped the enemy attack without a scratch.

How had this happened? Kang did not believe in luck. The terrorist attack was too well organized to fail this badly. He was missing something.

He handed the tablet to the colonel. "Show me your security logs again," he ordered.

Kang ran his eyes down the screen, hundreds of entries, most with clickable links. Every door that was opened, every time a sentry made a radio report—everything was captured, which made for a lot of noise hiding the signal he was seeking.

Kang went back to the first indication of an attack.

0300.37 – Radar contact, 197 degrees.

Another ten or so lines of automatic radar alerts. He scrolled down half a page until he found where the sentry reported the attack and triggered the air raid siren. That happened at 0303.19, less than three minutes later.

His gaze snagged on an entry a few lines above:

0301.00 – Sentry system activated.

He pointed at the line. "What does this mean?" he asked the colonel.

"The sentry system are the autonomous fighting vehicles."

"I know that," Kang said. "Who deployed them?"

"The system," the man said with a puzzled look on his face. "It's automatic."

"What system?" Kang pressed, annoyed now.

"Foresight." The base commander pointed at the Y-20 cargo plane. "Whenever we have a Y-20 on base, the system raises the base security posture. Part of the increased security is automatic deployment of the SAGs, the Sentry Autonomous Ground vehicles, in the event of an attack."

"You programmed the system to do that?" Kang asked.

The other man shook his head. "It just does it, sir. It's automatic."

It's predictive, Kang thought. The system recognized an increased threat profile and changed its own operating parameters.

He turned toward the foothills to the south. His eyes traced the tracks of the sentry vehicles across the grass and through the fence. He squinted up at the rocky face where the third wave of the attack was launched. His mind wrestled with the idea that a computer algorithm had saved this base.

Maybe his dismissal of Foresight was too hasty, he realized. The idea of turning over control of battlefield decisions to a computer was against everything he believed in, but here was proof that the system could work.

In a firefight, every second counted and Foresight had given them many, many seconds back when it mattered the most. The SIF should have laid waste to this airfield and instead they'd had to settle for a handful of destroyed helos in exchange for ten dead men.

Imagine what a system like that could do if given really good intelligence. The SIF would not stand a chance against the PLA. Their every move would be predicted and blocked...

Kang's gaze settled on the bloodstained concrete as he half listened to the colonel's ramblings.

"We'll see what the MSS interrogator can extract from the prisoners," the base commander said with a dark laugh.

Kang wheeled on him. "What did you say?"

"The survivors. The MSS are interrogating them."

"Take me there," Kang ordered. "Now."

19

Karshi-Khanabad Air Base, 12 kilometers east of Karshi, Uzbekistan

Even with the help of the base commander, it took Kang forty minutes to find out where the MSS had taken the SIF prisoners. Forty precious minutes.

They went to the detention center first. The PLA had built a new facility, complete with automatic cell doors, a solitary confinement area, and interrogation rooms wired for video.

The captain in charge of the military police assured them that the MSS had brought no prisoners into the facility, but Kang insisted on seeing for himself. The hurried tour ate up fifteen minutes. The SIF prisoners were not there.

They tried the infirmary next. Despite the assurances of the duty officer that there were no SIF prisoners on the premises, Kang again insisted on a visual inspection. He didn't know who to trust in this scenario, so he opted to trust no one.

Kang considered his next steps. Maybe they should check the morgue.

But when they emerged from the hospital, their driver asked to speak to the base commander privately. The corporal was young, his cheeks pitted with acne, his hair greasy, and he shifted his weight from one foot to the other as he spoke. The colonel took the young man aside.

When the base commander rejoined Kang, he had a smile on his face. He held open the door of the SUV for Kang. "Get in, sir."

Their destination was a low-slung Quonset hut located behind the new hangars. The building was at least twenty years old and in poor repair, but Kang's interest quickened when he saw two black SUVs parked outside. He led the way up the three metal steps to a set of double doors. He opened them and stepped inside.

At one time, the room had been a barracks, but now rusty bunkbed frames were stacked against one wall and the rest of the space was filled with boxes and crates. A storage room.

At the far end of the cluttered room, some forty paces away, was another set of double doors.

A scream rent the air. A male voice pitched high, soaked in pain. Kang felt the muscles of his belly contract in response.

He started for the next set of doors, breaking into a run. He pushed them open to find a washroom. White porcelain sinks lined each wall, and two rows of benches ran down the center of the room. High, rectangular windows illuminated the space with dirty morning light.

At the end of the room was an open doorway, then a cinder block privacy wall. The walls on either side of the door were adorned with hooks for towels.

Two men, posted on either side of the open doorway, startled as Kang burst into the room. There was a third man as well, seated on a bench and hunched over, his face in his hands. The man looked up and Kang recognized him. Timur Ganiev, the President of the Central Asian Union.

"What are you doing here, Mr. President?" he asked Ganiev.

The man's complexion was ashen, and he seemed to take a long time to process Kang's question. His pondering was interrupted by another scream that ended abruptly with a choking noise. Ganiev jumped to his feet and pointed at the shower room.

Kang advanced on the men posted outside the door. They were dressed in civilian clothes, but they were armed and Kang could tell by the way they moved that they could handle themselves. MSS agents, without a doubt. They separated so they were on either side of the approaching group.

"Let us pass," the base commander ordered.

The one on Kang's right seemed to be in charge. His eyes flicked from Kang to the base commander to Ganiev. "You have no authority here, Senior Colonel. Move along." He jerked his chin at Ganiev. "Take him with you."

Behind the cinder block privacy wall, Kang heard the sounds of a heavy object striking flesh. Then a noise like a whimpering dog.

"Jimmy Li," Ganiev said. His hoarse voice quavered with emotion. "He's in there."

Of course, Kang should have guessed it would be him. He raised his voice. "Jimmy," he called. "It's Kang. I want to come in."

The beating stopped, but the whimpering went on. There was a click of heels on tile, and Jimmy's head poked around the edge of the privacy wall. His hair was mussed, a dark wave draped over his forehead, and his cheeks were flushed. He panted, grinning. "Senior Colonel, what a pleasant surprise. Please, come in."

Kang turned to the base commander. "You're dismissed, Colonel."

"I'm coming in, too," Ganiev announced with a tone of finality.

Jimmy shrugged. Kang stepped past the security detail, ignoring the protests of the base commander. Ganiev followed him.

The inside of the room was all tile. Walls, floor, and ceiling were covered with industrial ceramic tile, the squares of dirty white separated by lines of mildewed grout. Along one wall stood a line of twelve freestanding toilets, on the other wall a row of showerheads. Fluorescent lights cast the room in a stark blue-white illumination.

One of the prisoners was slumped between two toilets, his outstretched arms lashed to the porcelain fixtures. Both of his arms were bruised and broken. His bare legs splayed out across the floor, and feces mixed with the blood between his legs.

This was not the man who had screamed. This man had a bullet hole in his forehead and red goo coated the white tile behind his shattered skull.

Kang's stomach lurched. Behind him, he heard Ganiev gag.

Across from the dead prisoner, a man was spread-eagled on the wall, his wrists raised and bound to two showerheads. His head lolled forward, and he sagged in his bindings, but Kang could see his chest rise and fall in short, rapid breaths.

The naked man had a gunshot wound on his right thigh just above the knee. Someone had applied a tourniquet and the wound had clotted into a clump of black blood. The muscles beneath his brown skin look stringy. Purple bruises bloomed on his rib cage, and his forearms were black and blue. The fingers on one hand curled forward and Kang could see where several of the fingernails were missing.

Jimmy Li had been a busy boy.

The MSS officer dipped a plastic cup into one of the toilets and dashed the water in the prisoner's face. The terrorist stirred, mumbling something. Jimmy nodded with seeming satisfaction at the response.

A flattened cardboard box covered one of the toilet bowls. The tools of Jimmy's trade were arrayed on the makeshift table: a rubber truncheon, needle-nose pliers, some scalpels, a handheld digital recorder, and a clear plastic box containing a pair of syringes.

Kang viewed Jimmy's crude tools with disgust. Those methods rarely worked. Past a certain pain threshold, the only information you got from torture was whatever the prisoner thought you wanted to hear. Kang had been trained in interrogation, and what he was seeing here was the mark of someone more interested in inflicting pain than gathering useful intelligence.

"You're just in time," Jimmy said in an enthusiastic tone. His eyes were bright, his grin stretching the limits of his face.

"Just in time for what?" Kang kept his voice level. They both knew he had no jurisdiction here. If Jimmy decided Kang was a problem, he would be forced to leave. As much as he disagreed with Jimmy's methods, he needed to know what that prisoner had to say.

"We've completed the initial phase of the interrogation," Jimmy said as if he was delivering an excellent financial report to a board of directors. "The softening-up phase. It's the fastest way to get past the preliminaries."

The prisoner whimpered and Jimmy turned. "They all go the same way. They resist at first. After we go at it for a while, they dish out some prepared story that's designed to mislead us. The first answer is never the right answer."

He walked to the prisoner and placed his hand under the man's chin. He lifted his face and spoke. "But we've worked through that part, right?" A line of bloody drool ran from the man's mouth. Jimmy nodded with satisfaction. "Yes, I believe we are ready to move on to phase two."

He dropped the prisoner's head and called out to the men guarding the door. When the security detail entered, the scene did not seem to bother them. They'd seen this before.

One of them opened a folding cot and camp chair while the other got out sheets and blankets. Together, they cut the prisoner's bindings and carried him to the cot. They laid him down gently and covered him with a clean sheet, then a blanket. The only exposed flesh was the man's battered face and his right arm, which they left on top of the blanket.

The man moaned softly as Jimmy perched on the camp stool next to him. He held one of the hypodermic needles in his hand.

"It's okay," he said in Russian. "We're done with all that nastiness now. I just want you to relax. I'll give you something to make the pain go away." His voice was low and soft, as if he was comforting a child. The sound sent a chill up Kang's spine.

Jimmy took the man's arm and turned it toward him. He found a vein, then inserted the hypodermic needle and pushed the plunger.

In a few seconds, the man's moaning ceased and his face relaxed.

"See?" Jimmy said in that singsong voice. "You feel better now, right?"

To Kang's surprise, the man gave a slight nod.

Jimmy placed the man's arm under the blankets and tucked them around his chin. He looked up, grinning again. "We'll just give him five minutes to ride the wave," he said in a tone of barely suppressed excitement. The soft bedside manner was gone. The sadist was back.

Kang pointed at the hypodermic. "What is that?"

Jimmy shrugged. "It's a cocktail. Works like a charm. We call it the tears of God. The real trick is that you have to know when to use it. Too soon, and they're stoned. Too late, and...well, you know." He cut a look at the dead man still lying between a pair of toilets.

Jimmy pulled out a pack of cigarettes and lit one. He extended the package to Ganiev, who took one. Ganiev's fingers shook as he held the cigarette.

Kang shook his head. "I don't smoke."

Jimmy grinned again. "I don't either, but it cuts down on the smell, you know?"

The MSS agent took his time finishing the cigarette, then dropped it to the floor and crushed it under his heel. He blew a column of smoke to the ceiling. "I think that's enough time," he said brightly.

Jimmy placed the digital recorder on the blanket next to the man's chin, then he gently woke him up. He asked a few easy questions, praised the responses. The prisoner even seemed to smile at one point.

"That's very good," Jimmy said in that creepy singsong voice.

Slowly, he moved the conversation toward a list of prepared questions and the words started to flow. Kang listened intently as the man told Jimmy the names of others in his cell, the location of their home base, and their weapons complement. He imagined feeding this gold mine of intelligence into the Foresight database.

Despite his brutal methods, it turned out Jimmy was a skilled interrogator. He went back over the questions multiple times, asking them in a slightly different way to make sure he was getting all the information.

The terrorists were using effective compartmentalization techniques, Kang realized. The prisoner told Jimmy everything about his own cell but knew little of the resistance movement beyond his own group. In the cell, only one or two others would be entrusted with knowledge of other cells.

No matter, Kang thought. We'll take down this cell, then climb the ladder until we get to the top of the SIF leadership.

The man said the word *ussat* again. It had come up twice before and Jimmy had not followed up.

"What is that?" he asked. "What is *ussat*?"

"It's not a what, it's a who," Ganiev answered. "*Ussat* is a Turkmen word. It means *master*. It's what they call Orazov."

Jimmy glared at Ganiev, who ignored him.

"That's the leader of the SIF?" Kang pressed.

"The SIF," Ganiev said in a scornful voice.

"That's enough, Timur." Jimmy was on his feet, his voice sharp.

Kang looked from Ganiev to the MSS agent. What was going on here? What was he missing?

"Senior Colonel," Jimmy said. "I think you have enough intelligence to keep you occupied for the foreseeable future. We're done here."

"Ussat," the prisoner said suddenly. "Ussat. U—"

Jimmy pulled a QSZ-193 pistol from his shoulder holster and fired it into the prisoner's face. The man's body convulsed once and then he lay still.

Ganiev doubled over and vomited.

The sound of the gunshot in the confined space was deafening. "Why did you do that?" Kang shouted over the ringing in his ears.

Jimmy grinned. His words were on the edge of Kang's deadened hearing.

"That was phase three."

20

Undisclosed location in Turkmenistan

The hot tea burned Harrison's tongue, but he didn't care. His body ached with cold and fatigue. He recrossed his legs and shifted his backside on the thin carpet in a vain attempt to find a more comfortable sitting position.

This farmhouse would be home for the next twenty-four hours. Harrison guessed they'd be moving again when darkness fell. In the three days since the failed attack on K2, Harrison had slept in a cave, in the back of a Land Cruiser, and in a very small hotel room that almost certainly had bed bugs.

But mostly, he didn't sleep. Every time he closed his eyes, he saw the faces of the men they'd left behind.

Twelve men. Twelve men missing—probably dead. For what? They'd damaged or destroyed a handful of PLA helicopters. Even the cargo plane, as big a target as it was, had gone untouched by their attack.

It was a humiliating result—and a dangerous one. They had to assume that some of the fighters inside the PLA airfield had been captured alive. They would be interrogated and they would tell what they knew.

After a narrow escape from their PLA pursuers, Akhmet spent the first hours communicating with his next level of leadership. In turn, they would communicate with their people, the next link in the chain. Any cells at risk were ordered to move immediately.

But while compartmentalized communications were secure, they also took time. Time Akhmet and his forces did not have. The unknown status of the fighters they had left behind meant there was a possible breach in the resistance network. Unless Akhmet could mend the breach before the Chinese could act on the intel they might gain from interrogating captured men, more of his men would die.

The morning sun streaming through the single window of the sitting room was bright and cheerful, but it did nothing to lighten the mood of the two brooding men.

Harrison studied Akhmet in the light of day. His head was down, his hooded eyes dark as pitch. His mouth appeared as a thin line of pressed white flesh in his gray beard.

The resistance leader had said little to Harrison since the attack, but Harrison knew his thoughts were with his men. Not the ones who were killed; they were beyond helping. He was thinking about prisoners.

Akhmet's men were tough, but eventually everyone broke. They would talk. Everyone talked. His men had prepared stories to dribble out over the course of an interrogation, designed to mislead their tormentors, but those stories would also fail and the truth would spill out.

Everyone talked. Eventually.

Harrison had heard the stories about the interrogation tactics of the Chinese security services and he offered up a silent prayer to those who might be in that dark place.

Maybe no one survived, Harrison thought, both ashamed and hopeful at the same time.

But they didn't know—they didn't really *know* anything—so they couldn't take that chance.

Akhmet raised his head. His eyes met Harrison's. There was fatigue and pain in that dark gaze.

"What happened?" Akhmet's voice was like sandpaper.

Every time they stopped, Harrison used his secure laser comms package to check in with Washington for their analysis of the battle. He'd sent them everything he'd recorded that night. Every radio comm, every scrap of video, and his own observations. They would marry his field data with whatever sensors or sources they had on their end and come up with an answer.

An hour ago, Harrison received a preliminary analysis from his colleagues at Emerging Threats Group. He could tell from the depth of the report that it had been an all-hands-on-deck effort in Washington.

"Nothing is definite yet—" Harrison began.

"But you have an idea," Akhmet interrupted.

Harrison nodded. "Just a theory, Ussat." He saw Akhmet wince at the use of his nickname. *Master*. With a dozen men dead or captured, the resistance leader surely did not feel like a master of anything.

"Tell me."

"The key element in the analysis is that the PLA response to our attack was too fast. It was like they were anticipating it."

Akhmet frowned. "You think we have a spy?"

Harrison shook his head. "As soon as the attack happened, there was a signal on the PLA communications network."

"An alarm?"

"Maybe, but my people think it was something else." Harrison hesitated. "They believe it was a signal to activate the assault vehicles."

He paused, recalling the tracked assault vehicles. The image of the small tank crashing through an eight-foot-high chain link fence all the while firing on their hillside position was not something he would soon forget. He could not even imagine what it must have been like for the fighters inside the perimeter of the PLA air base. He'd watched the video, and the automatic weapons fire on the drainage ditch had been murderous.

"What kind of signal are we talking about?" Akhmet asked.

"The assault vehicles were unmanned. It's possible the signal to release them was automated as well."

Akhmet's hooded eyes pinched shut. "You're saying that the PLA has a security system that can automatically trigger deadly weapons?"

"I'm saying it's possible, Ussat." Harrison kept his voice neutral.

The resistance leader stared at the bright square of yellow sunshine on the floor, considering this information. "If they were unmanned assault vehicles, how were they controlled? You think they have remote control drivers? Like a video game?"

"That's where we get into speculation," Harrison said.

Akhmet shrugged. "Then speculate."

"My people think they were autonomous, Ussat," Harrison said. "Their formation was too perfect to have been remotely controlled by multiple men—and they reacted too quickly. The assault vehicles were out of the garage before the second wave even fired a shot. There was no time for human drivers to react that quickly."

"Autonomous weapons," Akhmet whispered. "Is that possible?"

"It is possible." Harrison avoided the other man's eyes.

"There's more, Harrison. Tell me."

"Analysts like to extrapolate their findings, Ussat. They develop a theory and then they look for evidence to support their theory. Many times those theoretical frameworks fall apart under close scrutiny."

"You're avoiding my question."

Harrison hung his head. "The theory is far-fetched and I don't want to add to your burden with ideas that may not be relevant."

"Tell me."

"During the firefight, there was another burst of computer noise on the comms network. Immediately after the order, the assault vehicles split apart. Do you remember?"

Akhmet nodded. "They came right at us."

"Yes, they did. This action confirms the idea that the assault vehicles were computer controlled, but it leads to another observation."

Akhmet's eyes studied Harrison's face.

"The timing of the order happened *before* we opened fire, Ussat."

A frown creased his brow. "You're saying that they knew we were there? The PLA surveillance is that good?"

"That's one possibility," Harrison admitted. "But detailed analysis of the video shows the enemy vehicles changed course again after we opened fire, which indicates that they did not have an exact location when they split into two assault teams."

Akhmet rubbed his face. "I don't understand what you're trying to tell me, Harrison."

Harrison felt a flash of irritation. The idea was crazy. It never should have been in the CIA analysis report. He should not be discussing these science fiction fantasies.

"The theory is that the Chinese have developed a predictive algorithm. One that can direct battlefield assets without human intervention. The assault vehicles split off from the main attack because it predicted we would be there."

Silence fell in the room. Sunlight played across Akhmet's craggy features as he thought. The old man poured tea for both of them and handed a cup to Harrison. He sipped his drink in silence. For the first time since he'd known Akhmet, Harrison saw an old man sitting before him.

"You believe this is possible, Harrison?"

"It fits the observations from this single encounter," Harrison said. "The use of AI on the battlefield is still in its infancy. The amount of computing power needed for such a capability is immense, far beyond anything that exists today."

"What is the alternate explanation?"

Harrison shrugged. "The PLA got lucky. They were in an upgraded state of readiness because of the cargo plane, and their security team reacted very quickly." The explanation sounded weak and Harrison knew it, but next-gen computers driving battlefield movements was some armchair technocrat's wet dream.

Akhmet toyed with his teacup. "If there was such a system, how would it communicate with these autonomous weapons."

"Presumably through the Huawei network."

Akhmet nodded. "Then regardless of how the assault vehicles were controlled, the vulnerability of the enemy is the communications network, yes? That's the backbone of the whole system."

"True, but the communications system is protected by the surveillance network. Every day, the Chinese expand their surveillance capability. It's a chicken and egg problem, Ussat."

Akhmet grinned, the first time Harrison had seen him smile in days. "Then we need to have roast chicken and scrambled eggs at the same meal." He got to his feet. "Tell your people thank you for their hard work. I need time to think." He left Harrison alone in the room.

Harrison knew he should sleep, but his brain was too lit up to relax. He saw the TV remote on the low table and turned on the wall-mounted television.

The TV was tuned to a station in Samarkand and he left it there. A limousine pulled up to the curb in front of an impressive-looking building fronted by a wide plaza. The Russian headline read: *Constitutional committee resumes work.*

Harrison half listened to the commentary as he watched the screen. The door of the limo opened and Timur Ganiev emerged. He was dressed in a dark suit and overcoat with a cream-colored silk scarf, looking every bit the international diplomat.

On the right side of the screen, he caught a glimpse of Nicole Nipper, the only Western reporter allowed into Ganiev's inner circle. She filed periodic dispatches with Western news outlets and it was rumored she was working on a documentary about Ganiev and the Central Asian Union. As Timur started to make his way across the plaza, she directed two Chinese cameramen to follow him.

Just as the camera started to cut away, another man emerged from the limousine. If Harrison had looked away for even a second, he would have missed it. His fingers scrambled for the remote and he paused the newscast.

Carefully, he rewound until he found what he was looking for.

Jimmy Li. He'd first met Jimmy when he was investigating the death of his best friend. Jimmy worked for Surfan Oil and Gas, the same company that Tim had worked for. He'd suspected even then that Jimmy was part of the Chinese Ministry of State Security.

And here he was again, Harrison thought. Close to the center of the action.

He stared at the frozen screen. Was that useful? Maybe, but his brain seemed to be stuck.

He yawned, suddenly dead tired. He clicked off the TV.

21

South China Sea, 12 nautical miles southeast of Hainan Island, People's Republic of China

Commander Janet Everett was not superstitious, not even a little bit. Still, launching a sensitive and highly illegal exfiltration operation on Chinese soil on April Fool's Day seemed like they were just asking for trouble.

"Ship is hovering at five-zero meters, Captain," the Pilot said.

"Very well, Pilot," Janet replied. "Fathometer reading, please."

"One hundred eight meters under the keel, Captain," came the report.

As soon as they'd entered water depth less than two hundred meters, Janet had ordered the ship rigged for ultra-quiet and the fathometer watch manned continuously. Operating submerged in water this shallow made her skin crawl. The fact that they were skirting the territorial waters of the People's Republic of China did nothing to ease her anxiety.

Steady, she told herself. They're all watching you. You will be cool, you will be calm, you will be a professional.

"Sonar," Janet said in an even voice. "Contact report."

She studied the monitor as the Sonar Supervisor ran down the list of known contacts. He used a combination of shipboard sensors, mainly passive sonar, and two sail drones they had deployed six hours earlier.

The unmanned surface vehicles, known in Navy-speak as TASAs or Tube-deployed Autonomous Surveillance Assets, had been rechristened by the crew as Sharks. At sundown, when they were still more than twenty miles offshore, Janet had ordered the Sharks deployed. Released from two reconfigured VLS tubes, the twenty-five-foot canisters floated to the surface of the South China Sea. The canister unfolded into a configuration that resembled a windsurf rig with a twenty-foot-high triangular sail made of carbon fiber. The internal ballast system righted the craft and the upright mast established contact with a passing satellite.

Fifteen minutes after deployment, the *Illinois*, which was streaming a radio communications buoy, received confirmation that both Sharks were standing by for instructions.

The navigation system onboard the Sharks could be programmed to run a preset configuration, switched to autonomous mode, or receive orders from an ultra-secure satellite link. But repositioning the units took time and patience. There were no motors. The Sharks were high-tech sailboats, propelled by the wind. The Sharks were deployed with fully charged batteries, which recharged using an onboard wave-action generator. In theory, the units could stay on station indefinitely, but if all went well, she'd only need them for the next six hours.

And it all *will* go well, she told herself.

One of the Sharks was programmed to run a screen parallel to the shipping lanes that ran out of Yulin Naval Base on the southern tip of Hainan Island. The second unit patrolled closer to shore in a parallel racetrack, looking for ship traffic that did not show up on the sonar sensors of the *Illinois*, such as fishing boats not underway or pleasure craft.

She studied the six surface contacts. Two PLA Navy vessels were to the west, outbound from Yulin and operating within the normal shipping lanes. Four fishing vessels lay to the south of their position. There were no signs of subsurface contacts, but that was actually what worried Janet the most. She had read the intel reports of PLA underwater drones patrolling territorial waters outside sensitive naval installations. The deadliest threat to her submarine was another submarine, especially one she couldn't hear. Although the Sharks trailed a sensitive hydrophone behind them, she trusted her own onboard sensors for the task of ferreting out another submarine.

Janet rubbed the back of her neck and changed the display to show the weather report. Sixty-one degrees Fahrenheit, overcast with scattered rain showers, and a light six mph westerly wind.

Perfect conditions, she thought. Maybe April Fool's Day is taking the year off.

Janet turned to Lieutenant Rantz, who was studying the same information two screens down the stack of monitors. "I think this scenario is as good as we're going to get, Lieutenant," she said quietly.

Rantz, already geared up in his black neoprene wetsuit and boots, nodded. Rantz's chief stood behind him, watching the same screens to make sure they both had good situational awareness of what awaited them on the ocean's surface. Both men wore combat knives in sheaths lashed to their chests, and empty leg holsters. Their weapons were with the XO and the balance of the SEAL team who waited by the entrance to the SEAL delivery vehicle that was docked to the back of the *Illinois*.

"I agree, Captain," the SEAL team leader said. "Request permission to embark my team into the SDV."

"Permission granted, Lieutenant. Good hunting."

She watched him and his chief leave the control room, closing the door carefully behind them. Less than two minutes later, the request arrived in control from the XO to open the hatch to the SDV.

"Permission granted," Janet replied. She watched the status board change from a green circle to a red dot, then switch back as the watertight hatch was resealed.

"Green board, Captain," the Pilot reported.

"Very well."

They'd taken on the SDV and a team of twelve SEALs only five days earlier in Guam. The SEALs embarked a primary team and a backup team, five men in each, as well as two technical specialists in case anything went wrong with the submersible. No one was taking any chances with this mission.

At Janet's recommendation, the Special Forces assets were flown to

Guam to meet the *Illinois*. That allowed for a much faster, and quieter, transit for the submarine across the vast Pacific, buying them two extra days in their schedule. Once the SDV was locked on the back of the *Illinois*, the submarine's speed underwater was limited due to noise considerations.

Janet took full advantage of the extra time. On the trip from Guam to Hainan Island, her crew and both of the SEAL teams ran through the submersible docking and undocking sequence repeatedly until she was confident that the teams on both sides of the watertight hatch knew exactly what they were doing. There were not many variables she could control on this operation, but she was determined to ensure that the few within her sphere of influence would be letter-perfect.

"SDV requests permission to undock, Captain," called out the Pilot.

"Granted," Janet replied.

The control room was silent. Overhead, the constant white noise of the ventilation system shushed along. She waited for the very slight *clunk* as the submersible detached from the mother ship. She felt the deck tip down slightly.

"SDV is away. Adjusting trim."

"Very well, Pilot," Janet said. "Start the mission clock, Mr. Wilkins."

"Start the mission clock, aye, ma'am. Mission clock is running."

Lieutenant Brian Wilkins was one of her most promising junior officers, which was why she'd chosen him as her Junior Officer of the Deck for this evolution.

Two rows of monitors ran down the center of the control room, each display capable of being configured for any of the watchstanding functions, such as sonar, fire control, or the incoming tactical data stream from remote sensors, including the Sharks. At the top of each monitor, regardless of configuration, a countdown clock appeared.

4:00:00.

Four hours. That was how long Rantz and his team had to get to shore, pick up their passengers, and get back to the *Illinois* safely. Keeping a US submarine in the shallow coastal waters of China past sunrise was deemed an unacceptable risk. After four hours, her orders were to retreat to fifty nautical miles and wait until midnight to return.

Was four hours enough? She'd been over the mission details a hundred times and on paper it worked, but there were countless ways for an operation with this many variables to go sideways in a heartbeat.

A zodiac run to shore could be seen by a civilian and reported. The woman they were taking didn't know what was about to happen. What if she lost it? And there were kids—kids! On the return trip, Rantz's team needed to find the submersible and then the submersible needed to find the *Illinois*.

Four hours sounded like a lot of time until you added up all the things that could go wrong.

And if the SEALs missed their rendezvous with the *Illinois*, their orders were to put the submersible on the ocean floor and wait for midnight. Five SEALs, a kidnapped mother and two kids locked in a space the size of a walk-in closet for eighteen hours...

Janet took in a deep breath and let it out slowly. On this mission, everyone had a job to do and her job was to keep her submarine hidden and her crew on task.

They're all watching you, Janet thought. Set the example.

Rigging her ship for ultra-quiet meant that all nonessential personnel were supposed to be in their racks.

"Mr. Wilkins," Janet said, "you have the watch. I'll be in my stateroom."

"Aye, ma'am." The order seemed to take Wilkins by surprise, but he recovered quickly. "Attention in Control, this is Lieutenant Wilkins, I have the deck and the conn."

Janet listened for the acknowledgments from all the watchstanders in the room, then walked calmly to the door, turned. "Wake me if anything changes, Mr. Wilkins."

"Yes, ma'am."

Janet opened the control room door, took two steps forward, turned left and entered her stateroom.

She sat on her bunk, hands on her knees, and breathed.

In...out...in...out.

This was always the hard part. The waiting.

Janet forced herself to lie back on her bunk. She stared at the ceiling, but her eyes crept to the monitor on her stateroom wall. Then to the mission clock at the top of the screen.

3:48:16.

The SEALs had been gone a whole twelve minutes.

She blew out a long breath and closed her eyes.

22

Lingshui Nanwan Houdao Scenic Area, Hainan Island, China

Mei Lin felt the cool mist coat her cheek with dampness. She adjusted the hood over the baby sleeping in the carrier on her chest. What was she thinking bringing her children out on a night like this?

Lixin's slick hand pulled away from hers as he stamped his way through another puddle. His small form was clad in a yellow rain slicker and matching boots. So far, he was enjoying their midnight outing, but Mei Lin knew what was coming next. Soon, the boy would tire and his mood would change.

Although Mei Lin had taken care to dress her children for the weather, she had neglected to do the same for herself. Her wet windbreaker clung to her skin, her hair was as wet as if she'd just stepped from the shower, and her running shoes were soaked through.

She shivered, but only partly from the cold. She and the children had walked down this path three times since they'd come to the island. In the daytime, it was beautiful. Sundrenched beaches and gleaming white sand on one side. On the other side, a tropical forest of lush green trees bordered by a hedge of laurels. The smell of fresh flowers scented the air, and gibbons, called singing monkeys by the locals, swung from tree branches like miniature trapeze artists. People fed the monkeys—even though they weren't supposed to—and the little creatures responded by doing tricks.

Mei Lin recaptured her son's hand. This walk was different at night. She could hear the ocean off to her right, but thick fog obscured the view. The few meters of visibility she had in the darkness showed the beach as a smear of gray. She kept to the right side of the path, as far away from the forest as possible. The trees were shapeless, brooding black.

And the gibbons. A shadow slid across her path, bringing Mei Lin to an abrupt halt. The monkeys were terrifying. At any second, she expected one of them to leap down from the black trees and attack her and her children.

"Ow, Mama," Lixin protested, jerking his hand free again.

Mei Lin felt a moment of panic as the boy's hand slipped from hers. She seized his shoulder, felt her way down his arm, and took his tiny hand in hers.

"You must hold Mama's hand," she said. Why was she whispering?

"I'm tired," the boy announced.

"I know," Mei Lin said, still in a whisper. "But I need you to be my brave little soldier, just like Bába."

At the mention of his father, the boy straightened, gripped her hand with new fervor, and tugged her forward.

Mei Lin let him pull her into the night, her heart breaking a little in the process. She knew the boy didn't really remember Yichen. To Lixin, his father was more a symbol than a real person.

Mei Lin set her jaw and picked up the pace. Tonight, all that would be in the past. Tonight, she would be reunited with her husband. At least that was the plan.

If she stopped to really think about it, the set of circumstances that brought her to this rainy nature walk in the middle of the night was not logical. First, during a chance meeting with a stranger in a Beijing park she received a note, a folded square of paper tucked inside her daughter's clothing written in her husband's handwriting.

It instructed her to take a vacation in honor of their wedding anniversary. Immediately, Mei Lin booked three nights at Raffles hotel on Lingshui Beach on Hainan Island, the same resort where they'd honeymooned together three years ago.

She smiled to herself at the memory of those happier times with her husband. It was the finest resort she'd ever stayed at and Yichen indulged her every wish. The exquisite spa, the golf course, the many restaurants. And sex. They had a lot of sex on that trip.

The note was soon gone. The paper with Yichen's handwriting had been thin, like onion skin. As she handled it, the paper grew more flimsy until by the end of the day, it had dissolved to nothing.

There were days when she believed that she might have made the whole thing up in her head. There was no mysterious note with familiar handwriting, just a wish for the life that she'd lost and was never getting back.

But she went on the vacation anyway. Just in case.

When she and the children arrived at the resort, Mei Lin wasn't sure what to expect. Would her dead husband be waiting for her in the lobby? Would he fill her room with flowers and chocolates?

None of those things happened. Instead, she and the children spent the first two days of their vacation going to the pool and taking walks along the nature paths. Mei Lin's doubts piled up.

That afternoon, as she was putting Bai down for her nap, she saw a square of pink paper peeking out from under the baby's blanket.

With trembling fingers, she unfolded the note. It was a phone number, written in her husband's hand.

It took all of her willpower not to call right away. She managed to get both children down for a nap, then she picked up the receiver of the hotel phone and dialed the number. There was a pause, a click, then a man's voice began to speak.

Yichen's voice.

"My darling, it's me," he said. "I can't explain everything now, but I need you to trust me."

A pause, and Mei Lin heard the sound of her own breath on the line. She did not speak. She could tell it was a recording.

"Meet me at the overlook tonight at one a.m. Bring the children and dress warmly. Do not bring anything electronic, not even a flashlight—that's very important. I love you, Mei Lin. We will be together again very soon. I promise."

The line went dead. Mei Lin stared at the blank wall until the phone started to beep at her.

She hung up, then picked up the receiver again and redialed the number.

The line was disconnected.

She went to the sliding glass door and stepped onto the balcony. Sunlight warmed her face. The gentle ocean breeze caressed her cheek. She still held the square of pink paper in her hand, but she could already feel it starting to dissolve.

Four stories below her room was the hotel pool. A middle-aged man stood in the shallow end. He wore sunglasses and a bucket hat, his shoulders slathered white with sunscreen. He held out his arms to a small boy perched on the edge of the pool. She couldn't hear them, but she could imagine the words.

"I've got you," the father was saying. "Jump. Go ahead."

"I'm scared, Bába."

"Don't be scared, son. I'm right here."

Mei Lin found herself weeping. Lixin never had a father like that, an ordinary father who took his son to the pool and caught him when he jumped in the water for the first time.

Or could he? That had been Yichen's voice on the phone, she was sure of it.

She closed her eyes, willed herself to stop crying.

It was him, she decided. Only Yichen would know about the overlook.

Now, as she walked the dark, wet path in the middle of the night with her two children, she remembered the last time she'd been at the overlook with her husband.

It had been a very different night. Hot, sticky. They'd walked the moonlit path with their arms around each other, fingers always exploring. More than a little drunk, Mei Lin recalled how the sea had sparkled silver under a full moon and the beach gleamed like bone. The trees shushed in the breeze and the smell of flowers in the air was intoxicating.

Mei Lin felt a smile form and she bit her lip in recalled pleasure. Yichen led her off the overlook and laid her down gently on the sand. They made love in the moonlight, not caring if they were seen or heard...

She gripped her son's cold, wet hand. They used to joke that was the night Lixin was conceived. That was why Yichen chose this spot.

Tears stung her eyes.

"I'm tired, Mama," Lixin said.

Mei Lin blinked. They had arrived at the turnoff for the overlook. The trail, bordered by a thick hedge of laurels, curved off toward the ocean while the main path continued into the darkness.

Mei Lin forced brightness into her voice. "We're here, my brave boy."

Out of the corner of her eye, a shadow moved, and she jerked her head in that direction.

A monkey, she told herself. Keep going.

Lixin held up his arms. "I'm tired, Mama. Carry me."

Mei Lin was exhausted from carrying the baby and her muscles trembled with cold. "I can't, Lixin. Mama's tired, too. I need you to be a soldier, like your Bába."

The mention of his father didn't have the same effect this time. The boy hung his head, on the verge of tears. With a groan, Mei Lin reached down and hauled Lixin up on her hip.

She started down the path. It was not paved and she stumbled in the dark over the uneven ground. The laurels on either side had grown in and they seemed to claw at her jacket as she passed. Just as Mei Lin began to think that maybe she'd taken the wrong turn, the path widened. In the dim light, she could just make out the shape of a wooden bench.

The bench was empty.

Where was Yichen? She looked around, despair filling her thoughts.

"Yichen," she whispered. "Are you there?"

No answer. Beyond the curtain of mist, the waves shushed against the sand.

She filled her lungs. "Yichen!" she shouted. "Where are you?"

Mei Lin walked forward and collapsed on the bench. The wet wood soaked through her jeans and chilled her backside. Lixin wormed his way under her arm and she clamped him tight to her body.

She closed her eyes, taking deep gulps of air. Despair turned to anger—at herself. What had she expected, really? That Yichen would be waiting here and they would all suddenly, magically be warm and dry and happy again?

Phone calls and notes on disintegrating paper. I'm a fool, a stupid woman who will not accept reality.

A shred of movement caught her attention, a separation of shadow where the hedge of laurel bushes ended and the sand began. The shadow took the form of a figure.

She blinked, not believing her eyes. "Yichen?" she whispered.

The figure stepped closer and she said his name again.

"Don't be afraid," a voice said in Mandarin. But it was not Yichen's voice and Mei Lin felt a stab of panic.

She opened her mouth to scream, but a gloved hand snaked around her shoulder, clamped over her mouth. Mei Lin shot to her feet in panic, but the hand stayed in place. She twisted and fought. The sudden movement woke the baby and Bai shrieked.

Lixin tumbled to the ground and she saw his floppy rain hat fall off.

Mei Lin twisted her chin and sank her teeth into the gloved hand. The man holding her grunted in pain but did not let go. She jammed an elbow backward with all her strength and felt it slam into flesh. Still, he did not let go.

"I got her," said a voice in English, and the hand covering her mouth was gone.

A new face loomed in the darkness. A white face, wearing all black up to his chin.

Mei Lin sucked in a breath to scream. She heard a sharp *hiss*, felt a cold spray across her face.

Then everything went black.

23

Lingshui Nanwan Houdao Scenic Area, Hainan Island, China

Lieutenant Trevor "T-Bone" Rantz squatted with his back to the trunk of an ancient stone oak tree. The soft *drip-drip* of water falling from the canopy above punctuated the silence. The heavy smell of decaying leaves and monkey shit filled the damp air.

In the clarity of his night vision goggles, shapes moved among the tree branches above. Monkeys, dozens of them, nested in the large trees. A pale, wizened face peered down at Rantz, watching the intruder to his territory.

"The fucking monkeys are watching me." Trigger's voice came over his earpiece. "That sure as hell wasn't in the mission brief."

"They're not monkeys," Doc replied. "They're gibbons. You can tell because they don't have tails."

"Who gives a shit. They still weren't in the mission brief and I don't like how they're looking at me."

"Pipe down," Rantz replied.

He checked his watch. They'd been on the beach for thirty-four minutes and that was way too long for his liking. This lady had another twenty-six minutes to make an appearance and then he and his team were gone. There were no do-overs on this mission. If the lady was a no-show, they were going home.

The parameters of Rantz's mission were clear. The target had to come to them. If anything looked off about the encounter, he had strict instructions to pull out. While he watched the trail north of the overlook turnoff, he'd placed Trigger a hundred meters to his south, which was the direction where they expected their contact to approach. Doc, his team corpsman, waited at the overlook on the beach. He carried a set of three aerosol canisters of knock-out spray, each container shaped differently so he could tell by feel which one contained the calculated dose for a grown woman, a toddler, and an infant.

He'd left Rhino down by the water's edge with the zodiac, and Bojack was minding the store back at the SDV, which floated just below the waves two kilometers offshore.

Each man was armed with the weapons he felt most comfortable carrying—and they came loaded for bear. In Rantz's case, a suppressed HK universal submachine gun was his happy place. The UMP with the foldable stock and laser sights was compact and accurate, with good stopping power. A Glock 19 was holstered on his right thigh and a combat knife strapped across his chest, the knife grip angled down for a right-handed extraction. He had no idea what they'd find on the beach. If this was a trap, they'd fight their way out. There was no way he or his men were getting taken by the Chinese.

The weather worked in their favor. He'd pegged the overlook as a lover's lane, but no one wanted to get naked in this weather. They'd been warned that there might be a hotel security patrol in a golf cart, but so far it was just his team and the monkeys out here in the dark. Trigger was right about one thing: the monkeys had not been part of the mission brief.

Rantz sighed to himself and checked his watch again. They were kidnapping kids—one of them a baby—off the beach in China, not even twenty miles from a major People's Liberation Army Navy base.

The extraction targets drove so many critical mission decisions. Although the temperature on the beach was close to sixty degrees, it would be much colder on the water. Hypothermia was a danger, especially for the kids. His team all wore wetsuits, but they had stowed blankets and hand warmers on the zodiac for their passengers.

The fact that they were bringing out kids also meant that they needed to use a dry submersible for the extraction. There was food, including baby formula, and essentials such as diapers waiting on the minisub as well. There was always the possibility that they'd miss their pickup window with the *Illinois* and have to wait a full day on the ocean floor.

Rantz had a sudden thought: What if they had to change the baby's diaper on the SDV? That would be *awful*.

"I've got incoming," Trigger reported, his whisper taut with tension. "Chinese female with a baby in a front chest carrier and a small kid on foot. I think it's them."

"Any sign of surveillance?" Rantz asked.

"Nada," came Trigger's reply.

"The meeting spot is clean, T-Bone," Doc reported.

Rantz crawled toward the edge of the paved path so he had a good view of where the trail split off toward the overlook.

Two minutes passed, then three.

"Trigger, where are they?" he asked.

"This kid is walking through every fucking puddle along the way. Forward progress is *slow*, man."

Another two minutes crawled by before they finally came into sight. Rantz could see right away that even though the woman had bundled up her children for the weather, she had not done the same for herself. The jacket she wore was soaked through and her dark hair was plastered to her head.

The baby was asleep in the chest carrier. The kid wore a yellow rain slicker and matching floppy hat and rainboots. She held him by the hand, but Rantz could tell the kid was dragging.

Wonderful, a mom dressed for hypothermia and a toddler on the verge of a meltdown.

He froze as the woman looked up and seemed to stare right at him. The kid tugged his hand away and held up both his arms.

"I'm tired, Mama. Carry me." His voice came out as a whine.

The mother shivered with cold as she replied in Mandarin that she was tired too. The kid didn't care. He still held up his arms, and in the clarity of his night vision goggles, Rantz could see his small face twisted into a grimace.

Rantz flinched. Any minute now, this kid is gonna lose his shit.

The woman groaned, then bent down and hauled the boy onto her hip. She turned down the path toward the overlook and started to walk. She looked ready to collapse.

"She's coming to you, Doc," Rantz whispered into his mic. "I'm mobile."

"I'm on the move," Trigger reported.

As soon as the woman disappeared down the path, Rantz got to his feet and moved across the paved trail to the sand. He stayed close to the thick hedge of laurels, matching his pace so that he stayed about ten steps behind the woman on the opposite side of the foliage.

From the glimpses he got of her through gaps in the hedge, he could tell that she was unaware of his presence. Her face showed the strain of carrying two children.

When she arrived at the point where the trail widened into an oval clearing, Rantz moved to the end of the hedge where he had a clear view of the woman. A few meters away, Doc lay prone in the sand.

She paused at the end of the trail and peered into the darkness. Rantz could hear her ragged breathing.

"Yichen," she whispered. "Are you there?"

Her shoulders slumped. Then she straightened up, threw her head back and shouted, "Yichen! Where are you?"

Rantz tensed, ready to rush in, but the woman staggered forward and collapsed on the bench. The kid in the rain jacket slipped off her hip and she put her arm around him. On the far side of the clearing, Trigger moved into position.

Rantz stripped off his night vision goggles and stepped away from the hedge. He took a step forward and the woman's head came up. Her face was a pale disc in the dim light.

"Yichen?" she whispered.

Rantz took another step forward.

"Yichen?" she whispered again.

"Don't be afraid," he said in Mandarin. He tried to keep his voice low and calm, but his was not the voice she was expecting. Rantz saw her stand, head reared back, mouth open.

"Please," he pleaded in Mandarin. "I'm a friend."

Trigger loomed behind her. His gloved hand clamped over the woman's mouth, but he knocked the baby on the head with his elbow. The baby screamed, a high, piercing wail that sounded like an air raid siren in the night.

The woman shot to her feet, struggling in Trigger's embrace. The toddler tumbled to the ground.

"Doc!" Rantz said. "Any time now."

The corpsman raced past him, sprayed the baby in the face. The child stopped crying instantly. He dropped the smallest canister and pulled a second one from his chest pack. He held the woman's face by her chin. "I got her," he said to Trigger.

A single puff and the woman sagged in Trigger's arms. The SEAL gently placed her inert body on the bench.

"Mama?" The toddler stood looking at them. His hat had come off when he'd tumbled from the bench.

Trigger started to move toward him, but Rantz held up a hand. He squatted in front of the boy.

"Are you okay?" he asked in Mandarin.

The boy nodded. Rantz picked up the kid's yellow hat and put it back on his head.

"Mama?" the kid said again.

Rantz held up a finger to his lips. "Mama's sleeping. You must be very quiet."

The child mimicked his motion, putting his own index finger on his lips.

Rantz took a chance. "Bába sent us to get you. Are you ready to go on a trip?"

The boy nodded. Rantz held out his arms and the kid walked right up to him. He stood and settled the child on his hip.

When he turned around, Doc had resized the chest carrier and had the sleeping baby strapped to the front of his wetsuit. Trigger picked up the sleeping woman in his arms, then shifted her to a fireman's carry.

"The bitch bit me," Trigger said.

"Language," Rantz said. "The kid's listening."

"Vitals are good on the baby and her mother," Doc reported. "You want me to knock the kid out?"

Rantz could feel the dark eyes of the child watching him.

"I think he's good."

They headed for the water.

24

South China Sea, 12 nautical miles southeast of Hainan Island, People's Republic of China

Janet sat bolt upright in her bunk. The room was dark, lit only by the glow of the monitor showing the ship's status.

Bzzt. The insistent sound like the buzz of an angry murder hornet echoed in the room. She snatched the heavy plastic handset from the cradle on the wall by the head of her bunk.

"Captain," she said.

Her eyes found the mission clock at the top of the monitor. She was shocked to see that she'd been asleep for over an hour.

"Captain," Wilkins said, "we have a relayed message from the SEALs."

"I'll be right there."

Janet took a quick minute to splash water on her face and run a brush through her hair. The part about being the commanding officer that she was still getting used to was that everyone watched her every move. They took their cues from her, which meant she had to be one hundred percent on point all the time.

She entered the control room at a brisk pace and went straight to where

Wilkins waited with the XO. He handed her the secure tablet with radio traffic. The message was one word: *Rodeo.*

Janet smiled to herself. The mission called for single word signals that the SEALs could use to communicate their status back to the *Illinois* in the clear, if necessary. She and Rantz had joked that the whole operation—kidnapping a mother and two kids from Chinese sovereign soil—was a goat rodeo. *Rodeo* meant that they had all three passengers on board and they were enroute to the *Illinois* with no pursuit.

Janet checked the mission clock. Less than ninety minutes left. She estimated an hour for the SDV to transit back and dock, which left them twenty minutes in the mission window.

She breathed out a sigh of relief. Plenty of time. This was going to work.

"Officer of the Deck," the Sonar Supervisor said, "I have a new sonar contact bearing two-seven-three, one-five thousand yards, designate Sierra two-six. Correlates to tactical contact Tango one-five, identified as Type 054A frigate. Contact is headed our way, sir."

Janet, the XO, and Wilkins compared the sonar broadband display with the tactical picture being supplied by the satellite feed. Without prompting, Wilkins took the controls and projected the course of the new contact. If the PLA ship stayed on its present course, it would not cross the track of the inbound submersible. Unless the surface ship was using active sonar, it would not be able to detect the SDV.

Another bullet dodged, Janet thought.

"There it is again, Chief," she heard one of the sonar operators say.

Janet crossed the control room. The sonar chief sat between two of his operators. He stared at the center screen, bulky headphones clamped over his ears.

"Run it again," the chief ordered.

"Yes, Chief." The young sonar tech punched buttons on the touchscreen.

The sonar chief closed his eyes as he listened. He opened them again and shook his head. "I've never heard that before."

"Chief?" Janet asked. "Problem?"

"I honestly don't know, Captain," the chief said. "It sounds like UW comms from the PLA ship."

"Not sonar?" Janet asked.

"Definitely not, ma'am. Wrong freq. It's short-range underwater comms, but it's not voice. I don't know what it is."

Janet beckoned for the headphones and slipped them over her ears. The first time, she missed it. The chief rewound the recording and played it again. She heard a brief chirping noise. Once she parsed through the warble and echo characteristic of underwater communications, it sounded like a bird call.

"It's definitely coming from the PLA ship?" she asked the chief.

The sonar chief's nod was firm. "Yes, ma'am. Hundred percent."

A surface ship transmitting on UW comms but not by voice, then what?

A signal, she thought. Just like the one-word code she'd received from the SEAL team.

"Chief, can you dig up the intel brief on the latest PLA Navy UUVs?"

It took the sonar chief only a minute to call up the top-secret document they'd received just prior to leaving Pearl Harbor.

Designated *Nemo* by SUBPAC, the latest PLA Navy's unmanned underwater vehicle was nearly thirty meters long. Janet studied the line drawing and the attached grainy photo. Like other UUVs, this one had a radio mast that could be raised and lowered to communicate at periscope depth. Janet pointed at a hump, like a dorsal fin pushing out of the skin of the submarine, forward of the mast.

"What's that?" she asked.

The chief shrugged. "The intel weenies think it might be a new sensor. Maybe a receiver for a new kind of scanning sonar array?" The chief eyed her. "You're thinking it's a command receiver, ma'am?"

Janet nodded. A hydrophone designed to receive underwater signals from a nearby surface ship escort would be positioned on top of the submarine. Underwater signals were notoriously noisy, so using a shortened command code made sense. A tonal signal like a bird call would be perfect to transmit information underwater.

It also meant that if the Chinese frigate was directing an underwater drone, the sonar capabilities of the surface ship would be equivalent to a submarine.

"Mr. Wilkins," she ordered, "assume that the PLA frigate now has the sensor range of a submarine. Project that along their track."

On the monitor, Wilkins added a ring around the incoming PLA Navy frigate. It intercepted their position right about the same time as they projected the SDV to rendezvous with *Illinois*.

Standing next to her, his arms crossed, the XO grunted.

Janet scowled at the screen. She had no way to communicate with the SEALs, so they had no idea there was a PLA Navy hunter-killer sub in their path.

"Captain?" the XO said.

"I'm thinking, XO."

The XO stepped closer and lowered his voice. "Ma'am, we can't stay here. Even if the drone doesn't see us, docking the SDV is noisy. It'd be like broadcasting our position to the whole freaking Chinese Navy."

The XO was right. Their mission brief stated that if the *Illinois* was at imminent risk of detection, they were to clear the area and attempt another pickup in twenty-four hours. No one wanted to put a four-billion-dollar *Virginia*-class submarine and her crew at risk. On the other hand, if she abandoned Rantz and his team, there was a chance they'd be discovered by the underwater drone. That would be a disaster.

Janet ground her teeth. Run away or stand your ground and hope for the best were her two options. There had to be another way.

"Chief," Janet said to the Sonar Supervisor, "do we have a layer?"

The sonar chief consulted a screen. "We've got a slight layer at 110 meters, ma'am. It's not much, but it's there."

Janet turned to the XO. "How much line do we have on the radio buoy?"

"One hundred fifty meters, Captain." His flat tone told her what he thought of her idea.

Janet nodded her head slowly. A third way, she told herself.

"Mr. Wilkins," Janet said.

"Yes, ma'am."

"I relieve you."

"I stand relieved, Captain."

"Attention in the Control Room," Janet announced. "This is the Captain. I have the deck and the conn."

She could feel the tension in the room ratchet up as the pilot, copilot, sonar, fire control, and radio acknowledged the change in command of the submarine.

Janet crossed to the Pilot's station. She kept her voice conversational.

"Chief Hanley, I want to make a controlled depth change, operative word being *controlled*. Level trim, quiet as you can make it, and *slow*—no more than a few meters every ten seconds. Take us down to 150 meters. Can you do that?"

Hanley was a big man with a mustache like a dust brush and a matching beard. "You got it, Captain."

"Make it so, Pilot. One-five-zero meters, nice and easy."

"Aye-aye, ma'am. Make my depth one-five-zero, nice and easy."

"Mr. Wilkins," Janet said.

"Captain."

"Get the Radioman and adjust the line on our radio buoy. I want that line snug, but do not lose contact with the satellite. We need the tactical picture from the Sharks if we're going to pull this off."

"Yes, ma'am." Wilkins left Control.

"Five-five meters, Captain," called the Pilot.

"Very well, Pilot," Janet replied. "Sing out every ten meters, please."

"Aye-aye, Captain."

The XO approached. "Captain, I recommend we clear datum. The SEALs can wait a day for pickup. It's part of the mission brief."

"Agreed, XO, and your concern is noted, but I think we have to try to get them out of here tonight." She cut a look at the countdown clock. "We're still inside the mission window."

The XO nodded, but he was clearly not happy. He was about to get even unhappier, Janet thought.

"I have a job for you, XO. Wake up the torpedo gang and get tubes one and two ready in all respects. Do not open outer doors." Opening a torpedo tube door was a noisy evolution and the last thing Janet wanted was to broadcast their position to the PLA.

The XO stared at her.

"It's a last resort," Janet said, "but one I can't ignore."

"Make tubes one and two ready in all respects, aye, ma'am. Do not open outer doors."

Janet watched the XO depart Control. He'd disagreed with her, but he'd done it in private. Once she'd made her decision, he'd accepted it. That worked for her.

She looked around the control room. Every watch station was absorbed in the task at hand.

The enormity of what she was doing pulled at her like gravity. If the *Illinois* was discovered, anything could happen—none of it good. Hell, if a few decisions broke the wrong way, she might go down in history as the submarine captain who started World War Three.

She took a breath and held it, then let it out slowly.

Worrying is not going to solve anything, she told herself. Take that energy and give yourself more options.

"One-one-zero meters, Captain," the Pilot called out. "Nice and easy."

"Acknowledged, Pilot."

She studied the monitor. The sensor circle of the PLA vessel drew closer to their position. It was a close-run thing. Too close for her liking. She needed a distraction.

"Fire control."

"Yes, ma'am."

"Call up the technical specs on the Sharks, please."

Janet pored over the lines of text on the screen until she found what she was looking for. She switched to a map of the region, chewing her lip in concentration.

It might work, she thought.

"Attention in Control," she said. "Does anyone know if we have any crew who speak Vietnamese?"

One of the sonar operators raised his hand. "Nguyen, ma'am. Machinist mate. I think she speaks Vietnamese."

Janet cast a glance at Chief Hanley. "Have Nguyen lay to control, Pilot. ASAP."

Machinist Mate Third Class Diep Nguyen was a slip of a woman who might have weighed a hundred pounds if she carried a toolbox. Her dark hair was pulled back into a stubby ponytail and she had a grease stain on her chin. Her underway coveralls, cinched around a rail-thin waist, looked two sizes too large.

Still, her chin was up and she did not seem cowed by the fact that she'd been called by the captain to report to Control on the double.

"Captain," she said.

Janet handed her a sheet of paper. "Can you translate that into Vietnamese?"

She scanned the sheet. "Of course, ma'am."

"I want you to make a recording of it in Radio. Make it loud and rough, like you're in distress."

"Aye-aye, Captain."

Ten minutes later, Janet listened to a recording. Nguyen had dropped the tone of her voice so that she sounded almost like a man. It was perfect.

"Captain," the Sonar Supervisor reported, "Sierra two-six is changing course. Intercept in six minutes at current course and speed."

Now or never, Janet thought. She gave the order to transmit the recording to the satellite and download it to both of the Sharks.

"Sierra two-six is increasing speed, Captain. We are inside their detection range now."

Janet called up the control screen for the Sharks. She selected the unit closest to the PLA Navy shipping lane and shifted the communications suite to broadcast VHF Channel 16, the international distress frequency.

The recording was queued up. Janet's finger hovered over the touchscreen button labeled TRANSMIT.

She lowered her finger. The button blinked and went out.

Immediately, the speaker in the overhead blared out. The voice was garbled and in Vietnamese. It ran for about fifteen seconds, then repeated.

Janet switched to the tactical data display. The Shark she had used to broadcast the fake message was well inside the twelve-mile territorial boundary, a fact which would not escape the PLA Navy.

She turned down the speaker volume. The contact designated Sierra two-six had not changed course. Janet bit her lip as she willed the screen to update.

"Submerged contact!" the sonar chief called out. "I have transients bearing three-one-zero." The chief pressed the headphones against his ears. "Cavitation! Changing doppler, ma'am. Submerged contact is turning and hauling ass."

The tactical screen finally updated. The detection circle was swiftly moving away from the *Illinois*.

"Chief Hanley," Janet said, "energize the locator beacon for the SDV and take us up to five-zero meters. Quietly, but with purpose, Pilot."

"Aye-aye, Captain. Five-zero meters coming up."

It took fifteen more minutes to get back on depth and reattach the SDV to the hull of the *Illinois*. The SEAL team needed only one pass to dock successfully, something Janet attributed to the extra practice they had done on their transit from Guam.

"Green board," the Pilot announced when the SEALs had exited the submersible and resealed the hatch.

"Very well, Pilot," Janet replied. "All ahead one-third, come right to new course one-two-zero." When they had turned away from the Chinese mainland and settled on their new heading, she said, "Make your depth one hundred meters."

Janet sagged back against the row of consoles. It worked, she thought, it actually worked. Energy flooded her body and she felt buoyed by a sense of euphoria. She cast a look at the XO. "Shall we go meet our passengers, XO?"

He was smiling, too. "Great idea, Captain."

She turned over the watch to Wilkins and she and the XO made their way out of the Control room. They exchanged glances as they turned into the passageway outside the officer's wardroom. Behind the fake wood Formica of the door to the officer's mess came a strange sound.

A crying baby.

25

United States Cyber Command, Fort George G. Meade, Maryland

Gao entered the conference room as if he expected to find a firing squad waiting for him. His expression softened a fraction when he saw Don.

Don kept his own features impassive as he watched the man close the door and scan the room. They were in one of the many secure windowless conference rooms that populated the subbasement of US Cyber Command. The beige walls were bare of artwork and the only furniture in the room was a rectangular table and four rolling chairs. On the table, two laptops stood open. One in front of Don and the other facing an open chair.

Don knew the former Chinese General had not left Frosty Valley, the secure CIA facility in northeastern Pennsylvania, in months. The man had no idea why he'd been summoned to Washington, DC, and by his demeanor, he expected the worst.

Gao was off-balance, exactly where Don wanted him. He did not get up to greet the former PLA officer. Instead, Don dropped his eyes to the open chair across from him. "Have a seat, General."

Gao drew out the chair and sat. His back did not touch the back of the chair. He took in the laptop screen, a royal-blue background with the logo of US Cyber Command. He frowned, looked up at Don.

"Why am I here?"

Don ignored the question. He touched the space bar on his own laptop. "We're ready, operator," Don said.

"Standby, Mr. Riley," said a voice from the laptop speakers.

The logo on the screen cleared, replaced by a shaky image of a Chinese woman with a round face and messy dark hair. She held a baby on her lap and at her elbow stood a boy about three years old. The baby grunted and fussed, but the boy stared at the screen with quiet intensity.

Gao's jaw dropped in surprise. He leaned close to the screen. "Mei Lin?" he whispered.

Don sat back in his own chair and folded his arms. The earpiece in his right ear gave him a running translation of the conversation.

The woman stared at the screen. "Yichen? Is that you?" she said in Mandarin. Her face crumpled and she began to cry, which made the baby cry. The boy continued to stare without expression. "You're alive. How?"

Gao was thunderstruck. His mouth gaped. "Mei Lin?" he said again. "Is it really you?"

The woman did her best to control her tears. She bounced the baby on her lap to quiet her. "They told me you were dead. They buried you..."

Gao's eyes rose from the laptop. Don shook his head.

"That doesn't matter now," Gao said. "There will be time enough for that when you get here. Where are you?"

Mei Lin wiped tears from her cheeks with the back of her hand. "We're on a submarine, a US submarine. They gave me your note...and I did what you said."

Gao raised his eyes and Don shook his head again.

"Good, that's good. Are they treating you well? Are the children okay?"

Mei Lin nodded. "We're fine. They're very nice to us." She lowered her voice. "The captain said we're going to America."

Gao nodded, on firmer ground now. "That's right. You'll meet me here and we'll start a new life together."

"Yichen, why? What happened?"

Gao did not look up at Don this time. "That doesn't matter now, my love. All that matters is that you're safe and we will be together again. Soon."

"But they buried you—"

"Mei Lin," Gao interrupted, "you were right. You were right about everything, and...I'm sorry."

Don touched a button to mute the conversation. "You have sixty seconds left, General. Say your goodbyes."

Gao glared at him, then looked back at the screen.

"I have to go," he said.

"Yichen, wait." The baby started to fuss again and she bounced the child on her knee. "When will I see you?"

"Fifteen seconds, General," Don said.

Suddenly, the boy spoke up. "Bába!" He pointed at the screen. "Bába!"

"Yes, Lixin!" his mother said. "That's Bába."

"Time's up, General." Don killed the connection. He let the last image of Mei Lin and the children stay on Gao's screen.

"I never thought of you as a cruel man, Mr. Riley." Gao's voice was thick with emotion. He wiped his eyes before he looked up. "Where are they?"

"Your family is on a submarine in the middle of the Pacific Ocean. They should arrive in Pearl Harbor in ten days or so, which means you could see them in about two weeks. Or I could fly you to Hawaii to meet them." He paused. "If you cooperate right now."

"This is not what we agreed."

Don nodded. "That's true, but my needs have changed. I've done the hard part. I've gotten your family out of China and now I need you to play ball, General."

As painful as a two week wait might be for Gao, it was torture for Don. Gao was his magic bullet, his way to get inside the Chinese network and finally make some progress in Central Asia.

The struggle on the General's face was plain to see. If he gave Don access now, all his leverage was gone. How much did he trust Don? That was the question he had to come to terms with.

"Your son recognized you," Don said. "That's good."

Gao nodded, his face tight.

"I want to speak to my family every day," Gao said.

"Of course," Don said. "That's not an issue." It was a big issue, he knew. No submarine commander wanted to come to periscope depth every day and hold a family conference call, but he'd worry about that later.

"And I want them here as soon as possible," Gao continued. "No stalling. No matter what happens."

Don nodded.

Gao's eyes dropped back to the laptop screen for a long moment. "Can I trust you, Mr. Riley?"

Don did not move. "You have my word that your family will get here safely, General."

Gao pressed his lips together. "Don't call me that anymore."

"What?"

"I'm no longer a General." He exhaled deeply, then sat up suddenly, back straight. "Tell me what you need me to do."

Don wanted to jump to his feet and pump his fist in the air, but he stayed in his chair. The door to the room opened and two men walked in carrying open laptops. As they commandeered the two open chairs and positioned them on either side of the former General, Don spoke. "Tell these two operators the exact process for logging into the Huawei system."

Gao nodded and Don left the room. He needed to be far away from Gao for now. In the hallway, he took a deep breath and blew it out.

This is who you've become, Don. A guy who threatens a man's family.

He comforted himself with the reports he'd received from Janet. The woman and her family were comfortable on the USS *Illinois* and the baby was a huge hit with the crew. Gao's wife had no shortage of sailors willing to volunteer as babysitters.

Carroll Brooks came out of the adjacent room where she'd been monitoring the operation. "Nice work, Riley," she said.

Don studied her. It almost seemed like she meant it. "Thanks," he said.

Carroll leaned against the wall next to him. "Do you think he's got the goods?" she asked.

"I hope so. We don't have a plan B."

The briefing of the Cyber Mission Force team assembled to penetrate the Chinese network was conducted by a Navy officer named Jennifer Starr. She'd divided the pen team into four groups and the decision tree on the action plan ran for six pages.

Lieutenant Commander Starr had short blond hair and a no-nonsense attitude that reminded Don of Janet Everett. She was on the young side, in Don's opinion, but she'd been handpicked by the Commander of US Cyber Command for the job.

"The best I've seen in a long time, Mr. Riley," the General had said to Don. "Maybe better than you in your prime."

Don had laughed at the joke, but the comment made him feel old.

"As soon as we use the General's login, we're in enemy territory," Starr said. "We have to assume that if the PLA sees a new access point, they'll kill it. Therefore, our first order of business is to build our own back door into the system, so we can come and go as we please. Alpha Team, that's you. We will do no further exploitation until we have our new ingress point established."

Heads around the table nodded in unison.

"Next task is to locate our packages on the Chinese network and catalog them for future use. Bravo Team, that's you."

Don knew the packages were a series of computer chips that had been illegally imported into China after the technology was embargoed two years ago. What the Chinese didn't know about the chips they'd bought was that the entire lot had been modified by the NSA to allow them to be remotely controlled once installed. Locating those assets was a high priority.

"Phase Three is system mapping. We want to know how deep these guys have penetrated into Central Asia and where the physical nodes are located. This is strictly a no-touch operation, ladies and gentlemen. No exploitation is authorized, no matter how tempting the target. No cowboys on this op. Is that understood?"

Nods all around.

"Phase Four is penetration of the PLA command and control network. This is the Holy Grail, people, and Delta Team has point. Once we start that effort, everyone else will be in support, including the watch floors at Cyber Command and NSA."

As the meeting moved on, Don's thoughts drifted.

He was dead tired, but his job here was almost done. Gao's access would get them into the PLA command and control network. Finally, they'd be on offense against the Chinese in Central Asia. He breathed a sigh of relief.

The weight of responsibility felt heavy these days. Every time he talked with Harrison, he felt like he was letting him down. While his colleague and friend was putting his life on the line every day, Don was moving paper from one side of his desk to the other. Hell, he didn't even have the satisfaction of that now. The job had finally forced Don to move away from paper to online reports.

The meeting broke and everyone stood, buzzing with nervous energy. The teams, roughly half active-duty military and half civilians, were young, overly caffeinated, and ready for battle against this virtual enemy. Don got to his feet slowly, feeling his age.

"Director Riley?" It was Starr. "I'll keep you updated, sir. Thanks for sitting in."

Don hid his smile. He was getting the brush-off from this young officer. Thanks for showing up, sir. Here's your hat. What's your hurry?

But it was okay, Don thought. He was ready for a break.

26

Yekaterinburg, Russia

Nikolay Sokolov was surprised to find that his Russian Navy dress uniform still fit. A little snug around the middle, perhaps, but not enough to require alteration. His valet had purchased a new officer's cap and epaulets. Newly shined medals gleamed like rows of golden coins across his left breast.

On the boulevard below the reviewing stand, the 3rd Motorized Rifle Battalion of the 27th Separate Guards Motor Rifle Brigade passed. This unit had been brought in by train from the Western Military District, along with half a dozen other battalions from the ground, air, and naval branches.

The men and women of the Guards marched in ruler-straight formation, eyes right, weapons at port arms. The straight legs of the dark blue uniform trousers and polished knee-high black boots stepping in perfect unison. Nikolay could feel the pride emanating from their ranks like a blast of radiation. He rewarded them with a crisp salute.

This was a good idea, he thought. No, an excellent idea. Maybe he should break tradition every year.

Growing up in Russia, Nikolay had fond memories of Victory Day. His uncle had revitalized the celebration of the Soviet victory over the Nazis into a national holiday designed to showcase the modern military might of the Russian Federation.

Of course, the pinnacle of the holiday was the parade in Red Square. Nikolay had spent every Victory Day parade on the reviewing stand at his Uncle Vitaly's side. Pictures in his uncle's home near the Kremlin chronicled their time together. From a stripling of five years old trying to imitate his uncle's crisp salute, to Nikolay in his midshipman's uniform while at the Kuznetsov Naval Academy, and the years of progression through the naval ranks to admiral in command of the Russian Pacific Fleet.

And then his Uncle Vitaly disappeared from the photographs. After deposing Luchnik, Nikolay still reviewed the parade. His salutes were still crisp, and he still wore his admiral's uniform, but Nikolay was alone.

He breathed deeply. Here, in Yekaterinburg on the eastern side of the Ural Mountains, spring was in the air. The first buds of the season showed as a green haze on the branches of the beech trees in the park opposite the reviewing stand. In the watery spring sunshine, the columns of military hardware and Russian manpower stretched as far as the eye could see.

Nikolay stood in the center of Yekaterinburg, where the grand boulevards of the city converged. Historic markers, streets named after great leaders, and commemorative plaques told the history of the place.

It was the perfect location for this grand display of Russian patriotism.

Nikolay had waited until April first to announce that the President of the Russian Federation would not be attending the Victory Day Parade in Red Square. In the closed media ecosystem of Moscow, the news went off like a bomb in a glass factory. For twenty-four hours, it was the only story that mattered. It consumed the media, dominated the headlines.

The next day, Nikolay announced that he would choose a city in the Russian Federation where he would personally host a Victory Day celebration. The internet went bananas. Talk show hosts got into on-air arguments about which city should be chosen.

The odds-on favorite was Vladivostok, where Nikolay had spent a good portion of his naval career. Under Federov's prodding, the news media frothed with anticipation. Politicians lobbied behind the scenes for their city to host the President.

After three more days of relentless speculation, Nikolay made the announcement in a video released to all news outlets at the same time. The host of this year's Victory Day celebration was Yekaterinburg.

Nikolay popped a fresh salute at the 1st Battalion of the 31st Guards Air Assault Brigade, smiling at the memory of the engineered spectacle. Yekaterinburg had been on no one's short list as a host city. Yes, it was the fourth-largest city in Russia, and the administrative center of the Ural Federal District, but why had the President chosen a city in the middle of nowhere? Other than the site of the 1918 execution of the Romanovs, it held little cultural significance to the modern Russian Federation.

As the last rank of soldiers passed by, Nikolay dropped his salute. He knew this battalion had been nearly wiped out in Uncle Vitaly's pointless invasion of Ukraine. Probably none of these young men and women had seen combat. He smiled grimly to himself. That might change very soon.

Nikolay's reasons for choosing Yekaterinburg had to do less with history and more with location. It was the closest major Russian city to the Kazakh capital of Astana.

To his right, General Arkady Makashov, Commander of the Central Military District, mirrored his salute. Next to the commander was his deputy, and beside him, staff officers arranged according to seniority formed a line of military uniforms across the full length of the reviewing stand railing.

"Well done, General," Nikolay said. "This is exactly what I wanted."

Makashov allowed a tight smile on his blocky features. "It is my honor, Mr. President."

"And the rest of my orders? Are you ready?"

"Plans are in motion, sir. As soon as the troops complete the parade route, they head south." He nodded at the company from the 80th Guards Tank Regiment passing the review stand. "They'll be at the border by sundown."

"Excellent, General."

Nikolay glanced over his shoulder and caught Federov's eye. Then he leaned to his left, where the mayor of Yekaterinburg stood. He was a portly man with a mustache and round glasses who looked more like a bookkeeper than a government official.

"Mr. Mayor," Nikolay said, "would you mind trading places with President Karimov? We have some business to discuss."

The mayor looked surprised at the request, but he nodded and stepped back from the railing. Fedorov ushered the President of Kazakhstan to Nikolay's side. Another memory of his uncle struck Nikolay. The old man always called the left-hand side the sinister side.

How fitting, he thought.

Nikolai saluted as the 439th Rocket Artillery Brigade rolled by in a lengthy formation of mobile rocket launchers. Nikolay had ordered this unit shipped over from the Southern Military District. The smell of diesel exhaust wafted up to the reviewing stand.

"Are you enjoying the parade, Mr. President?" Nikolay asked.

Karimov was dressed in a dark business suit with matching overcoat and fedora. His stylish glasses caught the glare of the sun as he studied Nikolay. The only color on his outfit was a bloodred tie at his throat.

"Very much so, Mr. President." His voice was couched in caution. "The display is formidable."

It was not unusual for the Russian President to invite guests to the Victory Day celebration and Russia enjoyed a long history of good relations with Kazakhstan. But Karimov was no fool. He sensed there was more to this invitation than a simple diplomatic gesture.

Nikolay pointed at a heavy truck painted in green camouflage. On the bed of the vehicle, an armored box was raised to a forty-five-degree angle, revealing a grid of forty holes, each the diameter of a dinner plate. "Do you know what that is, Miras?"

Karimov shook his head. "I'm afraid not, Mr. President."

"A Spartak modular armored platform carrying a Tornado-G Multiple Rocket Launch System. Inside each one of those holes is a 122mm rocket that can hit a target with pinpoint accuracy from a distance of forty kilometers. It's really an amazing weapons system—and we have dozens of them in this unit alone."

Karimov licked his lips, said nothing.

"You lied to me," Nikolay said. He packed all of the frustration and anger of the last few months into four words.

Karimov's cheeks turned ashen. "Mr. President, I think there's been some sort of mis—"

"I came to you as a friend, Miras. As an ally. All I asked was that you allow me the right to ship arms through your country—and you refused me. You told me that you couldn't take sides."

"Mr. President, Nikolay—"

"Did you really think I wouldn't find out, you little turd?"

Their faces were close together, their voices low. Around them, the celebrations continued loudly.

Karimov tried one last time. "I didn't mean—"

"Here is what is going to happen, you little shit." Nikolay's words were like shrapnel. He swept his arm down the long boulevard at the military might laid out before them. "All of these troops will be on the border by nightfall. In my speech this afternoon, I will announce the commencement of Operation Siberian Steel, a military exercise to ensure pipeline security with our regional partner Kazakhstan." Nikolay bared his teeth. "Air power demonstrations, live fire exercises, it will be glorious."

Nikolay turned away from the Kazakh President. A tank battalion approached three abreast across the wide boulevard. The tank commanders of the first armored rank, standing upright in their cupolas, saluted in unison.

Nikolay returned the honor. Out of the corner of his mouth, he muttered, "Let's see how the Americans like that, Mr. President."

27

The White House

Don Riley served at the pleasure of the President. He knew that. It didn't matter whether he liked the President or which party the President was part of or whether the President was a man or a woman. Serving the President was his job. His duty. His honor. He'd taken an oath, and he'd lived by that oath every day of his career.

All the same, at this moment, Don really missed President Serrano.

It was a brilliant Washington, DC, morning, the kind that only came a few times a year. The cherry blossoms fell like snow around the Tidal Basin. Outside, the air was balmy and ripe with the smells of new growth. Warm golden sunlight streamed through the windows behind the Resolute desk, but inside the Oval Office the atmosphere was wintry with tension.

If you allowed yourself to think of politics as a game show, then this one would be called the Blame Game.

The contestants faced each other over a dark walnut coffee table set with a silver coffee service surrounded by six china cups and saucers like satellites, each bearing the seal of the White House. The cups were empty and the silver coffeepot untouched.

Don and newly confirmed CIA Director Carroll Brooks sat on one of the pale yellow couches, but his team was a man down. Following the delivery of the Presidential Daily Brief, President Cashman had excused the CIA briefer.

Facing Don and Carroll on the opposing sofa was National Security Advisor Todd Spencer, acting Secretary of State Abel Cartwright, and acting Secretary of Defense Robert Gable. Both of their confirmations were facing resistance in the US Senate.

As their host and referee, President Cashman occupied the armchair between the opposing sides.

They all held their briefing tablets, all of them showing the final slide of the PDB, a high-definition map of the border area between Kazakhstan and Russia. The Russian side of the border was a rash of red dots, each dot carrying a data tag. Don touched one of the tags. A pop-up box appeared on the screen.

"The 90th Guards Tank Division has dispersed across this area." Don's finger traced a segment of the border between Russia and Kazakhstan where these troops had taken up fighting positions. The trace on his own tablet was mirrored on the devices held by the rest of the attendees. "All told, the Russians have moved roughly 75,000 personnel, drawn from across the Western, Southern, and Central military districts to the Kazakh border for this snap exercise. They are already running near-constant air defense and air-to-air training drills. We've also detected communications for coordinated field artillery firing exercises."

Don scanned the faces for a reaction. "It's a logistical success, executed on short notice. Just yesterday, they were part of a Victory Day parade in Ekaterinburg, attended by President Sokolov himself."

The unexpected Russian troop movements were reason enough for the tension in the room, but other factors were at play. Although they were a few months into the new administration, key players in the room still had "acting" next to their title, lending an air of impermanence to their role.

The confirmation process in the Senate had been grueling for both Cartwright and Gable and both men seemed worse for wear. Cartwright was a thin man whose features seemed to have sharpened since Don had last seen him. His gray eyebrows bunched together as he glared at his tablet. Gable was measured but professional.

Don's gaze settled on the untouched coffee service before him. He desperately wanted a cup but did not dare serve himself. He realized this was another difference between the former and current Presidents. Serrano had used coffee like a prop. He'd often served it himself when he wanted to put people at ease or he'd refill a coffee cup as a way to take a break in a conversation.

Cashman did none of those things. In fact, she treated the presence of the coffee service as an intrusion and seemed to have no desire to put anyone at ease.

The silence lengthened as the contestants in the Blame Game considered their tablets and the red rash of Russian provocation.

President Cashman made a *tsk* sound. "I'd like to hear your thoughts on what we're dealing with here."

Secretary of State Abel Cartwright spoke first. Don had noticed that Cartwright always spoke first. "I have a meeting scheduled with the Russian ambassador in an hour, Madam President. I'll read him the riot act. We'll get to the bottom of this."

Cashman looked at her National Security Advisor. "Thoughts, Todd?"

"President Sokolov is a dictator, ma'am. He's taking advantage of the Chinese actions in Central Asia to put pressure on Kazakhstan."

"Pressure them to do what?" Cashman asked.

"I think we should wait for the readout on State's meeting, ma'am. It would be premature of me to speculate."

Don stifled a sigh. A cop-out. The President sees Sokolov as a dictator, so they're just telling her what she wants to hear.

"Mr. Riley, what do you think?" As Cashman's eyes scanned over to him, Don felt like she'd read his mind. "Of all the people in this room, you have the most direct and personal connection to the Russians. You've met both President Sokolov and FSB Chief Federov, isn't that right?"

Don nodded. "True, ma'am."

"What's your take on the situation?"

Don cleared his throat. The smart play was to follow Spencer's lead and mealymouth an answer. After all, everyone in the room outranked him. The three seated directly across from him didn't really care what he thought, he could see that from the look on their faces. Still, he couldn't stand by and not say his piece. He'd promised President Serrano that he'd always tell Cashman the truth—even if she didn't want to hear it.

"It's a message, ma'am," Don said. "President Sokolov is responding to our refusal to engage with him on shipping arms to Central Asia."

He wanted to add, *and he's right too*, but Don could see his unwelcome assessment had not earned him any new friends. Spencer glared at him, and Cartwright's lips were pursed like he'd just sucked a lemon. Don had no idea what the expression on Gable's face meant. Next to him, Carroll's spine went rigid as a fencepost and Don wondered if maybe he'd gone too far this time.

The National Security Advisor started to object, but Carroll beat him to it.

"May I interject, Madam President?" Carroll had her chin up and forward, her tell that she'd made up her mind about something. Don hoped that something wasn't him.

"I agree with Mr. Riley," she said in a firm voice. "We had the opportunity to work with President Sokolov and we refused him. Dictator or not, in the matter of the Central Asian Union, our interests are aligned with Russia against the Chinese. Our actions put him in a position of weakness and he's responding in the only way he knows how—with threats."

Cashman's face clouded. "I've made myself clear about my policy on working with dictators, Ms. Brooks," she said in an icy tone. "It's bad politics. Period."

Carroll did not back down. "I can't speak to the political concerns, ma'am, but we now have a sizeable Russian military force parked on the Kazakh border. That destabilizes the region further and it is putting our weapons supply routes into the Central Asian Union at risk."

Cashman ignored Carroll, focused back on Don. "Is this true? What is the status of the arms shipments into Central Asia?"

"The supply lines we have in place are working, ma'am," Don said, "but it's not enough. My man on the ground wants permission to move arms using black market operators."

"That doesn't sound like a good idea, Madam President," Spencer said. "We could be feeding a secondary market with American weapons."

"I don't know that we have much of a choice, ma'am," Don replied.

"Between the limited number of approved supply routes into the region and the increased PLA surveillance, we are not meeting our commitments to the resistance. The People's Liberation Army security network is getting stronger by the day. We're running out of time."

"So those are my choices, Mr. Riley?" Cashman snapped back, frustration evident in her tone. "I can work with the Russians or work with arms dealers?"

"Or both, ma'am."

"Are you serious?"

Carroll jumped in before Don could speak. "Before we go down that rabbit hole, ma'am, I think we should update you on our attempt to penetrate the Chinese command and control network in Central Asia."

"Attempt?" Cashman's eyes locked on Don. "That sounds ominous, Mr. Riley. I thought this Chinese spy was going to give us the keys to the kingdom."

Don hated the term *spy*, but this was not the time to argue about word choice.

"We have good news and bad news, ma'am," Don reported. "As promised, General Gao was able to get us into the Huawei network. This network serves as the communications backbone for Chinese operations throughout the region. Because of that access, we now have a detailed map of the PLA's surveillance nodes."

Cashman frowned. "That sounds like a success, Mr. Riley. What's the bad news?"

Don licked his lips, desperately wanting a cup of coffee now.

"During the invasion of Taiwan, the PLA used a battle network they called *Shandong*, or lightning. We expected to find some version of that same network in Central Asia. Perhaps better security, faster connections, more processing power, but the same basic structure."

"But you found something else," Cashman prompted.

"The Chinese have introduced a new command and control system, completely separate from the communications network. All the processing is done behind a multifactor security firewall. Ultra-secure, limited access, and an unbelievable amount of computing power." He hesitated, then plunged ahead. "It's possible the Chinese have developed a quantum-level capability."

"Hold on," Gable interrupted, "you're implying that the Chinese are using a quantum computer for military command and control in Central Asia?" His florid features darkened. "Why would you do that?"

Don cut a look at Carroll, who nodded.

"This is conjecture," Don continued, "but the theory fits. The system processes data from tens of thousands of sensors all over the region, yet the response time between data acquisition and analysis leads us to conclude the work has been automated. Second, the Chinese allow very few access points to the new system. We estimate there are less than a dozen individuals authorized to access the administrative functions of the upgraded command and control system."

"Twelve people inside Central Asia?" Gable asked.

"In the entire country of China, sir," Don replied.

"That's just ChiComm paranoia," Gable scoffed. "They know we broke into their system last time, so they're trying to make it harder for us."

"That was our first thought as well, Mr. Secretary," Don said. "Then we started to analyze what was coming back from the system. It wasn't analyst reports, it was orders. Orders issued directly to the field."

"You're saying that the Chinese have developed an autonomous command and control network?" Gable's face crumpled into a scowl.

"It's a working theory, sir," Don replied. "We think they're using Central Asia as a testing ground."

"Ma'am," Gable addressed the President, "if Riley's right and the PLA really has this capability, we have no way to counter this type of system. They might be years ahead of us. We need to redirect the resistance forces in Central Asia and take this facility out."

"Mr. Secretary," Carroll said, "I think you should let Mr. Riley finish."

"There's more?"

"We've located the Chinese command and control facility, sir," Don said. "It's not in Central Asia, it's in Xinjiang. Inside China."

28

Khujand, Tajikistan

It was about an hour after lunch when Harrison felt the first twinges in his stomach.

That damned goat stew, he thought. I knew it was off.

He'd eaten it anyway, as had all the other men in the group. He scanned the faces of the men squatting in a circle around him for any signs of gastric distress. Every pair of eyes was focused on the map spread on the bare concrete floor in front of them—except for one person. Sanjar caught Harrison's eye and gave him a lopsided grin as if they were sharing a private joke. He tossed his head to flip the fall of dark hair out of his eyes. Harrison smiled back, even as another stab of pain lodged in his gut.

Harrison had grown fond of Sanjar. The kid still had the cockiness of youth, but he was also courageous and resilient. A prankster, too. Not a man in their unit had escaped a Sanjar-inspired practical joke. But they all loved the kid like a son, especially Akhmet.

The great man himself squatted on the floor to Harrison's left. He had his arms folded across his knees and his narrowed eyes flicked over the laminated map. The chart was an old Soviet version blackened by a thousand grease pencils, the lamination worn away at the folds and corners.

One of the two men who'd joined them for lunch pointed at the map and spoke low and fast in a local dialect that Harrison could not follow. His Saiga-12 automatic shotgun lay on the floor next to his sandalled feet.

Harrison studied the weapon, desperate for anything to take his mind off his churning gut. The Saiga-12 was vintage 1990s, a favorite of the Russian military and police forces. A twelve-gauge shotgun, usually loaded with buckshot rounds. At close range, on the automatic setting, the weapon was beyond lethal. The Saiga didn't just stop a target, it blasted it to pieces.

No one bothered to translate for the American, but Harrison was used to this treatment. Akhmet would fill him in later on the parts that he wanted Harrison to know.

Even though the words went over his head, Harrison didn't need a translator to tell him that something was wrong. The warm breeze that wafted through the window openings in the concrete wall did nothing to ease the tension in the air. It was unusual for Akhmet to call two of his cell leaders to an in-person meeting at the same time and he seemed to be doing more listening than talking. Harrison tried to read the room. Were they planning another operation or was he getting more bad news?

He suspected the latter. The last month had been a tough one for the resistance. It seemed every day Akhmet received word that another cell had been rolled up—and the tempo seemed to be increasing.

As usual, Akhmet's demeanor gave nothing away. The reports he gave to Harrison were always the same: *We are making progress. Send more weapons.* Harrison dutifully passed on the information using the laser comms set. The black attaché case was propped against the wall a few paces away.

He knew that Washington was getting frustrated with Akhmet. Since the resistance leader remained evasive about the exact number and disposition of his forces, Don had done his own internal estimate. Using intel from desertions from the military ranks of the Central Asian republics following the PLA invasion and local recruitment estimates, Don came up with a resistance force of around 2,500 fighters. When Harrison shared the estimate with Akhmet for confirmation, the old man smiled at him.

"It's a good number," he said, without adding any additional details.

Whatever the size of his forces, they were under constant pressure from PLA raids. Harrison heard the whispered reports about compromised cells and the talk among the men about the deaths of friends. In rare quiet moments, Akhmet's face deepened in thought and he smiled less these days.

Even Harrison could not miss the additional security measures. A month ago, they might have stayed for two or three nights in a location, now they moved every day. Sometimes twice or even three times in the same day.

The Central Asian Union was a large area, but the PLA's surveillance network made the vast empty spaces seem very small.

They'd arrived in this half-constructed apartment building after dark the previous evening. There were signs of ongoing construction in the concrete shell of the building, but it was empty when they arrived and no one showed up for work this morning.

Akhmet set up in a room on the third floor of the five-story building. Security protocols included two watchers on the roof and a concealed IED with a tripwire on the second-floor landing. The emergency egress from the building was the steel ladder that ran down the wall of the open elevator shaft in the center of the structure. In the basement of the building was a connection to the city sewer network.

They ate cold rations in the dark and slept on blankets spread on the concrete floor. They did have running water on this level and two working bathrooms with squatter toilets, which was a luxury compared to some of the places they'd stayed.

Between the pain in his gut and the blazing gibberish around the old map, Harrison found his mind wandering. He shifted his feet. These men could squat in place for hours, but Harrison's legs ached after about fifteen minutes. He tried to sit up to take the pressure off his gut and felt something move like a slithering snake in his intestines.

That did it. He was going to shit himself if he stayed here another minute.

Harrison scrambled to his feet. The conversation ceased as all eyes focused on him.

"Toilet," he said and headed for the door, but not before a blast of fetid gas escaped his backside in a loud burst. He heard the chuckles behind him.

Harrison paused in the hallway, remembering that he'd left the comms set in the meeting room. Another intestinal twist told him that he didn't have time to go back for it. He fast-walked down the hall and caught the edge of the concrete doorframe as he swung into the bathroom.

Occupied. A huge bearded man squatted over the porcelain hole in the floor, grunting, his trousers in a heap around his ankles.

"I'll be done in a minute," the man said in Russian.

Harrison doubled over in pain, clenched his buttocks together. He couldn't last another minute. The other working toilet was on the far side of this floor. He crossed the large landing in front of the stairs and hobbled down the hall. Sweat popped on his brow from the effort of trying to hold his bowels for another few seconds.

The passageway outside the toilet was partially blocked by two pallets of steel studs stacked one on top of the other. Harrison turned sideways and shimmied through the narrow opening.

Inside, he fumbled with his belt, dropped to a squat, and released a watery blast into the porcelain basin. Harrison groaned, rested his sweaty forehead on his knees, and closed his eyes.

The feeling of relief was like heaven.

Ka-BOOM!

The blast knocked Harrison off his feet. Disoriented, he scrambled on the dirty floor, his ankles tangled in his pants. Showers of concrete dust created a gray veil in the air. Harrison's ears rang, then they popped and he could hear again. He struggled to his feet, jerked his trousers up to his waist.

His brain tried to process what had happened. The explosion had come from below…

The tripwire on the second floor. That had to be it.

They were under attack.

29

Khujand, Tajikistan

From the captain's chair in the armored Dongfeng CSK-131 command post vehicle, Senior Colonel Kang considered himself the master of his universe. His center display offered him a high-definition aerial view of the neighborhood in the southeast quadrant of Khujand. This part of the city was far from the river and the Old Town with its ancient mosques, minarets, and gardens. Here the low-slung buildings were closely packed together. The tight streets were crowded with people and cars, and shopkeepers showed their wares in elaborate displays that spilled from their narrow storefronts.

With the touch of a finger, he zoomed in on one section of the neighborhood. An unfinished apartment building poked like a concrete finger above the sprawl. Judging from the equipment secured behind a fence in an adjacent empty lot, the five-story building was still under construction. The ground floor had steel doors and shuttered windows, but the square openings in the rest of the building face were empty. Even though it was the middle of the work week, there was no sign of construction going on this morning. In fact, the only sign of life in the entire building was two men on the roof.

The men on the roof were spotters, Kang knew, and they were guarding the man he'd been hunting for months.

He twirled his finger on the screen, getting a 360-degree view of the building. Akhmet Orazov, the leader of the SIF, was somewhere in that building.

Kang could not remember the last time he slept, but he wasn't tired. He was the opposite of tired. Excited. Energized. Alive.

He expanded the image and switched to a top-down view. Red dots, each identified with a data tag, peppered the streets surrounding the apartment building. He touched one of the tags and it displayed the man's name and vital signs. Heart rate, respiration, blood pressure—he could see it all in real time.

Unfortunately, he could not get video. These men were in civilian clothes, doing their best to blend in with the neighborhood as they got close to the building. When it came time to strike, his men would have the element of surprise. That was worth all the video in the world.

Kang let out a controlled breath. They were so close now. All he needed was an exact location of the SIF cell inside the building and he would break the back of the terrorist network once and for all.

For the last month, his special forces teams had taken down cell after SIF cell. With each raid, he harvested the intel from the site—phones, computers, notes, information from interrogations—and fed the new data into the Foresight system. The output from Foresight gave him his next target.

It was a virtuous cycle: the more he fed the algorithm, the more accurate the algorithm output became. Find, fix, and finish. He'd learned that doctrine from studying American counterinsurgency tactics in Iraq and Afghanistan.

He had the SIF on the run—and the dragnet was closing on their leader. He knew it; they knew it. It was only a matter of time...and that time was today.

He just needed one last piece of data. Once he'd located Orazov and his men inside the building, he could release his raiders to finish the job.

"Sniper teams, report," he said over the net.

"This is Sniper One. I think I have them, Senior Colonel," said a calm voice. "Southwest corner, third level."

Kang paged through screens until he found the image. He squinted at the display. All he saw was a dark rectangle in sun-drenched concrete. "Do you have a shot?"

"Negative. I think they're sitting on the floor, below the level of the window, but I saw movement. There's multiple targets in the room."

Kang acknowledged the report and sat back in his chair, weighing his options. Foresight told him Orazov was in the building. His sniper had confirmed activity in a room inside the structure. He could wait for a positive ID of the target, but that might take another hour and he had men on the streets. Every minute he waited was a risk that they might be exposed as soldiers and his prey would be warned.

No, he decided. The time for action was now.

A surge of adrenaline coursed through Kang's body. His mind buzzed with excitement and relief. The end was in sight. In less than sixteen weeks, he'd dismantled an insurgency that spanned four countries and millions of square kilometers.

Almost, he reminded himself. Just one final step.

He rose out of the command chair and paced. "Spear Team One, this is Cobra actual. Proceed with the raid. Spear Two, you have perimeter security."

He waited for acknowledgments, then said, "I want them alive, One. That means you're going to have to move fast."

"Live capture, Cobra. Understand."

The team lead for Spear One was Lieutenant Wei. Kang touched the man's data tag on the screen. Wei's pulse was hammering away at 150 beats and his blood pressure was elevated. The man was ready for battle.

"Spear One, on the move."

On the aerial view, the red dots moved like ants converging on a picnic. The six members of Wei's team homed in on the steel doors blocking the entrance to the building. He'd done these types of raids a hundred times and he could picture every step.

Set breaching charges on the door hinges, while the rest of the team took cover around the corner. A civilian on the street might stop, wonder what was happening. They might even shout a warning, but it would be too late.

"Spear Two, in position."

The second team of ten red dots encircled the structure, covering any exit. If Orazov's team tried to escape, they'd be waiting.

"Breaching charges set."

Kang's throat was dry. In his own mind, he was in that alley with his men. He smelled the heavy odors of the close-packed neighborhood. Car exhaust, rotting fruit, woodsmoke. He felt the grit of the concrete wall under his shoulder blade, the checkered grip of the QBZ-95 Bullpup in his fist, heavy with a fully loaded magazine. The screaming tension as he waited for the breaching blast to release his coiled muscles.

"Proceed." Kang's voice was a rasp.

"Breaching."

The *bangs* came through the mic muted. He heard the heavy breaths of running men, the pounding of boots on concrete, then—

Ka-BOOM!

Silence.

"What happened?" Kang roared. He swiped to the screen monitoring life signs of the raiders.

The six members of Spear One were offline.

Kang closed his eyes. They'd walked into a trap. No, he'd sent his men into a trap.

"Spear Team Two, reinforce One. Send six more men inside. Exercise caution."

Three dots converged on the entrance to the building and three more fanned out across the front of the building. Kang heard the scuff of boots on concrete.

"IED," the team lead reported. "It's...fuck. They're all dead, Cobra."

"Proceed," Kang ordered.

30

Khujand, Tajikistan

The explosion had broken open the pallet of metal studs in the hallway outside the bathroom. The exit was closed off in an avalanche of gray steel.

Harrison felt a bubble of panic rise in his throat. He was trapped. He tugged one of the steel beams free and everything shifted in a clatter of metal. He ripped another length of steel away from the pile, and another. Precious seconds slipped away in a frenzy of activity until he had cleared enough space to worm his way into the hallway.

The way he had come to the bathroom was blocked. He'd have to go around the perimeter hallway to get back to the elevator shaft and safety. Harrison spun around and ran, bouncing off the walls as he took the corners. His boots slapped the floor, his breath came in ragged gasps.

The question loomed in his mind: Would Akhmet wait for him?

No, the resistance leader had been clear time and again. In a crisis, every man had a personal responsibility for his own safety.

You can't help your comrade if you get captured.

Akhmet drilled the words into them every day. You are responsible for your own safety. Know your escape routes. Know what to do if cut off from your team.

Akhmet would not wait. Harrison rounded the last corner. The elevator shaft was just ahead. He was going to make it, just a few more steps.

Then a thought stopped him. The transmitter. He'd left the comms set in the meeting room. Would Akhmet think to bring it?

A top-secret CIA communications package in the hands of the PLA would be a disaster beyond imagination.

I have to be sure, Harrison realized.

He turned away from the elevator shaft, raced across the landing in front of the stairs, and entered the corner room where they'd spent the night.

The black carbon fiber case leaned against the wall, right where he'd left it. Harrison crossed the room, reached for the case.

"Don't move." The voice spoke Russian, but with a heavy accent. A Chinese accent.

Harrison raised his hands slowly.

"On your knees."

If they wanted to kill you, he told himself, you'd already be dead. Even so, Harrison felt his arms quivering.

They came at him fast, two men flattening him to the floor, a knee between his shoulder blades. They pressed his face into the concrete. He tasted dirt and his own blood from a split lip. The man on top of him wrenched his arms back and zip-tied his hands behind his back.

Then they rolled him over. He lay in a square of sunlight streaming through the open window, squinting up at them.

If Harrison hadn't been in fear of his life, the reaction of the three Chinese men might have been funny. But he was terrified.

The trio looked at each other in gaping amazement. One of them spoke into a mic at his chin and Harrison caught the word *gweilo*. From his time in Hong Kong, he knew what that word meant.

White devil. Foreigner.

Shit, shit, shit, he cursed to himself.

They were dressed in civilian clothes, but these guys were military, and they were armed to the teeth.

"Who are you?" the soldier asked in English.

Harrison's mind raced.

"Where is Orazov?" he demanded.

Harrison feigned a look of confusion. "Who? I'm a real estate investor—"

His bullshit came to a quick end as the man on the right kicked him. The toe of his boot sank into the soft flesh just below Harrison's rib cage. He contracted into the fetal position. He felt his bowels let go, adding shame to his pain.

The leader was on the comms net again, giving orders.

Harrison tried to think. He was trussed up like a Christmas turkey, he'd just shit himself, and any second now, these goons were going to find the comms set. Then he'd be well and truly fucked.

Harrison clenched his eyes shut in pain and frustration. He had no idea what to do.

So, he yelled. He just opened his mouth and let all the pain and frustration out.

Mid-scream, the shooting started.

In the concrete room, the sound of a shotgun firing on full auto was deafening. And it seemed to go on forever.

One of the soldiers fell on top of Harrison, a warm wet mass of dead flesh. The one who'd kicked him, toppled to the floor next to him. His open eyes held a look of surprise and his chest was a bloody, pulpy mess.

Harrison squirmed out from under the dead man. The body was shredded, blood everywhere. He craned his head toward the hallway.

Sanjar stood just inside the door. He had a two-handed grip on the Saiga-12 and smoke curled from the muzzle of the weapon. He grinned and flipped his head back to get the hair out of his eyes.

"Harr-i-son!" His voice was joyful, joking.

Harrison moved his mouth, but nothing came out. Sanjar dropped to one knee and used his knife to cut Harrison's bonds.

"Harr-i-son!" he said again, exultant.

Harrison got to his hands and knees. He crawled to the comms case, threw the strap over his head and started to get up.

"We need to go now." His voice sounded shaky, like the voice of an old man.

Sanjar jogged a victory lap around the room, pumping his arms with the weapon held high, chanting, "Harr-i-son! I did it! I rescued you!"

He crossed in front of the open window. His boyish features, lopsided grin, pumping arms framed in golden sunlight.

The force of the sniper's bullet threw Sanjar's body back against the concrete wall with a wet slapping sound. He hung there for a long moment, then slid to the floor.

Harrison tried to yell, but nothing came out. He belly-crawled across the floor.

Sanjar was already gone. His head was thrown back so that for once, his long hair was not in his face. He still had that grin, but his eyes held all the life of shiny black marbles.

Harrison touched the kid's bloody neck. No pulse. His mind reeled. He couldn't breathe. His eyes scanned the room, refusing to process what he was seeing. In the space of less than a minute there were now four dead men in the room. Blood on the floor, blood on the walls. He'd never seen so much blood.

His breath returned to him in a rush, and he dragged air into his lungs that tasted of dust and burnt gunpowder.

Sanjar was dead, but he was alive. Akhmet's voice suddenly rang in his head.

You can't help your comrade if you get captured.

The comms set. He had to get out of here. Harrison crawled toward the open elevator shaft, but it was too late. Two PLA soldiers, dressed in camouflage uniforms and ballistic helmets, advanced up the steps, weapons raised.

Harrison froze. The pair moved into the space, flanking him. Two more flowed up the steps and advanced into the room Harrison had just left. A furious stream of angry Mandarin volleyed between the soldiers.

The one who seemed to be in charge motioned with the muzzle of his rifle for Harrison to stand. He got to his feet slowly, painfully aware of the slim black case slung over his shoulder. The soldier saw it, too. He motioned for Harrison to hand it over.

Harrison blinked slowly. He thought about making a futile run for the elevator shaft and a dive into oblivion. It wouldn't make a difference. He'd be dead, and the PLA would still have a top-secret CIA laser comms set in their possession.

And it was all his fault.

The rifle butt hit him in the small of the back, knocking him to his knees, then a knee in his back face-planted him into the dirty concrete floor. Through the waves of pain, he felt the sling being pulled over his head. Rough hands cuffed his arms behind his back for the second time in less than five minutes and hauled him to his feet.

The soldier opened the carbon-fiber case.

"Spear Two, report!" Kang shouted into the microphone.

"Cobra, Spear Two, three more dead." A pause. "We have a prisoner."

"Orazov?" Kang demanded.

"No, sir. The *gweilo*. I think he's American, and he has a communications package with him. High-end."

American...Kang's mind processed the new information. An American with a high-end comms set had been with Orazov.

"CIA," he whispered. He'd captured a CIA agent involved in a terrorist plot against the People's Liberation Army.

"Secure the building, Spear Two. I'm on my way." He mashed the intercom button that connected him to the driver. "Drive! Now!"

This was huge. Hard evidence that the Americans were running a covert action in the region was almost better than capturing Orazov himself. A live CIA agent would expose Orazov and the Americans to the world.

The vehicle swayed and bucked as the driver alternately accelerated and braked in the narrow streets. Kang braced himself in his command chair. He could hear the distant sound of the horn blaring as the driver tried to clear the road ahead.

The toes of Harrison's boots hit every concrete step as they hauled him down three flights and into the bright morning sunshine. The soldier ahead of him had Harrison's comms set slung over one shoulder.

When they stopped dragging him, Harrison managed to get his feet under him and he stood on the sidewalk. Six PLA soldiers had formed a perimeter outside the building entrance. Including the four that were with him, that made a contingent of ten. Dozens of civilians watched from doorways, windows, and alleys. Harrison scanned the people, desperately searching for a familiar face and seeing none.

He was on his own. Akhmet was gone, just as he'd promised.

You can't help your comrade if you get captured. Truer, more bitter words had never been spoken.

The one in charge, who held Harrison's comms set, was shouting into his mic.

Transportation, Harrison thought. They're waiting for a transport.

The full import of what was about to happen registered now and Harrison's mouth went dry. They'd want to know the details of the comms set and of his mission. Like every field operative, he'd been trained for this eventuality, but there was training, and then there was real life. Everyone talked. Sooner or later, everyone spilled their secrets.

And then what? Prison? A bullet in the brain?

Breathe, just fucking breathe, he thought. Don't get ahead of yourself. Deal with it as it comes. Stay alert.

He was so consumed with his own racing thoughts that Harrison didn't notice the sound at first. The soldier in front of him looked up. Like a swarm of bees, or a distant jet engine, the sound reverberated in the narrow street. It seemed to be coming from all directions.

The soldier in charge didn't like what he was hearing. He spun around, pointing back inside the building. He started to give an order, then he pitched forward, taking Harrison to the ground under his dead weight. Harrison fell straight back, hitting the concrete hard, his bound arms screaming under the strain of the combined weight of his own body and the soldier. For the second time that day, hot blood that was not his own flowed over his torso.

The soldiers flanking him collapsed to the ground.

Snipers, he realized.

The PLA soldiers on perimeter protection dove for cover, weapons high, looking for a target, firing wildly. The whining sound grew in pitch and intensity and a vehicle screamed down the narrow street at high speed. The PLA soldiers opened fire, some standing to get a better shot. Harrison saw two more fall to snipers.

The jet bikes, Harrison realized.

The soldier on top of him was dead weight. Harrison braced his feet and pushed with everything he had. He squirmed out from under the body.

Another jet bike roared down the street from the other direction, slower this time, with a fighter on the back. The rapid *boom-boom-boom* of an automatic shotgun reverberated in the space between the buildings. The PLA soldiers retreated around the corner of the building and Harrison heard more gunfire.

The scream of jet engines filled the air and a third jet bike descended. Akhmet was in the driver's seat. He shouted, but his words were lost in the noise. He held out his hand.

Harrison got to his knees, his hands still bound. The comms set was loose on the shoulder of the dead PLA soldier. Harrison seized it in his teeth, dragged it free, then staggered through the windstorm of dust and debris to the hovering jet bike. Akhmet took the case from him and looped it over his shoulder.

Harrison swung his leg over the seat and buried his face in Akhmet's broad back as the jet bike lifted off.

This high in the mountains, the Milky Way earned its name. Between the altitude, the lack of background light pollution, and the crystal-clear atmosphere, the countless stars of the Milky Way looked as dense as clouds in the night sky.

Akhmet hadn't said a word to Harrison after he landed the jet bike. He stalked away, leaving the CIA officer in the hands of a medic.

Not that Harrison noticed. His whole body shook from the adrenaline rush of the near-death experience. He was covered in his own shit and the blood of other men, and rife with bruises and cuts. His wrists were raw and bloody.

But he was alive. And he'd saved the comms set. That was what mattered, he told himself. He was alive.

And Sanjar was dead. It was hard to fathom a world without that goofy kid in it. His throat closed up when he thought about Sanjar prancing around the room seconds before the sniper's bullet took his life. It felt like a dream.

But it was real. And it was his fault. Sanjar had come back for him and he'd paid the price with his life.

Harrison startled as a shape loomed out of the darkness next to him. Akhmet's voice was low. "May I sit with you, Harrison?"

"Of course, Ussat." Harrison made room on the flat stone that formed his seat. He drew the collar of his jacket up. The night was getting colder, or maybe that was just guilt.

They sat in silence. It was just cold enough for their breath to form slight wisps of steam when they exhaled.

"Are you okay?"

"Yes, Ussat."

"Good."

Minutes passed. Harrison's ass had long since grown numb, but he dared not move, dared not break the spell.

"Sanjar saved my life," Harrison said finally. His voice sounded rusty and thick.

Akhmet sighed then, and Harrison felt the older man's body sag next to him.

"Sanjar was a fool." Akhmet's voice was heavy with emotion. Anger, sadness, regret. "I taught him better than that."

"It was impossible to teach Sanjar anything, Ussat."

"True." A bitter laugh. "He was brave, but he was still a boy."

More silence. Finally, Harrison couldn't take it any longer. "You came back for me, Ussat."

Next to him, Akhmet's shadow nodded.

"Why?" Harrison pressed. "Was it because of the comms set?"

Akhmet's sigh sounded again. "Perhaps. Or perhaps I'm as big a fool as Sanjar." He climbed to his feet. "Good night, Harrison."

Akhmet's steps faded in the darkness.

31

The Kremlin, Moscow

Federov did not look well. The FSB chief's suit jacket hung on him like a scarecrow and the gap between his shirt collar and his neck had grown since Nikolay had last seen him. But his eyes were clear and his chin was high. Two bright spots colored his sallow cheeks as he made his point.

"This is not a good idea, Mr. President." Federov coughed into his closed fist. "You had a relationship with Serrano, sir. I fear President Cashman will see this move as arrogant."

"Nonsense, Vladimir." Nikolay pointed at the secure video teleconference setup in his Kremlin office. "Eleanor Cashman is no different than any other American President. They understand strength, and right now we are strong. It's time to press our case."

The reception to his unannounced military exercises along the Kazakh border had gone even better than Nikolay had hoped. Everyone saw another Ukraine invasion in the making and they were desperate to stop it.

Protests were lodged at the UN Security Council. His phone rang with calls from leaders all over the European Union pleading for him to withdraw his forces. He even got subtle inquiries from the Chinese. But through it all, the Americans had not seen fit to reach out, not even through unofficial channels.

Meanwhile, Nikolay's mole inside the Kazakh government had been a busy boy. The report on Nikolay's desk offered a detailed accounting of US arms shipments through Kazakhstan. His eyes scanned the page, and he frowned.

"These numbers can't be right, Vladimir."

Federov raised his hands in frustration. "Yet another reason why this call is premature, Mr. President. We do not have a good understanding of the situation in Central Asia. The numbers of weapons that are going into the region are not consistent with our force estimates of the resistance. I need more time to sort this out."

"We have no more time, Vladimir," Nikolay snapped. "How long do you think I can leave eight divisions on the border of Kazakhstan before I begin to look foolish? You yourself have told me the precarious nature of our supply situation. How long before news reports leak out about Russian soldiers starving in the middle of field maneuvers?"

"I can handle the media, Mr. President," Federov replied. "But I urge you to wait—"

"Wait for what?" Nikolay shouted. "You keep saying *wait*. What are we waiting for?"

"To find out which way this goes. Let the Americans supply the resistance movement in Central Asia. Let them take on the full burden of fighting the Chinese. The Americans supply the resistance and the resistance creates chaos." Federov leaned across the desk. "There is opportunity in chaos, Mr. President."

"Now, you're quoting my uncle to me, Vladimir?"

"I only meant that—"

Nikolay's jaw clenched tight. "If you are going to invoke the wisdom of Vitaly Luchnik, then let's do it right, shall we?" He stood, planted his fists on the desktop. "President Luchnik did not *wait* for chaos to happen. He sowed the chaos and he reaped the reward. In his own time. On his own terms."

Federov dropped his eyes to the ground. Nikolay could see the blue veins tracing the pale skin of his scalp.

"With all due respect, Mr. President, these are different times."

"Ahhh!" Nikolay let out a growl of frustration and paced out from behind his desk. "And what about Kazakhstan? Do I wait to see what happens there as well? When the Chinese are finished in Central Asia, they will turn to Kazakhstan. The water resources alone are reason enough for them to invade the country. Every day, the Chinese grow stronger—and we grow weaker in comparison. No, I will not wait while the future security of the Russian Federation is in jeopardy."

"Mr. President," Federov said quietly, "I do not believe the Americans will be receptive to your proposal."

"You underestimate me, Vladimir. President Cashman understands the Chinese threat in the region. She will see the value of a partnership now. I can convince her it is in our mutual interest."

Fedorov knew he had lost. It showed in the set of his shoulders. "I understand, Mr. President."

While the technicians readied the secure video teleconference, Nikolay visited the en suite bathroom. He checked his appearance in the mirror and retied his silk tie until he had a perfect dimple just below the knot. He donned a freshly pressed suit jacket and inspected the result in the mirror.

Perfect, he decided.

Federov knocked on the door of the bathroom. "Five minutes, Mr. President."

Nikolay experienced the familiar rush of excitement just before a high-stakes meeting. It was at moments like these that he felt most alive, as if he was called to this job.

He strode into the office and seated himself behind the wide mahogany desk. Evening had fallen and the royal-blue brocaded curtains behind his chair were drawn, lending richness to the backdrop.

The coat of arms of the Russian Federation showed on the screen. A golden, double-headed eagle clutching a scepter and an orb, on a background of deep crimson. A fitting nod to the historical power of the Russian Empire and the bright future ahead.

"Connecting now, Mr. President," said the technician.

Nikolay nodded, let out an easy breath, and smiled into the camera.

You can do this, he thought. You can bring her over to your side.

The screen in front of him filled with a larger-than-life image of the President of the United States. Eleanor Cashman was dressed in a pale-yellow blouse and dark jacket with a string of pearls. Matching pearl earrings showed beneath her carefully styled short blond hair. For the first time, Nikolay noticed the elegant length of her neck. Her chin was angled down so that she stared directly into the camera.

What a handsome woman, Nikolay thought. He smiled.

"How good to see you again, Madam President."

32

The White House, Washington, DC

What an arrogant prick.

That was Eleanor Cashman's first thought when the Russian President's face appeared on the screen. Nikolay Sokolov's blond hair was turning silver. He wore it long and swept straight back from his forehead, like a gangster. He had thin facial features, a long straight nose, high cheekbones, and a sharp jawline. His thin lips were curved into a toothy, wolfish smile.

"How good to see you again, Madam President." His voice was a smooth baritone.

Cashman wanted to reply that they'd never met, but she checked herself. Instead, she mirrored his smile. "Likewise, Mr. President. To what do I owe the pleasure of your call?"

She felt more than heard the stirring of her advisors seated in the Oval Office beyond her screen. Secretary of State Abel Cartwright was seated next to Secretary of Defense—now newly confirmed—Gable on one of the sofas, both hunched forward studying the monitor that mirrored her own. Pens scratched on open notepads. National Security Advisor Todd Spencer had claimed the armchair at the head of the coffee table. On the opposite sofa sat CIA Director Carroll Brooks and CIA Director of Operations Don Riley. Neither was taking notes.

The peanut gallery would have comments about her directness, Cashman knew, but she didn't care. She hadn't wanted to take this call in the first place. The only reason she was sitting here at all was that all of her advisors—every single one—told her that refusing to take the Russian President's call would be a mistake. It was a sign. Her advisors never agreed on anything.

So here she was. But as soon as Sokolov bent his lips into an insincere smile, Cashman knew in her heart that she'd made a mistake. That was why she cut to the chase with her direct question.

To his credit, Sokolov didn't seem surprised or offended by her bluntness. "There seems to be concern about routine military exercises in central Russia," the Russian President replied. "I thought I would call and clear the air."

"Routine?" Cashman countered. "I believe that routine military exercises are normally announced well in advance so that there are no misunderstandings between countries. What you did was turn a victory parade into a military provocation on the border of a sovereign nation, Mr. President."

Sokolov's brow crinkled in feigned confusion. "Provocation? I see these events as a straightforward message meant to highlight our mutual interests in the Republic of Kazakhstan."

Cashman resisted the urge to scowl. She momentarily reflected on the fact that Riley had called it exactly right.

"I'm not sure I follow your logic, Mr. President," she said stiffly. "Exactly how are our interests mutual?"

"Did you really think I wouldn't find out about the arms shipments, Madam President?"

"I don't know what you're talking about, President Sokolov."

"I'm talking about your unwanted influence in my part of the world, Madam President. I'm talking about your threats to the national security of the Russian Federation."

"The United States is willing to support democracy wherever we find it —even if it is in your backyard, Mr. President."

"You are meddling where you don't belong," Sokolov replied flatly.

"Excuse me?" Cashman stopped herself from smiling. She'd gotten under his skin and now the gloves come off.

"My intelligence sources in the region are excellent, Madam President." He made a show of consulting a report on his desk, raised an eyebrow. "Four thousand Stinger missiles? You must have raided most of your own stockpile in the United States to ship that many to Central Asia. One would think you're trying to start a war." He leaned forward and the wolfish smile returned. "I could offer this information to the Chinese, but I came to you first, out of respect. After all, we have the same goal: Central Asian republics free of Chinese influence and restoration of the traditional relationship between Russia and Kazakhstan."

Cashman let the silence hang for a long moment. "Exactly what are you proposing, Mr. President?"

"A partnership." Nikolay spread his hands, palms up. "I have well-established supply routes into Central Asia. I can make your operation to supply the resistance much more efficient and secure."

"And what's in it for you?" Cashman asked.

"Regional stability," Sokolov said. "Together, we help the resistance drive out the PLA and we restore the natural political order of things."

Cashman smiled at the camera. "Would you excuse me for a moment, Mr. President?" Without waiting for an answer, she nodded at the technician. The screen switched back to the White House seal on a royal-blue background.

"We're secure, ma'am," the technician said.

Her advisors ringed the perimeter of the Resolute desk. Cashman leaned back in her chair.

"So, there we have it," Cashman said. "The President of Russia has come hat in hand to the United States asking for a *partnership*. What is my response?"

As he usually did, Abel Cartwright spoke first. "Ma'am, I think this is a serious offer. Keep your friends close and your enemies closer, I always say. If we work with the Russians, we can demand they move their troops off the Kazakh border."

"Strongly disagree," National Security Advisor Spencer said. "This is the last gasp of a desperate man. They're bluffing. We wouldn't even be having this conversation if they didn't have nuclear weapons. Russia is a joke, and we should treat this request the same way."

Cashman's gaze settled on the CIA contingent. The look on the Director's face was pensive, but Riley had that chin tilt that meant he had something to say. She decided to get it over with.

"Mr. Riley, you were the one who called it correctly. Where do we go from here?"

Riley cut a look at his boss and got a subtle nod. Somehow those two had managed to form an alliance.

"Ma'am," Riley said, "working with the Russians always carries a certain amount of risk. However, in this instance, I would have to agree with State. The devil we know is better than the alternative. A partnership might even give us greater insight into Russia's future moves in the region. The more we know about their operations, the better."

Cashman spun her chair so she was looking out the windows behind her desk. Heavy pewter clouds hung low over the city, adding to the oppressive humidity. It was going to rain. She could feel the clouds ready to burst.

Cartwright was correct. If she threw Sokolov a bone, she'd be able to demand that he move his troops off the border with Kazakhstan, but was that the right thing to do? Sure, she could play the statesman, but that was a double-edged sword. On the one hand, she might bring some order to an unstable region, which was a good thing. But what was on the other side of the equation bugged her. She'd be helping that arrogant Russian bastard out of a debacle of his own making.

He was the one who'd moved his troops to the Kazakh border and created an international crisis. Now he was asking her for a favor. Why was this her issue? Let that prick solve his own problems.

And then there was her own image to think of. For years she'd cultivated a persona as the tough-as-nails fighter, the hawk candidate who would not back down in the face of international pressure. It had been part of her campaign pitch. This was too early in her administration to go soft on Russia.

No, she thought, the right call was to stick it to Sokolov and let him choke on his political vomit. Even better, after she slapped him down, she could make sure a readout of this encounter leaked to the press. She'd not only burnish her own image as a hawk, but make Nikolay Sokolov look like an incompetent beggar.

Win-win, she thought, and this time she didn't bother to hide the smile.

She spun her chair around, focused on Riley. "If I refuse President Sokolov's request outright, what will he do?"

"Ma'am?" Riley's tone was cautious. "That's not really a question I can—"

"Bullshit, Riley," Cashman snapped. "Right now, in the Kremlin, Sokolov is sitting with his advisors and making the same calculations we are. If we refuse him, what will he do?"

Don dropped his gaze and thought for a moment.

"Nothing, Madam President," he said slowly. "At least for the moment, nothing. He doesn't have the military strength or the public support to invade Kazakhstan. He could expose our operation to supply weapons to the resistance, but that doesn't help him either. China is a bigger threat to him than we are right now. But, ma'am, in the long run, we're on the same side in Central Asia, which is exactly why I think we should be working—"

President Cashman interrupted. "You've answered my question, Mr. Riley. Thank you."

She squared her shoulders and faced the camera.

"I'm ready to resume the call," she said to the technician.

33

Ayni Air Base, Dushanbe, Tajikistan

The last time Kang had seen Lieutenant General Cheng had been his first day in the region. On that day, the Commander of the Western Theater of the People's Liberation Army had made a special trip to the forward operating base in Dushanbe for the express purpose of humiliating a roomful of subordinates.

Kang could still taste the disgust he'd felt for the man that day—and time had done nothing to dull his feelings.

Cheng was turned out in a freshly pressed, tailored dress uniform, with rows of colorful ribbons across his chest and gleaming golden epaulets on his square shoulders. His carefully styled hair bounced as he paced the floor of the operations center with Major General Wong following him like an eager puppy.

All of the ops center personnel had been ordered to wear dress uniforms in honor of General Cheng's visit. After months of wearing combat fatigues every day, Kang's dress uniform felt stiff and awkward.

"You see here, sir," Wong said, "Foresight has predicted an enemy weapons drop, right...here." Wong's arm lunged over the shoulder of one of the enlisted technicians manning a console. His stubby finger stabbed at a screen. A few stations away, Kang rolled a trackball to zoom in on the target location.

The aerial picture of Kyrkkyz, some eight hundred kilometers from their present location, showed a lonely outpost in western Uzbekistan. The highway that ran through the high desert made a ninety-degree turn, and the town grew there like a tumor. He guessed there were no more than fifty structures in the settlement, ranging from neat bungalow-style, single-family homes with small patches of green yard to bleak, poured-concrete tenement buildings. It was after midnight and few stirred in the town of less than a thousand souls. Cars lined the sleeping streets. In the infrared display, Kang saw ghostly white shapes flit between houses. Dogs, he supposed.

The nearest PLA installation was in Bukhara, three hours away by car. As soon as Foresight registered the predicted weapons drop, Kang had dispatched a full company of soldiers to deal with the potential threat.

Kang's terrorist-hunting operation was reliant on Foresight now. Ever since the raid in Khujand, he had become a believer in the power of the predictive AI battle system. The failure to capture Orazov was not a failure of Foresight, but his own lack of imagination in anticipating the terrorist leader. Kang now understood how tenacious and resourceful Orazov was. He was a formidable adversary.

But even Orazov was no match for Foresight. The abilities of the system grew by the day, as did Kang's reliance on the battle AI's intelligence. Foresight now predicted enemy supply drops and Kang routinely dispatched troops in advance of any firm intel of a weapons shipment.

"Senior Colonel?" he heard Major General Wong say.

"Yes, sir." Kang realized he'd been caught woolgathering and he put some extra force in his response. Behind Wong's shoulder, Lieutenant General Cheng studied him with eyes the color and warmth of obsidian.

"What is the status of the intercept team?" Wong asked.

Kang made a show of studying the screen. "One hour, sir. They're coming from Bukhara."

"Do you mean to tell me that you have enough confidence in this computer"—Cheng waved a dismissive hand at the row of monitors— "to put troops in the field ahead of time?"

"Absolutely, sir," Kang replied, and Wong beamed like a schoolboy.

"Not only that," Wong added, smacking his fist for emphasis, "but the system can recommend a course of action. It can even initiate an attack on its own—if we enable that feature, of course."

Cheng pursed his lips as he studied the computer screens.

Armchair generals should tread carefully, Kang thought. Wong was a true believer. He did not hide the fact that his goal was to take the soldier out of soldiering. Foresight was very capable, Kang knew that, but it still required guidance. He worried that the system was missing obvious signs that the tactics of the SIF were changing again. The last series of weapons drops, for instance, had been smaller and composed of older weapons. One reading of that data point was to assume that the terrorist supply lines were drying up. But there was another, less obvious answer: the SIF had switched tactics to a less traceable supply route and these less valuable air drops were a diversion.

No matter, Kang thought. We'll intercept the men who arrive to pick up the weapons and question them. Find, fix, and finish.

"I have an inbound aircraft," an operator called out.

Kang got to the operator first, but Wong elbowed him aside to give Cheng a clear view of the screen as he narrated the action.

"You see, sir," Wong said in a crowing voice. "Just as Foresight predicted."

"Contact is a probable twin-engine commercial craft. Identification system is deenergized," the operator reported. "Approaching from the west, flying at an altitude of 250 meters."

Kang's pulse quickened. Small aircraft flying across the Kazakh border in the middle of the night well below normal cruising altitude. This was the shipment.

"I have a visual on the bogey," another operator said.

"Put it on the wall screen," Wong demanded.

The infrared image from the high-altitude overwatch drone flying 10,000 meters over the target area showed a small white silhouette of a plane flying over the dark, cool expanse of the nighttime desert.

"Are you going to shoot it down?" Cheng asked. His eyes were fixed on the wall screen and his voice had a ring of excitement.

Kang saw the operators exchange glances. "We don't have a positive identification, sir," Kang said. "We can't just shoot down a civilian aircraft."

Cheng frowned and nodded, but he seemed unaware of the reaction to his words. "Look!" He pointed at the screen.

The overwatch operator zoomed in until the infrared image of the plane filled the wall screen. A side door on the aircraft opened. Kang could see two men in the opening. A package tumbled out, followed by another and a third. Parachutes deployed, arresting the fall of the cargo as it descended to the ground. The door on the aircraft slid shut and the plane banked into a wide turn.

"Track the outbound aircraft," Kang ordered. "I want to know where it lands."

"Yes, Senior Colonel," said the operator.

"How close is the intercept team?" Kang asked.

"Forty minutes out, sir," his comms operator said. "I've alerted them about the weapons drop."

"What do we do now?" Lieutenant General Cheng asked. Gone was the disinterested attitude. The General's beady eyes flitted from display to display, drinking in the information.

"We wait, sir," Kang said.

"Wait? For what?"

"Three vehicles are enroute from the town," the overwatch operator reported. "On screen, sir."

"That's what we're waiting for, General," Kang said.

Three vehicles, ghostly white with heat signatures, sped across the open desert trailing clouds of dust. Foresight automatically assigned data tags and calculated a firing solution for each target.

Minutes crawled by as the vehicles split up and hunted down the dropped crates. Two men disembarked from each truck and loaded the crates into the back. One by one, the trucks made a U-turn and headed back toward town.

"Track them," Kang ordered. "Do we have license plate numbers yet?"

"We have registration information on two of three contacts, sir. Uploading to Foresight now."

"Very well," Kang replied.

The three vehicles reached the main highway. They turned into the town and split up. Each truck ended its journey inside of a covered garage.

"Transmit coordinates for all three locations to the intercept team," Kang ordered.

"Yes, sir," the operator replied. "Intercept team is fifteen minutes out, Senior Colonel."

Kang sighed. Not ideal. He would have preferred to take the men picking up the shipment in the open desert. He overheard General Wong speaking to Cheng farther down the row of workstations. His voice held all the pride of a proud father.

"You see, sir, Foresight accurately predicted the weapons drop. We were able to track the shipment. When they arrive, the intercept team will take everyone in those buildings in for questioning."

"You said earlier that the system recommends a course of action."

Kang looked up to see Cheng frowning at the screen.

"Absolutely, sir." Wong's shock of iron gray hair bounced with the force of his agreement. "In this instance, Foresight recommends a drone attack to take out the target. Execution of the recommendation is at the discretion of the field commander." His gaze rested on Kang.

Cheng advanced, his dark eyes raking across the senior colonel's features. "Why?" he demanded.

Kang took a step back. "Why what, sir?"

"Why haven't you followed your instructions?"

"I don't understand your point, General," Kang said, although he understood the General's point perfectly well. He cut his eyes toward Wong, but the man just stood there, watching the exchange.

Cheng's voice grew sharp. "Foresight ordered a drone strike, correct?" Without waiting for an answer, he continued. "You have armed assets over the target. Why don't you follow through on your orders from Foresight?"

Kang wanted to say, *because I don't take orders from a computer*, but he took a deep breath instead.

"Sir, Foresight has provided a *recommendation*. In my experience, a drone strike is not the right course of action. We don't know what was in those crates. It could be anything."

Cheng's eyes narrowed further. "You're telling me that you trust Foresight enough to deploy a company of soldiers into the field based on a prediction, but you don't trust it enough to follow through on all the recommendations. Is that what you're saying, Senior Colonel?"

Kang felt a spark of anger, but he kept his voice even. "Yes, sir. That's exactly what I'm saying. As field commander, I have the option to take the system recommendations or not."

Cheng shrugged. "Very well, then. You are relieved, Senior Colonel Kang." He turned to Wong. "You're in charge of this operation now, General Wong. What are you going to do?"

Kang's irritation flared. "Just a minute, sir." He realized his tone did not carry the necessary respect for this man's rank, but he was past caring. "I am responsible for this mission, and we are not launching a drone strike on an unknown target. Sir."

Cheng turned very slowly, fixed his eyes on Kang. "You are relieved of your duties, Senior Colonel. You may go."

Frozen silence in the room. The operators stared at their screens. No one moved.

Cheng turned back to Major General Wong. Beneath the upturned puff of thick gray hair, Wong's forehead was slick with sweat. His eyebrows crushed together into a deep frown. Kang knew his boss had never seen combat of any kind. He was a systems analyst who knew more about computers than carbines.

"General Wong." Cheng's voice was silky with implied threat. "Either you believe in Foresight, or you do not. Which is it?" He raised his voice like he was performing for an audience. "You brought me here to convince me that Foresight is the future of the PLA. You said you would convince me beyond a shadow of a doubt that the billions we've spent building this computer system were worth it. So, this is your moment. Do you believe in Foresight or not?"

Wong looked at his boss, then looked at Kang, then looked at the floor. "Yes, sir."

Cheng spread his arms in an expansive gesture, palms up. "Well?"

"Drone operator," Wong said, his voice hoarse.

"Yes, sir?"

"How many armed aerial assets are available?"

The drone controller looked at his screen. "Sir, we have three armed assets in the area. All three can be in weapons range in the next ten minutes."

I have to stop this, Kang thought. I cannot let this happen. He opened his mouth, but Cheng held up a finger, shook his head in warning.

"Redirect all three drones to the target," Wong ordered. "Upload the Foresight attack parameters."

The young soldier worked at his terminal. He looked back at Wong. "Firing solution ready, sir." The kid's eyes ping-ponged between Generals.

Cheng smiled, and Kang did not like what he saw in his eyes.

This sick fuck is enjoying this, thought Kang. This was not the way to fight an insurgency. This was how you fed the resistance, by using brutal unthinking tactics from brutal unthinking men.

"Don't," Kang said. "Sir."

"Senior Colonel," Cheng snapped, "I will not warn you again."

"Drones are in positions, sir," the operator reported. "Firing solution is locked. Standing by." Kang thought he heard the young man's voice crack.

Wong looked like he wanted to disappear. He swallowed, licked his lips. Beside him, Cheng folded his arms.

"Execute," General Wong said.

"Missiles away," the operator reported.

The overwatch drone offered a bird's-eye view of the attack. The white contrails of twelve missile tracks zipped across the screen. They separated, each homing in on its own target, a thin white reticle hovering over the ghostly image of a building.

Blossoms of fiery white explosions saturated the screen.

"Foresight reports all targets destroyed, sir," the operator reported.

34

Kyrkkyz, Uzbekistan

As the sun rose over the horizon, Timur Ganiev's sleep-deprived brain realized where the aircraft was heading.

He leaned past Nicole for a better view out the window of the Harbin Z-20 transport helicopter. Keying his microphone, he said, "I know this place. Kyrkkyz." His voice sounded excited in the heavy plastic headphones.

He turned to look at Jimmy Li. The MSS agent's hair was a mess and his face haggard. He nodded, said nothing.

Then Timur saw the smoke. Dark columns rose above the landscape, hit a thermal layer, and merged into a thick ominous cloud that hung over the high desert town.

"What happened?" Timur demanded.

"Terrorist attack," Jimmy replied in English so that Nicole understood what he was saying. "Last night."

Terrorist attack. It made no sense. Why would the resistance fighters attack a town in the middle of nowhere? There were no PLA troops stationed here.

Then it clicked into place and he knew why Jimmy had rousted him in the middle of the night. The President of the Central Asian Union was here to denounce the violence, to smooth over the situation. The euphoria of only a moment ago evaporated and he slumped in his seat.

This had gone on too long, and he was tired. He was sick to death of seeing innocent people hurt and killed. And that feeling of sickness lingered in his body. It seemed to be a part of him now.

I never wanted this, he thought. I wanted to help people.

Nicole nudged him with her elbow as they passed over the town. Through the curtain of smoke, Timur could see multiple buildings—homes—had been bombed. The debris field splashed away from the bomb craters like some kind of sick modern art display. He remembered Kyrkkyz as a small town, no more than a village really, a waypoint on the highway through the high plains. The smoking bomb sites looked like raw wounds against the brown of the desert around them.

The town had been one of their first free clinics, his and Lila's. Those were heady days of young love and rampant idealism, a time when they were far richer in spirit than in purse. Every time he administered a vaccination or set a broken arm, he felt like a hero. Parents paid him in chickens and fresh baked bread and sweets and he didn't care. He had purpose. He had purity.

He looked down at himself. A bespoke wool suit jacket over a fine cashmere sweater. He wore hand-tooled Italian loafers. Was he even the same man he remembered?

The helicopter touched down next to the highway north of town where a pair of PLA military SUVs waited. Clouds of exhaust billowed silver into the still morning air.

Jimmy took the passenger seat in the first vehicle while Nicole and Timur got in the back. Nicole's ever-present camera crew piled into the second vehicle with their gear.

"Here's what I have planned, Doc," Jimmy began. He spoke to Timur in Russian so that Nicole couldn't understand. For some reason, Jimmy had taken to calling Timur "Doc" instead of Mr. President when they were alone. He seemed to think it was funny.

"We're going to tour the bomb sites first and get some camera footage of you in the wreckage. Maybe comforting an old lady or something. There's a press conference at nine. I need you to emphasize that innocent people died at the hands of the Seljuk Islamic Front and that you fully support the PLA in their quest to hunt down these vicious terrorists. You know the drill. We'll be back in Samarkand by dinnertime, Doc." Jimmy's voice was relaxed to the point of boredom, as if he was telling Timur about his latest trip to the barbershop.

They reached the edge of the town when a sudden thought struck Timur. "I have a better idea," he announced to Jimmy in English so that Nicole would understand. "I want to go to the clinic."

"The clinic?" Jimmy turned around in the seat. "What are you talking about, Doc?"

Timur ignored him, spoke to the driver in Russian. "Turn there." He pointed to a street on the left.

The driver looked at Jimmy, who gave a tired shrug, and the man turned the wheel. The street was paved but rough with potholes. Timur leaned forward between the seats and directed the driver to a side street at the edge of town that was clogged with cars and people. The SUV stopped.

"This won't work at all," Jimmy said. "I've got press coming in an hour and I need you fully briefed—"

Timur got out. If Jimmy called after him, Timur didn't hear him. He was lost in a memory.

The free clinic was a one-story, whitewashed cinderblock building with a red cross painted on the wall next to the glass front door. People were everywhere, sitting on cars, sleeping on the sidewalk, crowding around the door. They held each other; some wept, some just stared into space.

Timur angled his body sideways and pressed into the knot of people blocking the entrance.

"Please let me through," he said. "I'm a doctor."

Bodies moved aside and he made his way into the waiting room of the clinic. An avalanche of memories rolled over him. Everything was the same. The same scuffed linoleum floor, the same fake leather chairs, the same scarred wooden desk where the receptionist wrote down the names of patients in a heavy brown ledger.

The air in the packed waiting room was stuffy with the odor of too many bodies. A ripple of conversation met his arrival. "Mr. President," someone said in Uzbek.

Timur answered in the same language. "Today, I am a doctor," he replied. And when he said the words, he suddenly felt clean. For the first time in a long time, he felt like he had a purpose. Timur took off his jacket and draped it across the reception desk. Then he pushed open the door to the examination rooms in the back.

The smell made him want to gag. The meaty scent of blood, the sharpness of antiseptic, the sour smell of urine, and above all, the sickening heavy odor of charred flesh. It was not as noisy here, but the quiet was intense with muffled suffering.

There were four examination cubicles and they each held multiple patients. With the door closed behind him, Timur felt the eyes of the waiting patients on him.

"Where is the doctor?" he said.

As if in answer, a child's wail sounded from the closed door at the back of the room. Everyone's eyes turned toward the sound. It was the operating room. Timur knew that because he was the one who had set it up.

The child's cry suddenly stopped and it felt as if everyone held their breath.

He advanced to the door and pushed it open a few inches.

The room was small, no more than four meters square, and tiled all in white with a drain in the center of the floor. On one wall was a sink, on the opposite wall an autoclave for sterilizing instruments and a medicine cabinet. In the middle of the room was a stainless steel operating table illuminated by a bright overhead light.

A child lay on the table. Timur guessed the girl was four years old, and she was asleep. Her face was dirty and tearstains crossed her cheeks. Two women, both in scrubs with masks, bent over the girl's left leg, a bloody mess of tissue and bone. Someone had tied off the wound with a piece of baling wire wrapped around a blood-soaked makeshift bandage.

As he looked at the grievous wound, he realized what was about to happen.

An amputation.

The woman facing him looked up. She had large dark eyes that blazed with anger. "What do you want?" she demanded in a harsh voice.

"I'm a doctor," Timur said. "How can I help?"

She pointed a scalpel at him. "Triage the rest of the patients," she ordered.

Timur shut the door, faced the room. He felt the eyes of the patients looking at him, but for the first time in so long, he knew exactly what to do.

Timur lost all track of time as he buried himself in the work. He cleaned burns, stitched cuts, set a broken arm and a broken leg. He gave more tetanus shots than he could count. He told stories to the children as he plunged the needle in their arms. The doctor and her nurse performed a second amputation and sent both patients off in an ambulance to the hospital in Nukus some 135 kilometers to the southeast.

Slowly, the exam room emptied. More ambulances arrived and more of the badly wounded were transferred to Nukus. Timur followed the last transfer patient into the alley behind the clinic and slapped the side of the ambulance as it drove away.

He drew in a deep breath. The air still smelled of smoke, but the cloud over the city had dissipated. He raised his face to the sun and was surprised to see it was past noon. He looked at his watch. He'd been in the clinic for almost eight hours.

Timur watched the ambulance turn the corner and he waved. He felt alive, useful, fulfilled. More emotion than he'd felt in what seemed an eternity.

"Tea?"

The doctor held two cups and she handed him one. She was a plain-looking woman with bobbed dark hair and very large eyes. She considered him with a frank gaze.

"I'm sorry I didn't recognize you, Mr. President," she said finally, speaking in the local dialect.

Timur said nothing, sipped his tea.

"What are you doing here?" Her voice was sharp, accusing, and he looked at her in surprise. Her eyes held that same angry spark he'd seen when he'd interrupted her operation on the child.

"I—I—" Timur tried to find the words.

"I saw the cameras," she interrupted him. "Is this some kind of photo op?"

"No!" Timur found his voice. "My wife and I, we started this clinic. It was"—he tried to remember—"twenty-two, no, twenty-three years ago."

The doctor stared at him. Suddenly, the large, angry, dark eyes filled with tears. On instinct, Timur put his arms around her. Her shoulders shook as she sobbed.

"I'm sorry," she said into his chest, "but how could they do this?" She pushed back from him, swiped at her eyes with her fingers. "They're animals. In the middle of the night, they fired missiles into houses full of sleeping people. Families, children. Why? Why would the Chinese do such a thing?"

Timur blinked at her. Missiles? Jimmy said it was a terrorist attack. He grabbed her by the shoulders. "What happened? I was told this was a terrorist attack."

"Not unless the resistance suddenly started using drones and missiles." Her voice was bitterly angry again. "Twelve people died last night. Another thirty-seven wounded. I was hoping the President could tell me why."

Timur handed her the empty teacup. "I need to make a phone call."

He walked away, already dialing.

"Doc," came the answering voice, but Timur cut him off.

"You lied to me, you piece of shit."

"Hello to you, too. By the way, you look awesome on TV. Like Mother Teresa."

"Where are you?" Timur demanded.

"I took the helo back to Samarkand," Jimmy said in an airy voice. "I got a hot date tonight and I didn't want to miss it."

"You told me this was a terrorist attack. It was a drone attack. Carried out by the PLA."

"Now, Doc, we've already put out that it was a terrorist attack. That's our story and we're sticking to it."

Timur didn't say anything. He didn't know what to say.

"Doc? You still there?"

"What really happened?" Timur said. "Tell me."

Jimmy sighed. "The SIF got—"

"Stop it!" Timur interrupted. "There is no SIF. You know it and I know it, so just stop. Stop lying for one second and tell me what really happened."

"What happened?" Jimmy's voice grew testy. "What happened? The resistance got a weapons shipment in last night. Airdrop. Three trucks came out of the town, picked up the weapons, and went back home. We decided to take the necessary action."

Timur felt his stomach heave. "You shot missiles into homes? You had no idea who was in those buildings. There were children, old people, innocent people."

"Let's remember who the real enemy is here," Jimmy said. "You don't like it when I call them the SIF? Fine. Akhmet Orazov is a stone-cold killer who has murdered Chinese citizens. He's the criminal—and as long as he's alive, your people are going to continue to pay the price."

"You're an animal." Timur's voice shook.

"I think you're forgetting who you work for, Doc."

"Fuck you."

"You kiss your girlfriend with that mouth? By the way, speaking of Nicole, you and her'll need to drive yourselves back to Samarkand tonight. Who knows? Maybe you'll get lucky."

Jimmy's mocking laugh echoed in Timur's ears long after the line went dead.

35

Kyrkkyz, Uzbekistan

It was after eight in the evening when Nicole Nipper climbed into the back of the SUV with Timur Ganiev. Right away she could see there was something wrong with her traveling companion.

He was always solicitous to her—maybe a little *too* solicitous at times—but tonight it was as if she didn't exist. As their vehicle left the lights of Kyrkkyz behind, Timur stared out into the darkness of the empty desert plateau.

He was tired, she guessed, and who wouldn't be after the day he'd had. She'd seen a side of Timur she hadn't known even existed. She knew Timur the politician, the activist, and the orator, but until today she'd never seen Timur the caregiver.

Which one was the real Timur? she wondered. She'd followed him closely for almost a year now and had convinced herself that she knew the man. It disconcerted her that after all this time and effort she'd discovered in him something she hadn't seen before. If she wanted her documentary to really mean something, she needed to explore this new aspect of the man next to her.

At midday, Jimmy Li announced he was taking the helicopter back to

Samarkand. Nicole's camera crew, anxious to avoid a six-hour nighttime return trip by car, wanted to go with him.

Nicole refused. She was staying with Timur, she said, but the camera crew was not needed. Jimmy thought differently, of course—Jimmy Li always wanted someone with her—but Nicole dug in her heels. Her reporter's instinct told her that she needed to stay with her subject.

An argument ensued and Nicole was not proud of what happened next.

She threw a full-volume, prima-donna, privileged-Westerner, rich-bitch temper tantrum.

And it worked. The cowed crew left a small handheld camera and beat feet for the helo with creepy Jimmy Li.

Nicole spent the rest of the day on her own. Part of the time she spent watching Timur, trying to understand the change she saw in him. He truly cared for these people. She could see it in the way he spoke to them, and they responded in kind.

In the afternoon, she found a local teenager who spoke enough English for them to communicate. With his help, she managed to interview some of the people in the town. She heard the rumor that the attack was a false flag by the PLA to blame on the resistance, but that didn't make sense. She chalked it up to a translation issue. She'd pursue that lead later when she found someone who could do a proper translation of the interviews for her.

Nicole cut another look at Timur, who was still staring out the window, his outline dim in the soft dashboard lights. In the late afternoon, she interviewed an older woman who said that Timur had once been a doctor in the town. In fact, he and his late wife had opened the very clinic that he'd been in all day, caring for the wounded.

Maybe that was it, she wondered. Maybe the day brought back memories of his wife. This was good. It added another dimension to her documentary.

She startled when Timur touched her hand. In the dim light, his shadowed face looked haggard and worn. Normally, he came across as supremely confident, always cheerful and pleasant, but now he seemed hesitant. He leaned close to her.

"I'm going to tell the driver we want to stop for the night," he said in a low voice.

Nicole started to protest, but he held up his hand. "I need to speak with you. Privately. It's..." His voice trailed off as if he was searching for the right word, then he said, "...important. Please, Nicole."

The right answer was no. Ever since they'd met, Timur had made it clear he was interested in her. He made a few passes at her over the past year, but Nicole had stopped them all cold. Not that he wasn't an attractive man but sleeping with the subject of your story never ended well. Never.

"Timur," she replied in a whisper. "It's not going to happen."

Timur smiled, but it was a sad smile. "That's not what I'm after. I promise."

Nicole searched his face. Could she trust him? Finally, she nodded.

Timur returned to his side of the back seat. He spoke to the driver in Russian.

Nicole didn't know Russian, but she knew what *nyet* meant.

Timur spoke to him sharply and got another *nyet*. His face hardened and he made a show of dialing his mobile phone as the driver watched him in the rearview mirror. Nicole heard the faint voice of Jimmy Li answering, and the sound made her shiver with disgust. Slimy, arrogant prick who always seemed to be undressing her with his eyes. He liked to make comments to her camera crew in Mandarin while she was working. She didn't need a translator to know what they were saying.

Timur spoke in an angry voice and she heard Jimmy answer in his lazy, mocking tone that made her skin crawl.

Timur handed the phone to the driver and there was a short conversation in Mandarin. When he handed the phone back, he looked at Nicole and leered.

"Where you want to go?" he said in English.

These assholes thought they were arranging a booty call for Timur. Nicole opened her mouth, but Timur put a cautioning hand on her arm.

She bit her lip and said nothing.

Less than an hour later, Nicole sat on the bed in a hotel room. She had no overnight bag, but she always carried a toothbrush in her backpack, so that was something at least.

To call the hotel rustic was generous. As Timur checked in, she did the currency conversions in her head. The place was ten bucks a night. She'd checked her phone in the car and there were plenty of nicer places within a few minutes of this dump.

What was Timur after? He was a man who was used to the finer things in life. Why stay here?

Her room consisted of a double bed, a chair, and a nightstand with a lamp. No TV, no phone, not even an alarm clock. Facing the bed was a locked door connecting her room to the one next door, where Timur was staying.

When she realized they were staying in adjoining rooms, Nicole got that familiar queasy feeling, but Timur assured her.

"Please, trust me," he murmured to her in the hall. The driver was two doors down and across the hall. He threw her a knowing look as he entered his room.

Timur tapped on the closed door and Nicole blew out a long breath. She was putting a lot of trust in this guy, maybe too much.

She unlocked the door.

Timur had taken off his suit coat and tie and unbuttoned the top button of his shirt, but he looked far from relaxed. He paused in the doorway. "May I come in?"

Nicole hesitated again. This was a terrible idea. She stepped back from the door and sat on the edge of the bed. She gestured to the chair, to preclude him from joining her on the bed. He sat down in the chair and leaned forward, elbows on his knees. He breathed like he'd just run a race.

Nicole reached for her recorder on the nightstand, but Timur stopped her. "Please, I need to talk to you." He spoke softly, his voice pitched just above a whisper. "As a friend."

"I'm a reporter, Timur," Nicole said just as quietly, but with urgency. "I'm not your friend and we're not going to sleep together. I just want that to be clear before you say anything."

Timur barked out a laugh and she immediately regretted her words. His emotions seemed to boil just beneath the surface. Nicole sensed pain, anger—and fear. Lust was not in the mix.

Whatever he wanted to say, her reporter's instincts told her it was Big, with a capital B. She needed to tread carefully. Put him at ease, she told herself.

Nicole took a different tone. "You were magnificent today, Timur. I've never seen you as a caregiver. It was... inspiring."

Yes, she decided, that was the word. *Inspiring*. Damn, she wished her recorder was running. This stuff was solid-gold Pulitzer.

To her surprise, Timur's eyes filled with tears. His face was still as stone and he stared straight through her with glassy eyes.

Nicole held her breath.

"I need your help." Timur's voice came out in a choked whisper.

"I don't understand. Help with what?"

"I'm not the man you think I am." Timur licked his lips. He wiped his eyes, leaned forward on his elbows, then sat up straight again. She half expected him to jump out of the chair and rush back to his room.

Nicole sat perfectly still, silent. From hundreds of interviews, she knew the right thing to do in this moment was to do nothing.

Finally, whatever internal argument Timur was having with himself ended. His body stilled. He placed his hands on his knees and bent forward at the waist.

"I'm a Chinese agent," he said simply. "I've been one for as long as you've known me."

Nicole stared at him. This time, staying silent was not an interview tactic, it was shock.

Timur continued without any further hesitation, his voice pitched low, but clear and strong. He told her about his connection to the Chinese Minister of State Security and donations that later became bribes. He told her about the social media campaign to raise his profile across the region and promote the idea of a Central Asian Union. And he explained the Seljuk Islamic Front was a lie, another fabrication by the MSS.

Nicole raised her hand to make him stop. She looked around the room. Was it possible this place was bugged?

Timur seemed to read her mind. "We can talk here. That's why I chose this place."

Nicole nodded but did not relax. She'd been inside the Chinese surveillance state for too long.

When he finally finished talking, a full hour had passed and Nicole's brain was on fire. It made her furious that all the work she'd done so far was a waste—she was not going to make a propaganda film for the Chinese. But at the same time, *this*, this new story was HUGE. The story of the century. The man who would become the first President of the Central Asian Union was a Chinese spy, bought and paid for by the Ministry of State Security.

The story had everything: intrigue, international politics, a complex and compelling main character. And she had the exclusive.

"I can't do it anymore." Timur looked at the floor. "What I saw today... what the PLA is willing to do to my people. I can't be part of it anymore." He looked up, locked eyes with her. "I need your help."

"Of course," Nicole said. "I'll tell your story. Together, we'll—"

"No."

"No?"

He reached for her hand. "I don't want you to tell my story, Nicole. I want you to help me stop them."

"I'm a reporter." Nicole tried to extract her hand, but he tightened his grip.

"You're also a human being. Today, I watched a four-year-old girl lose a leg because of what I did three years ago. I need to make it right. I need your help. This is not a story, Nicole, these are peoples' lives."

"I—I can't get involved."

"Please."

She'd seen Timur Ganiev speak dozens of times and she'd seen his powers of persuasion. *Please*. The word rattled around in her mind and she thought about the people she'd seen that day and how he'd cared for them. Was it possible she'd finally met the real Timur?

Nicole pulled her hand from his. She took a deep breath.

"What do you need me to do?"

36

Tashkent, Uzbekistan

The United States Embassy in Tashkent looked like a prison. A nice prison, Nicole thought, as she surveyed the four-story limestone-and-glass structure behind layered defenses, but a prison all the same.

She parked her rental car in the visitor's parking lot and walked under the gaze of who knew how many cameras to the guardhouse. She walked through the retractable bollards designed to foil car bombers and approached the uniformed guard seated behind a shield of bulletproof glass. She dropped her passport into the open drawer and spoke into the microphone.

"Nicole Nipper. I have an appointment."

The bored Uzbek guard inspected the passport and pressed a button to buzz her through the steel door. Inside the gatehouse, she found a small waiting room and more cameras. A very efficient young lady had her sign in, took her picture, issued a visitor badge, then escorted Nicole out of the gatehouse.

Nicole's US passport looked brand-new, which made perfect sense because she rarely used it. Even though she had dual citizenship with the United States and the United Kingdom, she invariably traveled using her

UK identification. The US passport had visa stamps on fewer than six pages, which made the reason for her visit to Tashkent nothing short of ridiculous. Any moment now, she expected someone to leap out and cry, *Liar!*

As she followed the young woman across the courtyard to the main building, Nicole tried to get control of her emotions. In the moment when she'd agreed to help Timur, her actions felt right, noble. But now, when she was lying to gain entry into a US government facility, it seemed like the height of stupidity.

A man with blond hair and a big smile held the door for them. "Have a great day," he said in a cheerful voice.

Nicole thought her face might break if she tried to crack a smile, so she just nodded at the man and followed her escort inside.

Their destination was a window labeled Passport Services, located in a hallway off the main foyer. Two rows of vinyl-upholstered chairs lining the wall were empty. A middle-aged woman slid open the window and took her documents.

"How can I help you?" she asked.

"I, um, need new pages," Nicole said in a small voice.

The woman flipped the book open and compared Nicole to the photo. Then she flicked through the pages with practiced fingers. Most of them were blank.

Nicole leaned down. "That's not really why I'm here," she said quietly.

The page flicking ceased. The consular officer looked up. Nicole could not read her expression, but her hand moved under her desk.

Oh my God, she thinks I'm some kind of terrorist.

"I need to talk to someone in the CIA," Nicole blurted out in an urgent whisper.

"Excuse me?" The woman still had her hand under the desk.

"An intelligence officer," Nicole said. "I have...information."

The woman's squinting blue eyes relaxed the tiniest bit. She nodded at the chairs in the hall. "Have a seat, please." She slid the window closed and picked up the telephone handset.

Nicole sat. Her legs quivered, and she could not seem to stop sweating. Why had she agreed to do this?

She saw an armed Marine appear where she'd entered via the foyer. A second one posted at the other end of the hallway. Nicole stared straight ahead at the shuttered passport window.

Ten minutes dragged by before a new sound hit her ears. Whistling. Some jaunty tune that she sort of recognized, but she was so nervous now that her brain refused to work.

A young man passed by the stone-faced Marine in the foyer and walked toward her. He was dressed in khakis, a blue blazer, and a red tie, and he walked with a loose stride as he whistled. He came to a complete stop in front of Nicole and held up her open passport. His eyes traveled from the document to her face.

"Nicole Nipper," he announced.

Nicole tried to smile and failed.

"Jack Harris." He held out a large hand that engulfed hers and he used the connection to draw her to her feet. "Let's find a place to chat, shall we?"

He set off toward the foyer without waiting for an answer. "Do I know you from somewhere?" He nodded to the Marine as they walked past.

"I'm a reporter," Nicole said. "I used to be with the BBC. Now, I'm freelance."

He snapped his fingers. "That's it. You're the embed with the new President of the CAU, right? President Ganiev?"

She smiled weakly, exhaling. "That's me."

He waved a key card over the lock of a door near the main entrance. "We reserve these rooms for walk-ins," he said. "Like you."

The room was small, barely three meters square, with a round table and two chairs. Nicole noted the camera in the corner of the ceiling.

Harris dropped into his chair as if he was a puppet whose strings had been cut. He swung one leg over the other. "How can the United States government help you today, Ms. Nipper?"

"I have information that I need to get to the CIA," she said.

Harris's smile was plastic. "I see. What kind of information are we talking about, ma'am?"

Nicole took a deep breath, then plunged ahead. "Timur Ganiev sent me. He is a Chinese asset and he wishes to help the United States in any way he can."

Harris's mouth fell open, then snapped closed again. "Okay, then. Didn't see that coming." He uncrossed his legs, leaned his elbows on the table. "Why don't you start at the beginning, Ms. Nipper? Take your time and include as many details as you can remember."

Nicole nodded. Now that she'd actually said it out loud, the pressure in her chest eased and she could breathe again.

You're a reporter, she thought. Details are your job.

She began to speak, then immediately stopped.

"Are you going to write any of this down?" she asked.

"Don't worry, Ms. Nipper, everything you tell me is being recorded. Take your time and start at the beginning."

The beginning was her first interview with Timur Ganiev, over a year ago now. She described how she'd shadowed him before the terrorist attack at the Samarkand Jade Spike ceremony and how she'd been asked to stay on as an embed after the PLA descended on the region. She told them about how Timur had been blackmailed into inviting the PLA into Central Asia and how he was being managed by the Chinese MSS.

"You said his handler's name is Jimmy Li?" Harris said.

"Yes, he works for Surfan Oil and Gas. A Vice President, I think, but he's actually a case officer. Timur told me he really works for the Ministry of State Security."

Harris nodded, but she had the impression that this was not new information for him.

When she finished speaking, her throat was dry. "May I have some water?"

"Of course." Harris left the room.

Nicole let out a long sigh and closed her eyes. A strange sense of euphoria rose in her chest. It was done. They believed her and now they'd help Timur and she could go back to being a reporter again. The sweat that seemed to leak from every pore just a few minutes ago was drying, leaving her skin clammy in the air conditioning.

Harris returned after a few minutes and handed her a bottled water. Nicole opened it and drank greedily. Harris sat with folded hands, waited for her to finish.

"Wow," he said finally, "that is quite a story. Can I ask you a few questions?"

Nicole nodded. Somehow, she'd expected a more enthusiastic response.

"What is the nature of your relationship with Mr. Ganiev?"

"I told you. I'm a reporter. He's my story."

"Are you two...close?"

Nicole twisted the cap back on the water bottle. "You mean, are we sleeping together?"

"I mean how close are you with Mr. Ganiev? It's important that we understand why you're here today."

Nicole felt heat crawl up her neck. "I told you. He asked me to help him. I agreed. That's it."

"That's a big ask, Ms. Nipper. You're a reporter."

"I'm trying to do the right thing here, Mr. Harris," she said stiffly.

"I'm sure you are, ma'am. What about Mr. Ganiev? What does he want out of all this?"

"I told you: he wants to help."

Harris wrinkled his nose like she'd said something wrong. Then he sat up straight in his chair and clapped his hands together. "Well, thank you for coming in today, Ms. Nipper. I will review this information and we'll be in touch if we have any more questions. In the meantime, I'll keep your passport and get those pages added. You can pick it up tomorrow morning first thing."

"But I—"

Harris put out his hand. "Thank you for coming in, ma'am."

"Don't you need to—"

"Ms. Nipper, you've given us a lot to think about and I'm sure you're tired. If you need a hotel, I suggest the Intercontinental. If you mention the embassy, you can get a great discount."

He did the thing again where he used a handshake to pull her out of her seat and then urged her toward the door. Five minutes later, Nicole was standing in the sunshine next to her rental car.

What the hell had just happened? she wondered, feeling the rise of anger in her gut. Nicole turned around, started back for the gatehouse.

Maybe they hadn't understood that she was offering the President of the Central Asian Union as a spy for the United States.

After a few steps, she stopped. Harris had understood her perfectly well. He just hadn't believed her. She thought about his questions regarding their relationship. Was it so hard to believe that she hadn't slept with Timur? Maybe they thought she'd been jilted and this was a revenge play.

Fuck them, she thought, and their dirty minds. She toyed with the idea of just leaving her passport there and driving back to Samarkand tonight, but she was so tired. After a sleepless night, there was no way she could face a five-hour drive right now. What she needed was a drink or three and a bed.

She put the Intercontinental Hotel into her GPS app and laughed when she saw the location. The hotel overlooked the Amir Temur Square in central Tashkent, a park in honor of the fourteenth-century ruler so often invoked by supporters of Timur Ganiev.

Who says irony is dead?

She mentioned the embassy discount at the front desk and the young man helping her brightened. "Absolutely, madam." He tapped at his computer, then leaned across the desk. "I can offer you an upgrade to a penthouse suite for the same price as a regular room. It has a magnificent view. Truly magical."

"Well, if it's magical, I guess I can't refuse," Nicole replied. The young man didn't get the sarcasm. The failure of her visit suddenly weighed her down. "Yes, I'll take it. Thank you."

She waved off the porter since she had only her backpack and made her way to the elevator. She had to put her room key into the slot to gain access to the penthouse level.

The elevator doors opened onto a marble foyer. Straight ahead a set of carved wood double doors stood open, revealing a salon with white leather furniture. Nicole walked in, her feet sinking into the thick woolen carpet. To her right, the open bedroom door showed a massive four-poster king bed piled with pillows. To her left, a long bar, fully stocked, and a dining table.

"Holy crap," Nicole muttered. She dropped her backpack onto the leather sofa and kicked off her shoes. Her toes burrowed into the luxurious carpet.

A drink, a bath, and room service, she thought. A gentle breeze wafted through the open sliding door and she walked onto the patio. The sun was setting over Tashkent, turning the ancient city into a tableau of golden light and long shadows.

"Beautiful, isn't it?" The voice made her whirl around.

A man held up open palms. "Don't be afraid, Ms. Nipper."

He was her height, slim build, with ragged gray hair and beard. He was a white man, but deeply tanned, and he spoke with an American accent. He wore a plain white shirt and blue jeans, but his boots were scuffed and dusty.

Nicole swallowed. She'd left her phone in her purse. Behind the man, she could see that the heavy double doors leading into the apartment were closed. "Who are you?" she demanded.

He smiled, a slash of white in his tanned features. "My name is Harrison Kohl. I work for the CIA."

37

Van, Turkey

Using the telescope set up on the flagstone patio of the villa, Don studied the magnified image of the Fortress of Van in the brilliant morning sun. A pamphlet from his room informed Don that the massive stone fortification was one of the best-preserved examples of the power of the Urartu kingdom, which had ruled this region from the ninth to the seventh century BC.

Don had absolutely no idea what the Urartu kingdom was, but they clearly built castles to stand the test of time.

In this land where modern-day Armenia, Turkey, and Iran met, history oozed from the landscape. Don tried to wrap his mind around the fact that he was looking at a structure that was three thousand years old and he failed.

The modern villa, a private residence, had not been selected for its historic surroundings but rather for its proximity to Central Asia. The Director had insisted that Don's meeting with Harrison and Akhmet Orazov take place in Turkey, so Don had found a secluded location in the far east of the country.

And it was secluded. Although the city of Van, with a population of a half million people, was only twenty kilometers away, it might as well have been on another planet. The villa perched on a bluff overlooking Lake Van with million-dollar views of unspoiled landscape and ancient castles. The loudest sound was the soughing of the wind and there was zero light pollution out here. When Don arrived the previous night, the star scape looked like sequins on a black velvet dress.

He spied a plume of dust on the road leading up to the villa and swung the telescope to spy on his arriving guests. A black SUV with a driver and a security man in the front passenger seat was all that he could see.

He went back inside and hit the restroom. He splashed water on his face, finger-combed his hair, and tucked in his shirt. "You need to be firm with Orazov," he ordered his reflection. Information needs to flow both ways. With that affirmation in mind, he went to meet his guests.

The SUV entered the paved courtyard and pulled to a stop under the portico that sheltered the front door. The rear door opened and Harrison got out.

His friend had always been in good shape, but now Harrison was wiry and moved lightly on his feet as he crossed to Don. Harrison wore dusty jeans and boots, with a khaki shirt and earth-tone neckerchief. His deeply tanned face split into a smile.

"Don." He hugged his friend fiercely. "Good to see you, boss."

Don returned the embrace, then he stiffened as the driver shut the rear door of the vehicle.

"Where's Orazov?" he demanded.

Harrison stepped back, met Don's glare. "He won't leave the region, Don. I'm sorry."

How in the hell was he going to explain this back in Washington? The rebel leader that they'd been supporting with millions of dollars in weapons over the last six months refused to meet with the guy paying for his rebellion.

"Dammit!" he shouted, all his frustration packed into two explosive syllables.

"I tried to warn you, Don."

And he had, but Don assumed that when push came to shove, Orazov would realize how much he needed Don and he'd show up as directed.

Your bluff has been called, Riley, he thought bitterly. He turned on his heel and stalked inside.

Harrison followed him out to the patio. "Wow," he exclaimed when he saw the glassy expanse of Lake Van.

"Don't get too excited," Don snapped. "You're here to work."

Harrison paused at the railing. "You shouldn't have forced the issue, Don. You know what Akhmet's like."

Don ignored the comment. "I assume you can speak for him?"

Harrison shrugged. "I can speak *to* him and I'm pretty sure he'll listen to me, but that's all I can promise."

"I need real answers, Harrison. Akhmet needs to cooperate with us. Share information. I can pull the plug on this thing, you know."

Harrison walked to the bar. "I know. But you won't. You and I both know what's at stake."

Don watched as Harrison poured himself two fingers of scotch, then settled into the massive sofa. Don plopped down opposite Harrison, still miffed.

"It's five o'clock somewhere," Harrison said as he downed his drink.

Don studied his friend and colleague. Harrison had always been rough around the edges, a no-nonsense guy who didn't mind ruffling feathers if it got the job done. But the man who sat before him had changed. There was an air of bitterness that Don had never seen before.

He was also flat-out exhausted. Harrison had been in the field over a year and it showed.

"I'm bringing a doctor in to give you a full physical," Don said.

"We don't have time for that, Don. You know it and I know it." He set down the empty glass on the marble coffee table and pointed to the pile of papers between them. "Shall we?"

They talked for an hour, then moved to the dining room for lunch. They pushed their empty plates aside and kept talking.

"I need to know where these arms shipments are going, Harrison," Don insisted. "If these weapons show up on the black market somewhere, we're screwed."

For the last eight weeks, Orazov had put in place alternate shipping routes from depots in Kazakhstan across the border into Central Asia. Don had no visibility into where the weapons were going.

"The PLA surveillance network is getting more adept at predicting our shipping routes. He's taking precautions," Harrison said. The weariness in his voice told how tired he was to be going over the same issue again.

"They're Mafia!" Don said. "Literally, guys in black leather jackets are picking up Stinger missiles and driving away—and we're letting them do it!"

"Akhmet knows what he's doing, Don. I trust him, and you should, too."

"Trust." Don didn't even try to hide the condescension in his voice. "Trust works both ways."

Harrison shook his head. "C'mon, Don."

"We're working with a guy who won't even tell us how many men he actually has in the field, Harrison, much less where he has them positioned. Do you have that information?"

"You know I don't, Don," Harrison said patiently. They'd been over this, too.

"Why do you trust him?"

Harrison pivoted. "Tell me about the PLA network pen test."

Don sighed. "We're in the Huawei backbone, so we can see routine comms and assess the volume of traffic across the secure network, but we're locked out of Foresight."

"They actually call it Foresight?" Harrison asked.

Don nodded. "That's a rough translation, but yeah. Our best guess is that they have a predictive algorithm running on a quantum platform in Xinjiang."

"And we can't get inside? It's that secure?"

Don leaned forward. "Triple authentication procedures. Password, biometrics, then a voice print that has to be done over the Huawei backbone. The list of users is tightly controlled, so if anyone else is on the system they'll know. Oh, and the user has to be reauthenticated every twelve hours. Noon and midnight."

Harrison sat back in his chair. "Wow. I guess they learned their lesson after Taiwan."

Don's stomach churned with acid. It was hard to ignore the feeling of impotence that always lurked in the back of his mind these days. Every action he took seemed designed to draw them deeper into this conflict. Was this what the early days of Vietnam felt like? Or Iraq or Afghanistan? Was he doing the right thing?

"We're running out of time," Harrison said. "Every day, the PLA surveillance network expands, cuts down on our ability to operate. We need to change the variables in the equation, Don." Harrison looked out over the lake. "We need to shut it down."

"If you've got an idea, I'm all ears," Don said sullenly.

"An EMP device," Harrison said. "Wipe out the Huawei network. That gives Akhmet a chance to launch a counterattack."

Don shook his head before Harrison even finished. "No way. An EMP is like a billboard that says *The CIA was here*. Remember, the PLA was invited into the region. This is not Taiwan. Here the Chinese are the saviors, not the aggressors."

"What about Whisper?" Harrison said. Whisper was the codename for Timur Ganiev. "Can he uninvite them?"

Harrison was now the handler for the CIA's newest asset in Central Asia. With Nicole Nipper acting as their go-between, Ganiev had yielded useful intel, but nothing that was actionable yet.

They were playing a very dangerous game and Harrison was developing their asset with care. Ganiev had no training in operational security, and he was under the thumb of the Ministry of State Security.

"Right now, we need to make sure Whisper stays in place," Don said. "He's our best source for what's going on with the PLA. If everything else goes to shit, at least we'll have him as an asset."

"You mean if Akhmet gets wiped out." It wasn't a question and Don felt the edge of bitterness in his colleague's tone.

"Yeah, Harrison," Don snapped. "If Akhmet gets whacked, Whisper might be the only window we'll have into the Chinese takeover of Central Asia. We need to keep him clean."

Harrison got up and walked to the patio. The sun had set, leaving the dark horizon bruised with deep oranges and reds. Don joined him at the railing, looking out on the extraordinary natural beauty with a sour gaze. His head throbbed, maybe from the altitude or the stress or the fact that he was going to tell the President of the United States that after months of careful planning, they should abandon their operation in Central Asia.

The night air was sharp and still. Lake Van shone like quicksilver in the moonlight.

"Look, Harrison, this is not working out how—"

"What if we had another way into the Foresight network?" Harrison interrupted. He fished his mobile from his pocket and swiped to his saved photos. Don squinted at the glaring screen. It was a Chinese man. Young, styled hair, wearing Ray-Bans, a jacket thrown over his shoulder like he was a model for GQ.

"That's Jimmy Li," Don said.

"Does he have access to Foresight?" Harrison asked.

"Yeah, he's on the access list." Don's head ached and he wanted to go to bed. "Why?"

"If we got his cooperation, could we get into Foresight?"

"You think we can recruit Jimmy Li?" Don laughed. "Even if we could make an approach, it would take months. We don't have that kind of time."

"I didn't say recruit, Don. I said *cooperate*," Harrison explained. "If he's an authorized user, then he could get us inside Foresight, yes?"

Blobs clouded Don's vision from the bright light of the mobile screen. He could not see Harrison's face. "It's theoretically possible, yes."

Harrison's voice crackled with excitement. "Don, this is the break we've been waiting for."

38

8 kilometers east of Jyrgalan, Kyrgyzstan

All Serik Amangeldi wanted to do was drive his truck and get paid. No shady deals, no easy money, just regular work for regular pay. He'd told his uncle that a hundred times, but the old man would not listen.

"We need the money, Serik," he said. "Think of your poor mother."

"You think of my mother, you stupid bastard," he said out loud even though he was alone in the cab of the Hino 916 truck.

Serik hunched over the steering wheel and squinted into the darkness ahead. The fog rising off the Jyrgalan River reflected his headlights back at him, forcing Serik to slow down. Thick trees floated in the misty verge of the single-lane dirt track. He rolled down the window and let the moisture-laden air cool his sweaty face.

The illuminated face of his wristwatch glared at him. He was late and the people he was driving for were all about punctuality. The road started to rise out of the valley and he cursed as the grade forced him to downshift.

Then the truck broke through the fog and he saw a crescent moon hanging above the horizon. The trees thinned and a meadow appeared through his open window.

Was this it? Serik pulled the truck to the side of the road and picked up the map off the seat next to him. In the dim light of the cab, he studied the folded paper, his finger tracing his path of the last eight hours.

He'd picked up the load at Taldykorgan Airport in Kazakhstan promptly at five in the afternoon. As usual, while a crew loaded the soft-sided cargo container on his truck chassis, he was forced to surrender his mobile phone and GPS. In exchange, they handed him a paper map with his route traced in pencil.

The destination was his first clue that this run was different than the twenty or so deliveries he'd made over the past four months. Crossing the border from Kazakhstan into one of the Central Asian republics was normal, but on all the previous occasions, they'd specified a fixed destination. A garage in Bishkek or the parking lot of a tavern outside of Tashkent, all places with fixed addresses. As near as Serik could tell, this was just a random spot in the middle of nowhere.

The drill was always the same: park the truck, leave the keys in the ignition, and return in one hour to find an envelope of cash on the driver's seat and an empty truck. All he had to do was drive home.

Although he always picked up his loads *near* major distribution centers, they were never *in* the transportation hubs. Usually, the warehouses were a few blocks away in a secure building with lots of cameras and men with guns.

Serik wasn't an idiot. He knew his uncle was making deliveries for an organized crime ring, but there was more to it than that. While the guys who gave him the maps and delivery instructions were locals, he'd seen the English words on the crates and he'd heard American English being spoken in the warehouse.

It was only by accident that Serik figured out he was running guns across the border into Central Asia. One of his deliveries had been to a tavern. As usual, he followed his instructions and left the truck in the parking lot. It wasn't his fault that the men arrived to unload his cargo at the same time as Serik went to the restroom and just happened to peek out the open window.

The crew arrived in four Toyota pickups. They posted guards with AK-47s at either end of the parking lot and quickly divided up the load into the four waiting vehicles. They were gone in less than ten minutes.

The speed with which they unloaded his truck was not what made an impression at the time. He'd watched one of the men pry open one of the long crates and pull out a 1.5-meter object that looked like a length of heavy pipe with a box attached. He watched the man flip up the gunsight.

Serik stepped back from the window and flattened his sweaty back against the wall. He'd seen enough movies and played enough video games to recognize a Stinger missile when he saw one in real life.

His uncle was unperturbed by Serik's news. "Do you think they're paying us all this money to move watermelons across the border?"

"What if I get stopped?" Serik demanded. "There's PLA roadblocks everywhere."

His uncle sipped his tea and looked at Serik like he was an idiot. "Have you ever been stopped?"

"No." It was true. He'd never been held up at the border and he'd never been stopped at a PLA roadblock. At least, he hadn't been stopped on the way to make a delivery. He'd been stopped at least a half dozen times on the way back to Kazakhstan in his empty truck.

"Why not? Think about it, nephew."

Serik thought about the maps and the strict timetable and the specific routes he was given each time. He'd never delivered to the same place twice and never used the same route. "They're watching me," he said.

His uncle rolled his eyes. "They don't give a shit about you. They care about the cargo."

"I don't want to do it anymore," Serik said. "It's too dangerous."

"Think about your mother," his uncle replied. "What would your dear father want you to do?"

By the dome light in the cab of the truck, Serik read the scrawled note next to a circled village on the map. *10.5 km past town. Meadow at top of hill.*

He'd been so focused on making up lost time that he hadn't checked the odometer when he passed through the last town. He looked at his watch, trying to estimate how much time had passed, but even that was useless. The heavy fog in the river valley made him speed up and slow down.

Serik cursed to himself. Had he traveled ten kilometers? Maybe he should drive farther down the track to see if there was another hill and another clearing. But if he was wrong, he'd be even later.

Serik made up his mind. He turned off the dome light, shut off the truck engine, and killed the headlights. The night closed in around him like a fist. After being subjected to hours of diesel engine noise and rushing wind, his ears rang in the silence.

His instructions tonight were to stay with the truck until they asked him for the package, but his legs itched with anticipation, and he desperately wanted to get out and walk around.

Minutes passed and Serik's stomach curdled with rising panic. He'd missed them or they were waiting for him at some other clearing a few kilometers away. Then another thought struck him: If no one showed up, what was he going to do with a truckload of weapons? They'd taken his mobile phone, and besides, who would he call? He was going to be sick. His hand moved for the door latch, then he froze.

A light appeared on the road ahead. Not headlights, just one small light in the dark, bobbing like it was on the water. Too small for a motorcycle and too slow for a bicycle. It was a flashlight, he decided. Serik held his breath as the light drew closer.

Out of the darkness a man appeared riding a donkey, holding a flashlight, and leading a train of sixteen more pack animals. Serik was just about to call out to the man when a cold button of steel pressed against the base of his skull.

"Be silent," said a quiet voice in Russian. "Look straight ahead, put your hands on the steering wheel, and do not say anything. Do you understand?"

Serik wasn't sure if the "do not say anything" rule applied to saying yes, so he just nodded.

He heard car engines, at least three of them, approach from behind the truck. One of the donkeys made a braying noise and a man shushed him. The truck rocked as people got in the back and he heard and felt heavy boxes being shifted. Men's voices, low and urgent. The slam of a tailgate and ghostly red shadows from brake lights. Out of the corner of his eye, Serik saw the train of donkeys, now laden with smaller boxes, strike out across the meadow. Two Toyota Land Cruisers passed the truck headed down the dirt track. The third vehicle idled behind Serik's truck.

The man with the gun was still outside his window. He could hear his breathing, Serik didn't dare look back. Another man approached and there was a whispered conversation.

What were they talking about? They still hadn't asked for the package. Maybe that was it. The box was behind Serik's seat in the cab. He should tell them.

"Wait—" he began, but the man with the gun cut him off. The muzzle of the rifle ground into the skin behind his ear so hard that Serik felt tears spring into his eyes.

"I said be silent," the man growled.

Serik felt his bladder let go. Shame and fear and panic all mixed into one ugly emotion and he started to gag.

I'm going to die, Serik thought. I'm going to die by the side of the road in a foreign country and it's all my fucking uncle's fault.

The pressure on the base of his skull disappeared. Something lofted through the open window and landed in Serik's lap. He heard the tires of the last vehicle grind in the dirt as the taillights disappeared down the track behind him.

Serik gulped air. He was alone. Alive.

He picked up the object in his lap. An envelope, stuffed with money. He rested his forehead on the steering wheel and sobbed with relief. He reached for the keys to start the truck, then stopped.

What about the package? Serik felt behind his seat. It was still there, sealed in plastic. They didn't ask for the package. Serik had no idea what was in it, but there was no way he was going to cross the border with that in his truck.

The feeble dome light came on when he stumbled out of the cab. His limbs were weak and his hands shook as he reached behind the driver's seat and pulled out the package. He dropped it on the seat.

It was the size of a shoebox, but heavy and solid, like it was filled with bricks. There was no movement inside the container when he shifted it. The box was plain brown cardboard, no markings, sealed with tape on all edges and wrapped with heavy plastic.

They were supposed to ask him for the package. The instructions Serik had been given were crystal clear. But they hadn't asked, so what the hell was he supposed to do now?

Throw it away, he decided, and get out of here. And never, ever drive for these people again. If his uncle wanted the money, he could drive.

He gripped the edge of the seat and dug his fingernails into the cracked vinyl. That would never work.

Bury it! He'd bury the package. That way, if they wanted to know where it was, he could tell them.

"*Zdravstvuyte*," said a voice behind him.

Serik screamed and spun around. The man who stood a few paces away was shorter than Serik and thin. A fringe of gray hair poked out from beneath a black watch cap and his unshaven face was gaunt. He wore a rucksack on his back with an aluminum frame that poked up over his head.

"Sorry to startle you," the man said in Russian.

Serik blinked. The man was obviously ethnic Chinese, but he was speaking in schoolboy Russian.

"What do you want?" Serik said in the same language.

"Pick up package."

"Package?" The word took a moment to register, but then relief flooded into Serik's body and he broke into a grin. "Of course." He seized the box on the seat and practically threw it at the man.

"*Spasibo*."

The man weighed it in his hands, then slipped the backpack frame off his shoulders. He secured the box inside the pack, then hoisted the rucksack back into place. He nodded to Serik.

"Good luck, young man." He disappeared into the darkness of the meadow.

Serik blinked. His gut churned with fear, his pants were damp with piss, and his whole body shook.

None of that mattered. He was alive.

He scrambled into the cab, started the engine, and drove away.

39

10 kilometers sought of Dzarkutan, Tajikistan

The back seat of the minivan smelled of dust, cigarette smoke, and some sort of barnyard animal. The dust was from the dirt road they'd been on for the last twenty minutes and the driver smoked like a chimney.

The van drew to a halt. The driver's side door opened and she heard him get out. A few seconds later, the sliding door next to her head ground open.

"You can sit up now, miss," the driver said in English.

Nicole pulled the blanket off her head and sat up in the darkness. Fresh air flooded into the vehicle and she breathed deeply of the damp night air. She heard the rush of a stream and the distant sound of bleating sheep.

Barnyard animal identified, she thought.

The driver walked away, lighting yet another cigarette, and another man took his place in the open doorway. She recognized Harrison Kohl's slim figure.

"Sorry about all the cloak and dagger, Nicole," he said and she could hear the humor in his voice. "We felt it was necessary."

"Why?" Nicole wasn't sure if she was annoyed or intrigued. After all, this was their fifth meeting. All her prior debriefs with Harrison had gone off without a hitch. Why was this one different?

"You'll see," Harrison said, holding out his hand to help her out of the van.

Typical, thought Nicole, she was the one taking all the risks—and not just security risks either. These people were dragging her reputation through the mud.

An affair with Timur had been Harrison's idea. He convinced her it was the perfect cover for Timur to pass her the intel and for her to slip away to brief her CIA handler. Harrison selected the hotels for their supposed trysts. She and Timur arrived separately, always at night, knowing that he was under surveillance by the MSS. After she had the intel from Timur and he'd departed, she met Harrison for a debrief. Sometimes in another room at the same hotel, sometimes in a nearby location.

The only drawback to the subterfuge was the knowing looks she got the next day when her camera crew asked her how she'd spent her evening. Her face burned when she lied and even though she knew her embarrassment only improved her cover story, it made her hate the whole process.

At first, she'd worried that Timur might try to take advantage of the situation and tell her they needed to sleep together for the sake of their cover. Her fears proved groundless. Timur was a changed man, a man whose only goal was atoning for the sin of betraying his people.

He took risks to get the intelligence Harrison pressed him for. He asked to tour the PLA operations center in Ayni Air Base and provided detailed descriptions of everything he saw, including sketches of interior layouts. He went drinking with Jimmy Li and pumped the MSS agent for information. Over the protests of his closest advisors, he gave press conferences in support of PLA operations. But the most galling to Nicole was how he played along when the camera crew leered at Nicole after their nights together.

In spite of all that, Nicole felt herself growing closer to Timur in a way that surprised her. The impartiality that she'd worked so hard to maintain between them eroded to the point that she thought she would sleep with him if he asked her.

But he didn't. Somehow, that made him even more desirable.

"Nicole," Harrison asked.

"What?" she said, realizing she'd missed his question.

"How is Timur tonight? What's his mood?"

"What's his mood?" Nicole considered the question. He'd been different tonight, she realized, but she struggled to come up with the right description. At peace, maybe? Happy?

"He seems content," she said finally.

"Hmm." Harrison slid the door of the van closed. It sounded loud in the quiet night. He didn't elaborate further on Nicole's assessment. Instead, he said, "Are your eyes adjusted? We have a bit of a walk ahead of us."

He took a path through the tall grass on the side of the road, heading toward the sound of rushing water. They passed through a fringe of trees. "Watch your step on the bridge, please."

"Where are we going?" she asked.

"You'll see," Harrison called over the rush of the stream.

"What time is it? I have to get back." They had taken her phone.

Harrison continued on without answering. They walked through another line of trees into an open meadow. A hundred meters distant, by the light of the moon, she could make out a small cabin. There was a dim yellow light in the window and solar panels gleamed silver on the roof.

Harrison strode along, head down, and Nicole hurried to keep up with him.

"You're not answering my questions, Harrison."

"You're right. I'm not." They were less than twenty meters from the front porch of the cabin. Someone moved across the light inside. She'd never been debriefed by anyone other than Harrison.

Then a terrifying thought struck her. She was in the middle of nowhere with a man she barely knew. A man who *said* he was from the CIA and had asked her to spy for the Americans, but did she really *know* he was from the CIA? It wasn't like she was going to start googling CIA operatives from the computer that the MSS was surely monitoring.

What did she really know about Harrison Kohl? What if this was an elaborate sting operation designed to entrap her for some reason she didn't even understand?

"Stop!" Her voice was sharper and louder than she intended and she could hear the fear there.

Harrison paused on the steps. He turned. "Nicole, it's all right. I promise."

"I'm not going anywhere or telling you anything until I know why I'm here." Her breathing was heavy and ragged. Her mind clicked through possibilities. Assuming she could find the trail through the forest in the dark, she could get back to the road. Then what? She hadn't seen the way they'd come and she didn't have her phone.

"Nicole." Harrison's voice was warm and comforting—exactly the way a killer might sound before he stuck her with a knife. "Trust me."

"No! I—"

The door behind Harrison opened and warm yellow light poured into the night. A man stood in the doorway. He was on the shorter side, but heavily built with the shoulders of a wrestler. He had short gray hair and a carefully trimmed gray beard. His eyes were hidden in shadow.

"Ms. Nipper, my name is Akhmet Orazov. It is a pleasure to make your acquaintance."

Nicole's breath hitched. She was meeting with the head of the resistance forces. Was that a good thing? Her adrenaline-stressed brain struggled to make a decision.

Orazov stepped outside and walked down the steps. He extended his hand and Nicole took it. The callused palm felt like she was shaking hands with a bear. He put an arm around her shoulders and urged her forward.

"Please," he said. "It is a chilly night. I have prepared hot tea for you."

Nicole allowed herself to be escorted up the steps and inside the cabin. Harrison closed the door behind them.

It was a war room, she realized. The walls were covered with maps tacked in place with nails. Mug of tea in hand, she walked the perimeter of the room. The laminated maps were creased and worn and covered in black grease pencil marks.

She paused at the detailed topographical map of the area around Ayni Air Base near Dushanbe. There was a neat list adjacent to the outlined base.

Nicole moved closer to read the words: two squadrons of combat aircraft, including how many fighters and ground attack jets. Two divisions of PLA soldiers, with exact tallies of armor, infantry fighting vehicles, and artillery. Further out from the base, she noticed black X marks and abbreviated names with numbers in parentheses. She pointed at the marks. "What are these?"

Harrison started to shake his head, but Orazov held up a hand. "Those are my men," he said. "The code name of the cell leader and the number of men in his command."

Nicole moved to the next map and scanned it. Khujand Air Base in Tajikistan had two squadrons of PLA attack and transport helos and two brigades of ground troops. Fuel depot, ammunition warehouse, and other notes described the base.

Nicole's eyes jumped from one X to another, but it took her a moment to see the pattern. The resistance cells surrounded the PLA bases, taking advantage of the rough mountain terrain. She did a rough estimate of the force numbers on that map alone. They numbered in the hundreds and there were at least ten maps on the walls of this room. That was thousands of men in Akhmet's resistance forces.

She turned to Orazov. "Why did you bring me here?"

The resistance leader cradled a teacup in his heavy palm. "I wanted to meet you."

Nicole waited. He was lying and making no attempt to hide it. She heard Harrison chuckle softly.

"Ussat," he said, "I don't think she's buying what you're selling."

"No, I'm not," Nicole said, making a mental note to ask about the name Ussat.

Orazov sighed, but they all knew it was mostly for show. "If you have brought us what we expect, this will be our last meeting."

"Last meeting?" Nicole said. "What does that mean?"

"Perhaps we should see the information first, then we can talk."

Harrison extracted Nicole's mobile phone from an EM-proof mesh bag and handed it to her. She powered it on, logged in, and called up the calculator application. She typed in a mathematical formula and pressed the minus sign three times. The screen cleared and a cursor blinked in the upper-left corner. She handed the phone to Harrison.

Nicole didn't understand exactly how the secret app that Harrison had installed on her and Timur's phones worked, but she knew how to use it. Timur could put whatever he wanted into a file—photos, voice memos, emails, anything. For her part, all Nicole had to do was remember two codes. One for data transfer from Timur's phone and one to allow Harrison to move the file off her phone. If her phone was ever taken, a simple, seemingly harmless sequence of touches would erase the file and the app from her device.

Harrison opened a slim black attaché case on the table in the center of the room. It looked like a laptop with a telephone handset. He attached her phone to the case with a cord and tapped on the keypad. The room was silent as he concentrated. Finally, he looked up at Orazov and nodded. "It's uploaded, Ussat. It'll take them a few hours to do a full breakdown, but everything we need is there."

Harrison spun the case around so Nicole and Orazov could see the screen. A woman with luxurious red hair and smoldering emerald-green eyes filled the screen. Her full red lips curved with a secret smile.

"That's her?" Orazov asked.

Instead of answering, Harrison looked at Nicole.

"Her name is Daria Volkov," Nicole said, recalling the dinner she and Timur had had with Jimmy Li and his girlfriend. It had been an excruciating three hours. "Timur told me that Jimmy sees her every Tuesday and Thursday at ten. He stays the night. Always."

"Tomorrow night, then," Harrison said to Orazov, a note of excitement in his voice. "It's our best chance."

"Let's wait for the analyst report, Harrison," said Orazov.

"I know what it's going to say already." The CIA operative's tone held a note of finality. "And you do, too. The PLA network is nearing completion. Once they have full surveillance in place, we are screwed. Everything we want to do—everything—gets a lot harder. We can't wait any longer, Ussat."

Nicole realized that they weren't trying to hide anything from her. The resistance had an attack planned and that woman on the screen had something to do with it.

This was the story, she realized. *Her* story. Somehow, she needed to convince Harrison to let her embed with the resistance forces and witness the attack firsthand.

Orazov nodded. “It is time, Harrison. I agree.”

Harrison turned back to his comms set and placed three calls, then he packed up the attaché case and turned to Nicole.

“I’m sorry,” he said, “but I can’t let you go back to Samarkand. It’s too dangerous. If what we’ve planned works, you’ll be free to leave the region. If it doesn’t...” He gave her a wry smile. “If it doesn’t, then Samarkand is the last place you want to be.”

“I understand.” Nicole did her best to suppress the grin that threatened to break out. She nodded at Orazov. “I’ll stay with Ussat.”

40

Tashkent, Uzbekistan

When Daria Volkov opened the door to her apartment a few minutes before ten, she wore an emerald-green robe the exact shade of her eyes, loosely belted at the waist. As she swung wide the heavy door, her red hair swirled and the robe slipped off her shoulder revealing toned muscles the color of bone china.

Her wide smile evaporated. Clearly, the dramatic door open was not intended for a delivery man. Her gaze dropped to the enormous bouquet of red roses cradled in the man's left arm, and her red-painted lips formed a pout.

Harrison wore a cap pulled low and kept his eyes down. He stepped forward, pushing the bundle toward her. "Special delivery, madam," he offered in Russian.

She bent her head down to smell them, and his right hand came up spraying the hypo directly in her face. As her body went limp, he caught her and continued his forward progress into the room. He kicked the door closed behind him and deposited Daria on an overstuffed sofa.

Quickly, he extracted the suppressed Glock 9mm from the pancake holster at the small of his back and cleared the apartment. As he'd anticipated, they were alone. Back in the living room, he checked Daria's vitals.

Strong pulse, regular breathing. She was out cold. The dosage he'd given her should keep her that way for at least two hours.

Harrison sent a text via the secure app to update his team and waited for acknowledgments. Phase One was complete.

Soft cello music played from hidden speakers and the lights were turned low. Harrison walked to the windows that spanned one wall and hit the button to close the drapes. When the heavy fabric had swept across the dark glass, he turned up the lights and took stock of the room.

Ms. Volkov had a thing for gold. Both of the low sofas were covered in some kind of soft velvety fabric with glinting gold threads. The same gold-threaded motif continued in the plush area rug. The coffee table was antiqued gold paint and the expansive mirror on the far wall had a gold leaf frame. Neo-Italian whorehouse was the thought that crept into Harrison's mind as he took it all in.

On the sofa, Daria snored gently. A thin line of drool escaped her red lips and pooled on the golden cushion. Harrison surveyed her skimpy outfit with a critical eye. Had he interrupted her dressing or was Jimmy Li a man who liked to get down to business right away? He found a light blanket and covered the woman's inert body.

He paced, watching his phone for an update. Jimmy should be leaving the Grand Surfan office any moment now. Timur had told them he visited Daria every Tuesday and Thursday and stayed the night. Every week, he said, without fail. Keeping a predictable schedule in a combat zone was idiotic, a level of arrogance that showed Jimmy did not see the resistance movement as a threat.

Harrison prayed the MSS agent wouldn't suddenly get a renewed sense of operational security tonight.

He certainly had reason to. Harrison switched channels on the app and scanned the updates. Akhmet's men were moving into position all over the region. It was impossible to move that many men and not tweak the PLA surveillance network. Additional PLA drones were up and they'd added extra security patrols, but the enemy had not raised the overall threat level in the region.

How long would that hold? Harrison wondered. There was surely a tripwire programmed into the Foresight system that calculated the security posture of the region. In fact, he and Akhmet were counting on it—but not just yet.

Harrison's nightmare scenario was a premature security call that kept Jimmy at the office. He tapped out a message to the team monitoring their target's movements. The MSS agent still had not left his office.

Harrison checked the time. Jimmy was ten minutes off schedule. Not good, but not a catastrophe. Yet.

He paced and breathed deep, regular breaths. Everything depended on Jimmy Li coming through the gold-painted door of Daria Volkov's apartment. In this entire operation, the variable that Harrison could not control was Jimmy Li's libido. The thought made him want to laugh and throw up at the same time.

His phone buzzed with a message from the interrogation team. *In elevator.*

Harrison crossed to the door and put his eye to the peephole. The elevator doors parted, and two men dressed in workmen's coveralls and caps entered the hallway. They carried heavy toolboxes.

Harrison let them in and quickly shut the door. He saw them exchange glances at the golden apartment and the redheaded woman asleep on the sofa.

"Set up there." Harrison pointed to the glass-and-gold dining table under a gold chandelier.

It took only a few moments to unpack their gear. Knockout spray, a tray of pre-loaded hypodermic needles, duct tape, flex cuffs, earmuffs, blackout goggles, and Harrison's laser comms set.

He saw one of the men check his watch. They all knew the timetable.

"He's late," Harrison said. "While we're waiting, put her in the bedroom. Cuffs, goggles, and earmuffs. I don't want her to hear or see anything."

As one of the men gathered the gear, the other lifted her off the couch. Her head lolled back, her hair spilling like a red waterfall off his arm. The blanket slipped off her and her robe gaped open.

The man froze, not sure what to do.

"Get her into the bedroom," Harrison ordered sharply. "And cover her up."

They were back in five minutes and Harrison read the worry on their faces. "He's running late, that's all," he assured his men with a confidence that he did not feel. Jimmy was now more than twenty minutes off schedule.

All three men sat on the sofas without speaking. Harrison knew his nervous tell was bouncing his right leg and he forced it into stillness. The room filled with brittle silence.

When Harrison's phone pinged, it sounded like the gong of a church bell.

Target en route.

"He's on his way," Harrison announced with relief.

The ten minutes it took for Jimmy to drive from his office to Daria's apartment seemed an eternity. Harrison posted by the windows, parting the heavy fabric of the drapes with his hand so he could watch the front entrance with one eye and his phone with the other.

Arrival from north, one minute, the message read. *Black SUV.*

Headlights approached the building from the north. A black SUV came into view. Harrison wanted to pump his fist. This was going to work.

The SUV continued past the front entrance of the building.

Harrison parted the drapes further so he could see more of the street. He must have spotted the wrong car. He scanned the street again and saw his trail car pass. A new message arrived on his phone:

Target stopped at restaurant, 2 blocks south.

Harrison craned his face against the window. Two blocks down, he could see brake lights and someone getting out of the SUV. The car drove away.

"No," Harrison whispered. "No, no, no."

A ping sounded from the other room. Harrison was through the door before his team even left their seats.

The bedroom was like something out of Midas's wet dreams. Any surface that wasn't covered in gold fabric, leaf, or paint was mirrored, including the ceiling and one entire wall. Daria Volkov lay curled in the fetal position on the expansive gold bedspread, covered with a yellow-gold fleece blanket.

The ping sounded again and Harrison homed in on the nightstand drawer. Nestled amid fuzzy handcuffs and other tools of her trade was an iPhone. There was a text from Jimmy waiting on the home screen.

Meet me at Chez Henri.

Harrison cursed. Then he paused. The text was in English. Jimmy's Russian was terrible—he was much more comfortable in English—but the profile he'd read on Daria did not list her as a fluent English speaker. Maybe there was still a way to salvage this thing.

"Get the goggles off her eyes," he ordered. He opened Daria's phone with facial recognition and quickly scrolled through the texts between Jimmy and Daria.

His eyebrows went up. Jimmy liked dirty talk and Daria was a woman who delivered whatever her man wanted. The messages were sexually explicit and heavy on emojis, but Daria's English was rudimentary. He scanned the texts for phrases that she liked to use.

The phone pinged again.

Im waiting, Jimmy wrote.

Harrison took a deep breath. They never covered sexting in CIA tradecraft training.

NO!!!!! he texted in all caps with a pouty face and lots of exclamation points. *I am waiting. I want my dessert. NOW.* He threw in a peach emoji and a rhinoceros for good measure. He was only guessing about the meaning behind the rhino, but Daria seemed to use it a lot.

Harrison walked back to the window overlooking the street. They were running out of time and he was sexting with an MSS case officer.

It took Jimmy a full minute to answer.

Lets eat first. Dinnerplate emoji, coffee emoji, then an eggplant.

Shit, shit, shit, Harrison thought. Time to go all in. He took one last scroll through the old messages before he composed his reply.

Get ur ass up here or I will never suck ur dick again, Mr BIG. Kiss emoji, kiss emoji, kiss emoji, rhinoceros, eggplant.

Harrison hesitated on the Mr BIG, but that seemed to be her nickname for the MSS agent. He sent the message and waited.

C'mon, you horndog, he thought. It was hard to believe that the success or failure of the resistance movement in Central Asia might come down to how badly an MSS officer wanted to get laid.

Harrison's breath fogged the cold glass of the window as he squinted at the distant door of the restaurant. A man appeared in the doorway, he held a phone in his hand, a tiny blip of glowing light at this distance.

Daria's phone buzzed in Harrison's hand.

Im coming, the message read. *Right now*.

Harrison wondered if Daria would have gotten the double entendre. Probably not.

The tiny man two blocks away pocketed his phone and turned in Harrison's direction.

"He's on his way," he announced.

They dimmed the lights again and took places at the entrance to the apartment.

Seven minutes later, the doorbell rang followed by a firm knock.

Harrison waited a beat, then turned the doorknob.

Jimmy Li was stripped to his underwear, his ankles flex-cuffed to the legs of a dining room chair but his arms hung at his side. His head dipped forward, his chin resting on his chest, his thick black hair hanging like a dark veil obscuring his face.

The lights in the room were on full brightness, illuminating the articles arrayed on the glass dining room table. Jimmy's mobile phone, his secure tablet, money clip, ID papers, and a security badge were neatly arranged. On the other side of the table, Harrison's attaché case was open and the secure comms set had a good link to US Cyber Command in Fort Meade, Maryland.

The woman running the op in Cyber Command had identified herself as Jennifer Starr. Harrison didn't know her, but he had faith that Don Riley would make sure whoever was on the other end of their secure connection was the best.

"We're standing by," said Starr.

Harrison's mouth was suddenly very dry. "Acknowledged," he said. He checked his watch. Five minutes to midnight.

"Wake him up," he ordered.

This was the tricky part, he knew. They'd used a knockout spray on Jimmy when he'd come in the door. After stripping him and tying him up, they administered a cocktail that would put him in a compliant state, essentially an industrial-strength date rape drug with CIA chemical enhancements. But for this next part, they needed him awake and functioning. The stimulant was carefully calibrated to Jimmy's weight, but there were so many factors to take into account: how much he'd eaten, how much sleep he'd had, what other drugs he might be taking.

Harrison held his breath as one of the team emptied the contents of a hypodermic needle into the MSS operative's arm.

A beat passed, then another. The drug should take effect almost immediately, Harrison knew.

Jimmy's head rose from his chest, his eyes snapped open, but his stare was vacant.

"Jimmy?" Harrison said in a soft voice. "Can you hear me?"

"I...can...hear you."

"That's very good, Jimmy. It's almost midnight. Do you know what you're supposed to do at midnight, Jimmy?"

"Sign in...security check."

"That's right," Harrison said. "Look down at the table in front of you."

The dark hair angled down a few degrees.

"I want you to show me how you log on to the system, Jimmy. It's almost midnight."

Slowly, the MSS officer picked up the tablet and held it up to his face. Harrison saw the screen clear, replaced by a countdown timer. Jimmy put the tablet back down.

Harrison swallowed. "What happens now, Jimmy?"

"Wait."

Harrison wanted to ask what they were waiting for, but he held his tongue. The timer on the tablet was a three-minute countdown and they were already well into the second minute. He sensed the tension in the other two men in the room.

The timer passed one minute.

"Jimmy, what are you waiting for?" Despite the sick feeling in his stomach, Harrison kept his tone measured and calm.

"Wait." The voice was vacant of emotion.

At thirty seconds, the mobile phone on the table buzzed. Slowly, Jimmy reached for it and slid his finger across the screen. He held it up in front of his face. Harrison stepped back and pressed a finger to his lips.

A female voice said something in Mandarin. A challenge phrase? Harrison wondered.

Jimmy responded, slowly, distinctly. Harrison bit his lip. Would the system be able to detect that Jimmy was drugged?

Another phrase came out of the speaker and Jimmy responded.

It felt like time stopped. Jimmy stared at the mobile phone in front of his face. Hair wild, jaw slack, vacant gaze. Harrison closed his eyes and prayed.

A tone sounded from the phone and Jimmy placed the device back down on the glass tabletop. Harrison picked up the tablet. The countdown timer was replaced by a dashboard screen with Chinese characters. He plugged the device into the comms set.

"Receiving," he heard Starr say over the speaker.

A pause, then, "We're in. Mission clock is running. We'll take it from here. Mr. Riley said that he owes you a beer."

The feeling of relief was so overwhelming that Harrison had a hard time talking. "You can tell Don Riley that he owes me an entire bar. Good hunting."

41

PLA Headquarters, Ayni Air Base, Dushanbe, Tajikistan

A tapping sound snapped Senior Colonel Kang out of a deep sleep. He sat up, his eyes flashing around the dark room as he tried to remember where he was.

Tap-tap-tap.

He swung his feet to the floor and the feel of the close-cropped industrial carpet on his toes grounded him.

His office. A cot. His eyes found the red digits of the clock on the wall above the door.

0302.

Kang stood. “Come,” he called.

The door cracked open. “Senior Colonel,” a woman’s voice. “It’s Second Lieutenant Chin, sir.”

“Enter, Lieutenant,” Kang barked.

Bright light filled his dark office and the young officer stood in silhouette. She cleared her throat.

“Well?” Kang didn’t bother to hide his irritation at her hesitant manner. He’d seen Chin at work on the ops floor. She was technically savvy and smart, but she lacked the command presence of a field officer.

"You said you wanted to be notified if there was a change in the security situation, sir."

Kang rubbed his face, feeling stubble on his chin grate against his palm. "Lieutenant."

"Yes, sir."

"If you're going to wake up a senior officer at"—Kang made a show of consulting the digital clock over her head— "zero-three-oh-five, it's best to have a complete verbal report ready to present."

"Yes, sir," she replied. "The new surveillance network reports eleven terrorist cells active across the region. Foresight recommends a full offensive response."

Kang was fully awake now. "*Eleven?*"

"Eleven, sir. Six of them just popped up in the last twenty minutes and the Foresight offense recommendation just landed in the last five." She paused. "I think the insurgents are on the move, Senior Colonel." Her voice held a note of excitement.

Kang grunted to hide his disdain. She was a staff officer who might go an entire career without ever seeing a shot fired in anger. To her, war was a video game. "I'll be out in five minutes. Have a full briefing ready."

"Yes, sir." The door closed.

Kang pulled on socks and zipped up his combat boots. In the bathroom, he splashed water on his face and bare chest and rinsed out his mouth.

Eleven terrorist cells? That had to be a mistake. He'd been hunting down Orazov's men for months. Their ranks were depleted. He scrubbed his face and chest with a rough towel as he considered the problem.

Maybe this was Orazov's last gasp, his final push. Maybe this was his chance to break the terrorist network once and for all. Kang pulled on a fresh battle dress tunic and strode onto the watch floor.

The energy in the room had changed over the last few hours. He could hear it in the crisp exchanges between operators and the way the techs sat up at their workstations.

Chin waited for him, tablet in hand. She started to speak, but Kang held up a hand. He walked to the center of the room and folded his arms, studying the wall screen.

Red dots showed up all over the region. Anywhere there was a PLA forward operating base, Kang saw the red presence nearby. The enemy was challenging the PLA. Orazov was challenging *him*.

"Lieutenant Chin," he said. "Report."

Chin was ready for him this time. "At 0230, sir, we began to see major activity across the region. In Safirkon, north of Bukhara, we spotted enemy troop movements of estimated thirty fighters—"

"Thirty?" Kang interrupted. "That's impossible."

"Actually, that's the lower band of the force strength, Senior Colonel. Some of the hits are estimated at up to fifty men. That's only the discrete signatures our sensors can detect. There may be more."

Kang narrowed his eyes. It wasn't possible. His men had degraded the terrorist forces to the point that they were barely operational.

"I can show you the raw intel, sir," Chin said. "These numbers are real."

"That's not necessary," Kang said. "Continue."

As Chin carried on with the briefing, Kang's skepticism changed to frustration, then to anger. He'd been chasing these terrorists for months. It was time to end this. If they wanted to challenge the PLA, then he would give them the fight they were asking for. He had the men and the means to crush them once and for all.

"Wake up General Wong," Kang ordered. "I need to brief him."

"He's in Beijing, sir," Chin said. "For the technology summit. He's briefing the Foresight program to the Central Military Commission."

"Then get him on video," Kang snapped. "Now."

Thirty minutes later, Kang was looking at the General's very sleepy face on a screen in his office. He kept the briefing high level. If Wong wanted the details, he could access the Foresight system himself.

"It's a major offensive maneuver, General," he said. "I'll be mobilizing forces from every operating base in the region. Battalion strength movements, sir. This is our chance to finish off the terrorist insurgency in one action."

Wong blinked at the screen. "I don't understand. Our estimates of the enemy strength were much lower. How do we explain this sudden change?"

Kang heard the question behind the question. For months, the General's reports to Beijing told of glowing progress, with heavy praise given to Foresight. Now that same system was reporting radically different results and recommending a full-scale offensive action in response. There was no way the force movements Kang was proposing could be hidden from the Party. There would be questions.

"This is the action recommended by Foresight, General," Kang said. "I believe this may be the SIF's last gasp. If we respond with full force, we will break the terrorist network for good." He added, "I concur with Foresight, sir."

The warring emotions played out on his commanding officer's face. Kang had called the man's faith in his creation into question. Finally, he nodded. "Agreed, but I want you to oversee the operation personally, Senior Colonel."

"Of course, General, I will be in—"

"You will be in the headquarters bunker for the entire operation, Senior Colonel," Wong ordered. "You are my counterinsurgency expert. I want you guiding the action. That means you are not to go out in the field."

"But, General, I work best—"

"You have your orders, Senior Colonel."

Kang stiffened in his chair. "Yes, sir."

"Keep me updated." Wong ended the call.

Kang scowled at the screen. He belonged in the field with his men, but orders were orders. He checked the clock over the door. 0515.

Kang strode on to the ops center floor and called for silence.

"I've just conferred with General Wong and we have orders to execute the Foresight battle plan. As of this moment, all PLA forces in the region are on high alert, ready for immediate deployment. Issue Foresight battle orders to individual unit commanders and inform them that I want to hear their mission briefs at 0700, complete with air asset laydown." Kang paused, surveyed the room. He was suddenly painfully aware that at forty-seven, he was the oldest person in the room by at least a decade. The faces looking back at him belonged to children. He shook off the feeling. They were soldiers in the greatest military force on the planet, and every last man or woman in the room stood ready to do their duty this day.

"Are there any questions?"

No one moved.

Kang nodded. "Carry on."

The room exploded into activity. Kang watched as dozens of techs and operators sent out orders to field commands, updated screens, relayed information. The atmosphere was electric with barely contained euphoria.

He nodded with satisfaction. Maybe General Wong was right after all. He did belong here.

Time passed swiftly as Kang dealt with the myriad of decisions required to deploy thousands of troops and billions of dollars of hardware to the field of battle. He listened to mission briefs from operational commanders and offered his experience. To a person, they expressed confidence and he encouraged it. They were a modern-day fighting force—the best in the world—going up against a ragtag band of terrorists led by a former Russian soldier whose glory days were decades behind him. This was not a fight, it was a slaughter.

"Senior Colonel Kang?" It was Lieutenant Chin again. The hesitation from earlier had vanished. Her face glowed and she had a gleam in her eye. "I have something you should see, sir."

She handed him a tablet. Kang quickly scanned it and oriented himself. It showed a topographical map of the border between Uzbekistan and Kyrgyzstan. The village of Iordan was technically in Uzbekistan, but due to the crazy political boundaries in this part of the world, the place was surrounded by Kyrgyzstan, like a cul-de-sac in a suburban neighborhood.

The valley where the village lay was bowl-shaped, surrounded by steep mountains, with a single road leading to where a red dot pulsed. The town of Iordan.

Kang exhaled in frustration. "I have another briefing in three minutes, Chin. What am I looking at?"

"The data tag, sir. It's him."

"It's who?" Kang snapped.

"Orazov. We just got a drone hit. It's him."

Akhmet Orazov. Kang felt the buzz of the room fade away. They'd located the leader of the resistance. The head of the snake.

"Shall I call in an air strike, sir?"

Kang started to nod, then paused. Why make Orazov a martyr? It would be much better to take him alive.

Crushing the terrorist fighters was a foregone conclusion, but if he had their leader as his prisoner, that would drive a stake through the heart of the resistance for good. If he could capture Orazov, the entire region would be under absolute Chinese control by day's end.

"Sir?" Chin pressed.

"No," Kang said in a curt tone. "No air strike."

"Sir?" Chin's tone was uncertain now. She'd expected her news to have a positive impact on her boss, but instead, he seemed angry.

"Chin, what would it take for me to go mobile?"

"I don't understand the question, sir."

"I want to remain in overall command, but I want to operate from a mobile command post in the field." He pointed at the village of Iordan in the isolated valley. "I want to operate from here."

Chin's moon-shaped face split into a wide grin.

"No problem, sir. I'll get you set up right away."

42

US Cyber Command, Fort Meade, Maryland

Don nursed a cup of cold coffee and an increasingly insistent headache. The headache was both an actual pain at the base of his skull and metaphorical pain caused by the sheer number of competing bureaucratic interests that milled around him.

His grandmother had a saying that she trotted out around holidays about cooks and kitchens and broth, but he was too distracted to recall the full phrase. He dropped the half-empty paper cup into the trash. He needed to pace himself. It was after eight in the evening, and if all went well, he had a long night ahead of him.

Don had commandeered the entire ops floor at Cyber Command and every workstation was manned by a hand-picked technician. Operation Rampage had the potential of being the most high-profile operation in the history of Cyber Command and everybody wanted a piece of the action. It also had the possibility of becoming a monumental disaster that would end his career and the careers of all those closely associated with him.

But right now, Don had no time to consider failure.

He and Lieutenant Commander Starr had carefully negotiated the plan of attack on the Chinese battle network. Entire forests had been felled in the processing of interagency agreements and planning documents.

Throughout the entire planning process, Don had been firm in his decisions and he was backed up by General Jeff Ondich, a US Air Force four-star general and a recognized expert in cyber operations across the entire Department of Defense. Don thanked the nameless bureaucrat in history who had decided that the same person should oversee US Cyber Command and the National Security Agency. Combining the intelligence operations at NSA with those at CYBERCOM made the decision tree that much simpler. Both organizations maintained their separate missions, but General Ondich had the ability to combine forces when required.

And it was most definitely required for Operation Rampage. Don and Starr organized the ops floor into teams. Each member, carefully selected for their skillset, was networked with a team lead who monitored the flow of the operation, reporting to Starr, who manned the Watch Floor Supervisor's desk.

Across the span of the ops center floor layout, Don could pick out the individual teams. The first step in the plan was mostly CIA personnel, many of them drafted from Emerging Threats Group, Don's former home in the CIA. They were in charge of disseminating preplanned disinformation to the PLA surveillance network in the Central Asian Union. Their job was to draw the PLA forces out of their bases and onto chosen fields of battle.

It was a straightforward call-and-response play. They were there to bait the trap. The surveillance network provided the inputs, the raw material, to tweak the Foresight algorithm. The team assessed which sensors had picked up Orazov's troop movements and they amplified or erased the signal according to the attack plan.

The second group was called ReaD, short for reactive disinformation, staffed by handpicked members from CIA, NSA, and Cyber Command. These were Mandarin-speaking analysts with native-level fluency who monitored the real-time comms inside the PLA network. Like their colleagues on the disinformation team, they chose to either amplify, reduce, or disrupt communications to propel the PLA forces toward the intended goal. This was the trickiest part of the operation. For starters, the communications methods could be anything from official encrypted comms from headquarters to text messages between soldiers or even social media posts. The twenty-person team was networked into an AI assistant that combed the Huawei communications backbone for anything that might be relevant. Possible targets were queued and suggested responses attached. Still, every outgoing piece of disinformation was released by a team member, Don insisted on that. He had a lot of respect for AI as a tool, but he was not about to put the operation on autopilot.

Another joint team of a dozen technical experts waited for their turn to take a deep dive into the quantum network. There were a number of classified quantum R&D projects across the NATO alliance, but none of those projects had been operationalized like Foresight. The penetration team hoped to find clues about how the Chinese had managed to make their system work.

The last three teams were smaller, fewer than ten people in each, and much less active than the disinformation side of the operation. Systems analysis, signals intelligence, and imagery collection and distribution were there to make sure they gleaned every possible scrap of intel from the penetration of the Foresight quantum computer network. Don had been clear to these exploitation teams. They might only get this one chance to see inside the PLA network. Make the most of the opportunity.

Every team had back-up personnel on standby, ready to take over as needed. Although Don did not expect the operation to last more than the planned twelve hours, he wanted to be ready for anything.

At the front of the room, the mission clock blazed with foot-high red numbers. The clock had been started the moment they entered the Chinese network using Jimmy Li's access code at midnight in Tashkent. It read 05:31.

Even though every workstation on the ops floor was manned and the atmosphere buzzed with nervous energy, the noise level in the room was manageable. Don nodded his approval. Lieutenant Commander Starr ran a tight ship. She'd selected and trained the teams well, and so far, the operation was working as planned.

He studied the wall screens, which Starr had configured to mirror the displays in the PLA headquarters bunker at Ayni Air Base. They could see in real-time the effect their control of the information flow was having on the PLA decision-making process.

"Excuse me, Director Riley?" The young man looked young enough to be a high school student, but he wore a badge that gave him access to the ops floor. "Commander Starr would like to speak with you, sir."

Don followed his escort to the ropes that kept the observers off the ops floor and passed through. He immediately sensed the difference. One side of the ropes was packed with high-level visitors from all over the Washington, DC, intel community. CIA, NSA, FBI, the White House, two people on the China team from the National Security Council staff, even the chairs of the Senate and House intel committees were there. They drank coffee, talked shop, shared jokes, and ate food catered from a local Greek restaurant.

It was like a holiday for them because they had nothing to do. All of the decisions were made in advance and the operational commands had control. The observers were what Don's grandmother would have called lookie-loos, people who showed up to see history being made or to watch a slow-motion trainwreck. He sincerely hoped that as the evening wore on, they would choose to go home.

Don walked up the four steps to where Jennifer Starr stood behind her desk in the supervisor's command post. From this elevated position, she could monitor the whole floor. In front of her were three touch screens from which she could access any display in the room. Two assistants sat at the ten and two positions in front of her, each with three screens and wireless headsets. Don knew from experience that the information flow in the ops center went from operator to team lead to assistant supervisor to Starr, with any level in the chain of command able to make decisions on the spot so that only the most critical issues reached the level of floor supervisor.

Starr greeted him with a distracted smile. She muttered something into her headset and gave her attention to Don. "We have a new intel feed, sir." She cast a look over Don's shoulder to the high-level gathering behind the ropes. "I wanted your thoughts on what to do with it."

She touched an icon on one of her screens and an image popped up with live video. The image was in high definition and color, but no sound. It showed a room very similar to the one they were in now, filled with workstations manned by men and women in camouflage battle dress uniforms. Don leaned in. A young woman with short black hair spoke to a tall, well-built officer with a buzzcut. They were both Chinese. Everyone in the picture was Chinese.

"Is that...?" Don let his voice trail off.

"Yes," Starr said. "It's the ops bunker at Ayni Air Base. One of our guys hacked a security camera."

Don let out a long breath. "Wow."

He studied the screen. The wall monitor in the video mirrored the one at the front of the room. Red dots with data tags in Mandarin. Don watched the officer in charge, a senior colonel with a spec ops badge on his uniform. He nodded at the screen.

"That's him?"

Starr tapped her center console. "Senior Colonel Hao Kang. Mid-forties, career in PLA special operations with combat experience during the Taiwan debacle. His official job in the Central Asian Union is head of PLA special operations forces. Intel says he's the field commander in charge of taking the fight to the resistance."

This was the guy Orazov wanted to target, but he was in the wrong location. "What's he doing in the ops center?"

Starr switched screens. "According to our intel, General Wong is in Beijing for a technology summit with Party officials."

"And that leaves Kang in charge," Don said.

"We intercepted video traffic. Wong ordered Kang to stay at HQ and run things from there. He was very clear about that."

Starr turned away to deal with another issue. Don watched the mission clock as the last digit flashed. 05:43. It was early morning in Central Asia, the sun would be up soon. What would this day bring?

Another thought nagged at him. Senior Colonel Kang was a potential problem for the operation. The plan assumed General Wong would be running the ops center during the escalation. Wong was a technocrat, completely dedicated to the success of Foresight. Whatever the system told him to do, he would execute it.

But Senior Colonel Kang had real field experience. Their plan depended on drawing the bulk of the PLA forces into the field for a series of decisive battles. Would Kang smell a rat? An experienced commander overseeing the conflict might choose to override the Foresight orders. If he saw through Orazov's plan, he might have the wherewithal to rally forces and stage a counterattack.

Don felt a tingle of anxiety. A man like Senior Colonel Kang could spell disaster for Operation Rampage. They needed to isolate him.

But to do that would require Kang to disobey a direct order from his superior officer. The senior colonel was a career army officer. Expecting him to take a possibly career-ending step was a big ask.

Don thought about it: Could they bait him into chasing Orazov? Kang was no fool, but he was human. Orazov had bested the PLA officer multiple times. That had to sting a little.

What Don had in mind was a risk. Kang might see through their plan, or worse, he might assign another unit commander to prosecute the new mission. Still, it was the best—and only—card he had left to play.

"Commander Starr," Don said. "Release the kraken." He pointed to the spot on the map that Orazov had chosen in advance. "Here."

Starr turned, her skepticism evident. "Are you sure, sir? We're not even six hours into the problem and that's a one-and-done move. Once it's out there, we can't use it again."

Don studied the video image of the PLA bunker. Kang was a career soldier who followed orders. He wasn't going to leave his post unless they drew him out with an irresistible target. Even this might not be enough, but it was better to find that out now than regret it later. Now or never, Don decided.

"Do it, Commander."

She held his eyes, making it plain that she did not agree.

"Aye-aye, sir. Releasing the kraken." She turned back to her screens and spoke into her headset. "ReaD Team Leader, this is Supe."

"Go ahead, Supe," came the reply from the reactive disinformation team leader.

"Execute package Kraken Delta. Release in the village of Iordan. Confirm."

Don saw the ReaD team leader stand up at his workstation and turn toward the command post. "Supe, we planned to hold Kraken in reserve until we saw which way the action breaks. We're rolling out our biggest gun in the arsenal in the first quarter of the Superbowl."

To her credit, Starr did not turn toward Don. She stared her team lead down across the busy floor. "Execute your orders, ReaD Team Leader."

The guy gave a mock salute. "Release the Kraken, aye, ma'am," he said in a tone that showed he also did not agree with Don's decision.

Starr looked up from her screen. "It's done." She stepped aside so that Don could see the video of the PLA HQ. "Let's see how long it takes for their fancy quantum computer system to process the intel and give an order."

Less than sixty seconds later, Don noticed a young second lieutenant sit up at her workstation.

"Holy shit," Starr said under her breath, "that was fast."

The Chinese officer rushed up to Kang and spoke with him. She held a tablet as a prop. Kang took the tablet and zoomed in. His face crumpled in a scowl. He gave an order to the comms workstation.

Starr was on it, pinging the team lead for a readback on the outgoing communications from the PLA ops center. She pressed her headset against her ear as she listened.

Lieutenant Commander Starr turned to Don. "Congratulations, Director Riley. Colonel Kang just ordered up a mobile command post."

43

8 kilometers north of Iordan, Uzbekistan

From the air, the sight of a People's Liberation Army armored battalion on the move made Kang's heart swell with pride. This was why he was a soldier. China was ascendant, the most powerful military in the history of the world, and he was a part of it.

The lead element, four tanks and six infantry fighting vehicles, was at least a kilometer ahead of the main column. His orders to the vanguard element were clear: get onto the objective with all haste and capture the SIF contingent.

The full battalion, including self-propelled artillery and more armor, was doing its best to keep up, but the winding road that led up to Iordan slowed them down. The terrain favored Orazov, that was obvious, but a force of this size could handle anything the terrorist leader could muster. Kang might have waited for nightfall and used a company of his special operations troops to hunt down the terrorist leader, but this was better. A daylight attack using overwhelming firepower was a fitting way to end Orazov's reign of terror in Central Asia.

He sat back so that Lieutenant Chin could see out the window of the Z-

20 Harbin transport helo. She looked up from her tablet, took in the view, then dropped her gaze to the screen again.

"Senior Colonel, two of the other battalions are reporting light resistance. They're moving forces into position for a full-scale attack."

Chin's helmet and flak jacket were both too large for her small frame. She looked ridiculous.

"Very well," Kang said, not really listening. His field commanders were trained soldiers; they knew what they were doing.

He leaned forward again, his attention still on the rapidly moving lead element. His own tablet sat in his lap, the screen dark. His excuse for bringing Chin with him was so that she could experience actual combat, but the real reason was that he wanted someone to keep track of the operations all over the region while he focused on the prize:

Akhmet Orazov.

How many times had that slimy bastard slipped away from him? Too many, but that ended today. This time, Orazov had underestimated his enemy and overplayed his hand. The latest surveillance nodes were a gold mine of intel, by the time the terrorist cells realized they'd been targeted, it would be all over.

Kang felt strangely disconnected from the action. He'd been a soldier all of his adult life, trained to rely on his personal assets: his five senses, his rifle, and the soldiers by his side.

But with Foresight, he'd seen a new side of warfare. This technology changed everything. Remote sensors found the enemy and a computer told him the best way to attack for maximum effect. Before the enemy even knew he was under surveillance, Kang had troops closing in.

He lifted his own tablet now and reviewed the tactical picture.

Orazov had set up a command post in Iordan, that much was clear. Kang laughed to himself. It was obvious why he'd chosen this spot. The valley in which the village of Iordan lay was tucked deep in the mountains. Through some extraordinary political error when the Soviet Union collapsed, this place was part of Uzbekistan but surrounded on all sides by Kyrgyzstan. Orazov surely knew that the PLA commanders were assigned to Central Asian countries. By hiding in this little out-of-the-way Uzbek cul-de-sac, Orazov assumed he'd be overlooked by the PLA regional commanders in both countries.

The ploy might have worked except for the power of the surveillance network. An overwatch drone picked up Orazov by facial recognition. In the normal military intelligence human bureaucracy, that nugget of vital intel would have been chopped through channels for action at the country level, a process that might take a day or more.

But Foresight accomplished that work in minutes. Kang had been alerted to Orazov's presence and had a recommended plan of attack in less time than it took to drink a cup of tea.

And now, Kang not only had the opportunity to take the leader of the resistance off the board, but to capture him alive. General Wong would be ecstatic at how his quantum pet had performed. Surely, when Kang presented his boss with the terrorist leader, he'd forgive the fact that his subordinate had disobeyed a direct order.

"Sir," Chin interrupted, pointing out the window of the helo, "there's our mobile CP. I'll tell the pilot to put us down." Kang spotted a modified ZBL-08 command vehicle parked next to a clearing by the side of the advancing column.

The helicopter descended, alighting in the grassy clearing. Kang popped open the helo door, swung to the ground, and loped under the still-spinning rotors toward the waiting command vehicle. He had no time to waste.

It was a magnificent day. The morning sun was warm on his back and the cloudless sky was the delicate blue of a robin's egg. It was still early enough—just after 0900—that the morning dew held the dust in check from the passing column.

Lieutenant Colonel Ming, the battalion commander, waited for him next to the open door of the 8x8 wheeled command post. Ming popped a crisp salute. On any other day, Kang might have reprimanded Ming for saluting in the field during combat operations, but not today. Kang returned the honor and shook the man's hand with warmth.

Ming's eyes slipped past his commanding officer to where Chin came to a stumbling halt behind Kang.

"Lieutenant Chin is from headquarters," Kang said, raising his voice to be heard over the passing vehicles. "She's here to see a real combat operation."

Ming raised an eyebrow and gestured at the open door. "After you, sir."

Kang gripped the handrail and swung up into the mobile command post. Ming and Chin clambered in behind him and the door swung closed, cutting off the sound of the outside traffic.

The ZBL-08 was a state-of-the-art, mobile C6ISR platform. From this armored vehicle, Kang had every communications channel and command-and-control function at his fingertips as well as access to any intelligence, surveillance, and reconnaissance asset he desired. From here, he could stay in immediate contact with all of his field commanders and view the exact same sensors they were seeing. Kang passed through an aisle with four computer workstations on either wall, manned by technicians. There were no windows and the indirect lights were dimmed to allow better viewing of the computer displays.

"This way, Senior Colonel." Ming touched an intercom on the wall. "Driver, move us forward. I want us in a position behind the vanguard element as quickly as possible."

Kang felt a rumble under his feet and a gentle swaying as the vehicle turned, but the ride was smooth. It felt odd, not being able to see outside, like he was cut off from his senses. The filtered air, cooled for the benefit of the electronics, tasted dry on his tongue and the only sound was the clicking of computer keys.

Past the narrow aisle between the computers, the room opened up to the full width of the vehicle. In the center of the space stood a 3D map table. An operator, tablet at the ready, waited at attention.

"At ease," Ming ordered. "Bring up the area of operation."

The operator worked his tablet and the map table sprang to life. Kang immediately didn't like what he saw.

The two-lane highway they were on ran like a funnel from the wide-open Fergana Valley into the mountains, becoming more constricted the farther they went. After two kilometers, the road made a ninety-degree turn following the bank of a river. The highway wound through a narrow causeway before entering a bowl-shaped valley and the town of Iordan.

"The enemy is here, sir." Ming pointed to a structure on the outskirts of the town. "We estimate approximately forty hostiles, small arms only."

"Orazov?" Kang asked.

Ming nodded and passed a tablet to Kang. It was a grainy picture of a man standing outside a one-story building in the early morning sunshine, smoking a cigarette. The time stamp on the image told Kang it was less than an hour old. He squinted at the picture but could not make out the man's features. Still, the data tag identified the subject as Orazov, Akhmet, with a probability of eighty-four percent.

Kang drew in a deep breath. Four out of five: he'd take those odds.

"A drone strike would be the most efficient means of target elimination, sir," Ming ventured.

"No," Kang said sharply. "I want Orazov alive."

"Of course, sir," Ming demurred. "I just wanted to make sure we have all the options on the table. Per your instructions, I've made arrangements to contain the target."

Ming pointed to the east on the topographical map. "We have a road up to this reservoir. I've deployed ten infantry fighting vehicles to cut off any escape route. To the west and south there are no roads, so I moved two special forces platoons in by helo, with the third platoon in reserve. All of these activities were screened by the mountains around the valley. Orazov has no idea that he's in a box."

Kang nodded. It was a good plan, as good as anything he could have devised. When the PLA forces rolled into the valley by road from the north, Orazov would try to run—right into a trap.

"Show me the terrain around the town," Kang ordered. The operator zoomed in and Kang studied the map. The valley was mostly flat farmland and orchards, but a big chunk of rough land, rolling hills and gullies filled with low scrub and small trees jutted into the valley like a thumb on the far side of the town.

Kang pointed at the patch of rough terrain. "He'll try to escape through here, and then into the mountains. I want the lead element to bypass the town and cut off his escape." He dropped his finger on the interactive map, leaving a yellow pulsing dot. "Tell me about air assets, Colonel," Kang ordered.

"An overwatch drone has had continuous coverage on the target. We have four Falcon UAVs loitering in range and six attack helos on standby. Air superiority is a given, Senior Colonel."

One of the techs spoke up. "Colonel Ming, the enemy is on the move, sir!"

Kang felt his pulse quicken and his face tightened into a smile. The PLA lead element had entered the valley and Orazov's lookouts had seen them. This was the moment he'd been waiting for.

"Move this vehicle to the head of the column, Colonel," Kang ordered.

"Sir," Ming said, "we have him contained—"

"Get this vehicle forward. Now! I want to be there when we take down Orazov."

Ming stepped aside to order the slowly advancing main column to clear the road ahead. Kang felt the vehicle sway as they increased speed. He wished again for a window.

On the 3D map, a swarm of red dots moved from the building on the edge of town into the rough terrain. They moved quickly, bunched into pairs, an indication that they were riding dirt bikes or ATVs.

Too late, Kang thought.

From the north, the lead element moved rapidly across the map as ten blue squares. A diamond formation of tanks led the way, followed by a double file of six armored infantry fighting vehicles. Trailing behind the lead element was a blue star, moving very fast as if trying to catch up.

"Is that us, sir?" Chin asked, pointing at the blue star.

Kang nodded and bared his teeth in a savage smile.

The end was close at hand, he could feel it.

44

Iordan, Uzbekistan

Nicole Nipper had been a war correspondent for decades. Over the years and various conflicts, she'd been embedded with both Royal Marines and US Marines. She'd interviewed special forces operators and Taliban warlords in the wilds of Afghanistan.

But the thing she realized now was that in all those previous encounters, she'd always perceived an invisible shield around her. She was part of the press corps. She was on the side of telling the story, not doing the fighting, and that made her feel safe.

In all those prior encounters, she'd also been outfitted with the best possible physical protection. Body armor with the word PRESS in bold white letters across the chest and back, a ballistic helmet, kneepads, gloves, eye protection—everything a person needed to prevent death from a stray bullet or fragment of shrapnel.

At this moment, she had none of those things. She wore the same blue jeans, T-shirt, and hiking boots that she'd had on when she met Harrison Kohl two nights ago. It was just lucky that she'd chosen to wear hiking boots to the meeting instead of sandals.

The first night, before they left the cabin, Akhmet gave her a heavy jacket that smelled like it had been worn by a cigarette-smoking billy goat. It kept her warm during the nighttime hike, but the only personal protection it offered was to shield her bare arms from being scratched by the branches of trees along the mountain pathways.

Now she sat cross-legged on the dusty floor of a cave, hunched in the smelly jacket, her back to the wall. A few paces away a half dozen men, all dressed in clothes the color of sand and dirt, squatted in a rough circle around a laminated map.

Akhmet was holding court, using a stick to point out features marked in black grease pencil on the map, talking in low urgent tones in a local language that Nicole did not understand. No one offered to translate. No one even acknowledged her presence. She watched and listened, seeking to glean something from the gestures and the stoic faces.

Akhmet had not given her phone back to her, and she had nothing to write with, so she just tried to take in as much as possible and store it in her memory. The physical details set the scene, grounded her description. The layer of dust that covered everything and everyone, the morning chill that was rapidly dissipating under the heat of the rising sun, the smell of body odor and gun oil. Personal hygiene was optional, but these men knew how to take care of their weapons.

A long overhang of rock formed the mouth of the cave. She guessed it was about eight o'clock in the morning—Akhmet had kept her wristwatch, too. A sentry crouched inside the cave, his eyes roving across the terrain outside. The man's gaze locked on something and he called out.

Conversation ceased and the group tensed. Akhmet stood. Nicole knew he'd not slept a wink, but he was light on his feet, no sign of fatigue. The sentry called again and everyone removed their fingers from the triggers of their weapons. Nicole wouldn't call it a relaxed posture, but at least she didn't feel like gunfire was imminent.

Harrison Kohl slipped around the cave wall. He paused for a moment, blinking in the dimness of the cave interior. He was dressed like all the men in the cave, in a loose-fitting tunic, dark pants, desert boots, and a scarf. The only thing out of place was the sleek black carbon fiber attaché case slung over his shoulder. He was deeply tanned and dusty. If Nicole hadn't known him, she would have assumed he was one of the fighters.

Akhmet wrapped Harrison in a bear hug. The CIA officer responded in kind and Nicole felt the warmth between the two men. Akhmet kissed Harrison on both cheeks and gripped his biceps as he spoke to him in low tones. Harrison smiled and she heard him say, "It is done, Ussat."

She had no idea what the "it" was, but it meant a lot to Akhmet. The older man closed his eyes and sighed. Harrison put his hand on the man's grizzled cheek and they touched foreheads.

Nicole watched them. This was the story of her career, she realized. Two men from backgrounds as different as night and day bonding on the battlefield. Her fingers itched for her camera, or at least a scrap of paper and a pencil to capture this moment.

Harrison spotted her and came over. He dropped to the floor next to her as Akhmet returned to his strategy circle.

"How was your night?" Harrison asked.

"How was yours? That was some greeting from the big boss."

He offered her a tired smile. "We did what we needed to do," he said. "I just hope it's enough." Harrison opened the attaché case and powered up the laptop inside.

Nicole nodded her head toward the men gathered around the map. "Do you know what they're saying?"

"They're probably talking about what they want to order in for lunch."

"Very funny," Nicole snapped back. "Look, if you're going to hold me as a prisoner, the least you can do is let me get a story out of it."

Harrison carefully moved the case off his lap and turned toward her. His face was calm, but his eyes blazed with emotion. He spoke in a low voice. "I don't think you understand where you are or what you're caught up in, Nicole. You want to know what I was doing last night? I was pissing on a hornet's nest, and let me tell you, we've got 'em all riled up.

"In about an hour, they're gonna come rolling up that valley. One of the finest military operations in the world will be right outside and we're going to kick their asses and then repeat the process all over the Central Asian Union." He leaned back against the wall, suddenly deflated. "Or not. I don't know if this plan will work, but I do know one thing. Those men and all their fighters hidden all over this valley." He jabbed his finger at the gathering around Akhmet. "They're not a story. This is their lives."

As he finished speaking, Akhmet looked up as if he'd overheard them. He locked eyes with the CIA officer, and Nicole felt again the intensity of the connection.

"I'm sorry," she said.

Harrison went back to the comms set. "It's okay."

"How many men does he have?" Nicole asked.

Harrison laughed, a genuine chuckle that broke the tension between them. "Ask him that. If he tells you, let me know. I've got a boss in DC who would love to know the answer to that question."

"He keeps you in the dark?" Nicole was surprised.

Harrison laughed again. "Not exactly. He tells me everything I need to know to do my job—and nothing more. And I do mean nothing."

"So, it's operational security?"

"I don't think so." Harrison's face softened. "It's just how he is. He takes the responsibility on himself. It's..." He seemed to search for the word.

"Pride?" Nicole suggested, thinking of Timur. "Ego?"

Harrison shook his head. "Respect. He doesn't share anything unless absolutely necessary because if this all goes to hell, he doesn't want anyone else to be blamed. He plans to shoulder the burden alone."

"What about the glory? He'll shoulder that burden alone, too?"

"I don't think so. This has always been about his country, these people. Never about personal gain."

Nicole let the words hang in the air between them. Did she believe that? She couldn't help but compare Akhmet Orazov to Timur Ganiev, a man who professed to love his country but had turned out to be a fraud.

"What about your guy, Timur?" Harrison asked as if reading her mind. "What's in it for him?"

"I don't know for sure. I think they want the same thing, but they took very different paths. I hope Timur's for real. I care about him." As she said it, she realized it was true. She did care what happened to him.

"For what it's worth, his intel on Jimmy Li was spot on. We couldn't have taken him down without Timur's help."

Nicole looked at him. "You killed him?"

Harrison did not answer. He stared at his laptop screen. "Ussat," he called out. "They're here."

Nicole managed to get a look at the screen before Harrison carried the case into the circle of men. It was an aerial view of the landscape outside and the surrounding mountains. A two-lane highway ran into the broad valley. The road ran next to a wide river and had steep mountains on either side. It was clogged with military vehicles in double file. Tanks, armored fighting vehicles, and trucks covered with antennae and satellite dishes.

Ahead of the main column was a smaller element. She counted ten vehicles moving fast with specks of crimson flying above them. The national flag of the People's Republic of China.

The effect on the gathering of men was immediate. Akhmet rapped out orders and the meeting broke up abruptly. One by one, the men slipped out of the cave into the morning sunlight.

It was a beautiful day, Nicole realized. Warm sun, a gentle breeze, and a cloudless sky of soft blue. The kind of day to have a picnic, not a war.

The exodus of fighters made the cave feel suddenly empty. Harrison, Akhmet, and a young man who carried a compact radio set were all that remained.

"Would you like to see the town?" Akhmet asked her.

Nicole nodded and they crept to the edge of the cave mouth, protected from above by the rocky overhang. Morning sun streamed from over the mountains behind them, leaving half the valley lit and half in shadow. Akhmet handed her field glasses and she studied the town below them. It was about the size of the bombed village she'd visited with Timur. She imagined people in the town going through their morning routines, oblivious to what was coming.

"The name of the town is Iordan," Akhmet told her. "More than five hundred people live there."

His voice held such a note of sadness that she looked up. He pointed down the mountainside. "You see the one-story white building with the red door, next to the orchard?"

"Yes."

"My people are there," he said. "Only six of them, but Harrison's computer friends will make them seem like many more."

"Why are they there?" Nicole asked.

"They are bait."

"Bait for what?"

Akhmet pointed to the far end of the valley. "For them."

Nicole swung the glasses to the break in the mountains that ringed the valley. Military vehicles poured into the valley, spreading out as they reached open ground and speeding up. Four tanks in a diamond formation, followed by six infantry fighting vehicles, advanced on the village.

Nicole focused on the white building with the red door. Six men emerged and mounted dirt bikes. They rode down a slope and Nicole lost sight of them when they entered an area of rolling hills and gullies. The PLA column had almost reached the town, but they had not slowed down.

"Harrison?" Akhmet called. His voice was steady. "What is the status?"

Harrison crawled between them, pushing his laptop. He pointed to the screen, where Nicole could see the progress of the PLA main column had slowed along the narrow road that led into the valley.

Akhmet sighed and said to the radio operator, "Tell Farhod to proceed."

Harrison and Akhmet stared intently at the screen. Nicole heard Harrison's sharp intake of breath and saw what looked like puffs of dust rippling along the mountainside above the advancing PLA main column. In the distance, she heard a series of booms like the beating of a faraway bass drum.

Then the mountain moved. It slid sideways, covering the road leading into the valley. Dust clouded the screen.

Akhmet watched, his face unmoving.

"Harrison?"

"Yes, Ussat."

"Tell Mr. Riley the time has come."

45

US Cyber Command, Fort Meade, Maryland

Don Riley focused on the screens across the front wall of the operations floor.

Each one was a different location in Central Asia, the names showing up in black boxes with white letters in the lower right corner of the screen. Bukhara, Karshi, Khujand, Namangan, Kokand, Fergana, Turkmenabat, and Iordan.

They were just names to Don, but the screens told a story. The aerial images, landscapes of forest green and dusty brown, were littered with hundreds of thick blue squares and triangles advancing on a thin scattering of red dots. The blue signified the PLA forces—squares for ground forces, triangles for air assets—and the red was the resistance forces.

Here, on the huge wall screens in Fort Meade, Maryland, he was seeing the exact images taken from the PLA ops center in the headquarters bunker in Tajikistan.

And it was a complete and utter lie. A total fabrication spun from digital thin air. The US penetration into the enemy systems was breathtaking in scope and audacity. It would rank in his memory as one of the most amazing sights Don had ever seen.

They *owned* the PLA sensor network. If Don ordered it, he could make the Chinese sensors show a sparkly unicorn shitting rainbows run across the screen.

"Director Riley?"

Don blinked, his runaway thoughts crashing to a halt. His eyes found the mission clock on the wall. In a few hours, the Foresight network would force a reauthorization of security protocols and they would be locked out of the system. If only they had more time, he thought, maybe they could have found a way to disable the Foresight system permanently.

"Director?" Starr said again.

Don turned to face her. Her skin was sallow and her face haggard, but she wore a broad smile. The woman was running on pure adrenaline, Don knew, and why not? She'd quarterbacked the greatest hack in history. All she had to do now was spike the ball.

"Incoming message from your officer in the field. Standby to pull the pin. That's a quote, sir."

Don felt his lips bend in a slight smile. Harrison always did have a sense of humor. "Is the Burn Team ready?"

The grin widened. "Yes, sir."

Don cut a look across the ops floor to where three operators manned workstations. They all sat straight in their chairs, all turned toward where Don stood with Starr, waiting.

Under the Serrano administration, the President had put an embargo on a specific type of high-speed computer chip used in state-of-the-art computer servers. Of course, the Chinese had found a way around the restrictions and smuggled in a supply of the chips. Anticipating this, the CIA had worked with the Taiwanese manufacturer to design in a feature that allowed outside control of the devices. Someone with a sense of humor had named the covert operation Yankee Swap.

Naturally, the CIA had no control over where the chips ended up being installed, so one of the first actions during the initial penetration was to map the location of the smuggled chips inside the PLA network. Yankee Swap was a raging success: the smuggled chips were installed everywhere in Central Asia.

Don eyed the three operators. Only one was required for what came next. Queue up a few lines of code, push a button, and watch every PLA server in Central Asia melt into slag. But there were three operators: one to load the program, one to check his work, and a supervisor to make sure everything happened as planned. Don wondered if they flipped a coin to see who got to push the button.

But none of that would happen unless he gave the order.

He slipped on a spare headset. "Connect me with Director Brooks, please."

"Don," said Carroll's voice almost immediately. He hadn't even heard the phone ring.

"They're ready, Director," Don replied. "I'm expecting the request to disable the network any moment now, ma'am. Do I have clearance?"

Don was glad this decision had been taken out of his hands. There was no right answer. The short-term win would be sweet. Akhmet's men could score a decisive win over the PLA—maybe even enough to drive them out of the region. But they'd be back. The Chinese were relentless. They would rebuild their network and resupply their forces and retake the ground they'd lost. It would take time. Months at least, maybe years, but they would be back.

And the Chinese would still have Foresight. Don's team could kill the Huawei communications network, but they couldn't touch the brain behind the battlefield AI. The quantum computer was safely located in Xinjiang, China, shielded from harm by distance and firewalls.

Even if they could reach it, the US had no computer virus that was guaranteed to take out a quantum computing platform. A direct-action mission inside China was not even up for consideration.

If Don gave the order to destroy the Huawei network in Central Asia, Foresight would live to fight another day. Not only that, but it would be enriched by the experience it had gained in Central Asia. Battle-hardened and prepared for the next Chinese conflict.

There was another way. The US could leave the Huawei network intact. They had the ability to build in access points. With enough time, they might be able to find a fatal flaw in Foresight. But that would take time. Months, maybe years. Maybe never.

And if they did not destroy the Huawei network today, then he was condemning Orazov's resistance fighters to a slow and painful death against a much larger and well-armed PLA force.

The bureaucratic battles around this decision were unlike anything Don had ever experienced. Until twelve hours ago, when Harrison got them access into the network, it was an academic exercise.

But now, it was all too real. President Cashman decided that the CIA Director would make the final call based on the conditions at the time of the decision.

Which was now.

"Tell me what's going on out there, Don." Carroll's voice was cool.

"We've been feeding the Chinese battlefield AI bullshit for the last ten hours and they've fallen for it. Battalion and brigade-level troop mobilizations at nine different locations across the region, every single one of them chosen by Orazov. If we kill the network, the PLA will take a serious beating."

"Enough to force them out of the region?"

Don shrugged, a pointless gesture since he was on the phone. "I can't answer that, ma'am."

"What about the other alternative?"

Don let out a slow breath. There it was: preserve the network and abandon the resistance. "We have established an entry point that *could* give us long-term access to the network. It's not a guarantee, but it looks promising." He kept his voice neutral, but he emphasized the word *could*.

It didn't really matter, he'd been over this with Carroll at least a dozen times. She knew the trade-offs.

The line was silent.

Starr turned and whispered to Don. "We have a go signal from the field, sir."

Don nodded that he understood. "They're calling for an answer, Director," he said into his mic.

"What's the right call, Don?" Carroll said. "I trust your judgment."

Don scanned the wall screens. Blue blocks and triangles advancing on a smattering of lonely red dots. The Chinese had brought this on themselves. Whatever happened, they deserved it.

"You already know what I think, ma'am," Don said. "My recommendation stands."

He heard Carroll's breath catch and he was glad he didn't have her job. Whatever call she made, she'd be second-guessed by everybody. There truly was no right answer.

"Do it, Don. You have clearance to take down the PLA network."

"Aye-aye, Director." He killed the connection.

Starr looked at him. "Well?"

"Burn it to the ground," Don said.

46

Iordan, Uzbekistan

The command vehicle swayed as their speed increased. Kang gripped the edge of the map table to steady himself.

It was surreal, he thought, like playing god. On the three-dimensional rendering of the battlefield, Kang had reduced the scale of the visual image to about two square kilometers. He tracked the progress of the tiny blue image that represented their vehicle as it hurtled over the exquisitely depicted landscape. At this scale, the mobile CP was about the size of the first joint of his pinky finger and clearly recognizable as the modified ZBL-08 he was riding in. Kang wondered if he picked it up and opened the tiny doors if he'd find tiny soldiers inside.

His ears popped and he felt the vehicle swerve as if they'd been hit by an unexpected gust of wind. Kang gripped the table harder, focused only on the scattering of red dots rapidly traversing the patch of rough ground. The PLA vanguard of tanks and armored fighting vehicles raced on an intercept course, but they weren't going to get there in time. Orazov and his men were getting away.

"Tell the lead element to open fire on these coordinates." Kang stabbed a finger down at the map. His touch left a glowing yellow dot. He bared his teeth at the display. Cut off their escape route, give his troops enough time to disembark and close in by foot. A short firefight and Orazov would be his prisoner.

Kang suddenly realized that he'd not heard an acknowledgment of his order. "Colonel Ming!" he roared. His head snapped up and he whirled around.

Ming was bent over the shoulder of a technician, absorbed in a computer display. Lieutenant Chin stood next to him. They looked up at Kang at the same time, their faces blank and pale.

Kang bit back the hot flash of anger. "What?" he demanded.

Ming moved to the map table, expanding the field of view to encompass the whole valley and surroundings. He pointed at the narrow road leading from the mountains to the town of Iordan. The long double line of blue squares that had clogged the road only a few moments ago were gone.

"A landslide," he said, his voice choked.

Kang stared at the map. It made no sense: a landslide was a localized event; this was more than a kilometer long. Then his brain locked on what he'd felt just minutes ago. A change in air pressure and the swerve of the heavy vehicle.

An explosion. Orazov used explosives to trigger the rockslide, to bury Kang's reinforcements, to cut off his escape.

It was a trap. He and the advance guard—a fraction of his full fighting force—were trapped inside this valley. The full impact of what he'd done hit him now. All he'd seen was the chance to capture Orazov and crush the resistance. Exactly what Orazov wanted him to do.

Instinct took over.

Fight the battle in front of you. Do it now.

Kang leaned over the table, his finger stabbing positions on the mountainside above and around them. If he were leading an ambush, this is where he would put men. He did not think; he let his years of experience dictate his choices.

"Order the lead element to open fire on these positions. Hold nothing back." He heard the icy calm in his own voice. This was a setback, he told himself, nothing more. What mattered now was how quickly he could bring his superior fighting force to bear on the enemy. "Bring all air assets forward now. Transmit these coordinates. I want a full-scale attack on these positions."

Outside, he heard a distant explosion. It was close, which meant it was not one of theirs. The enemy was attacking. He heard the muffled rattle of heavy-caliber machine gun fire, but he could not tell if it was the enemy or his own forces.

"Ming!" he roared again. "Order the lead element to open fire now!"

No response.

He spun away from the map table. "What is the matter with you, Colonel!"

Ming wore a headset. His eyes were wide. "There's no response, sir. I don't know—"

"Use the tactical data channel, damn you! Attack!"

Ming pointed wordlessly to the map table and Kang spun around. The table was blank. The intricate topographical detail, the blue squares, and red dots were all gone. Kang's gaze cut to the nearest computer display. It was blank, too.

Another explosion outside, this one so close that the room rocked like they were in an earthquake. The CP vehicle jerked to a stop.

Chin's voice cut through the silence. "All communications channels are down, sir."

Another explosion, much closer. The heavy vehicle reared up sideways, almost tipping over, then crashed back down to earth.

Kang looked around wildly. The vehicle had no windows, no way to see what was going on outside. He needed to get out of here and lead the battle.

He grabbed Chin by the shoulder, pushed her toward the door at the rear of the armored vehicle. "Everyone out."

His foot was in midair when the missile hit them. The room lifted, tilted, then broke into two pieces. Kang felt his body levitate, slam into the ceiling, then bounce off the wall. His head snapped back, connected with something solid. Stars burst across his vision, then nothing.

When he opened his eyes, Kang saw sunlight and blue sky. He was on his back, and above him the dark walls of the CP had split open. Above the ringing in his ears, he could hear the distant shriek of alarms and see pulsing red light from the darkness beyond the breach. He breathed in a lungful of sharp smoke, laden with ozone from burning electronics.

A face blocked the patch of blue sky. Round, pale, framed with dark hair and a too-large ballistic helmet. "Can you move, Senior Colonel?" Chin shouted at him. He could just barely hear her.

Kang moved his arms and legs, then tucked his chin and sat up. The room swam for a second, then steadied. "Help me up," he said.

Chin gripped his forearm and hauled him to a standing position on what had once been the wall of the CP. She handed him his helmet and he put it on. He could feel clotted blood matted on the back of his scalp, but that would have to wait.

His senses were sharpening. Outside, the battle raged. He heard and felt the concussion of explosions and the brisk punching of machine gun fire. Four soldiers stared at him with terrified eyes. Someone had wet themselves and the hot, sharp scent of urine reached his nostrils.

"Where's Ming?' he rasped out.

"Dead," Chin announced. "Broken neck."

A blast of heavy-caliber bullets drummed against the side of the CP. The percussions making everyone cower. They were lucky, Kang knew. If the armor-piercing missile that had capsized this vehicle had been a direct hit, they'd all be dead. If they stayed, they'd be dead, too.

"We need to get out of here." Kang pushed toward the rear of the vehicle, crawling over computer workstations. Behind him, he heard Chin giving orders to the soldiers to follow. When he reached the heavy door at the back of the command post, he saw the hinges were on top. Kang undogged the handle and pushed at the door. It was unblocked, but there was no way to hold the door open. The best he could do was slip through the opening, but into what?

"I'm going out," he called back to Chin. He poked his feet out the door and dropped to the ground.

Kang hit the dirt and rolled behind the vehicle, putting the heavy-armored carcass between himself and the fire fight. He blinked in the impossibly bright sunlight. A corporal scrambled out of the door, followed by another and another. They saw Kang and joined him behind the overturned CP. Chin was the last one out. She sprawled in the dirt next to him.

Kang felt naked. He only had his sidearm. Chin was unarmed. The command post troops were also unarmed. He needed to find them all weapons.

"Wait here." Kang ran to the front of the vehicle, got low to the ground and peered around the corner.

The CP was still thirty meters behind the lead element of the vanguard forces. They'd just topped a crest in the road when the enemy missile struck. All of this—the distance from the fighting and the overlook position—gave Kang an excellent view of the battlefield. A gentle wind cleared heavy gray smoke from the scene.

And what he saw made him sick.

All four tanks were out of commission. On two of them, the turrets had blown off completely, another was hidden under a pall of black, oily smoke. As Kang watched, the ammunition in the final tank began to cook off, igniting a ripple of secondary explosions that made him take shelter.

Kang lay on his back, breathing heavily, staring at the sky. Where the hell was his air support? Drones and attack helos should be shredding the mountainside with rockets and cannon fire.

The secondary explosions ceased and Kang rolled back into his observation position.

The infantry fighting vehicles had fared better than the tanks. Two were smoking hulks, but the other four were still in the fight. The gunners in the IFVs were hard at work as evidenced by the sounds of the 30mm autocannons echoing across the battlefield. The open doors at the rear of the vehicles told Kang they'd deployed their troops.

There were casualties. He could see at least a dozen bodies, a few of them still moving. Two figures were on fire, twisting on the ground in agony. He blocked out the sound of their screams.

He studied the mountainside, looking for the enemy positions. Kang cursed his own arrogance. They were in a bowl, trapped like goldfish, enemy fire raining down on them from high ground. As he watched, a streak of bright light lanced down from a rocky outcropping, scoring a direct hit on one of the remaining IFVs. The other PLA units trained their fire on the attacking position. Kang watched the boulder on the mountain disintegrate under a rain of bullets.

Then two more missiles shot down from a new position, taking out another fighting vehicle. The explosion made Kang duck his head.

They were getting slaughtered. His first instinct was to order a retreat, but he had no communications with the remaining men on the battlefield. Even if he gave the order, where would they go?

He cut his gaze to the patch of rough ground some hundred meters to the left. If he could get Chin and the rest of these survivors in there, at least they'd have some cover. But that would be like sprinting across a wide-open soccer pitch. Orazov's men had the high ground and they were well armed.

No matter how fast they ran, they'd never make it.

Then a rhythmic sound hit his ears. The sweetest sound he'd ever heard in his life. Kang rolled over to scan the sky.

Two Z-19 Harbins flew over the town behind them. They came in low and hot, the blazing 23mm cannons making the helos look like they were spitting fire. As they roared over Kang's position, they rose in the air and each released a full spread of HJ-8 missiles.

The resulting explosions rocked the valley. Plumes of dust and rock rose over the mountainside.

Kang pumped his fist. Salvation, at last.

The helos abruptly broke off their attack. They peeled off and separated, racing away from the battlefield.

From at least four places on the mountain, Kang saw surface-to-air missiles being fired. They corkscrewed up, leaving crazy smoke trails behind as they chased the fleeing helicopters. One of the helos jinked and spewed out a silver cloud of chaff and flares. The pursuing missile slewed by, but the success was short-lived. A second missile, only seconds behind, exploded, shredding the aircraft. The burning carcass cartwheeled to the ground.

The second helo dove for the deck, flying so low that Kang could see clouds of dust in its wake. The tactic fooled the pursuing missiles. Both of them impacted the ground.

The helo pilot spun to the right, trying to use the rough land mass to obscure its escape. Then the machine gun emplacements on the mountain opened fire. The effect was like flying into a buzzsaw. The aircraft jittered and the front windshield disappeared as the helo flew out of sight. A fireball rose into the air over the rise of rough ground.

Lieutenant Chin crashed to the ground next to him, startling Kang. "What are your orders, sir?"

47

Iordan, Uzbekistan

Nicole trained her field glasses on the oncoming PLA military vehicles. The four tanks ran straight at them in a diamond formation. They moved much faster than she'd expect a vehicle that size to move, leaving a cloud of dust in their wake. The lead tank had a crimson flag flying from a whip antenna and she made out a man wearing goggles and a ballistic helmet standing in the cupola. A second PLA soldier manned a machine gun.

The long barrel of the lead tank was trained forward, but the barrels on the flanking units angled out to the side, casting back and forth as if searching for targets. Behind the tanks, she counted six infantry fighting vehicles in a double file. As she watched, the IFVs broke formation, spreading out and speeding forward along the flanks of the tank formation. It was clear to Nicole that they were moving to intercept Akhmet's fleeing men.

Nicole instinctively lowered her head. She'd seen what a tank could do to a battlefield target kilometers away and a shell fired from one of those PLA tanks could easily reach this cave. If Akhmet was going to attack, what the hell was he waiting for?

A flash of movement near the edge of town caught her eye and she focused the binoculars. It was a lone PLA vehicle, an eight-wheeled armored combat vehicle similar to the IFVs but larger, with an array of satellite dishes and antennae on the roof. This vehicle also flew a red flag.

Harrison saw it, too. "Ussat," he said pointing. "Command vehicle."

Akhmet nodded. "Has Mr. Riley responded?"

"Yes. It is done, Ussat."

"What's done?" Nicole asked. "What is happening?"

"Did it work, Harrison?" Akhmet asked.

"I can't tell, Ussat." Harrison's voice was taut with tension.

Akhmet stood and held out his hand. The radio operator passed him a stubby plastic pistol with a wide muzzle. A flare gun, Nicole realized. He moved to the edge of the cave, aimed the flare gun at the sky and pulled the trigger.

A bright red flare arced over the valley and drifted, a spot of smoking red against a soft blue sky.

"What does that mean?" Nicole asked.

The hillside below them erupted in gunfire.

Streaks of silver smoke blazed down from all directions on the diamond formation of tanks. Almost at the same time, three of the tanks erupted in flames. The tank commander that Nicole had seen riding so proudly only a few moments prior was ejected from his cupola. She lost track of his body in the smoke and dust.

The fourth tank at the base of the diamond managed to get off one round before the next volley of Javelin missiles tore it apart.

The armored personnel carriers skidded to halt, disgorging soldiers under covering fire from the weapons mounted on top of the IFVs. The PLA soldiers fired wildly, unsure of where Akhmet's men were in the surrounding hills above them. Tracer rounds lanced down from all directions and she saw PLA soldiers cut down under withering crossfire.

The deafening sounds of automatic weapons fire, exploding mortars, and secondary explosions from the burning tanks made Nicole want to retreat to the deepest part of the cave, but she stayed in place. She tried to estimate the number of men and positions Akhmet had placed on the hillside, but gave up. As soon as she counted one sector, a new position opened up.

She also saw a tandem firing strategy take shape. Missile and gun positions on the west side of the hill concentrated on a single PLA target. Once they drew fire from all the active Chinese shooters, new positions in the east opened up.

She watched the PLA vanguard force go from four tanks and six IFVs to three functional armored troop carriers in the space of minutes. She searched through the smoke for the command vehicle that had been speeding to catch up with the advance units before the attack.

The mobile CP lay on its side like a wounded animal. It was not burning, but she could see lazy smoke drifting up from the wreck. As she watched, the back door swung open and a man dropped to the ground. He rolled behind the vehicle. Five more soldiers followed.

She belly-crawled back to Harrison, who was hunched over his comms set. "What are you doing?"

He turned the screen in her direction. "This is happening all over the region. Ambushes like this one are going on in another eight locations. It's a bloodbath."

As Nicole sat up to get a better look, Harrison looked over her shoulder. Suddenly, he shouted, "Incoming!" and tackled her to the ground.

The shockwave forced the air from her lungs. A wall of fire blotted out the blue sky outside the cave. Inside, rocks fell from the ceiling and walls. When Nicole opened her mouth to breathe, she choked on a mouthful of dust.

Harrison's body weight lifted off her. "You okay?"

She nodded, still gagging. She tried to wipe the dirt off her face but only managed to rub it into her eyes.

"Hold still." Harrison tilted her head back and poured water over her face.

Nicole blinked. Her vision cleared. "What happened?"

"Rocket attack." Harrison wiped the dirt off his laptop. "Helo."

Outside, she saw the fiery outline of a helicopter cartwheel into the floor of the valley.

Nicole crawled back to the front of the cave. Smoke drifted over the hillside and she spotted multiple fresh bomb craters, but the fighting raged on unabated as far as she could tell.

There was only one PLA armored fighting vehicle left, but it was immobile. Two of the wheels on one side were gone. The machinegun on the top of the vehicle stopped firing and she saw a soldier bail out of the back entrance and take cover. Two Javelin missiles streaked down, scoring direct hits. The IFV exploded.

Akhmet got to his feet and called for another flare. He moved to the edge of the cave and fired it into the air. Yellow light arced over the battlefield and drifted to the ground in a trail of yellow smoke.

Gunfire from the hillside stopped. The few remaining PLA soldiers continued to fire, but slowly they stopped too.

Silence descended over the scene of destruction. The black smoke from the burning vehicles tasted like soot on her tongue and she could hear the distant screams of wounded men.

"Play the recording," Akhmet ordered and the radio operator spoke into his microphone. It took Nicole a moment to realize that Akhmet had given the order in English. He wanted her to know what he was doing.

Far down the mountain, she heard words being broadcast in Mandarin through a bullhorn. "What are they saying?" she asked Akhmet.

He looked at her with eyes as cold as winter. Here was a man who knew exactly what he'd done and made no apologies for it.

"Surrender or die. You have one minute."

48

Iordan, Uzbekistan

When Kang saw the second helicopter go down in flames, he knew it was over. The road into the valley was blocked. There were no reinforcements coming. Somehow, they'd lost air superiority. He had no way to communicate with headquarters, and even if he did, there was no one to save him.

In his heart, he knew he was defeated. But his brain refused to accept what he was seeing.

It was inconceivable. These terrorists were peasants, and yet they'd annihilated an armored element of the People's Liberation Army and a pair of state-of-the-art attack helicopters in a matter of minutes. The enemy obviously had access to modern weapons—and lots of them—but Kang was a seasoned soldier. Superior weapons were not the deciding factor here.

He thought back to the intel that had brought him to this unlikely place in the middle of the mountains. He'd marched his men right into an ambush, willingly ignoring every lesson he'd learned from decades of military service. He'd been outfoxed—and not just here, either. Kang was willing to bet that all the other battles he'd committed troops to around the region had gone just as poorly as this one.

His brain ached with the enormity of the loss. How many men? He didn't even want to guess.

This was all his fault. Every death was on his head.

"Senior Colonel," Chin shouted at him, shaking him by the shoulder. "What are your orders?"

He looked at her. He'd even dragged this greenhorn into the field with him. He'd wanted to show this inexperienced young officer what real combat looked like. Well, now she knew and she'd be lucky to live to tell about it.

Kang looked past her to the wild area a hundred meters away. Rough terrain, some trees and scrub brush. If they could get in there, maybe they'd stand a chance. Maybe. What other option did they have? They were in an exposed position. Any second now, another missile might come flying down from the high ground and blow them all up.

Kang got to his knees and pointed to the area of rocks and brush rising out of the plain, but before he could say anything, a yellow flare soared into the sky.

The gunfire from the mountainside stopped. The return fire from the PLA petered out.

Silence fell across the valley. It was an unnerving sensation. Kang lay back down in the dirt and peered around the front of the CP.

He saw the fires and smoke, but no sign of armed men trying a flanking maneuver. What was the enemy doing now?

"Surrender or die. You have one minute." It was a recording, a man's voice speaking in Mandarin. The message repeated three times, then it stopped.

Kang sat up, rested his back against the armored skin of the CP.

Surrender or die. He was a decorated officer in the People's Liberation Army of China. An elite special operations soldier. Surrender was not an option.

His eyes were closed against the bright sun, but he could hear Chin getting to her feet, hear her giving orders. With an effort, he opened his eyes—just in time to see her sprint into the open ground.

"No!" he shouted, but it was too late. Before he even heard the report of the rifle shot, he saw her body spin and crash to the ground. She did not move again.

Kang scrambled to his feet. “Get up!” he shouted at the four remaining soldiers. “Who has something white on them?” He was aware that his shouting sounded unhinged, but he couldn’t stop himself.

One of the soldiers had a white cotton handkerchief and Kang snatched it out of his hand. “Follow me,” he ordered in the same loud voice. “Single file.” His eye strayed past the row of terrified soldiers to Chin’s dusty, still form. This was all his fault.

He turned, held the handkerchief over his head, and stepped out from behind the cover of the overturned vehicle. He marched forward, his footfalls making little dust clouds in the dirt. The handkerchief fluttered in the breeze above his head.

It was only about thirty meters between the CP and the rest of the devastated column, but it felt like he was walking through deep sand. With every step, he expected a sniper bullet. Part of him wanted it to happen.

But no bullet came for him.

“This is Senior Colonel Kang,” he shouted. “I am your commanding officer and I order you to throw down your weapons and form on me.” He said it over and over again until his voice was hoarse.

Slowly, he saw soldiers stand up, raise their hands. He counted six. He’d led a battalion of soldiers into this valley and they now numbered eleven effective troops. The cries of wounded men echoed around him. The sound cut him to his core, but there was nothing he could do for them.

Kang skirted the worst of the fires and stayed upwind of the smoke. When he reached a point that was clear of destruction, he stopped his march. Let the enemy come to him.

Flickers of movement on the mountainside and armed men dressed in dirty clothes emerged from the rocky landscape. He stopped counting when he got to thirty, any hopes of a last-ditch counterattack evaporated. Orazov was no fool. If he put thirty men in the open, he had at least twice that many still in hiding.

The bitterness of the loss made Kang want to gag, but he clamped his jaw shut and held his body at rigid attention. “Fall in,” he said to his soldiers. They formed two ranks of five behind him.

A contingent of enemy fighters advanced on them, circled them. From the corner of his eye, Kang saw more of the enemy filter through the smoking wreckage like wraiths, looking for remaining PLA soldiers.

A shot rang out, then a quick three-round burst. The armed enemy around Kang raised their weapons. This is it, Kang thought. They're going to slaughter us.

"Wait!" he said, holding up open palms. "Please."

The three rifle barrels on him did not waver.

Kang cupped his hands around his mouth and roared into the smoke. "This is Senior Colonel Kang, your commanding officer. I order you to surrender immediately."

A few moments later, a young man stumbled out of the smoke, hands up and trailed by two enemy fighters. He looked very young and he was shaking like a scared puppy.

"Fall in, Corporal," Kang ordered.

The young man joined the last rank. They now numbered twelve.

Kang eyed the enemy fighters who stared back at him with hard, dark glares. What happened now?

He didn't have long to wait. The breeze blew away a veil of smoke and Akhmet Orazov stood a few meters away. He was a trim man in his mid-sixties, with short gray hair and beard. His hooded eyes were unreadable as he studied the remaining PLA soldiers. Orazov gestured to Kang to step forward.

Kang advanced in two stiff steps. He'd read Orazov's file and he knew about his Russian special operations experience in Afghanistan. Kang had heard the stories of what the Spetsnaz did to their prisoners.

Orazov turned his back to him and walked away. The enemy fighter nearest to Kang indicated with his rifle muzzle to follow. Orazov led him away from the smoke, far enough that they were out of earshot of his men, then he turned. His piercing gaze raked over Kang's features.

"You're a long way from home, Senior Colonel Kang." He spoke in English, which seemed an odd choice to Kang. Not that it mattered; he was not going to give this terrorist the satisfaction of an answer.

"Would you like to live, Senior Colonel?" Orazov pressed.

Kang's stomach tightened. There it was: the threat. What did they want from him? A video statement to embarrass his country? He would take whatever humiliation they heaped on him. He would show them how a true soldier handled pain.

Orazov studied him. “Do you want your men to live, Senior Colonel?”

“What do you want?” Kang demanded, in English.

“I want you to leave my home and never come back.”

Kang said nothing. He was not going to let this old man toy with him.

“You’re fighting a phantom, Colonel Kang. There is no SIF. There never has been. It was created by your own Ministry of State Security as a reason for the PLA to invade my homeland.”

“That’s a lie,” Kang said. “You are the leader of the SIF.”

“You don’t believe that,” Orazov returned. “You’ve seen with your own eyes PLA operations that were blamed on the SIF. Why would Jimmy Li do that? My men have attacked legitimate military targets, but our own people? Never.”

“You’re lying.”

Orazov laughed, but it was brittle. “I don’t need to lie. I have the truth on my side.”

The strands of doubt that he’d harbored in the back of his mind for months suddenly formed a pattern. It was all a lie…and that meant all these soldiers had died for no reason. It was his fault. He’d given the orders. He’d sent them to their deaths in service of a lie.

He looked at the battlefield around him, aware that Orazov was tracking his gaze. “Is it like this everywhere?” Kang’s voice was hoarse.

“Yes,” Orazov said in a quiet voice. “We carried the day.”

“How many…” Kang could not form the words.

“Too many.” Orazov looked past Kang and nodded. “We’re out of time, Colonel. Have you considered my offer?”

Kang’s brain was stuck in neutral. He blinked. “What offer?”

“Do you promise to leave my home and never come back?”

“And then?”

“And then I let you and your men live.”

“That’s it?”

“There’s been enough killing today, Kang. I don’t want to add more bodies to the pile.”

Kang felt the heat of the older man's gaze.

"If you agree to leave my home and never come back, I will let you and your men live."

"What if I continue the fight from beyond your borders?" Kang demanded. Why was he arguing with this man? Tell him what he wanted to hear and live to fight another day.

He felt like Orazov was looking through him.

"I am confident that you will do the right thing." He gestured behind them. "I also have a reporter with me."

Kang turned to find a blond woman with a mobile phone recording the conversation.

"You can't win," Kang said. "The PLA will be back. More men, more weapons, more technology. They will crush you."

Orazov's smile was grim. "The battle is not over."

Kang found his men seated in the dirt with zip ties on their hands and feet. He held out his own hands to be bound and sat on the ground, facing away from his men.

The enemy soldiers faded into the landscape. They were alone.

No one spoke as the shadows grew long. Then, in the distance, he heard the beat of helicopter rotors. The men began to speak in excited tones. They were the survivors. They were going to live.

Kang stayed quiet. He was alive, but his mind was numb, his heart sick. He should be thankful for being spared, he knew that, but the question remained.

Why? Why would a man who had slaughtered thousands of PLA soldiers this day spare Kang's life?

The PLA helo hammered up the valley, passed over them, then returned and hovered. Slowly, it descended to the ground, throwing up billows of dust over the scene of carnage.

49

US Cyber Command, Fort Meade, Maryland

Don sat at one of the open workstations on the now mostly empty ops floor at Cyber Command. Since they'd taken down the Huawei network four hours ago, there was no need for a full cyber penetration team. In its place, Don commandeered a grouping of computers and technicians to coordinate the flow of intel streaming from the multiple battlefields in Central Asia. They were no longer active participants in the bloody work of the day. They were spectators now.

His eye crept up to the clock on the wall. It was almost seven in the morning in Washington, DC, which made it four in the afternoon in Central Asia. The end of a very bad day for the People's Liberation Army.

"The next round of intel from NGA is coming to you, Director Riley," reported one of the techs.

"Thank you," Don said, unable to remember the young man's name and unwilling to show his ignorance. He'd been up all night and his thoughts felt fuzzy. He closed his eyes for a ten-count of deep breaths to clear his mind. He opened them again and didn't feel any better.

Don focused on the satellite image of a battlefield. Blackened carcasses of military vehicles littered the sand-colored ground, some still burning, and the whole scene was hazy with smoke. He scanned the accompanying written report:

...ground forces of the People's Liberation Army located in the Central Asian Union are estimated at 25% of original strength. Casualties are difficult to estimate at this point, but could be as high as 26,000–33,000 personnel killed and wounded...

Don paused in his reading. Tens of thousands dead or wounded in a single day? Those were World War One trench warfare numbers.

...With respect to air power, the PLA air force suffered an estimated 30% loss in aircraft. The Central Asian resistance fighters have advised the PLA that they will not attack transport helicopters engaged in medical evacuation; however, the PLA remains justifiably wary of the MANPAD threat that the resistance fighters have demonstrated. It is important to note that there was virtually no reduction in the PLA unmanned assets. When the Huawei network went offline, aerial assets executed a return-to-base program. The Chinese are engaged in strenuous efforts to restore a regional communications network and their military command and control systems...

Don sat back in his chair. And then what? he wondered. Despite the horrific losses on the battlefield, all they'd really managed to do was slow the Chinese down. A decisive day, yes, but it was unlikely to cause Beijing to throw in the towel. There was far too much at stake in Central Asia.

Within a day or so, the Chinese would have a rudimentary comms network running again. Within a week, maybe less, they'd have a secure command and control network back online. A network that they could reconnect to Foresight, which was still running in Xinjiang, well inside the territorial borders of China, untouchable by US assets.

What would the Chinese do then? They still had a functional air force and a full fleet of armed drones. Would they use Foresight to wage an air war on Orazov's resistance fighters?

Don rubbed his eyes. Those were the questions that President Cashman wanted him to weigh in on at the meeting of the National Security Council in—he stole another look at the clock—less than three hours from now.

He stared at a dark smear across a brown landscape, the remains of a destroyed helicopter. His eyes picked out shattered tanks, smoking IFVs and troop carriers, and the twisted bodies of fallen soldiers.

Don tried to imagine the mental calculus taking place in the minds of Chinese Communist Party leaders. The PLA had been routed, suffered a devastating and humiliating defeat on the battlefield by a smaller, less capable enemy. But they were not destroyed as a fighting force—far from it.

The PLA still had legions of soldiers and enough weaponry to flatten all of Central Asia multiple times over. More importantly, they still had a predictive battlefield AI which could deploy those forces with pinpoint precision. Don's side had managed to fool the AI once, but they'd burned that bridge.

His shoulders sagged with fatigue and disappointment. The best-case scenario was if Party leaders grew wary of the Foresight platform. But how long would that last? The genie was out of the bottle. The Chinese possessed military technology that put them years ahead of the United States. Sooner or later, they would come back to Foresight, he was sure of it. The question wasn't *if*, it was *when*.

"Director Riley?"

Don roused himself from his train of unproductive thoughts. "Yeah?"

"We're seeing a lot of chatter on the PLA secure military comms network," the operator reported. "From inside China," he added.

"Do you have a nexus?"

"Western China, sir. Xinjiang."

Don sat up. "Get the NGA back on the line. Tell them I need emergency satellite tasking on—" He looked up the coordinates and read them off.

Fifteen minutes later, Don was staring at a new image on his computer screen, a square of white concrete set in a flat, barren landscape of brown desert. There was a parking lot, a barracks, a guardhouse, and a huge round water tower on top of a hill with a white pipe running down to the building.

Smoke poured out of the concrete structure on multiple sides. The thick pipe that ran from the tower to the building had been severed and a dark stain expanded across the brown landscape.

How was this possible? was Don's first thought. The intelligence officer in him wanted to find the answers, but he pushed that instinct aside. There was a much more pressing matter to deal with right now.

Unless they moved fast, the United States was going to be blamed for this.

"Get me Director Brooks on the phone. Now."

50

Western Yarkant County, Kashgar Prefecture, Xinjiang, China

Arafat Memet pushed his cart of cleaning supplies into the security queue waiting to enter the compound. He kept his eyes down, occasionally looking up to scan the scene.

Everything looked normal. The two PLA guards on duty were the ones he expected to see this morning and they were using the X-ray machine that he'd planned for.

The young Muslim woman ahead of him in line reached the head of the queue. Her name was Fatima, but since that name was banned by the Chinese, she went by Akdan to everyone except her friends and family. She was petite and attractive and the guards made no attempt to hide the fact that they were undressing her with their eyes as Fatima bent over to load her boxes onto the X-ray conveyor. One of them looked at the other, raised his eyebrows and thrust his hips in a crude gesture.

Arafat looked away. This was part of the plan, to distract the bored guards with a pretty face, but it still disgusted him. The woman had a master's degree in microbiology, not that it mattered to these morons.

As her boxes disappeared into the X-ray machine, Arafat pushed his cart forward and opened the top carton. Two rows of sealed plastic pouches of thick, pink liquid filled the box.

"Four cartons of hand soap," he said.

The guard, his eyes still on Fatima's backside as she took her time reloading her cart, nodded to Arafat to put them through the X-ray. He offered up a prayer as he hefted the boxes onto the moving conveyor belt. Murat had done the calculations. The small squares contained inside the bottom layer of pouches in the third box should not be easily visible to the operator as long as they used this older X-ray machine.

Of course, that was just a hypothesis. A real scientist would have tested that working theory in the real world. But there was no time for them to test anything, so Arafat volunteered to take the precious cargo through the security checkpoint himself.

He gripped the handle to stop his hand from trembling as he pushed the cart to the end of the X-ray conveyor. A few meters away, Fatima was still creating a distraction, bent at the waist as she rearranged the boxes on her own cart. She had the attention of the PLA guard directing traffic, but the one operating the X-ray machine was doing his job.

The first box came out and Arafat loaded it onto his cart immediately. The second box followed quickly. Then the conveyor stopped and Arafat's heart skipped a beat.

He pasted a look of irritation on his face as he looked up. The two guards were both watching Fatima now. She straightened up, giving them a profile view as she straightened her dress.

Arafat cleared his throat and Fatima moved away. The guard on the X-ray machine advanced the belt so quickly that both boxes came out at the same time.

He had his hands on the precious third box when the guard called out, "Wait!"

Arafat froze. The guard walked over and flipped open the lid of the third cardboard box. He palmed a pouch of pink liquid and tossed it to Arafat, who caught it solely by reflex.

"Our latrine needs more soap," he ordered, pointing across the hall to the door marked as a toilet.

Arafat couldn't speak, so he just nodded. And stood there, staring.

The guard stared back. "Are you stupid? Get your shit off my machine, old man!"

Arafat nearly stumbled as he threw the two remaining boxes onto his cart and wheeled to the closed door. He refilled the empty soap dispenser and continued on his way to his workstation.

Fatima was waiting for him in the cramped janitor's storage closet. Neither of them said anything as he shut the door. Arafat leaned back against the cold steel and closed his eyes. His heart raced, his face slick with sweat.

The room was four meters square, lined with metal shelves stacked with the many cleaning supplies required to service a large government facility. It smelled of disinfectant and dampness. Fatima went to the deep sink and turned on the tap.

"Hurry," she whispered.

Arafat unloaded the third box and removed the first level of pink plastic pouches. He took the first container from the second layer and passed it to Fatima. She sliced it open, dumped the pink soap into a waiting empty bucket and extracted a sealed rectangle about the size of two decks of playing cards.

"It's heavy." She rinsed it off and passed it to Arafat.

He said nothing, just dried each package with a paper towel and stacked them. Inside of ten minutes, they had recovered all twelve of the precious bricks. There was a mountain of suds in the sink and a full bucket of liquid soap but that could not be helped.

"Get the detonators," he said to Fatima as he climbed to the ventilation shaft where he had hidden the timers.

The long, thin metal detonators had been smuggled into the facility inside a shipment of ball point pens, and the timers, each the size of a coin, had gone through the X-ray machine as fake bottlecaps on plastic bleach bottles.

Arafat assembled the explosives quickly, according to the instructions that had been inside the box he'd picked up and hand carried from Kyrgyzstan. The box and the paper had long since been burned, but Arafat had committed the instructions to memory.

It was a simple procedure. Connect the timer to the detonator and insert the long metal tube into the block of plastic explosive. Select the timer setting by dialing the face to how many hours you wanted to wait before the package exploded.

They knew today was the day because Hoshur, who cleaned in the communications center, had heard the PLA officers talking about the battle with Orazov's resistance forces. He only overheard bits and pieces, but it was enough. The PLA forces had been dealt a serious blow by the resistance.

Arafat looked at Fatima. It was almost noon. "Four hours?" he asked and she nodded. He set all the timers, except for one. Then they each took six devices and loaded them into their own carts.

Over the next hour, they made their rounds. They had set up this routine weeks ago so their PLA security team would be used to seeing the janitorial staff meet in the open and restock each other's carts with fresh cleaning materials. After the resupply, the Uighur janitors dispersed on their normal routes. Some went to the control room, others to communications or to the maintenance areas. Some passed by the outside cooling towers on their way to the dumpsters.

In the hallway, Fatima passed him, pushing her own cart, nodding to indicate all her devices were delivered.

At quarter to four in the afternoon, the janitorial staff took their afternoon break outside the staff entrance where Arafat had come in earlier that day. The PLA security guards ignored the gathering of the cleaning crew. They were invisible, Arafat knew. In fact, he was counting on it.

One by one, each member of the team reported that they had placed their devices successfully. There was only one device left, the one in Arafat's lunch bag.

At ten minutes to four, the twelve staff members got to their feet and walked toward the main entrance of the compound. The guards took no notice. Every day at this time, the group walked the half kilometer to the main gate and back.

The afternoon was overcast and oppressively hot. It was just possible to see the white caps of the western mountain range through the hazy afternoon. The water that supplied this facility came from those mountains via the Yarkant River. To the east, there was nothing but desert plains. Dust puffed with each footstep and rose in a cloud around them on this windless afternoon.

Behind them, the concrete bulk of the Kashgar Research Center loomed out of the flat dry earth. The facility had been built a decade ago by the Beijing Institute for Theoretical Computer Science, but it was under the jurisdiction of the People's Liberation Army now. Apart from the security staff and the electric fence that ringed the property, there was nothing to indicate this was a top-secret military installation. From outside, the Kashgar facility looked plain and unassuming, but looks were deceiving. Most of the operation was located below ground. In the bunker, at the protected heart of the facility, was the quantum computer. The one the Chinese called Foresight.

The computer itself was about the size of a small bungalow, a tiny fraction of the surrounding building. Most of the facility was needed to support the power and cooling requirements of the quantum computer. From his university degree that he was no longer allowed to use, Arafat knew that quantum computing generated incredible amounts of heat. Heat that must be removed or the computer would literally melt down.

The Chinese designers knew this, which was why the Kashgar facility had three independent cooling systems. The primary cooling towers were located on the surface level. Erkin, who had a degree in electrical engineering, had placed an explosive in the main power distribution panel. A second device was located on the primary cooling water supply into the facility.

The second cooling system ran off a series of diesel generators. Explosives had been placed on the power distribution bus, the fuel supply tanks, and the secondary cooling water supply line into the facility.

The third and final cooling system was a fail-safe. Entirely manually operated and gravity fed from a reservoir on top of the manmade hill next to the facility. The supply line into the facility was a meter-wide pipe that ran along the road where the janitorial staff took their afternoon stroll.

They walked past a gate valve sandwiched between two bolted flanges. The manual indicator on top of the valve showed it was closed. Arafat reached into his lunch sack and took out the final device. He set the timer for ten minutes, and using his fellow janitors as cover, he wormed his way under the pipe and jammed the explosives into the gap between the two heavy metal flanges.

He surveyed his work. The package looked tiny compared to the huge pipe, but he trusted his calculations. It would be enough. Arafat offered up a silent prayer as Fatima helped him to his feet and the group continued their stroll.

The first explosion happened at one minute past four. It sounded to Arafat's ears like a distant thud, as if someone had slammed a heavy door. If he hadn't been expecting it, he might not have even looked up.

Maybe the control room, he thought.

An alarm sounded and the guards in the gatehouse looked up, concern on their faces.

Then explosions happened in rapid succession. A bright fireball erupted into the overcast sky.

"The power distribution panel," Erkin said, a note of pride in his voice. Another explosion. "The cooling tower," he added.

A new alarm, a rapid bleating sound. Fatima said, "Loss of primary cooling alarm—"

But her words were cut short by the explosion of the diesel fuel supply. Even though the tanks were on the far side of the large building, Arafat felt the shock wave in his gut. A fireball rose over the low concrete structure.

The alarm changed again. A blaring up-down tone.

"Loss of secondary cooling," Fatima shouted over the noise.

All eyes shifted to the gate valve fifty meters down the track. It was a fail-open solenoid valve, designed to open if the power holding the valve closed went away. They watched the spindle begin to turn, opening the valve.

Nothing happened.

The valve was a quarter of the way open and Arafat could hear water moving inside the huge pipe.

"Something's wrong," he said. "I must have screwed up the timer."

He started to run, his feet throwing up clouds of dust. He felt like his heart would burst. This had to work, it had to—

The explosion knocked him backward and off his feet. He was looking up at the lead-gray sky...and he was soaked.

Fatima reached him. "Are you all right?" she asked.

Arafat saw the river of water flooding out of the broken pipe. It filled the road and ran into the adjoining field where the thirsty sand soaked it in.

His ears rang and he had a nosebleed, but he laughed out loud.

51

Samarkand, Uzbekistan

Timur Ganiev stepped from his limousine onto the wide plaza in front of the Congress Center. He was wearing his favorite charcoal suit, a blue silk tie, and cordovan Italian loafers that gleamed in the morning sun. He looked every bit the international diplomat and politician that he was.

The gaggle of reporters usually kept at bay by a screen of People's Liberation Army security personnel crowded up to his vehicle when it pulled to the curb. In fact, there was a noticeable lack of Chinese military personnel anywhere in the Silk Road Samarkand resort complex that hosted the proceedings of the Committee for the Constitution of the Central Asian Union.

There were other differences, unnoticed by the reporters, but significant to Timur. Normally, Jimmy Li was somewhere nearby. Not always seen, but always close. Timur had not heard from his MSS handler in over seventy-two hours. Also, on any other day, there would have been a Chinese camera crew following Timur and led by the only Western reporter with access to the President of the Central Asian Union.

Timur had not seen or heard from Nicole since she'd left to meet Harrison Kohl two nights ago.

But the reporters who met Timur on the plaza didn't care about Jimmy or Nicole. They had their own, more pressing questions for the President.

"We've had reports of extensive fighting between PLA forces and Seljuk Islamic Front resistance movement, Mr. President. Do you have any comment?"

The reporter was with the *Gazeta*, one of the few independent news sources in Uzbekistan. She had close-cropped dark hair with frosted tips and trendy, heavy-framed glasses that looked too large for her face. She pushed an iPhone toward him. "Do you have any comment, Mr. President?" she asked again.

Timur stopped walking and locked eyes with the reporter.

"I have much to say. I will speak to the regional situation at the opening of the session today." He smiled at her, but she glared back at him.

The rest of the reporters chimed in. "Can you confirm the fighting?" "Do you support the resistance movement?" "Mr. President, what's going on?"

The last question was the right one, he thought, but no one—not even him—*really* knew what was happening. And that appeared to be how the PLA wanted it. Yesterday afternoon, Chinese authorities had shut down all local and regional radio and TV stations. Mobile phone service throughout the region was down as well, although it was unclear whether that was deliberate or due to an accident.

But the rumor mill demanded to be fed and people were resourceful. Landlines went back into service, people dusted off old shortwave radios, and the lucky few who had satellite TV or internet service helped to fill the information gap.

The picture was confusing, but some facts started to emerge. The PLA had engaged in heavy fighting with the resistance at multiple locations around the region—as many as nine different battles, if the rumors were correct. The outcomes were not clear, but the consensus was that the PLA had not fared well.

Where there's smoke, there's fire. It was a saying he'd heard Nicole use. Standing on the balcony of his penthouse suite this morning, Timur smelled smoke, literally and metaphorically. A smudge of darkness on the otherwise crystal-clear sunlit horizon had not been there the previous evening and the morning breeze carried the acrid scent of smoke.

He hoped Nicole was safe. He hoped Jimmy had somehow gotten what was coming to him. He mourned for his countrymen who were injured or killed in the fighting. How many? he wondered. A hundred, a thousand, ten thousand? He'd seen what PLA weapons could do and the thought made him sick to his soul.

Inside the glass doors of the Congress Center the air vibrated with rumors. Delegates and staffers alike rushed up to him with more questions. "Mr. President, what's going on?" "Where are the Chinese security forces?" "Will we be in session today, sir?"

Timur gave them a confident smile. "I will be making remarks at the start of the session this morning," he said. "All of your questions will be answered then."

He made his way to his office and closed the door behind him. He needed to shut out the world for a few moments to gather his thoughts. He sat down in the leather chair behind his desk and took in the room. Soft Persian rugs, glass-fronted bookshelves, an entire wall of photos of him posing with famous people, an antique globe in a heavy brass holder. The custom suit hugged his shoulders just so as he ran his hand across the smooth desktop.

Will I miss these things? He knew in his heart that the answer was yes, a response that made him sad and angry at the same time.

He punched the intercom button on his desk phone. "Please have coffee for two brought in," he said. "And find the Vice President immediately. I need to speak with him before the opening session."

Firuz Sharipov arrived ten minutes later carrying a silver tray with the coffee service. "Good morning, Mr. President," he said from the door. "You wanted to see me?"

Timur rose from behind his desk and ushered the younger man to the leather armchairs in the sitting area. He insisted on pouring coffee for both of them. Now, with the niceties accomplished, Timur felt awkward, unsure how to begin.

"Do you know what's happening with the PLA forces, sir?" Firuz asked, his voice full of concern. "I have confirmed reports that there was significant fighting yesterday afternoon and there were heavy losses."

Timur stared at the younger man. His green eyes were keen with intelligence and his every movement spoke of his vitality—and his innocence. Timur contrasted that energy with the secret that had been dragging him down for the past three years.

"Mr. President—" Firuz began, but Timur cut him off.

"Timur. Please, call me Timur this morning."

The sharp eyes raked over Timur's features. "Is everything okay, sir?"

"I need to tell you something, Firuz," Timur said quietly. The Vice President put down his coffee cup. Timur could see that the other man sensed the tension in the room, but he had no idea what was coming.

"I am not who you think I am," he began.

The opening of the General Assembly to the Committee for the Constitution of the Central Asian Union started fifteen minutes late. The large room was over capacity. Every seat was taken and people crowded in the aisles and lined the back of the hall.

From the President's chair to the left of the speaker's podium, Timur studied the sea of assembled faces. Intellectually, he knew he was about to deliver the most important speech of his career, probably the most important of his entire life, and yet he was calm. After years of hiding, his mind was at peace. Telling Firuz unburdened him. Now, he was ready to tell the world the truth.

He felt the Vice President's gaze and Timur turned to him. The younger man was holding up well. Others would miss the signs that were evident to Timur: the bloody red tinge in the whites of his eyes, the subtle ashen pallor of his pale skin, the determined set of his jaw.

Timur nodded. *I am ready.*

Firuz Sharipov rose and strode to the podium. He snatched up the gavel and rapped it once, calling the session to order. In a voice clear and commanding, he announced, "The Honorable Timur Ganiev wishes to address the General Assembly."

Probably no one noticed that he used only Timur's name and not his title, but when historians analyzed this moment, they would note that fact.

Timur rose and walked to the podium. He rested his hands on either side of the heavy wooden lectern and looked out over the sea of faces. He saw every shade of skin and every color of eye. They were all gathered here, every part of a once proud people who had been invaded and divided and set against each other by outside forces for centuries.

He had no notes, and the teleprompter was blank, but Timur felt the words rise out him.

"I had a dream once," he began. "I believed that in my lifetime, we could reunite and rebuild that which politics and wars have done to divide us. The people of Central Asia are made up of different tribes, but once upon a time we were a proud people, a united people. Though from different backgrounds, we recognized each other and acted as one. Like the leader before me, I bore the name Timur proudly. I saw myself as a man who could unite us again."

The room was so pin-drop quiet that Timur heard himself swallow.

"I believed nothing was more important than this dream. I told myself there was no sacrifice too great as long as it served the goal I had set out to achieve." Timur paused, feeling the knife-edge of tension in the room. He felt the intake of a collective breath.

"I was wrong," he said in a flat voice. "I sold my soul for that dream and only now have I realized that the price was too high." A stirring in the sea of faces. "I have not been honest with you, my countrymen. The presence of the People's Liberation Army in Central Asia is a fraud. A fraud perpetrated by me. For years, I have been an agent of the Ministry of State Security of the People's Republic of China. I have taken their money, I have used their influence, and I became your President by false means."

A collective gasp rippled through the room. Timur pressed forward, the words coming fast and strong now.

"I told myself I was doing it for the right reasons, but I was wrong. I lied to you and to myself. There is no shortcut to the creation of a Central Asian Union. If we want a democracy, we need to fight for it. Together. On our own, not using the military of some foreign power. I have allowed our beautiful land to become a war zone, and for that, I beg your forgiveness."

Timur bowed his head. He sighed and he heard the amplified sound echo around him. He felt the room begin to buzz with energy.

He looked up. "A few moments ago, I resigned as President of the Central Asian Union. All of my duties and responsibilities have been turned over to Vice President Sharipov. He is an honest man and a fine leader. Please give him your full support."

He stepped back from the lectern. For a few beats, shocked silence gripped the room. Firuz brushed past him. He did not look at his mentor or even acknowledge him. He stood at the lectern and took up the gavel.

The room erupted in shouts. The bang of the gavel sounded like a gunshot in the chaos.

"There will be order!" Firuz shouted, banging the gavel again and again.

Timur backed away. Clamor filled the air around him, and he felt a prickle of shame creep across his skin. Through his pride and greed, he had created this mess, and there was nothing he could do to fix it.

"Order!" Firuz shouted again.

No one noticed when Timur exited through the side door.

52

Beijing Miyun Mujiayu Airport, 68 kilometers northeast of Beijing

No matter how hard he tried, Nikolay Sokolov could not sit still. So, he paced and he studied the office of the airport administrator—anything to burn away the restless energy that threatened to overwhelm him.

The absence of family pictures told him the man was a confirmed bachelor. Most of the photographs were of military units, with one exception. The centerpiece of the wall display was an 8x10 photograph of the administrator shaking hands with the man Nikolay had flown all this way to meet.

The two men were roughly the same age and Nikolay saw a familiarity in the way they held themselves that indicated a personal connection. Friends, perhaps. Maybe classmates.

The photograph was at least thirty years old, but the Chinese General Secretary looked remarkably unchanged. He still had the same heavy features and deceptively sleepy eyes. His doughy lips were curled into a smile that looked genuine. He even had the same hairstyle, a heavy pompadour sculpted with hair gel.

Nikolay resumed his pacing. He'd flown seven hours for a thirty-minute meeting. Everything rested on the outcome of the next thirty minutes.

At least Nikolay had insisted on the General Secretary making the trip to the airport at two in the morning. It was petty, he knew that, but it was also the barest show of mutual respect. If Nikolay could fly seven hours each way, then asking the second-most powerful man in the world to make a forty-five-minute car trip was objectively fair. It also served as a subtle signal that the Chinese were willing to listen to what he had to say.

Nikolay stopped his pacing and closed his eyes. He drew in a deep breath and held it.

Focus. There is opportunity in chaos. Seize it.

He smiled to himself as he recalled the words of his late Uncle Vitaly. At any other time, what he was about to propose would seem ludicrous. But his political instincts told him this was a unique moment in history, and Nikolay intended to take full advantage of it.

The Chinese Communist Party and their leader General Secretary Yi Qin-Lao had a lot on their plate at the moment. Orazov's forces had handed the PLA a humiliating and costly defeat, followed by the destruction of their quantum computer facility in Xinjiang. That final indignity had come as a surprise to Nikolay and he wondered how Orazov had managed to pull it off.

No matter, he would have Federov suss out the details later. For now, the added stressors worked to Nikolay's benefit.

As if on cue, there was a tap at the door and Federov entered. It seemed like every time Nikolay saw the FSB chief, the man looked more diminished. His suit jacket hung on his bony shoulders, and he'd developed a runny nose during the long flight from Moscow. Federov swiped at his nose with a white handkerchief. "He's here, Mr. President."

Nikolay nodded. "I'm ready. The arrangements in Astana are set?"

"All that is required is a phone call, sir."

"Good, good." As Federov turned to leave, Nikolay said, "Are you okay, Vladimir? Healthwise."

"It's nothing, sir. What matters is the work."

Nikolay nodded. Federov had always been about his work, even at the expense of his own health. Nikolay had benefited from that singular dedication many times, including right now.

"Have a good meeting, Mr. President." Federov withdrew.

Nikolay let the tingle of nervous energy flow through his body. He shot his cuffs, smoothed his lapels, and inspected his appearance in the small mirror on the inside of the closet door.

"Showtime," he said to his reflection.

There was a single knock on the door and Yi Qin-Lao, General Secretary of the People's Republic of China, entered.

The second-most powerful man in the world wore the cares of his office on his face. His skin had a waxy cast and his heavy eyelids drooped lower than normal. He walked with a leaden tread and his firm handshake was clammy.

A second man followed the General Secretary. Yan Tao, the Minister of State Security, was a thin, ascetic contrast to the fleshiness of his boss. He turned to close the door behind him, but Nikolay intervened.

"I think this would be more productive as a private meeting, Mr. General Secretary."

Yan turned, clearly surprised, anger flushing his thin cheeks. Nikolay smiled at him, enjoying the moment. Excluding Yan was necessary to his plan, but it was also satisfying on a personal level. The man had embarrassed Nikolay during the presidential election in Russia and it was time he returned the favor.

Yan opened his mouth, but Yi waved a heavy hand dismissively. "Go," he said.

Nikolay watched the door close, then indicated the two armchairs in front of the desk. The General Secretary sat down with a weary sigh.

Before the other man could speak, Nikolay asked, "What are you going to do?" He spoke in English, their only common language. Nikolay did not want a translator in the room.

His tone was abrupt, borderline rude. It was a dangerous way to start, but time was not on his side. He and Federov had strategized about how to open the meeting and decided the best method was a frontal assault. This was also the reason why he'd wanted Yan out of the room. With just Nikolay and Yi, there was no need for the General Secretary to posture in front of his subordinate.

Yi Qin-Lao's face flushed red, his jaw clamped shut. "What is that supposed to mean?"

"You just got your ass handed to you by a bunch of natives," Nikolay said, without backing off the aggressive tone. "I want to know your next move."

Don't explain yourself, Federov had counseled. Demand an answer.

"This is a setback." Yi had regained his composure now and he relaxed back in the chair. "Costly, but temporary. We have air superiority and we will regarrison our ground forces. The resistance movement will pay a heavy price."

"Why?" Nikolay challenged.

Yi looked confused again. "Why what?" His voice was testy and he glanced at the door.

"You already have what you want in the region," Nikolay said. "The Belt and Road is a success and the resistance would be fools to destroy their own infrastructure. Akhmet Orazov is many things, but a fool is not one of them."

"You're suggesting we abandon our position in Central Asia?" The pouchy cheeks flushed red again. "We let them get away with it?"

A perfect opening. Nikolay softened his tone. "On the contrary, I'm suggesting you expand your position." He leaned forward, elbows on knees. "Timur Ganiev has exposed you. The new President is demanding that Chinese military forces leave the Central Asian Union. If you regarrison your ground forces now and go after Orazov, you will only draw criticism from the international community. Every attack, no matter how justified, will be litigated by reporters and talking heads and the UN. You will be seen as the aggressor. It will be Taiwan all over again. You don't need that."

"And you have a better plan?" The General Secretary's tone held a hint of a sneer.

"I do." Nikolay sat back in his chair, crossed his legs. He could hear Federov's voice in his head: *Make him ask for it*.

Yi sighed with more than a little theater in the action. "Tell me your plan and tell me what's in it for you."

"You already have what you want—the Belt and Road connection to Tehran—so let me give you what you need: Kazakhstan."

Yi chuckled darkly. "You are wasting my time, Nikolay. I already own Kazakhstan."

Nikolay smiled without humor. "No, you own the *President* of Kazakhstan, who, as of an hour ago, is in jail on embezzlement charges. Unfortunately, the Vice President was also implicated in the scandal and has resigned. The new President of the country is Sergei Musayev."

Yi closed his eyes. "I assume from your energetic description that Sergei is a Russian agent?"

"We have a...pre-existing relationship," Nikolay acknowledged.

"What do you want?" the Chinese leader replied. "You didn't fly all this way to tell me you screwed me over."

"I want an understanding that benefits us both," Nikolay said. "Abandon your military efforts in Central Asia and move your forces into Kazakhstan. At the same time, I will move Russian troops into the region from the west and north."

Nikolay extracted a printed map from his inside pocket. "I've proposed a division of territory that is in both our interests. I will control the north with our oil and gas infrastructure as well as our space assets. The capital of Astana will become a Russian city. You will control the southern part of the country, including the water resources there. To seal the deal, we sign a non-aggression pact."

He sat back, watching the General Secretary study the map. He could see the wheels in the man's brain grind through the implications of the deal.

Nikolay's proposal neatly sidestepped a rematch with Orazov and the inevitable international outcry that would follow any increased PLA military activity in the region. With Timur Ganiev's disclosure, the Chinese had gone from saviors to invaders overnight.

On the home front, Yi could sell the plan to the Chinese people as an expansion of territory into Kazakhstan. In his revision of events, the losses in Central Asia were a necessary step to secure their future in the region.

And then there was the water. That was what the Chinese really wanted.

If Russia and China invaded Kazakhstan at the same time, they would share the global opprobrium as partners. No one could play one country off the other in the UN Security Council or any other forum.

Most importantly, Nikolay's agreement would lock the United States out of the entire region for a generation. President Eleanor Cashman could go fuck herself.

Yi looked up. "This is a very good deal for Russia, Mr. President."

The General Secretary's eyes had all the liveliness of a lizard as he studied the Russian President's face.

Nikolay returned the searching gaze. Time and political pressure worked in his favor. By taking out the President of Kazakhstan, he'd put the deal on a clock. If China wanted to negotiate better terms, Nikolay would move into Kazakhstan on his own. In addition to the ongoing debacle in Central Asia, the Chinese would face a new military threat in their backyard.

"It's a very good deal for both our countries," Nikolay replied.

The General Secretary nodded slowly, his reptilian gaze never leaving Nikolay's face. He leaned forward and held out his hand.

"I agree."

53

The White House, Washington, DC

"How. Could. This. Happen." President Cashman's voice wore an edge of bright steel.

On the sofa across from Don, Secretary of State Abel Cartwright, for the first time since Don had known him, had nothing to say.

The President pointed at the stack of newspapers on the coffee table. The headline on the *Washington Post* told the story:

China, Russia reach deal on Central Asia. US excluded.

"The headlines should be saying *China gets her ass handed to her in bloody conflict engineered by the CIA.*" Cashman held up her right hand, fingers spread, ticking off points as she continued. "Instead, China takes a victory lap, Russia and China seize sovereign territory, and we lose Kazakhstan as an ally. You call that a successful foreign policy, Abel?"

"No, Madam President."

Cashman closed her eyes and took a deep breath. "Do you know what they're calling this?" She barreled on without waiting for an answer. "A modern-day Molotov-Ribbentrop Pact. Do you remember that one from history?"

"Of course, ma'am," Cartwright said, once again loving the sound of his own voice. "It was the agreement signed between the Nazis and the Soviets in 1939 to divide up Poland."

Cashman glared at him. "Do you know what that makes me in that analogy?"

Cartwright opened his mouth and then closed it again.

"It makes me Neville Fucking Chamberlain, Abel, which as I'm sure you can appreciate, is not the historical parallel I'd like to put on my political tombstone."

Secretary of Defense Robert Gable tried to step into the line of fire. "Ma'am, the PLA losses are much more significant than these news stories make it appear. And don't forget the attack on the quantum computer facility has set them back significantly."

"Good point," the President replied in a voice dripping with sarcasm. Her gaze swung to Don and Carroll. "Are we trying to start World War Three? How exactly did an attack inside the borders of China take place without our knowing about it?"

"Our intel—" Carroll began, but Cashman cut her off.

"I'd like to hear what Mr. Riley has to say, Director," Cashman replied. "It was his operation and his agent on the ground, correct?"

"Yes, ma'am, but—"

Cashman stopped her again. "I'll come back to you, Director, but first, I'd like to hear from Mr. Riley."

Don cleared his throat. "It was an independent operation conducted by a group of Uighurs that worked inside the facility. Quantum computers require a tremendous amount of cooling to operate efficiently, and if the heat is not removed promptly, it can cause a runaway thermal reaction. From our analysis, it appears that they disabled all three cooling systems—a primary and two backups—and the entire system melted down."

Cashman's lips twisted into a wry smile. "That sounds ingenious."

"It was the ultimate inside job, ma'am," Don continued. "A dozen or so blocks of plastic explosive in the right places took out the world's most advanced AI."

"And we had nothing to do with it?"

"Nothing, ma'am."

The President cast a baleful eye on the stack of newspapers. "I'd like to give that story to the *Post*."

Carroll Brooks shifted in her seat.

"I know, Director." Cashman rolled her eyes. "We don't want the world to know that the PLA actually built a functional battlefield AI, so we have to pretend we know nothing."

"That information has the potential to be very destabilizing, Madam President, especially with respect to Taiwan."

Cashman closed her eyes, blew out a long breath. "All right, I'm done venting. Let's get to work. Abel, tell us how we're going to deal with this disaster."

Don listened to the discussion, but his expertise was not required for a diplomatic strategy session. In fact, apart from the explanation about the attack on the Chinese quantum computer facility—which could have been delivered by Carroll—Don shouldn't even be in this meeting.

He studied the now much calmer President Cashman as she engaged with her cabinet. This was the first serious setback for her administration and would not be the last. He'd been in the room with three other Presidents operating in adverse conditions and none of them handled their first crisis well. But the most important thing was that they all released their anger and got back to work, just as Cashman was doing now. In a world where he dealt with critical situations every day, that type of leadership felt reassuring to Don.

Cashman ended the meeting and everyone stood. As they gathered up their folders and tablets, the President caught Don's eye and motioned for him to stay. Carroll raised her eyebrows in a question and Don shrugged a reply.

Cashman waited for the heavy door to the Oval Office to close before she resumed her seat and gestured for Don to do the same. She stared at the untouched coffee service as if gathering her thoughts, and Don said, "Can I pour you a cup, ma'am?"

She nodded, her eyes still unfocused. "Please."

Don poured two coffees and handed one to Cashman.

"Thank you, Donald." She sipped and put the saucer on the table. "I got a phone call this morning from President Serrano."

Don didn't hear a question, so he said nothing.

"He wanted to know how I was doing," she continued.

"He still gets regular intel briefs, ma'am," Don said.

"Yes, he does, and he reads the papers. He told me to hang in there. He said even if it feels like a bad week, don't worry, it'll get worse." She barked out a short laugh.

"That sounds like him, ma'am."

"He told me I should have listened to you about Nikolay Sokolov," Cashman continued in a casual tone. "What do you think, Donald?"

Don swallowed.

"I think it was a strategic error, Madam President. You put Sokolov in a corner and that forced him to get creative. He saw an opportunity with China and he took it. It worked out well—for him."

Cashman laughed, a genuine expression this time. She leaned back in her chair. "For God's sake, that cheeky bastard was right again! I bet that you'd kiss my ass and tell me I made the right choice. Serrano said that you'd let me have it with both barrels. Now I owe him a hundred bucks."

"I'm sorry, ma'am."

Cashman drained her cup. "Don't be. I can be my own worst enemy sometimes." Her look turned pensive. "Donald, I don't want to be Neville Chamberlain."

"If it makes any difference, ma'am, the Nazi-Soviet nonaggression pact didn't last long. History shows us that autocrats don't keep their commitments."

Cashman smiled ruefully. "Any way you can accelerate that process, Donald?"

Don matched her smile. "I'll see what I can do, Madam President."

54

Islam Karimov Tashkent International Airport, Uzbekistan

The private air terminal at the Tashkent airport still smelled new, a combination of fresh paint and floor wax. The room was tastefully decorated in shades of blue. Dark blue Berber accent rugs, blue leather seats trimmed in shiny chrome, and a long bar made entirely of some kind of bluish-gray stone. A flat-screen TV occupied an entire wall next to the door. One panel showed arrivals and departures, but the rest of the wall displayed a sweeping landscape in vivid color with accompanying nature sounds playing softly in the background.

A waiter, dressed in a blue waistcoat and dark trousers, set two coffees on the low table between Harrison and Akhmet. The young man's dark eyes flickered over Akhmet. It looked like he might be working up the courage to speak to him, so Harrison intervened.

"Thank you," he said. "That will be all for now."

The waiter got the hint and left. Harrison watched him go, allowing his amusement to show. "You're a celebrity, Ussat."

Akhmet curled his lip in a mock show of disgust. "You can't call me that anymore, Harrison. The resistance is disbanded, and once again, I am master of nothing."

"Somehow I doubt that," Harrison shot back.

But the comment picked at the worry lurking in the back of his mind these past weeks, ever since what the new President of the Central Asian Union had taken to calling their Independence Day.

Where did he fit in now? Did he really expect to return to his desk at ETG and pick up his life where he'd left it?

Harrison was determined to try and he'd dressed for the part. He'd gotten a haircut and a shave and bought a new wardrobe. His uniform was business casual now. Dark blue blazer, khakis, an open-necked white shirt, and loafers. But the clothes felt like a costume and hung on his lean frame awkwardly. His face was still sunburned in places that were normally exposed and his newly shaved cheeks were pale and tender.

For his part, Akhmet dressed the same as he had in the field, albeit in cleaner clothes. The loose tunic was pushed up to the elbows, exposing corded forearms, and the thick belt cinched his trousers to a lean waist. His battered leather jacket was thrown across the chair next to him. A black *doppa* covered his head and the scarf wound around his neck made him look ready for action, as if he might step from the filtered air of the terminal into a violent sandstorm.

"What will you do, Ussat?" Harrison blurted out.

Akhmet let the name pass this time. He shrugged. "I will return home. Like you."

"What about your security?" Even today, Harrison had tried to convince Akhmet that coming to a public place, especially one with a Chinese security presence, was not a good idea. It was too soon, he argued.

The resistance leader was unmoved. "If the PLA wanted to kill me, they would have done it already. They have decided I am not worth the trouble. They have moved on, Harrison, and so have I."

The political changes following the defeat of the PLA was remarkable. Harrison had expected a full-scale Chinese military response. Instead, in a head-snapping turn of events, the Chinese announced the Kazakhstan Accord, a Russian-Chinese pact to carve up the country they had just mutually invaded. Before a gathering of the Chinese Communist Party, General Secretary Yi Qin-lao proclaimed "mission accomplished" in Central Asia. The thousands of PLA casualties merited only a single line in his speech and received only minor coverage in the state-controlled media.

Overnight, in Central Asia, the inertia of normality took over. People resumed their lives as if the battles and the deaths and the destruction had not even happened.

As Harrison studied Akhmet now, he still had a hard time reconciling that just weeks before they had both been in a cave not sure if they would live to see the end of the day. Now, they drank coffee in a Chinese-built terminal of a Chinese-built airport waiting for a Chinese-built airplane to lift off from a Chinese-built concrete runway.

Maybe the General Secretary was right, he mused. Maybe the Chinese won after all. Mission accomplished.

Then again, the Chinese certainly had not planned on the destruction of the Foresight computer facility in Xinjiang. Something that Akhmet had never come clean about. Harrison turned to the older man.

"I only have a few minutes, Ussat. Can I ask you a question?"

Akhmet nodded.

"The attack on the Foresight facility. How did you do it? Don Riley will ask me. It would be nice to give him a straight answer."

"I owe Mr. Riley my thanks," Akhmet conceded. "He has been very patient, but I have been a good investment for him, I think."

"That's true." Harrison studied this man that he'd come to admire, and he knew that he was not going to get an answer.

"The enemy of my enemy is my friend. My friend had motive. I gave him the means."

Harrison laughed in spite of himself. It was the perfect Akhmet answer that somehow left him wiser without making him at all smarter.

"Can I ask you a question, my friend?" Akhmet said.

Harrison sat up straight. "Of course."

"Why did you stay? This was never your fight and the outcome was always in doubt, but you stayed."

Harrison felt the prickle of heat in his eyes and he looked away, struggling for words. He could say that he'd stayed to avenge the death of his best friend. That was true. He could say that he stayed because the CIA needed an experienced asset on the ground, which was also true.

But neither of those were the real reason. He turned back to Akhmet and looked him in the eyes. How could he explain that he loved this man like a father and a brother and a comrade in arms? Even though they had nothing in common, he would follow him anywhere if he asked. Akhmet Orazov was the reason he'd stayed.

"Ussat, I—I—" Harrison began.

Akhmet gripped his forearm. "Thank you, Harrison. I owe you my life."

"Damn right," Harrison said, swiping at his eyes.

"Mr. Kohl?" the waiter was back. "Your flight is ready to board, sir."

Harrison got up and slung his duffel over his shoulder. When he turned back to face Akhmet, the older man gripped him by the shoulder and kissed him on both cheeks. His eyes shone like glass.

"Goodbye, my friend."

"Goodbye, Ussat." Harrison managed to get the words out.

They walked to the door together with heavy steps.

"You did not tell me before," Akhmet asked. "What will you do when you get home?"

"I've had my fill of field operations," Harrison replied with a laugh. "I think I'll ride a desk until I can retire."

Akhmet held the door open for him.

"I do not believe that, Harrison."

55

Wolong Special Administrative Region, Wenchuan, China

Kang Hao leaned back against an oak tree, breathing heavily from the climb. The rough bark dug into the ridge of scar tissue on the back of his head. He was well above three thousand meters on this climb—he could feel it in the thinness of the air—and had only a vague idea of where he was in the wildlife preserve. Although he started this morning by following the track of the big male up the narrow game trail, he kept going long after he lost sign of his quarry.

It didn't matter. He worked alone, and he reported to a man who got winded climbing a single flight of stairs. As far as his boss was concerned, as long as Kang was out in the preserve, he was doing his job.

He closed his eyes and breathed in the smells of the hushed forest. In December, this part of the Yangtze River Basin turned cold and damp. Wintry fog drifted through the forest like ghostly remnants, leaving a sheen of moisture on everything and dampening the sounds of nature.

The weather matched his mood. Isolated, dark, quiet. He had no friends in his new job and he wanted none. Wandering the hills looking for wildlife was just what the doctor ordered. Technically, the doctor had ordered him into intensive therapy for battlefield trauma, but after the court-martial and Kang's dismissal from the Army, the doctor's orders held no power over him.

Kang pushed off the tree and trudged forward, head down. Until his discharge, the only constant in his life had been the military. He'd been raised in a military family, attended military schools for his education, and had built a career as a respected officer. The very thought of being outside the military should have terrified him, but instead something different happened.

It emptied him. It gave him perspective. And what he saw from this new vantage point changed him.

He loved his country, but his country did not love him in return.

The truth was that Kang's survival was inconvenient. The Party needed scapegoats, and he was useful to them in that capacity. His court-martial lasted a single afternoon, resulting in a discharge from military service, immediate and unappealable. The speed of the proceedings should have astonished him, but nothing surprised him anymore. The Party wanted to move on. They wanted to celebrate the annexation of Kazakh territory and ignore the devastating losses in the mountains of Central Asia.

It was odd to Kang how the scale of the losses was less impactful to him than the loss of individuals. Somehow, his mind gave more weight to the death of one young second lieutenant staff officer than to hundreds of troops who had been buried in a massive rockslide.

Lieutenant Chin was never far from his thoughts. In his dreams, he talked to her, laughed with her. And nights when the dreams turned dark, he saw her die again and again.

He paused on the trail and swung his rucksack off his shoulders. The woodland camouflage backpack and his combat boots were the only remnants of his military service that he'd kept after his discharge. Everything else—uniforms, medals, awards, pictures—had gone into a dumpster. The backpack, which he'd owned since his days as a cadet, was well used and patched in places. Not unlike his life, he reflected. Battered and worn, but still of service.

He pulled out his canteen and drank deeply. When he returned the bottle to the pack, his hand touched the GPS receiver. Kang looked at the gray sky—he didn't bother wearing a watch anymore—and saw the afternoon was waning.

What he should do was get a GPS location and find the nearest trail down the mountain to overnight accommodations, but he zipped up the pack instead. He'd spend the night out here. He had everything he needed and it wasn't as if he slept much anymore.

Kang settled the pack on his shoulders and trudged on. Thirty minutes later, he came to a clearing just as the overcast sky melted under watery afternoon sunshine.

This will do, he thought, dropping his pack under the cover of a large dove tree. It was a beautiful specimen, one that he would mark with a GPS location. In the spring the dove tree would bloom with white flowing flowers that moved in the breeze and gave the tree its name. For tonight, it would give him shelter from a rainstorm.

His back against the trunk, Kang pulled a military ration from his pack and ripped it open. Stewed beef and fried rice combination. He assembled the self-heating kit and waited for it to warm the stew. He chewed methodically, without pleasure, and washed down the spare meal with a swig of water from his canteen.

Across the clearing stood a lush grove of bamboo. The narrow leaves shimmered with moisture in the waning sunshine.

Just as he was reaching to zip up his pack, Kang heard a chuffing sound to his right. He froze, then slowly turned his head to study the undergrowth. Kang relaxed back against the tree and waited.

The low bushes rippled, and into the clearing stepped a full-grown panda. It was a magnificent animal. A boar, and a big one, at least 150 kilos and two meters in length. Powerful muscles rippled under the heavy black-and-white coat.

It made its way to the grove of bamboo and sat down on its haunches. Using razor sharp claws, the beast expertly sliced off a bamboo stalk, held it in his paw and fed the green leaves and stems into its mouth. The rhythmic sound of the animal's methodical chewing reached Kang's ears.

He studied the creature. It did not wear a radio collar or any kind of tag, so he knew that this animal had probably never been sighted before.

Looking closer, he noted scars on the animal's face and right shoulder. This boar had seen some battles.

Kang's job was to track wild pandas and catalog the interactions. Since it was extremely rare to see wild pandas, his job mostly entailed setting up trail cams and taking scat samples for DNA analysis. In the unlikely event that he did see a wild panda, he was supposed to document it on video.

The top of his pack was unzipped. Pandas had poor vision. It would be simple to ease the camera out of the rucksack and make a recording.

But Kang left the camera where it was. As the light faded, he watched the big boar fill his belly, listened to the rustle of the foliage and the sound of powerful jaws crushing the bamboo to pulp. He tasted the dew on his tongue and smelled the woody scent of damp leaves. The curve of the tree trunk fitted to his spine and his insulated coveralls kept him warm and dry.

As the dark closed in around him, the panda faded into the shadows. Only the sounds of chewing let him know that his wild companion was still there.

Kang closed his eyes and slept.

56

Varganza, Uzbekistan

The sun was fully over the mountains when the Land Rover made the final turn into the valley.

It had snowed overnight and the tops of the armored hulks next to the highway were sugared with a dusting of white, softening the harsh, soot-black lines of the burned-out tanks and infantry fighting vehicles.

Nicole tried to estimate how many soldiers these vehicles had carried when they were struck with armor-piercing missiles. The math made her head hurt.

The Land Rover topped a rise and she saw the village of Varganza come into view. Or what was left of it. This had been the scene of an intense firefight between PLA forces and Orazov's resistance fighters. The plan had been to take the Chinese forces in the open and spare the town, but a PLA company officer on the flank of the advancing force must have sensed a trap. On his own volition, he moved his infantry company into the shelter of the town, forcing the resistance fighters to engage in urban warfare.

It had been more than three months since that bloody, destructive day, but she saw the scars everywhere. A wide gap in a stone wall, a blue tarp tent next to a flattened house, scaffolding surrounding a three-story brick structure, a shattered minaret on the mosque that poked above the roofline of a building.

On the back seat next to her, Barry snored. Yes, Barry was back, as slovenly as ever, but just as devoted to her as the day he'd left. Nicole patted his arm.

"Barry, we're here. Wake up."

His eyes snapped open and he startled awake. He yawned, rubbed his eyes. "Wow. How long was I out?"

"Not long," Nicole said. It had been three hours, but she was grateful for the solitude of the predawn drive. It gave her time to collect her thoughts before the meeting. Maybe her feelings, too.

She leaned between the seats, pointing to a group of young men sitting under an apple tree surrounded by baskets of ripe red fruit and ladders. The orchard around them had seen some damage, but there seemed to be fruit left to harvest. "Ask them," she said to the driver.

The driver pulled to the side of the road and rolled down the window. He called to the group in their local dialect. The young men shook their heads when the driver mentioned the name of the man they were looking for.

"They do not know him, madam," the driver said in English.

Nicole threw herself back in her seat and blew out a breath of frustration. It was the same everywhere they went. The most famous man in all of Central Asia had disappeared. But she'd had a feeling about this place.

Then an idea occurred to her. "Ask them if there's a doctor in this town," she said.

The driver asked and this time they nodded.

"They say yes. The clinic was damaged but the new doctor is rebuilding it. They say he's usually there in the morning."

She passed him some money for a tip. "Tell them thank you."

The Land Rover left the highway for a dirt road that ran around the town. The driver took his time navigating around potholes and other road hazards. A herd of sheep blocked their way, a boy of ten or so eyeing their vehicle until the driver rolled down his window and shouted for him to clear the path.

The men in the orchard undersold the level of damage to the clinic. The building was destroyed, the whitewashed bricks salvaged and stacked into neat piles. A few meters away, a knee-high wall showed the progress of the new clinic. A man, bent over at the waist, trowel in hand, laid bricks.

The man must have heard the approaching car, because he straightened up. The morning sun caught his face. His hair was longer now, more gray than black and tied back in a short ponytail. His beard had streaks of silver. He was leaner than she remembered. His eyes met hers and he stooped down for another brick.

"Stop the car," Nicole said. "Wait here," she told Barry.

"Is that him? Doesn't look like him."

Nicole got out of the car and shut the door behind her. The fresh morning breeze knifed through her jacket and she wrapped her arms around her body. She picked her way across the rock-strewn ground.

"Hello, Nicole," the man said without looking up.

"Timur." In her mind, she'd imagined this reunion a hundred times and she always said something witty like, *You're a hard man to find*, or *What's a guy like you doing in a place like this?*

But in the emotion of the moment, all she managed to get out of her mouth was his name. She couldn't even process what she was feeling. Relief that he was alive, maybe, coupled with anger that he'd just walked away and left everything behind. Left her behind.

"Why did you leave?" she demanded.

He straightened up. "Haven't I done enough damage already?" He swept his arm toward the town. "They didn't ask for any of this."

"You did the right thing in the end," Nicole said. "That's what matters."

"Twenty-six people from this town were injured or killed, including ten children. I don't feel like I did the right thing, Nicole."

"Your heart was in the right place," she insisted.

Timur's lips twitched with a smile. "I used to believe that, you know. I told everyone who would listen, including myself, that I was doing the right thing. I gave up medicine to try to convince even more people that I was doing the right thing. And I was good at it—my words moved people." He broke off, looked out over the valley. "I was wrong, Nicole."

"You weren't wrong, Timur. You weren't perfect, but you weren't wrong.

You just made a mistake." She hesitated. "You need to tell the end of your story."

His face hardened. "That's why you're here." It was a statement, not a question.

Even in the cool morning air, she felt her cheeks burning. "I need a final interview, Timur. You just disappeared; there's no end to your story. I need you to fill in the blanks, tell me why you left, what you plan to do next."

Timur bent down, picked up a brick, and scooped mortar on his trowel. She saw the sureness of his movements, the economy of motion. "What I plan to do next is finish this wall"—he pointed the tip of the trowel to the right—"then finish that wall."

"Timur, you owe people—"

He stood suddenly, looming over her. "The people in this town, they don't know who I am and they don't care. I'm the doctor. I'm also the guy who knows how to lay bricks—and that's good enough for them." He smoothed the mortar over the brick and placed it on the wall. He used the handle of the trowel to tap the brick level.

"You're right about one thing, Nicole, I do owe them. I owe these people my life—and I'm going to give it to them one brick at a time and one sick child at a time. Maybe someday, if I'm lucky and I work hard, I'll get to the point where no one even remembers the name Timur Ganiev."

He straightened, breathed deeply. "It's funny, you know. All I ever wanted was to be so famous that people would never forget my name. Now, all I want is for them to forget I ever existed."

Nicole tried to reach for his arm, but he twisted away.

"You need to go, Nicole. I have nothing to say to you or anyone else. I'm sorry about your documentary."

He bent over for more bricks and mortar.

Nicole stepped back. "Goodbye, Timur."

"Goodbye, Nicole." He did not look up.

She got back in the car. Barry had his camera ready. "Well?"

Nicole summoned up a smile. "It's not him."

57

Cozumel, Mexico

Don was just a face in the crowd as he walked down the ramp of the ferry. The mass of people compressed into the width of the pier, and Don let himself be carried along. Off to his right, a massive Carnival cruise ship, docked to the deepwater pier, glistened in the late afternoon sun.

The pier funneled onto the Malecon, which was thronged with pedestrians getting into position for sunset. Don stepped out of the flow of humanity, and with the sun at his back, energized the burner phone. He'd found the device sitting on the desk in his hotel room when he returned from lunch. The note underneath the phone read: *Take the 4:30 ferry from Carmen del Playa to Cozumel. Turn the phone on when you land.*

The note wasn't signed, of course, but Don had a pretty good idea who had left it there. He'd come to the G20 in Cancun as part of his normal duties, but also on the off chance that behind-the-scenes outreach might be possible.

It was certainly needed. In the months following the Central Asian crisis, as it was now referred to in National Security Council meetings, President Cashman's hard line with Russia and China had not fared well. It turned out that their allies were alarmed to see the United States frozen out by a China-Russia alliance. As a smaller country, the only thing worse than having to deal with China *or* Russia was having to deal with China *and* Russia, together. Their expectation was that the US would find a way to drive a wedge between the two countries. Not only was President Cashman not meeting that expectation, she was viewed as the proximate cause of the troublesome alliance.

The mysterious burner phone offered Don a ray of hope. He waited as the mobile went through the startup sequence and connected to the local network. When the screen cleared, he saw he had a text message waiting. The message consisted of a link that opened the map application on the phone. A red pin rested on a location only a few blocks away.

La Cocay.

Don searched his memory for the meaning of the Spanish word and came up with nothing. It didn't matter anyway. The little symbol next to the red pin had a martini glass, so he was headed to a bar.

He set off down the Malecon, pausing occasionally to look in store windows to see if he had a tail. Who was he kidding? He wasn't a case officer. He'd never been trained in spotting surveillance. Besides, if he was meeting who he thought he was meeting, then he was definitely being followed. Even if Don couldn't detect them, he knew they would be there. It was no accident that he'd arrived just as the cruise ship docked and the streets of the tiny island town were flooded with tourists.

Don decided it didn't matter. They knew where he was going anyway. He'd just have to trust that his host was watching Don's back for any unwanted followers.

The crowds thinned considerably when he turned right into the town itself. By the time he'd walked two blocks, the streets were all but empty. Don knew that was not unusual. Apart from the outdoor activities, the main attraction at western facing beaches on Cozumel was watching the sun set.

La Cocay was a one-story building with the name of the establishment in playful script and a cartoon firefly. In the tall open windows looking over the narrow street, billowing white curtains framed linen-covered tables.

Don passed through wide-open French doors into a cool, tiled hallway and made his way past the dining room to a patio that opened onto a walled garden. Brilliant red flowers from a huge bougainvillea covered one entire wall of the garden. A long bar was staffed by a young man with skin the color of mahogany, long dark hair, and a snow-white dress shirt open at the neck.

Don paused at the empty bar. “Beer, please,” he said.

The young man went to work while Don took in his surroundings. The house was designed to funnel a pleasant sea breeze through the patio and into the garden. The lights in the covered patio were dim and the angle of the sun meant the garden was falling into shadow.

“Here you are, sir.”

Don turned to find a copper mug garnished with lime and a sprig of mint. The cold drink made the side of the mug sweat with condensation.

“What is this?” Don asked. “I ordered a beer.”

“Compliments of the gentleman, sir.” He pointed behind Don.

Vladimir Federov stood in front of the wall of red flowers, dressed in a linen suit with a matching fedora and leather sandals. Despite the dapper clothing, he looked gaunt and he leaned on a cane with a stiff left arm. He extended his hand as Don approached.

“Donald, thank you for coming.”

Federov’s grip was strong. Even though Don could see he was sweating, his skin was cold to the touch. The Russian pointed at the Moscow mule. “You don’t have to drink that. It was a joke.” He stifled a cough when he laughed.

Don followed him to a table in the corner of the patio. The FSB chief walked with a limp and used the cane liberally for support. He sat down with the only sunny corner of the garden at his back, so Don had to squint to study him.

“How are you, Vladimir?”

Federov looked up at the waiter who had followed them to the table. “Club soda, por favor.”

“Same,” Don echoed.

Federov removed his fedora and dropped it on a vacant chair. His bare scalp glistened with rivulets of sweat.

“I’m dying, Donald.”

Don laughed nervously. He hadn’t expected an honest answer.

"Liver cancer."

"I'm sorry," Don said earnestly, and strangely enough, he was. "How much time have the doctors given you?"

Federov laughed, which devolved into a coughing fit. "Always the intelligence officer, eh, Donald?"

"I'm sorry," Don said again.

The drinks arrived and Federov took a sip to calm the coughing fit. "I'm jesting, Donald. It's better if you know. It might cut down on miscommunications in the future."

Don said nothing, sipped his drink.

Federov looked into the garden and scowled. "The doctors say two years. I think they're full of shit. I'll be dead by Christmas."

"Vladimir—" Don began.

"It's fine." Federov waved a bony hand. "I've made my peace with it, Donald, and you should too. Anyway, we have things to discuss." The Russian's gaze pierced the gloom. "Your President made a strategic error in Central Asia. You forced my hand."

Now it was Don's turn to study the garden. "Yes," he said finally. "The agreement in Kazakhstan was an unexpected turn of events."

Federov's smile was wolfish. "Your work with Orazov was masterful. The Chinese never knew what hit them—and the destruction of the quantum computer facility. How did you pull that off? Tell me."

"Maybe next time," Don said.

"Touché," Federov replied. "Nevertheless, your actions provided the perfect opening for an agreement with Beijing. They were desperate for anything to change the subject. Do you know that Sokolov negotiated that deal in thirty minutes? Think of the years we spend negotiating treaties, when all you really need is two motivated leaders in a room face-to-face."

"Can we do that, Vladimir? Can we get my President and yours in the same room again?"

Federov sighed. "It pained me to have to align with the Chinese, Donald, but you left me no choice."

"That's not an answer." Don's voice was sharp. Federov was after something, but what? "Why did you invite me here, Vladimir?"

"You're not asking the right question," Federov replied.

Don turned in his chair and called to the bartender. "I'll have that beer now. Whatever you have on draft." He eyed Federov. "Do you want something?"

The Russian shook his head.

Don waited for the beer to arrive, then took a long pull and carefully placed the mug on the table between them.

"What is the right question?" he asked.

"My President aligned with China because it was in his interest to do so. That alliance will remain in place until outside forces create a reason for it to change. There is a sorting going on in the world, Donald. I know you see it, too. It's evident at the G20 meeting right now. Smaller countries are being forced to choose between the United States and my side."

"You're talking about a Cold War," Don replied. "That's better than a shooting war."

"Not if you're one of those small countries," Federov returned. "Central Asia was a proxy war between the US and China, but tell me, Donald, how many American soldiers died?"

Don took another drink of his beer, thinking about the thousands of casualties that resulted from the Central Asian covert action. "None."

"Exactly. The smaller countries don't want to choose sides and they certainly don't want to be the next proxy war battlefield between the US and China. They want to be left alone to build their own futures."

Don sighed. "And how do we do that?"

"You will have to do it without me, Donald." Federov got to his feet, his body swaying until he planted the cane to steady himself. "The American side tends to view the idea of a Cold War with a certain amount of nostalgia. You won the last one, so you assume it will turn out the same way this time. I would encourage you to examine that assumption. China is a very different beast than the former Soviet Union."

Don stood. "Is there anything I can do for you, Vladimir? Arrange for medical care, maybe."

"My course is set, Donald." His handshake was like ice. "My time is over, but you have many good years left, I think. Use them well."

Don watched him leave, an old, frail man in a too-large linen suit and reliant on his cane to stay upright. Anyone who saw him on the street would not recognize him as one of the most powerful intelligence operatives on the planet—which is exactly the way Vladimir Federov would want it.

The garden fell into darkness as Don nursed his beer. His thoughts drifted back to his first days during the Serrano administration. Not so different from Cashman's time in office. Yes, she'd made mistakes, but so had Serrano, and so had every other President. He took comfort that the Presidents he'd served during his time at the CIA were people of conviction who tried to put the good of their country above themselves.

Don drained his glass. He leaned back in the wicker chair, suddenly tired. Seeing Federov as a dying man had taken Don by surprise. They were more alike than he cared to admit. Both single men, married to their job, dedicated to the service of their country.

As noble as that sounded in his head, it was hard not to feel like he was running on the hamster wheel of history. Maybe it was time to get off the wheel.

Don laughed out loud at the thought. The smile was still on his lips when the bartender appeared. He picked up Don's empty glass. "Can I get you another, sir?"

Don stood, peeled off a twenty-dollar bill, and handed it to the bartender.

"No, thanks. I have to get back to work."

Line of Succession
Command and Control #7

In the wake of a global crisis, a covert action team goes to work on behalf of an enemy of the United States.

When a failed assassination attempt on the Russian President rocks the global stage, U.S. President Eleanor Cashman, a hardline Russia hawk, faces a brutal decision: watch a nuclear-armed Russia destabilize, or prop up a weakened Russian leader to prevent the collapse.

CIA officer Harrison Kohl, fresh off a year of intense paramilitary operations in Central Asia, is tasked with the urgent mission to stop the powerful ultranationalist faction from taking control ahead of Russia's impending elections.

But covert ops under pressure rarely go as planned—and Kohl's mission is no exception.

When his operation spirals out of control, Kohl finds himself in the crosshairs, his career in jeopardy. With time running out, Kohl devises a bold, last-ditch plan—one that puts him at the heart of the action. Victory could restore a fragile balance between the U.S. and Russia. Failure could mean an emboldened Russia on the march across Europe—and the end of the line for Harrison Kohl.

ABOUT THE AUTHORS

David Bruns

David Bruns earned a Bachelor of Science in Honors English from the United States Naval Academy. (That's not a typo. He's probably the only English major you'll ever meet who took multiple semesters of calculus, physics, chemistry, electrical engineering, naval architecture, and weapons systems just so he could read some Shakespeare. It was totally worth it.) Following six years as a US Navy submarine officer, David spent twenty years in the high-tech private sector. A graduate of the prestigious Clarion West Writers Workshop, he is the author of over twenty novels and dozens of short stories. Today, he co-writes contemporary national security thrillers with retired naval intelligence officer, J.R. Olson.

J.R. Olson

J.R. Olson graduated from Annapolis in May of 1990 with a BS in History. He served as a naval intelligence officer, retiring in March of 2011 at the rank of commander. His assignments during his 21-year career included duty aboard aircraft carriers and large deck amphibious ships, participation in numerous operations around the world, to include Iraq, Somalia, Bosnia, and Afghanistan, and service in the U.S. Navy in strategic-level Human Intelligence (HUMINT) collection operations as a CIA-trained case officer. J.R. earned an MA in National Security and Strategic Studies at the U.S. Naval War College in 2004, and in August of 2018 he completed a Master of Public Affairs degree at the Humphrey School at the University of Minnesota. Today, J.R. often serves as a visiting lecturer, teaching national security courses in Carleton College's Department of Political Science, and hosts his radio show, *National Security This Week*, on KYMN Radio in Northfield, Minnesota.

You can find David Bruns and J.R. Olson at
severnriverbooks.com